Quickly, brav~~ely,~~ ~~for th~~e record, Joe, it isn't true."

He turned, looking at her intently. "What do you mean?"

His blue eyes seemed to penetrate all the way to her soul. Her heart began to gallop. She couldn't back down now that she'd begun.

"What you said before—that I can't bear the sight of you—it's not true." *So not true*.

"That's the way it comes across."

"I know. I'm sorry. Really sorry."

She could feel the sudden stillness in him, almost as if she'd shot him. He was staring at her, his eyes burning. With doubt?

Ellie's eyes were stinging. She didn't want to cry, but she could no longer see the paddocks. Her heart was racing.

She almost told Joe that she actually *fancied* the sight of him. Very much. Too much. *That* was her problem. That was why she was tense.

But it was too late for personal confessions. Way too late. Years and years too late.

Instea~~d~~ ~~...~~ ~~...~~ about ~~...~~ ~~... ...~~ e I can't ~~...~~ ~~? ...~~

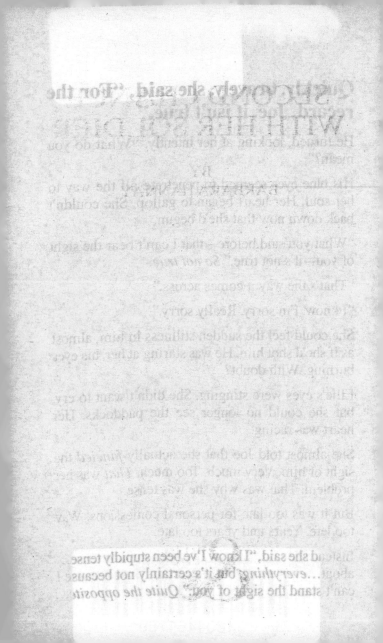

SECOND CHANCE WITH HER SOLDIER

BY
BARBARA HANNAY

MILLS & BOON

Reading and writing have always been a big part of **Barbara Hannay**'s life. She wrote her first short story at the age of eight for the Brownies' writer's badge. It was about a girl who was devastated when her family had to move from the city to the Australian Outback.

Since then, a love of both city and country lifestyles has been a continuing theme in Barbara's books and in her life. Although she has mostly lived in cities, now that her family has grown up and she's a full-time writer she's enjoying a country lifestyle.

Barbara and her husband live on a misty hillside in Far North Queensland's Atherton Tableland. When she's not lost in the world of her stories she's enjoying farmers' markets, gardening clubs and writing groups, or preparing for visits from family and friends.

Barbara records her country life in her blog, *Barbwired*, and her website is: www.barbarahannay.com.

PROLOGUE

CORPORAL JOE MADDEN waited two whole days before he opened the email from his wife.

Avoidance was not Joe's usual MO. It went against everything he'd learned in his military training. *Strike swiftly* was the Australian Commandos' motto, and yet…here he was in Afghanistan, treating a rare message from Ellie as if it were more dangerous than an improvised explosive device.

Looming divorce could do that to a guy.

The fact that Joe had actually offered to divorce Ellie was irrelevant. After too many stormy years of marriage, he'd known that his suggestion was both necessary and fair, but the break-up certainly hadn't been easy or painless.

Now, in his tiny hut in Tarin Kot, Joe scanned the two other email messages that had arrived from Australia overnight. The first was his aunt's unhelpful reminder that she never stopped worrying about him. The other was a note from one of his brothers. This, at least, was glib and slightly crude and elicited a wry chuckle from Joe.

But he was left staring at Ellie's as yet unopened email with its gut-churning subject heading: *Crunch Time*.

Joe knew exactly what this meant. The final divorce

papers had arrived from their solicitor and Ellie was impatient to serve him with them.

Clearly, she was no longer prepared to wait till the end of his four years in the army, even though his reasons for suggesting the delay had been entirely practical.

Joe knew no soldier was safe in Afghanistan, and if he was killed while he and Ellie were still married, she would receive an Army widow's full entitlements. Financially, at least, she would be OK.

Surely this was important? The worst could so easily happen here. In his frequent deployments, Joe faced daily, if not hourly, danger and he'd already lost two close mates, both of them brilliant, superbly trained soldiers. Death was a real and ever-present danger.

Joe had felt compelled to offer Ellie a safety net, so he'd been reassured to know that, whatever happened to him, she would be financially secure. But, clearly, getting out of their marriage now was more important to her than the long-term benefits.

Hell, she probably had another bloke lined up in the wings. Please, let it be anyone but that damn potato farmer her mother had hand-picked for her.

But, whatever Ellie's reasons, the evidence of her impatience sat before Joe on the screen.

Crunch Time.

There was no point in avoiding this any longer. The coffee Joe had recently downed turned sour as he grimly clicked on the message.

It was a stinking-hot day at Karinya Station in Far North Queensland. The paddocks were parched and the cattle hungry as Ellie Madden delivered molasses to the empty troughs. The anxious beasts pushed and shoved at her, trying to knock the molasses barrel out of her hands, so of course she was as sticky and grimy as a candy bar dropped in dirt by the time she arrived back at the homestead.

Her top priority was to hit the laundry and scrub up to her elbows. That done, she strode through the kitchen, grabbed a jug of chilled water from the fridge, filled a glass and gulped it down. Taking another glassful with her to the study, she remained standing in her molasses-smeared jeans as she fired up her laptop.

Tension vibrated and buzzed inside her as the latest messages downloaded. Surely Joe would send his answer today?

She was so sick with apprehension she closed her eyes and held her breath until she heard the ping of the final message's arrival. When she forced herself to peek at the screen again, she felt an immediate plunge of disappointment.

Nothing from Joe.

Not a word.

For fraught minutes, she stood staring at the screen, as if somehow she could *will* another email to appear. She hit 'send and receive', just to be sure.

Still nothing.

Why hadn't he replied? What was the hold-up? Even if he'd been out on a patrol, he was usually back at camp within a day or two.

A ripple of fear trembled through her like chilling wind over water.

Surely he couldn't have been injured? Not Joe.

The Army would have contacted her.

Don't think about that.

Ever since her husband had joined the Army, Ellie had schooled herself to stomp on negative thoughts. She knew other Army couples had secret 'codes' for when they talked about anything dangerous, but she and Joe had lost that kind of closeness long ago. Now she quickly searched for a more likely explanation.

Joe was probably giving her email careful thought. After all, it would have come as a shock, and no doubt he was weighing up the pros and cons of her surprising proposal.

Wanting to reassure herself, Ellie reread the email she'd sent him, just to make sure that it still sounded reasonable.

She'd tried to put her case concisely and directly, keeping it free of emotion, which was only fitting now they'd agreed to divorce. Even so, as she read, she found herself foolishly trying to imagine how Joe would feel as her message unfolded.

Hi Joe,
I hope all is well with you.

I'm writing on a practical matter. I've had another invoice from the fertility clinic, you see, and so I've been thinking again about the frozen embryos. (Surprise, surprise.)

Joe, I know we signed that form when we started the programme, agreeing that, in the case of divorce, we would donate any of our remaining embryos to another infertile couple. But I'm sorry—I'm having misgivings about that.

I've given it a lot of thought, Joe. Believe me, a LOT of thought.

I'd like to believe I would be generous enough to

hand over our embryos to a more deserving couple, but I can't help thinking of those little frozen guys as MY babies.

I've thought around and around this, Joe, and I've decided that I really do want to have that one last try at IVF. I know you will probably be horrified. You'll tell me that I'm setting myself up for another round of disappointment. I know this will come as a shock to you, and possibly a disappointment as well.

However, if by some amazing miracle I did become pregnant, I wouldn't expect to change our plans re the divorce. I promise I wouldn't try to use the baby to hold on to you, or anything manipulative like that.

As you know from past experience, success is EXTREMELY UNLIKELY, but I can't go ahead with IVF without your consent and I wouldn't want to, so obviously I'm very keen to hear your thoughts.

In the meantime, stay safe, Joe.
All the very best,
Ellie

Joe felt as if a grenade had exploded inches from his face.

I know this will come as a shock to you…

Hell, yeah. Never in a million years could he have imagined this possibility…

He'd assumed that the stressful times when he and Ellie had tried for a family were well and truly behind him.

Since he'd left Karinya Station, he hadn't allowed himself to give a single thought to those few remaining embryos. How many were there? Two? Three?

A heavy weight pressed against his ribs now as he

remembered the painful stretch of years when the IVF clinic had dominated his and Ellie's lives. All their hopes and dreams had been pinned on the embryos. They'd even had a nickname for them.

Their *sproglets*.

So far, none of them had survived implantation…

The ordeal had been beyond heartbreaking.

Now… Joe had no doubt that Ellie was setting herself up for another round of bitter disappointment. And yet, for a crazy moment he almost felt hope flare inside him, the same hope that had skyrocketed and plunged and kept them on edge through those bleak years of trying.

Even now, Joe couldn't help feeling hopeful for Ellie's sake, although he knew that her chances of a successful pregnancy were slimmer than a hair's breadth. And it stung him to know that she planned to go ahead this time on her own.

Truth was, he didn't want to think about this. Not any aspect of it. He'd joined the Army to forget his stuffed-up life. Here, he had a visible, assailable enemy to keep him focused day and night.

Now Ellie was forcing him to once again contemplate fatherhood and all its responsibilities. Except, this time, it would be fatherhood in name only. She'd made it very clear that she still wanted the divorce, and Joe totally understood why. So even if there was an against-all-the-odds miracle and he found himself technically a father, his kid would never grow up under his roof.

They would be more or less strangers.

Almost as an accompaniment to this grim thought, an explosion sounded outside, too close for comfort. Through the hut's window Joe saw bright flashes and smoke, heard frantic voices calling. Another rocket-propelled grenade had dumped—a timely reminder that danger and death were his regular companions.

There was no escaping that and, if he was honest, there was absolutely no point in going over and over this question of Ellie's. It was a waste of time weighing up the pros and cons of his wife's request.

Already Joe knew his answer. It was a clear no-brainer.

CHAPTER ONE

Three years later...

'ELLIE, IT'S MUM. Do you have the television on?'

'Television?' Ellie's response was incredulous. 'Mum, I've just come in from the paddocks. Our dams are drying out. I've been wrestling with a bogged cow all afternoon and I'm covered in mud. Why? What's on TV?' The only show that interested Ellie these days was the weather.

'I just saw Joe,' her mother said.

Ellie gasped. 'On TV?'

'Yes, darling. On the news.'

'He...he hasn't been hurt?'

'No, no, he's fine.' There was a dismissive note in her mother's voice, a familiar reminder that she'd never approved of her daughter's choice of husband and that, eventually, she'd been proved right. 'You know he's home for good this time?'

'He's already back in Australia?'

'Yes, Ellie. His regiment or squadron or whatever it's called has just landed in Sydney. I caught it on the early news, and there was a glimpse of Joe. Only a few seconds, mind you, but it was definitely him. And the reporter's saying these troops won't be going back to Afghanistan. I thought you should know.'

'OK. Thanks.' Ellie pressed a hand to her chest, caught out by the unexpected thud of her heart.

'You might be able to catch the story on one of the other channels.'

'Yes, I guess.'

Ellie was trembling as she hung up. Of course she'd heard the news reports about a staged withdrawal of Australian troops, but it was still a shock to know that Joe was already home. For good this time.

As a Commando, Joe had been on dozens of short-term missions to Afghanistan, returning each time to his Army base down in New South Wales. But now he wouldn't be going back.

And yet he hadn't made any kind of contact.

It showed how very far apart they'd drifted.

Almost fearfully, Ellie glanced at the silent blank TV screen in the corner of the homestead lounge room. She didn't really have time to turn it on. She was disgustingly muddy after her tussle in the dam with the bogged cow and she needed to get out of these stinking clothes. She wasn't even sure why she'd rushed inside to answer the phone in this filthy state, but some instinct had sent her running.

She should get changed and showered before she did anything else. She wouldn't even look for Nina and Jacko until she was clean.

But, even as she told herself what she *should* do, Ellie picked up the remote. More than one channel would cover the return.

It took a few seconds of scrolling before she found a

scene at Mascot Airport and a journalist's voiceover reporting an emotional welcome for the returning troops.

The screen showed the airport crowded with soldiers in uniform, hugging their wives and lifting their children high, their tanned, lean faces lit by unmistakable excitement and emotion.

Tears and happy smiles abounded. A grinning young man was awkwardly holding a tiny baby. A little girl hugged her daddy's khaki-clad knee, trying to catch his attention while he kissed her mother.

Ellie's throat ached. The scene was crammed with images of family joy. Tears pricked her eyes and she wondered where Joe was.

And then she saw him.

The man who would soon be her ex.

At the back of the crowd. Grim-faced. He was skirting the scenes of elated families, as if he was trying to keep out of camera range while he made his way purposefully to the exit.

He looked so alone.

With his green Commando's beret set rakishly on his short dark hair, Joe looked so tall and soldierly. Handsome, of course. But, compared with his laughing, happy comrades, he also looked very severe. And so *very* alone.

Ellie's mouth twisted out of shape. Tears spilled. She didn't know why—she simply couldn't help it.

Then the camera shifted to a politician who'd arrived to welcome the troops.

Quickly, she snapped the remote and the images vanished.

She let out her breath in a despairing huff. She felt

shaken at seeing Joe again after so long. To her dismay, it had been more like a horse kick to her heart.

She drew a deeper calming breath, knowing she had to set unhelpful sentimentality aside. She'd been braced for Joe's return and she'd known what was required.

Their divorce would be finalised now and it was time to be sensible and stoic. She knew very well there was *no* prospect of a happy reunion. She and Joe had made each other too miserable for too long. If she was honest, she wasn't surprised that Joe hadn't bothered to tell her his deployment was over. She didn't mind really.

But she *did* mind that he hadn't even asked to see Jacko.

Joe stood at the motel window on Sydney's Coogee Beach, looking out at an idyllic moonlit scene of sea cliffs and rolling surf.

So, it was over. He was home—finally, permanently. On the long flight back from Afghanistan he'd been dreaming of this arrival.

For most Australians, December meant the beginning of the long summer holidays and Joe had looked forward to downing a cold beer at sunset in a bar overlooking the beach, and sitting on the sand, eating hot, crunchy fish and chips straight from the paper they were wrapped in, throwing the scraps to the seagulls.

This evening he'd done all of these things, but the expected sense of joy and relaxation hadn't followed. Everything had felt strangely unreal.

It was unsettling, especially as his Commando training had taught him to adapt quickly to different environments and to respond effectively to any challenges. Now he was home, in the safest and most welcoming of environments, and yet he felt detached and disconnected, as if he was standing on the outside, watching some stranger trying to enjoy himself.

Of course, he knew that the transition to civilian life would be tricky after years of strict training and dangerous combat. At least he'd been prepared for the Happy Family scenes at the airport today, but once he'd escaped those jubilant reunions he'd expected to be fine.

Instead he felt numb and deflated, as if nothing about this new life was real.

He stared at the crescent of pale sand below, silvery in the moonlight, at the rolling breakers and white foam spraying against the dark, rocky cliffs, and he half-wished he had new orders to obey and a dangerous mission to fulfil.

When his phone buzzed, he didn't have the heart to answer it but, out of habit, he checked the caller ID.

It was Ellie.

His gut tightened.

He hadn't expected her to call so soon, but perhaps she'd seen the TV news and she knew he was back in Sydney. No doubt she wanted to talk, to make arrangements.

His breathing went shallow as hope and dread warred inside him. Was he ready for this conversation?

It was tempting to let her call go through to voicemail, to see what she had to say and respond later. But in the last half-second he gave in. He swallowed to clear his throat. 'Hi, Ellie.'

'Oh? Hello, Joe.'

They'd spoken a handful of times in the past three years.

'How are you?' Joe grimaced, knowing how awkward he sounded. 'How's the kid?'

'We're both really well, thanks. Jacko's growing so fast. How are you?'

What could he say? 'Fine. Home in one piece.'

'It must be wonderful to be back in Australia for good,' she said warmly.

'Yeah, I guess.' Too late he realised he should have sounded more enthusiastic.

'I…ah…' Now, it was Ellie who seemed to be floundering for words.

They weren't good at this. How could they be? An unhappy silence ticked by.

'I hear you've had a very dry year up north,' Joe said, clumsily picking up the ball.

'We have, but the weather bureau's predicting a decent wet season.'

'Well, that's good news.'

Joe pictured Karinya, the Far North Queensland cattle station that he and Ellie had leased and set up together when they'd first been married and afloat on love and hope and a thousand happy dreams. In his mind's eye, he could see the red dirt of the inland and the pale, sparse grass dotted with cattle, the rocky ridges and winding creeks. The wide blue overarching sky.

When they'd split, Ellie had stubbornly insisted on staying up there and running the place on her own. Even when the much-longed-for baby had arrived she'd stayed on, hiring a manager at first while she was pregnant, and then a nanny to help with the baby while Ellie continued to look after the cattle business as well as her son.

His son. Their son.

'Joe, I assume you want to see Jacko,' Ellie said quickly.

He gritted his teeth against the sudden whack of emotion. There'd been opportunities to visit North Queensland between his many missions, but he'd only seen their miracle baby once. He'd flown to Townsville and Ellie had driven in to the coast from Karinya. They'd spent an awkward afternoon in a park on Townsville's Strand and Joe had a photo in his wallet to prove it.

Now the kid was two years old.

'Of course I'd like to see Jacko,' he said cautiously. How could a father not want to see his own son? 'Are you planning to come in to Townsville again?'

'I'm sorry, Joe, I can't. It's more or less impossible for me to get away just now. You know what it's like in December. It's calving time, and I'm busy with keeping supplements and water up to the herd. And Nina—that's the nanny—wants to take her holidays. She'd like to go home to Cairns for Christmas, and that's understandable, so I'm trying to manage here on my own. I…um…thought you might be able to come out here.'

Joe's jaw tightened. 'To the homestead?'

'Yes.'

His brow furrowed. 'But even if I fly to Townsville, I wouldn't be able to make it out to Karinya and back again in a day.'

'Yes, I know…you'd have to stay overnight. There… there's a spare bed. You could have Nina's room.'

Whoa.

Joe flinched as if he'd been hit by a sniper. He held the phone away at arm's length as he dragged a shaky breath. He'd been steeling himself for the heart slug of another meeting with his son, but he'd always imagined another half hour in Townsville—a handover of gifts, maybe a walk in the park and another photo of himself with the kid, a memory to treasure.

Get it over, and then goodbye.

He wasn't sure he was prepared to stay at Karinya, spending all that time with young Jacko, as Ellie called him, spending a night there as well.

That had to be a bad idea.

Crazy.

'Joe, are you still there?'

'Yeah.' The effort to sound cool and calm made him grimace. 'Ellie, I'm not sure about going out there.'

'What do you mean? You *do* want to see your little boy, don't you?'

The hurt in her voice was crystal freaking clear.

'I…I do… Sure, of course I want to see him.'

'I thought you'd want to at least give him a Christmas present, Joe. He's old enough now to understand about presents.'

Joe sighed.

'But if you'd rather not…' Her voice was frosty now, reminding him of the chill factor that had caused him so much angst in the past.

'Look, I just got back. I'm jet-lagged, and there's all kinds of stuff to sort out here.' It wasn't totally the truth and Ellie probably guessed he was stalling.

'You and I have things to sort out, too.'

Joe drew a sharp breath. 'Do you have the papers from the solicitor?'

'All ready and waiting.'

'OK.' He felt the cold steel of a knife at his throat. 'Can I call you in the morning?'

By then he'd hopefully have his head together.

'Sure, Joe. Whatever.' Again, he heard the iciness that had plunged their once burning passion to below freezing point.

'Thanks for the call, Ellie.' With an effort he managed to sound non-combative, aware they were already falling into the old patterns that had eroded their marriage—constantly upsetting each other and then trying to placate, and then upsetting each other yet again. 'And thanks for the invitation.'

'No worries,' she said, sounding very worried indeed.

Damn him!

Ellie stood beside the phone, arms tightly crossed, trying to hold herself together, determined she wouldn't allow her disappointment to spill over into tears. She'd shed enough tears over Joe Madden to last two lifetimes.

It had taken considerable courage to ring him. She was proud she'd made the first move. But what had she expected? Warmth and delight from Joe?

What a fool she could be.

If Joe came to Karinya, it would be to sign the papers and nothing more. He would be businesslike and distant with her and with Jacko. How on earth had she once fallen for such a cold man?

Blinking and swiping at her eyes, Ellie walked softly through the house to the door to Jacko's room. Her little boy slept with a night light—an orange turtle with a purple and green spotted bow tie—and in the light's glow she could see the golden sheen of his hair, the soft downy curve of his baby-plump cheek.

He looked small and vulnerable when he was asleep, but in the daytime he was a ball of energy, usually good-natured and sunny, and gleefully eager to embrace life—the life he'd been granted so miraculously.

Ellie knew Joe would melt when he saw him. Surely?

Perhaps Joe sensed this possibility. Perhaps he was afraid?

Actually, that was probably close to the truth. The Joe Madden she remembered would rather face a dangerous enemy intent on death and destruction than deal with his deepest emotions.

Ellie sighed. This next phase of her life wasn't going to be easy, but she was determined to be strong while she and Joe sorted out the ground rules for their future. The impending divorce had been hanging over them for years like an axe waiting to fall. Now, she just wanted it to be over. Finalised.

But she planned to handle the arrangements with dignity and good sense, and she aimed to be mature and evolved in all her dealings with Joe.

It probably helped that they were more or less strangers now.

This was a bad idea. Crazy.

The more Joe paced in his motel room, the more he was sure that going back to the homestead was a risk he didn't want to take. Of course he was curious to see his son, but he'd always anticipated that his final meeting with Ellie would be in a lawyer's office. Somewhere neutral, without memories attached.

Going back to Karinya was bound to be painful, for a thousand different reasons.

He had to remember all the sane and sensible reasons why he'd suggested the divorce, beginning with the guilty knowledge that he'd more or less trapped Ellie into marriage in the first place.

The unexpected pregnancy, their hasty marriage followed by a miscarriage and a host of fertility issues.

Now, since Jacko's arrival, the goalposts had shifted, but Joe had no illusions about a reconciliation with Ellie. After four years in the Army, he was a hardened realist and he'd seen too much injury and death to believe in second chances.

Of course, today hadn't been the only time Joe had landed back in Australia to find himself the sole father in his unit with no family to greet him. He was used to seeing his mates going home with their wives and kids, knowing they were sharing meals and laughter, knowing they were making love to their wives, while he paced in an empty motel room.

Until today, his return visits had always been temporary, a short spot of leave before he was back in action. This time, it was unsettling to know he wouldn't be going back to war. His four years of service were over.

Yeah, of course he was lucky to still be alive and uninjured. And yet, tonight, after one phone conversation with Ellie, Joe didn't want to put a name to how he felt, but it certainly wasn't any version of lucky.

Of course, if he hadn't been so hung up on leaving a widow's pension for her, they would have been divorced years ago when they'd first recognised that their marriage was unsalvageable. They could have made a clean break then, and by now he would have well and truly adjusted to his single status.

Almost certainly, there wouldn't have been a cute complication named Jackson Joseph Madden.

Jacko.

Joe let out his breath on a sigh, remembering his excitement on the day the news of his son's birth came through. It had been such a miracle! He'd even broken his habitual silence about his personal life and had made an announcement in the mess. There'd been cheering and table-thumping and back slaps, and he'd passed his phone around with the photos that Ellie had sent of a tiny red-faced baby boy wrapped in a blue and white blanket.

He'd almost felt like a regular proud and happy new father.

Later, on leave, when his mates quizzed him about Ellie and Jacko, he was able to use the vast distance between the Holsworthy Base and their Far North Queensland cattle station as a valid excuse for his family's absence.

Now that excuse no longer held.

He and Ellie had to meet and sign the blasted papers. He supposed it made sense to travel up to Karinya straight away.

It wouldn't be a picnic, though, seeing Ellie again and looking around the property they'd planned to run together, not to mention going through another meeting with the son he would not help Ellie to raise.

And, afterwards, Joe would be expected to go home to his family's cattle property in Central Queensland, where his mother would smother him with sympathy and ply him with questions about the boy.

As an added hurdle, Christmas was looming just around the corner, bringing with it a host of emotional trapdoors.

Surely coming home should be easier than this?

CHAPTER TWO

When Ellie's phone rang early next morning, Jacko was refusing to eat his porridge and he was banging his spoon on his high chair's tray, demanding. 'Eggie,' at the top of his voice.

For weeks now, Nina, the nanny, had supervised Jacko's breakfast while Ellie was out at the crack of dawn, delivering supplements to the cattle and checking on the newborn calves and their mothers.

Now Nina was in Cairns with her family for Christmas and as the phone trilled, Ellie shot a despairing glance to the rooster-shaped kitchen wall clock. No one she knew would call at this early hour.

Jacko shrieked again for his boiled egg.

Ellie was already in a bad mood when she answered. 'Hello? This is Karinya.'

'Good morning.' It was Joe, sounding gruff and businesslike. Very military.

'Good morning, Joe.' Behind Ellie, Jacko wailed, 'Eggie,' more loudly than ever.

'Would Friday suit?'

She frowned. Did Joe have to be so clipped and cryptic? 'To come here?'

'Yes.'

Friday was only the day after tomorrow. It wasn't much warning. Ellie's heart began an unhelpful drumming, followed by a flash of heat, as if her body had a mind of its own, as if it was remembering, without her permission, the fireworks Joe used to rouse in her. His kisses, his touch, the sparks a single look from him could light.

In the early days of their marriage, they hadn't been able to keep their hands off each other. Back in the heady days before everything went wrong, before their relationship exploded into a thousand painful pieces.

'I could catch a flight that arrives in Townsville around eight a.m.,' Joe said. 'If I hire a car, I could probably get to Karinya around mid-afternoon.'

'Eggie!' Jacko bawled in a fully-fledged bellow.

'Is that the kid crying?'

His name's Jacko, Ellie wanted to remind Joe. Why did he have to call him 'the kid'?

Holding the receiver to one ear, she filled a cup with juice and handed it to Jacko, hoping it would calm him. 'He's waiting for his breakfast.'

Jacko accepted the juice somewhat disconsolately, and at last the room was blessedly silent.

'So how about Friday?' Joe asked again.

At the thought of seeing him in less than forty-eight hours, Ellie took a deep, very necessary breath. 'Friday will be fine.'

It would *have* to be fine. They *had* to do this. They had to get it over and behind them. Only then could they both finally move on.

Joe was an hour away from Karinya when he noticed the gathering clouds. The journey had taken him west from Townsville to Charters Towers and then north through Queensland's more remote cattle country. It was an unhappily nostalgic drive, over familiar long, straight roads and sweeping open country, broken by occasional rocky ridges or the sandy dip of a dry creek bed.

The red earth and pale, drought-bleached grass were dotted with cattle and clumps of acacia and ironbark trees. It was a landscape Joe knew as well as his own reflection, but he'd rarely allowed himself to think about it since he'd left Queensland five and a half years ago.

Now, he worked hard to block out the memories of his life here with Ellie. And yet every signpost and landmark seemed to trigger an unstoppable flow.

He was reliving the day he and Ellie had first travelled up here, driving up from Ridgelands in his old battered ute. No one else in either of their families had ventured this far north, and the journey had felt like an adventure, as if they were pioneers pushing into new frontiers.

He remembered their first sight of Karinya—coming over a rise and seeing the simple iron-roofed homestead set in the middle of grassy plains. On the day they'd signed up for the long-term lease they'd been buzzing with excitement.

On the day their furniture arrived, Ellie had raced around like an enthusiastic kid. She'd wanted to help shift the furniture, but of course Joe wouldn't let her. She was pregnant, after all. So she'd unpacked boxes and filled cupboards. She'd made up their bed and she'd scrubbed the bathroom and the kitchen, even though they'd been perfectly clean.

She'd baked a roast dinner, which was a bit burnt,

but they'd laughed about it and picked off the black bits. And Ellie had been *incredibly* happy, as if their simple house in the middle of hundreds of empty acres represented a long and cherished dream that had finally come true.

When they made love on that first night it was as if being in their new bed, in their new home, had brought them a new level of connection and closeness they hadn't dreamed was possible.

Afterwards they'd lain close and together they'd watched the stars outside through the as yet uncurtained bedroom window.

Joe had seen a shooting star. 'Look!' he'd said, sitting up quickly. 'Did you see it?'

'Yes!' Ellie's eyes were shining.

'We should make a wish,' he said and, almost without thinking, he wished that they could always be as happy as they were on this night.

Ellie, however, was frowning. 'Have you made your wish?' she asked.

'Yes.' He smiled at her. 'What about you?'

'No, I haven't. I...I don't know if I want to.' She sounded perplexingly frightened. 'I...I don't really like making wishes. It's too much like tempting fate.'

Surprised, Joe laughed at her fears. He ran a gentle hand down her arm and lightly touched her stomach, where their tiny baby lay.

'Do *you* think I should make a wish?' Ellie's expression was serious now.

'Sure.' Joe was on top of the world that night. 'What harm can it do?'

She smiled and nestled into his embrace. 'OK. I wish for a boy. A cute little version of you.'

Three weeks later, Ellie had a miscarriage.

Remembering, Joe let out an involuntary sigh. *Enough.*

Don't go there.

He forced his attention back to the country stretching away to the horizon on either side of the road. Having grown up on a cattle property, he was able to assess the condition of the cattle he passed and the scant remaining fodder. There was no question that the country needed rain.

Everywhere, he saw signs of drought and stress. Although Ellie would have employed contract fencers and ringers for mustering, she must have worked like a demon to keep up with the demands of the prolonged drought.

He found himself questioning, as he had many times, why she'd been so stubbornly determined to stay out here. Alone.

He stopped for bad coffee and a greasy hamburger in a tiny isolated Outback servo, and it was only when he came outside again that he saw the dark clouds gathering on the northern horizon. Too often in December, clouds like these merely taunted graziers without bringing rain, but, as he drove on, drawing closer to Karinya, the clouds closed in.

Within thirty minutes the clouds covered the entire spread of the sky, hovering low to the earth like a cotton wool dressing pressed down over a wound.

As Joe turned off the main road and rattled over the cattle grid onto the track that led to the homestead, the first heavy drops began to fall, splattering the hire vehicle's dusty windscreen. By the time he reached the house the rain was pelting down.

To his faint surprise, Ellie was on the front veranda, waiting for him. She was wearing an Akubra hat and a Drizabone coat over jeans but, despite the masculine gear, she looked as slim and girlish as ever.

She had another coat over her arm and she hurried down the front steps, holding it out to him. Peering through the heavy curtain of rain, Joe saw unmistakable worry in her dark brown eyes.

'Here,' she yelled, raising her voice above the thundering noise on the homestead's iron roof, and as soon as he opened the driver's door, she shoved the coat through the chink.

A moment later, he was out of the vehicle, with the coat over his head, and the two of them were dashing through the rain and up the steps.

'This is incredible, isn't it?' Ellie gasped as they reached the veranda. 'Such lousy timing.' She turned to Joe. Beneath the dripping brim of her hat, her dark eyes were wide with concern.

He wondered if he was the cause.

'Have you heard the weather report?' she asked.

He shook his head. 'Not a word. I haven't had the radio on. Why? What's happening?'

'A cyclone. Cyclone Peta. It started up in the Gulf yesterday afternoon, and crossed the coast mid-morning. It's dumping masses of rain further north.'

'I guess that's good news.'

'Well, yes, it is. We certainly need the rain.' She frowned. 'But I have a paddock full of cattle down by the river.'

'The Hopkins paddock,' Joe said, remembering the section of their land that had flooded nearly every wet season.

Ellie nodded.

'We need to get them out of there,' he said.

'I know.' Her soft pink mouth twisted into an apologetic wincing smile. 'Joe, I hate to do this to you when you've just arrived, but you know how quickly these rivers can rise. I'd like to shift the cattle this afternoon. Now, actually.'

'OK. Let's get going, then.'

'You don't mind?'

''Course I don't.' In truth, he was relieved to have something practical to do. A mission to rescue cattle was a darn sight more appealing than sitting around drinking tea and trying to make polite conversation with his beautiful soon-to-be ex.

'It's flat country, so we won't need horses. I'll have to take Jacko, though, so I thought I'd take the ute with the trail bike in the back.'

Joe nodded.

'One problem. I'd probably have to stay in the ute with Jacko.' Ellie swallowed, as if she was nervous. 'Would you mind…um…looking after the round-up?'

'Sure. Sounds like a plan.' He chanced a quick smile. 'As long as I haven't lost my touch.'

As he said this, Ellie stared at him for longer than necessary, her expression slightly puzzled and questioning. She opened her mouth as if she was going to say something in response, but then she shook her head as if she'd changed her mind.

'I'll get Jacko. He's having an afternoon nap.' She shrugged out of her coat and beneath it she was wearing a neat blue and white striped shirt tucked into jeans. Her waistline was still as trim as a schoolgirl's.

When she took off her hat, Joe's gaze fixed on her

thick dark hair, pulled back into a glossy braid. Her hair had always been soft to touch despite its thickness.

'Come on in,' she said awkwardly over her shoulder. 'You don't mind if we leave your gear in your car until later?'

He shrugged. 'It's only Christmas presents.'

'Would you...ah...like a cup of tea or anything?'

'No, I'm fine.' The muddy coffee he'd had on the road would take a while to digest. 'Let's collect the kid and get this job done.'

They took off their boots and hung their wet coats on the row of pegs that Joe had mounted beside the front door when they'd first moved in here. To his surprise, his own battered elderly Akubra still hung on the end peg.

Of course, he'd known it would feel strange to follow Ellie into the house as her guest rather than her partner, but the knife thrust in his gut was an unpleasant addition.

The house was full of the furniture they'd chosen together in Townsville—the tan leather sofa and the oval dining table, the rocking chair Ellie had insisted on buying when she was first pregnant.

Joe wouldn't take a stick of this furniture when they divorced. He was striking new trails.

'I'll fetch Jacko,' Ellie said nervously. 'I reckon he'll be awake by now.'

Unsure if he was expected to follow her, Joe remained standing, almost to attention, in the centre of the lounge room. He heard the creak of a floorboard down the hall and the soft warmth in Ellie's voice as she greeted their son. Then he heard the boy's happy crow of delight.

'Mummy, Mummy!'

Joe felt his heart twist.

Moments later, Ellie appeared in the doorway with Jacko in her arms. The boy was a sturdy little fellow, with glowing blue eyes and cheeks still pink and flushed with sleep. He was cuteness personified. Very blond— Joe had been blond until he was six and then his hair had turned dark.

The last time Joe had seen his son, he'd been a sleepy baby, barely able to hold his head up. Now he was a little man.

And he and Ellie were a winsome pair. Joe couldn't help noticing how happy Ellie looked now, with an extra aura of softness and womanly warmth about her that made her lovelier than ever.

She was complete now, he decided. She had what she'd so badly wanted, and he was truly happy for her. Perhaps it was fitting that this miracle had only occurred after Joe had stepped out of the picture.

Jacko was grinning at him. 'Man!' he announced in noisy delight.

'This is Joe,' Ellie told him, her voice a tad shaky. 'You can say *Joe*, can't you, big boy?'

'Joe!' the boy echoed with a triumphant grin.

'So he's going to call me Joe? Not Dad?'

Ellie frowned as if he'd let fly with a swear word.

'You've been away,' she said tightly. 'And you're going away again. Jacko's only two, and if you're not going to be around us he can't be expected to understand the concept of a father. Calling you Daddy would only confuse him.'

Joe's teeth clenched. He almost demanded to know

if she had another guy already waiting in the wings. A stepfather?

'Jacko's bound to understand about fathers eventually,' he said tersely.

'And we'll face that explanation when the time is right.' A battle light glowed in Ellie's dark eyes.

Damn it, they were at it already. Joe gave a carefully exaggerated shrug. *Whatever.* He'd had enough of war at home *and* abroad. On this visit he was determined to remain peaceful.

He turned his attention to his son. 'So how are you, Jacko?'

The boy squirmed and held out his arms. 'Down,' he demanded. 'I want Man.'

With an anxious smile, Ellie released him.

The little boy rushed at Joe's legs and looked up at him with big blue eyes and a grin of triumph.

What now? Joe thought awkwardly. He reached down and took his son's tiny plump hand and gave it a shake. 'Pleased to meet you, Jacko.'

He deliberately avoided noting Ellie's reaction.

They drove down to the river flats with their son strapped into the toddler seat between them, and Ellie tried not to mind that Jacko seemed to be obsessed with Joe.

The whole way, the little boy kept giggling and making eyes at the tall dark figure beside him, and he squealed with delight when Joe pulled faces.

A man's presence at Karinya was a novelty, of course, and Ellie knew that Jacko had been starved of masculine company. He was always intrigued by any male visitor.

Problem was that today Ellie was almost as intrigued as her son, especially when she watched Joe take off on the trail bike through the rain and the mud. He looked so spectacularly athletic and fit and so totally at home on the back of a motorbike, rounding up the herd, ducking and weaving through patches of scrub.

He certainly hadn't lost his touch.

'Show-off,' she muttered with a reluctant grim smile as he jumped the bike over a pile of fallen timber and then skilfully edged the stragglers forward into the mob, heading them up the slope towards the open gate where she was parked.

'Joe!' Jacko cried, bouncing in his car seat and pointing through the windscreen. He clapped his hands. 'Look, Mummy! Joe!'

'Yeah, he looks good, all right,' Ellie had to admit. In terms of skill and getting the job done quickly, Joe might never have been away.

And that felt dangerous.

Out of the blue, she found herself remembering their wedding day and the short ceremony in the register office in Townsville. She and Joe had decided they didn't want to go through awkward explanations about her pregnancy to their families, and neither of them had wanted the fuss of a big family wedding.

They'd both agreed they could deal with their families later. On that day, all they'd wanted was to commit to each other. Their elopement had seemed *soooo* romantic.

But it had also been reckless, Ellie thought now as she saw how brightly her son's eyes shone as he watched Joe.

'Don't be too impressed, sweetheart. Take Mummy's word; it's simply not worth it. That man will only break your heart.'

Jacko merely chortled.

It was dark by the time Joe came into the kitchen, having showered and changed into dry clothes. Outside, the rain still pelted down, drumming on the roof and streaming over the edge of the guttering, but Ellie had closed the French windows leading onto the veranda and the kitchen was bright and cosy.

She tried not to notice how red-hot attractive Joe looked in a simple white T-shirt and blue jeans, with his dark hair damp from the shower, his bright eyes an unforgettable piercing blue. The man was still unlawfully sexy.

But Joe seemed to have acquired a lone wolf aura now. In addition to his imperfect nose that had been broken in a punch-up when he was seventeen, there was a hard don't-mess-with-me look in his eyes that made her wonder what he'd been through over the past four years.

Almost certainly, he'd been required to kill people, and she couldn't quite get her head around that. How had that changed him?

The Army had kept the Commandos' deployments short and frequent in a bid to minimise post-traumatic stress, but no soldier returned from war unscarred. These days, everyone knew that. For Ellie, there was the extra, heavily weighing knowledge that their unhappy marriage had pushed Joe in the Army's direction.

And now, here they were, standing in the same room, but she was painfully aware of the wide, unbridgeable chasm that gaped open between them.

She turned and lifted the lid on the slow cooker, giving its contents a stir, wishing she was more on top of this situation.

'That smells amazing,' said Joe.

She felt a small flush of satisfaction. She'd actually set their dinner simmering earlier in the day, hoping it would fill the kitchen with enticing aromas, but she responded to Joe's compliment with a casual shrug and tried not to look too pleased. 'It's just a Spanish chicken dish.'

'Spanish?' Joe raised a quizzical eyebrow.

No doubt he was remembering her previously limited range of menus. 'I've broadened my recipe repertoire.'

Joe almost smiled, but then he seemed to change his mind. Sinking his hands into his jeans pockets, he looked around the kitchen, taking in the table set with red and white gingham mats and the sparkling white cupboards and timber bench tops. 'You've also been decorating.'

Ellie nodded. 'Before I became pregnant with Jacko I painted just about every wall and cupboard in the house.'

'The nesting instinct?'

'Something like that.'

Joe frowned at this, his eyes taking on an ambiguous gleam as he stared hard at the cupboards. His Adam's apple jerked in his throat. 'It looks great,' he said gruffly.

But Ellie felt suddenly upset. It felt wrong to be showing off her homemaker skills when she had absolutely no plans to share this home with him.

'Where's Jacko?' he asked, abruptly changing the subject

'Watching TV. Nina's recorded his favourite programmes, and he's happy to watch them over and over. It helps him to wind down at the end of the day.'

This was met by a slow nod but, instead of wandering off to check out his son, Joe continued to stand in the middle of the kitchen with his hands in his pockets, his gaze thoughtful.

'He doesn't watch a lot of TV,' Ellie felt compelled to explain. 'I…I usually read him story books as well.'

'I'm sure he loves that.' Joe's blue eyes blazed. 'Chill, Ellie. I'm not here to judge you. I'm sure you're a great mum. Fantastic.'

Her smile wobbled uncertainly. Why would this compliment make her want to cry?

They should try to relax. She should offer Joe a predinner beer or a glass of wine.

But, before she could suggest this, he said, 'So, I guess this is as good a time as any for me to sign those divorce papers?'

Ellie's stomach dropped as if she'd fallen from the top of a mountain. 'Well…um…yes,' she said, but she had to grip the bench behind her before her knees gave way. 'You could sign now…or after dinner.'

'It's probably best to get it over with and out of the way.'

'I guess.' Her reply was barely a whisper. It was ridiculous. She'd been waiting for this moment for so long. They'd arranged an out of court settlement and their future plans were clear—she would keep on with the lease at Karinya, and Joe had full access to Jacko, although she wasn't sure how often he planned to see his son.

This settlement was what she wanted, of course, and

yet she felt suddenly bereft, as if a great hole had opened up in her life, almost as if someone had died.

What on earth was the matter with her? Joe's signature would provide her with her ticket of leave.

Freedom beckoned.

The feeling of loss was nothing more than a temporary lapse, an aberration brought on by the unscheduled spot of cattle work that she and Joe had shared this afternoon. Rounding up the herd by the river had felt too dangerously like the good old days when they'd still been in love.

'Ellie?' Joe was standing stiffly to attention now, his eyes alert but cool, watching her intently. 'You're OK about this, aren't you?'

'Yes, of course. I'm totally fine.' She spoke quickly, not quite meeting his gaze, and then she drew a deep, fortifying breath, hoping it would stop the trembling in her knees. 'The papers are in the study.'

'Ellie.'

The unexpected gentleness in his voice brought her spinning around. 'Yes?'

'I wish…'

'What?' She almost snapped this question.

What do you wish? Tell me quickly, Joe.

Did he wish they didn't have to do this? Was he asking for another chance to save their marriage?

'I wish you didn't look so pale and upset.'

Her attempt to laugh came out as a hiccup. Horrified, she seized on the handiest weapon—anger. It was the weapon she'd used so often with this man, firing holes into the bedrock of their marriage. 'If I'm upset, Joe, it's because this is a weird situation.'

'But we agreed.' He seemed angry, too, but his anger

was annoyingly cold and controlled. 'It's what you want, isn't it?'

'Sure, we agreed, and yes, it's what I want. But it's still weird. How many people agree to a divorce and then put it on hold for four years?'

'You know why we did that—so you'd be looked after financially if I was killed.'

'Yes, I know, and that was generous of you. Just the same, it hasn't been a picnic here.' Suddenly, Ellie could feel the long months of tension giving way inside her, rushing to the surface, hot and explosive. 'While you were away being the hero in Afghanistan, you were distracted by everything over there. But I was *here*, supposed to be divorced, but surrounded by all of this.'

Flinging her arm dramatically, she gestured to the homestead and the paddocks beyond. 'Every day, I was left with the remnants of our lives together. A constant reminder of everything that went wrong.'

'So why did you stay?' Joe asked coolly.

Ellie gasped, momentarily caught out. 'I'm surprised you have to ask,' she said quickly to cover her confusion.

He shrugged a cool, questioning eyebrow.

And Ellie looked away. She'd asked herself the same question often enough. She knew exactly why she'd stayed. Even now, she could hear her dad's voice from all those years ago. *If you start something, Ellie, you've got to see it through.*

Her dad had told her this just before her thirteenth birthday. She'd been promised a horse for her birthday and he'd been building proper stables instead of the old two-sided tin shelter they'd had until then.

Ellie had helped him by holding hammers or the long

pieces of timber and she'd handed up nails and screws. While they worked her dad had reminded her that owning a horse was a long-term project.

'You can't take up a responsibility like a horse and then lose interest,' he'd said. 'I've known people like that. They never stick at anything, always have to be trying something different, and they end up unhappy and wondering what went wrong.'

Tragically, her father had never finished those stables. He'd also he'd been mending a windmill and he'd fallen and died three days before Ellie's birthday. In the bleak months that followed, Ellie's mum had sold their farm and moved into town, and the horse that should have been Ellie's had gone to another girl in her class at school.

In a matter of months, Ellie lost everything—her darling father, her beloved farm, her dreams of owning a horse. And the bittersweet irony of her father's words had been seared into her brain.

If you start something, you've got to see it through.

Years later, with a failed marriage and failed attempts at parenthood weighing her down, she'd been determined that she wouldn't let go of Karinya as well.

'So why did you stay here?' Joe repeated.

With her arms folded protectively over her chest, Ellie told him. 'I love this place, Joe. I'm proud of it, and I've worked hard to improve it. It was hard enough giving up half a dream without giving up Karinya as well.'

Joe's only reaction was to stand very still, watching her with a stern, unreadable gaze. If Ellie hadn't been studying him with equal care, she might have missed the fleeting shadow that dimmed his bright blue eyes, or the telltale muscle twitching in his jaw.

But she did see these signs, and they made something unravel inside her.

Damn you, Joe. Tell me what you're thinking.

Painful seconds ticked by, but neither of them moved nor spoke. Ellie almost reached out and said, *Do we need to talk about this?*

But it wasn't an easy question to ask when it was Joe who'd originally suggested their divorce. He'd never shown any sign of backing down, so now her stubborn pride kept her silent.

Eventually, he said quietly, 'So, about this signing?'

Depressed but resolute, Ellie pointed to the doorway to the study. 'The papers are in here.'

As she reached the study, she didn't look back to check that Joe was following her. Skirting the big old silky oak desk that they'd bought at an antique shop in Charters Towers, she marched straight to the shelves Joe had erected all those years ago and she lifted down a well-thumbed Manila folder.

She sensed Joe behind her but she didn't look at him as she turned and placed the folder on the desk. In silence she opened it to reveal the sheaf of papers that she'd lodged with the courts.

'I guess you'll want to read these through,' she said, eyes downcast.

'There's no need. Geoffrey Bligh has sent me a copy. I know what it says.'

'Oh? All right.' Ellie opened a drawer and selected a black pen. 'So, I've served you with the papers, and all you need to do now is sign to acknowledge that you accept them.' She still couldn't look him in the eye.

She was trembling inside and she took a deep breath.

'There,' she said dully, setting the appropriate sheet

of paper on the desk and then stepping away to make room for Joe.

His face was stonily grim as he approached the desk, but he showed no sign of hesitation as he picked up the pen.

As he leaned over the desk, Ellie watched the neat dark line of his hair across the back of his neck and she saw a vein pulsing just below his ear. She noticed how strong his hand looked as he gripped the pen.

Unhelpfully, she remembered his hand, those fingers touching her when they made love. It seemed so long ago and yet it was so unforgettable.

There'd been a time in their marriage when they'd been so good at sex.

Joe scrawled his spiky signature, then set the pen down and stood staring fiercely at the page now decorated with his handwriting.

It was over.

In the morning he would take this final piece of paper with him to their solicitor but, to all intents and purposes, they were officially and irrevocably divorced.

And now they had to eat dinner together. Ellie feared the Spanish chicken would taste like dust in her mouth.

CHAPTER THREE

IT SHOULD HAVE been cosy eating Ellie's delicious meal in the homestead kitchen to the accompaniment of the steadily falling rain. But Joe had dined in Kabul when a car bomb exploded just outside and he'd felt more relaxed then than he did now with his ex.

It shouldn't be this way.

All their tensions were supposed to be behind them now. They were no longer man and wife. Their marriage was over, both in reality and on paper. It was like signing a peace treaty. No more disputes. Everything was settled.

They were free. Just friends. No added expectations.

And yet Ellie had barely touched the food she'd taken so much trouble to prepare. Joe supposed she wished he was gone—completely out of her hair.

As long as he hung around this place, they would both be besieged by this edgy awareness of each other that kept them on tenterhooks.

Ellie was meticulously shredding the tender chicken on her plate with her fork. 'So what are your plans now?' she asked in the carefully polite tone people used when they were making an effort to maintain a semblance of normality. 'Are you staying in the Army?'

Joe shook his head. 'I have a job lined up—with a government team in the Southern Ocean—patrolling for poachers and illegal fishermen.'

'The Southern Ocean?' Ellie couldn't have looked more surprised or upset if he'd announced he was going to mine asteroids in outer space. 'So…so Jacko won't see you at all?'

Annoyed by this, Joe shrugged. 'If you plan to stay out here, it wouldn't matter what sort of work I did—I still wouldn't be able to see the boy very often.'

'There's an Army base in Townsville.'

This was a surprise. He'd expected Ellie to be pleased that he'd be well away from her. 'As I said, I'm leaving the Army.'

Ellie's eyes widened. 'I thought you loved it. I thought it was supposed to be what you'd always wanted.'

'It was,' Joe said simply. For possibly the first time in his life, he'd felt a true sense of belonging with his fellow Commandos. He'd grown up as the youngest in his family, but he'd always been the little nuisance tagalong, hanging around his four older brothers, never quite big enough to keep up, never quite fitting in.

In the Army he'd truly discovered a 'band of brothers', united by the challenge and threat of active service. But everything about the Army would be different now, and he couldn't bear the thought of a desk job.

Ellie dipped her fork into a pile of savoury rice, but she didn't lift it to her mouth. 'I can't see you in a boat, rolling around in the Southern Ocean. You've always been a man of the land. You have all the bush skills and knowledge.'

It was true that Joe loved the bush, and he'd especially loved starting his own cattle business here at

Karinya. But what was the point of rehashing ancient history?

'I guess I feel like a change,' he said with a shrug.

'When do you have to start this new job?'

'In a few weeks. Mid-January.'

'That soon?'

He shrugged again. He was pleased he had an approaching deadline. Given the mess of his private life, he needed a plan, somewhere definite to go with new horizons.

'Will you mind—' Ellie began, but then she swallowed and looked away. 'Will it bother you that you won't see much of Jacko?'

Joe inhaled a sharp, instinctively protective breath. He was trying really hard not to think too much about his son, about all the milestones he'd already missed and those he would miss in the future—the day-to-day adventure of watching a small human being come to terms with the world. 'Maybe I'll be more use to him later on, when he's older.'

It was clearly the wrong thing to say.

Ellie's jaw jutted. She looked tenser than ever. Awkward seconds ticked by. Joe wished he didn't have to try so damn hard, even now, after they'd broken up.

'What about you?' he asked. 'I haven't asked how you are now. Are you keeping well?'

'I am well, actually. I think having Jacko has made a big difference, both mentally and physically. I must admit I'm a lot calmer these days. And I think all the hard outdoor work here has paid off as well.' She touched her stomach. 'Internally, things…um…seem to have settled down.'

'That's fantastic.' He knew how she'd suffered and he was genuinely pleased for her. 'So, do you have plans?'

'How do you mean?'

'Are you planning to move on from here?' Joe steeled himself. If there was a new man in her life, this was her chance to say so.

But her jaw dropped so hard Joe almost heard it crack.

'You're joking, aren't you?'

'Not at all.'

'You really think I could willingly leave Karinya?'

'Well, it's got to be tough for you out here on your own. You need help.'

'I hire help if I need it—fencing contractors, ringers, jillaroos…'

The relief he felt was ridiculous. He covered it with a casual shrug. 'I've heard it's hard to find workers these days. Everyone's heading for the mines.'

'I've managed.'

Joe couldn't resist prying. 'I suppose you might have a boyfriend lined up already?'

'Oh, for pity's sake.' Ellie was angry now.

And, although he knew it was foolish, he couldn't help having one last dig. 'I thought your mother might have had a victory. What was the name of that guy she picked out for you? The potato farmer near Hay? Orlando?'

'Roland,' Ellie said tightly. 'And he grows all sorts of vegetables—lettuce, pumpkins, tomatoes, corn—much more than potatoes. He's making a fortune, apparently.'

'Quite a catch,' Joe said, more coldly than he'd meant to.

'Yes, and a gentleman, too.' Ellie narrowed her eyes

at Joe. 'Do you really want me to give up this lease? Are you worried about the money?'

'No,' he snapped tersely. He couldn't deny he was impressed by Ellie's tenacity, even if it suggested that she was prepared to work much harder at the cattle business than she had at their marriage. 'I just think it's too big a property for a woman to run on her own, especially for a woman with a small child to care for as well.'

'Nina will be back after Christmas. She's great with Jacko.'

Joe recognised a brick wall when he ran into it and he let the subject drop. He suspected Ellie was as relieved as he was when the meal was finally over.

With the aid of night vision goggles, Joe made his way through a remote Afghan village, moving with the stealth of a panther on the prowl. In every dark alley and around every corner the threat of danger lurked and Joe was on high alert, listening for the slightest movement or sound.

As forward scout, his responsibilities weighed heavily. Five Australian soldiers depended on his skills, trusting that he wouldn't lead them blindly into an ambush.

As he edged around another corner, a sudden crash shattered the silence. Joe's night vision vanished. He was plunged into darkness.

Adrenaline exploded in his vitals. How had he lost his goggles? Or—hell—had worse happened? Had he been blinded?

He couldn't even find his damn rifle.

To add to the confusion, a persistent drumming sounded above and around him.

What the hell had happened?

Even more bizarrely, when Joe stepped forward he felt carpet beneath his feet. His *bare* feet. What was going on? Where was he?

Panic flared. Had he gone raving mad? Where were his boots? His weapon?

Totally disoriented, he blinked, and at last his vision cleared slightly. He could just make out the dimmest of details, and he seemed to be naked apart from boxer shorts and, yes, his feet were bare and they were definitely sinking into soft carpet.

He had absolutely no idea where the hell he was, or how he'd got there.

Then he heard a small child's cry and his stomach lurched. As a Commando, in close contact with the enemy, his greatest fear was that he might inadvertently bring harm to Afghan children.

It was still difficult to see as he made his way through the pitch-black night, moving towards the child's cry, bumping into a bookcase.

A bookcase?

A doorway.

Ahead, down a passage, he saw a faint glow—it illuminated painted tongue-and-groove timber walls. Walls that were strangely familiar.

Karinya.

Hell, yeah. Of course.

A soft oath broke from him. He'd woken from a particularly vivid dream and he was back in North Queensland and, while he couldn't explain the crashing sound, the crying child was…

Jacko.

His son.

Joe's heart skidded as he scorched into Jacko's room. In the glow of a night light, he saw the toddler huddled and frightened on the floor in the wreckage of his cot. Without hesitation, Joe dived and swept the boy into his arms.

Jacko was shaking but, in Joe's arms, he nestled against his bare chest, a warm ball sobbing, seeking protection and clearly trusting Joe to provide it.

'Shh.' Joe pressed his lips to the boy's soft hair and caught the amazing smell of shampoo, probably baby shampoo. 'You're OK. I've got you.'

I'm your father.

The boy felt so little and warm in Joe's arms. And so scared. A fierce wave of emotion came sweeping through Joe—a surge of painful yearning—an urge to protect this warm, precious miniature man, to keep him safe at all costs.

'I've got you, little mate,' he murmured. 'You're OK.' And then he added in a soft, tentative whisper, 'I'm your dad. I love you, Jacko.' The words felt both alien and wonderful. And true.

'What happened?' Ellie's voice demanded from the doorway. 'I heard a crash.'

Joe turned and saw her in the dimmed light, wearing a white nightdress with tiny straps, her dark hair tumbling in soft waves about her smooth, bare shoulders. She looked beautiful beyond words and Joe's heart almost stopped.

'What happened?' she asked again, coming forward. 'Is Jacko all right?'

'I think he's fine, but he got a bad fright. Looks like his cot's collapsed.'

Jacko had seen Ellie now and he lurched away from Joe, throwing out his arms and wailing, 'Mummy!'

Joe tried not to mind that his Great Three Seconds of Fatherhood were over in a blink, or that Jacko, now safely in Ellie's arms, looked back at him as if he were a stranger.

Ellie was staring at Joe too—staring with wide, almost popping eyes at his bare chest and at the scars on his shoulder. Joe hoped her gaze wouldn't drop to his shorts or they'd both be embarrassed.

Abruptly, he turned, forcing his attention to the collapsed cot. It was a simple timber construction with panels of railings threaded on a metal rod and screwed into place with wing nuts. Nothing had actually broken. It seemed the thing had simply come apart.

'Looks like the wing nuts in the corners worked loose,' he said.

'Oh, Lord.' Ellie stepped forward with the boy on her hip. 'Jacko was playing with those wing nuts the other day. He was trying to undo them, but I didn't think he had a hope.'

'Well, I'd say he was successful. He must have strong little fingers.'

Ellie looked at her son in disbelief and then she shook her head and gave a wry smile, her dark eyes suddenly sparkling. Joe so wished she wouldn't smile like that, not when she was standing so close to him in an almost see-through nightdress.

'You're a little monkey, Jacko,' she told the boy affectionately. Then, more businesslike, she turned to Joe. 'I guess it shouldn't be too hard to fix?'

'Piece of cake.' He picked up one of the panels. 'A

pair of pliers would be handy. The nuts need to be tight enough to stop him from doing it again.'

Ellie nodded. 'I think I have a spare pair of pliers in the laundry, but don't worry about it now. I'll take Jacko back to my room. He can sleep with me for the rest of the night.'

Lucky Jacko.

From the doorway, she turned and frowned back at Joe. 'Do you need anything? A hot drink or something to help you get back to sleep?'

She must have seen the expression on his face. She quickly dropped her gaze. 'I keep forgetting. You're a tough soldier. You can sleep on a pile of rocks.'

With Jacko in her arms, she hurried away, the white nightdress whispering around her smooth, shapely calves.

Joe knew he wouldn't be sleeping.

Jacko settled quickly. He was like a little teddy bear as he snuggled close to Ellie and in no time he was asleep again. She adored her little miracle boy, and she relished this excuse to lie still and hold him, loving the way he nestled close.

Lying in the darkness, she inhaled the scent of his clean hair and listened to the soft rhythm of his breathing.

His perfection constantly amazed her.

But, tonight, it wasn't long before she was thinking about Joe and, in a matter of moments, she felt a pain in her chest like indigestion, and then her throat was tense and aching, choked.

She kept seeing Joe's signature on that piece of paper.

And now he was about to head off for the Southern

Ocean. Surely, if he wanted adventure, he could have caught wild bulls or rogue crocodiles, or found half a dozen other dangerous activities that were closer to home?

Instead, once again, he was getting as far away from her as possible, risking his life in stormy seas and chasing international poachers, for pity's sake.

Unhelpfully, Ellie recalled how eye-wateringly amazing Joe had looked just now, standing bare-chested in Jacko's room. With the little boy in his arms, he'd looked so incredibly strong and muscular and protective.

Man, he was *buffed*.

He'd always been fit and athletic, of course, which was one of the reasons the Army had snapped him up, but now, after all the extra training and discipline, her ex-husband looked sensational.

Her ex.

The word hit her like a slug to the heart. Which was crazy. *I don't want him back. Looks aren't everything. They're just a distraction.*

Tonight, it was all too easy to forget the pain she and Joe had been through, the constant bickering and soul-destroying negativity, the tears and the yelling. The sad truth was—the final year before their separation had been pretty close to hell on earth.

Unhappily, Ellie knew that a large chunk of the tension had been her fault. During that bleak time when she'd been so overwhelmed by her inability to get pregnant again, she'd really turned on Joe until everything he'd done had annoyed her.

Looking back, she felt so guilty. She'd been a shrew—constantly picking on Joe for the smallest things, even the way he left clothes lying around, or the way he left the lid off the toothpaste, the way he'd assumed she was happy to look after the house and the garden while he swanned off, riding his horse all over their property, enjoying all the adventurous, more important outdoor jobs, while she was left to cook and clean.

Ellie hadn't been proud of her nagging and fault-finding. As a child, she'd hated the way her mother picked on her dad all the time, and she'd been shocked to find herself repeating that despicable pattern. But she'd become so tense and depressed she hadn't been able to stop herself.

Naturally, Joe hadn't accepted her insults meekly. He'd slung back as good as he got. But she'd been devastated when he finally suggested divorce.

'It's clear that I'm making you unhappy,' he'd said in a cold, clipped voice she'd never heard before.

And how could Ellie deny it? She *had* been unhappy, and she'd taken her unhappiness out on Joe, but that hadn't meant she wanted to be rid of him.

'Do you really want a divorce?' she'd asked him and, although she'd been crying on the inside, for the sake of her pride, she'd kept a brave face.

'I think it's the only solution,' Joe had said. 'We can't go on like this. Maybe you'll have better luck with another guy.'

She didn't want another man, but why would Joe believe that when she'd been so obviously miserable?

'What would you do?' she'd asked instead. 'Where would you go? What would we do about Karinya?'

He'd been scarily cool and detached. 'You can make up your mind about Karinya, but I'll apply to join the Army.'

She hadn't known how to fight this. 'The Army was what you wanted all along, wasn't it? It was what you were planning before we met.'

Joe didn't deny this.

It was then she'd known the awful truth. Falling for her had been an aberration. A distraction.

If she hadn't been pregnant, they wouldn't have married…

The bitter memories wrung a groan from Ellie and, beside her in the darkness, Jacko stirred, throwing out an arm and smacking her on the nose. He didn't wake up and she rolled away, staring moodily into the black night, thinking about Joe lying in his swag on the study floor. He'd insisted on sleeping there rather than in Nina's room.

'It's only for one night,' he'd said. 'Not worth disturbing her things.'

Ellie wondered if Joe was asleep, or whether he was also lying there thinking about their past.

Unlikely.

No doubt he was relieved to be finally and permanently free of her. He certainly wouldn't be as mixed-up and tied in knots as she was.

Joe didn't want to think about Ellie. She was part of his past, just as the Army was now. Every time visions of her white nightdress arrived, he forcibly erased them.

He'd signed the final papers.

Ellie. Was. No. Longer. His. Wife.

And yet…

Annoyingly, he felt a weight that felt like grief pressing on his chest. Grief for their loss, and for their failure, for their past mistakes and for how things used to be at the beginning.

And, despite his best efforts, he couldn't stop the blasted memories.

He'd been a goner from the moment he first saw Ellie, which was pretty bizarre, given that his first sighting had been at long distance.

Ellie had been walking with her back to him at the far end of their tiny town's one and only shopping street. And, from the start, there'd been something inescapably alluring about her. The glossy swing of her dark hair and the jaunty sway of her neat butt in long-legged blue jeans had completely captured his attention.

Of course, it was totally the *worst* time for Joe to become romantically entangled. He'd been on the brink of joining the Army. After struggling unsuccessfully to find his place in the large Madden family, overrun with strapping sons, he'd been lured by the military's promise of adventure and danger.

So, on that day that was etched forever in his memory, he should have been able to ignore Ellie's attractions. He should have finished his errands in town and headed back to their cattle property. And perhaps he would have done that if Jerry Bray hadn't chosen that exact moment to step out of the stock and station agency to speak to Ellie.

Jealousy was a strange and fierce emotion, Joe swiftly discovered. He hadn't even met this girl, hadn't yet seen her front-on, hadn't discovered the bewitching sparkle in her eyes. And yet he was furious with Jerry for chatting her up.

To Joe's huge relief, Jerry's boss interrupted his employee's clumsy attempts at flirtation and called him back inside.

Alone once more, Ellie continued on to the Bluebird Café, and this was a golden opportunity Joe couldn't let pass.

After a carefully calculated interval, he followed her into the café, found her sitting alone at one of the tables, drinking a milkshake and engrossed in a women's magazine.

She looked up when he walked in and Joe saw her face for the first time. Saw her eyes, the same lustrous dark brown as her hair, saw her finely arched eyebrows, her soft pale skin, the sweet curve of her mouth, her neat chin. She was even lovelier than he'd imagined.

And then she smiled.

And *zap*. Joe was struck by the proverbial lightning flash. His skin was on fire, his heart was a skyrocket.

'So what d'ya want?' asked Bob Browne, the café's proprietor.

Joe stared at him blankly, unable, for a moment, to think. It was as if his mind had been wiped clean by the dark-eyed girl's smile.

Bob gave a knowing smirk and rolled his eyes. 'She's not on the menu.'

Ignoring this warning, Joe shrugged and ordered a hamburger and a soft drink. Unable to help himself, he crossed the café to the girl's table. 'Hi,' he said.

'Hello.' This time, when she smiled, he saw the most fetching dimple.

'You must be new around here. I don't think we've met. I'm Joe Madden.'

'Ellie Saxby,' she supplied without hesitation.

Ellie Saxby. Ellie. Had there ever been a more de-lightful name?

'Are you staying around here?' he asked super-casually.

'I'm working for the Ashtons. As a jillaroo.'

Better and better.

There was a spare chair at Ellie Saxby's table. 'OK if I sit here?' Joe was again carefully, casually polite.

Ellie rewarded him with another dazzling smile. 'Sure.'

Her eyes were shining, her cheeks flushed. The at-mosphere was so electric, Joe felt as if he was walk-ing on clouds.

And yet there was nothing remarkable about that first conversation. Joe was too dazed to think of any-thing very clever to say. But he and Ellie chatted easily about where they lived and why they'd come to town.

By the time his hamburger arrived, he was halfway in love with Ellie and she was giving out all the right signals. They left the café together and Joe walked with her to her vehicle.

They exchanged phone numbers and Ellie remained standing beside her car, as if she wasn't ready to drive away.

She looked so alluring, with her sparkling eyes and shiny hair, her soft skin and pretty mouth.

Joe had never been particularly forward with girls, but he found himself saying, 'Look, I know we've just met, and this out of line, but I really need to—'

He didn't even finish the sentence. He simply leaned in and kissed her. Ellie tasted as fresh as spring and, to his amazed relief, she returned his kiss with just the right level of enthusiasm, and a simple hello, exploratory kiss became the most thrilling, most electrifying kiss ever.

It was the start of a whirlwind romance. Before the week was out, he and Ellie had found an excuse to meet again and, within the first month, they drove together to Rockhampton for dinner and a movie, followed by a night in a motel, which proved to be a night of blazing, out of this world passion.

When Ellie discovered she was pregnant, Joe had to make a quick decision. Ellie or the Army?

No contest.

In a blinding flash of clarity, he knew without question that his plan to join the Army had been a crazy idea. In Ellie he'd found his true reason for being. He asked her to marry him and, to his delight, she readily agreed.

The ink on their marriage certificate was barely dry before they headed north in search of their very own cattle property and the start of their bright new happy-ever-after.

When Ellie miscarried three weeks after they'd moved into Karinya, they'd been deeply disappointed but, in the long run, not too downhearted. After all, they were young and healthy and strong and in love.

But it was the start of a downhill run. A diagnosis of endometriosis had followed. Joe had never even heard of this condition, let alone understood how it could blight such a fit and healthy girl. Ellie was vivacious, bursting with energy and life and yet, over the next few years, she was slowly dragged down.

He remembered finding her slumped over the kitchen table, her face streaked with tears.

He'd touched her gently on the shoulder, stroked her

hair. 'Don't let it get you down, Ellie. It'll be OK. We'll be OK.'

We still have each other, he'd wanted to say.

But she'd whirled on him, her face red with fury. 'How can you say that? How can you possibly *know* we'll be OK? I'm sorry, Joe, but that's just a whitewash, and it makes me *so* mad!'

She'd lost all hope, had no faith in him or their future. He'd felt helpless.

Now, with hindsight, he could see the full picture. He and Ellie had rushed at marriage like lemmings to a cliff, expecting to build a lasting relationship—for richer or poorer, in sickness and in health—having based these expectations on little more than blazing lust.

It was his fault.

Joe had always known that. Looking back, it was blindingly obvious that he hadn't courted Ellie properly. They hadn't taken anywhere near enough time to get to know each other as friends before they became life partners. They hadn't even fully explored their hopes and dreams before they'd embarked on marriage.

They'd simply been lovers, possessed by passion, a heady kind of madness. And Ellie had found herself trapped by that first pregnancy.

Small wonder their marriage had hit the rocks as soon as the seas got rough and, instead of offering Ellie comfort, Joe had taken refuge, working long hard hours in Karinya's paddocks—fencing, building dams, mustering and branding cattle. Later he'd joined the Army. Had that been a kind of refuge as well?

Whatever. It was too late for an extensive post-mortem. Tomorrow he'd be leaving again and Ellie would finally be free. He wished he felt better about that.

CHAPTER FOUR

NEXT MORNING IT was raining harder than ever.

Out of habit, Ellie woke early and slipped out of bed, leaving Jacko curled asleep. She dressed quickly and went to the kitchen and, to her surprise Joe was already up, dressed and drinking a mug of tea.

He turned and greeted her with only the faintest trace of a smile. 'Morning.'

'Good morning.' Ellie flicked the kettle to bring it back to the boil and looked out of the window at the wall of thick grey rain. 'It's been raining all night. You won't want to waste time getting over the river.'

Joe nodded. 'I'll need to get going, but I'm worried about you and Jacko. You could be cut off.'

'Yeah, well, that happens most wet seasons.' She reached for a mug and a tea bag. 'I'm used to it and we're well stocked up.'

Joe was frowning, and Ellie wondered if frowning was his new default expression.

'It's hardly an ideal situation,' he said. 'A woman and a little child, isolated and alone out here. It's crazy. What if Jacko gets sick or injured?'

'Crikey, Joe. Since when has that worried you? We've been living here since he was born, you know.'

'But you haven't been cut off by flood waters.'

'I have, actually.'

He glared at her, and an emotion halfway between anger and despair shimmered in his eyes.

Ellie tried for nonchalance as she poured boiling water into her mug.

Joe cleared his throat. 'I think I should stay.'

Startled, Ellie almost scalded herself. 'You mean stay here with us?'

'Just till the river goes down again.'

'Joe, we're divorced.'

His blue eyes glittered. 'I'm aware of that.'

'And…and it's almost Christmas.' Last night they'd struggled through an unbearably strained meal together. They couldn't possibly manage something as festive as Christmas.

Ellie was supposed to be spending Christmas Day with her neighbours and good friends, the Andersons, although, if the creek stayed high, as well as the river, that might not be an option.

Of course, her mother had originally wanted her to go home to New South Wales, but Ellie had declined on several grounds. Number one—she wasn't comfortable around her stepfather, for reasons her mother had turned a deaf ear to. As well as that, up until yesterday, she'd been dealing, ironically, with drought. Her priority had been the state of her cattle—and then clearing things up with Joe.

The Joe factor was well and truly sorted, and sharing Christmas with him would be a disaster. Being divorced and forced to stay together would be a thousand times bigger strain than being married and apart.

'There's absolutely no need for you to stay, Joe. I really don't think it's a good idea.'

'It was just a suggestion,' he said tightly. 'I was only thinking of your safety.'

'Thanks. That's thoughtful.' Feeling awkward, Ellie fiddled with the handle of her tea mug. 'You know drought and floods are part and parcel of living in this country.'

With a brief shrug, Joe drained his mug and placed it in the sink. 'I should head off then, before the river gets any higher.'

'But you haven't had breakfast.'

'As you pointed out, it wouldn't be wise to wait. It's been raining all night and the river's rising every minute. I've packed the solicitor's papers. I'll drop them in at Bligh's office.'

'Right.' Ellie set her tea mug aside, no longer able to drink it.

Joe's duffel bag was already packed and zipped, and the swag he'd used for sleeping on the study floor was neatly rolled and strapped. Seemed the Army had turned him into a neat freak.

'I've also fixed Jacko's cot,' he said.

'You must have got up early.'

Without answering, he reached for his duffel bag and swung it over one shoulder. 'I wasn't sure where to put the Christmas presents, so I stowed them under the desk in the study. Hope that's OK?'

'That…that's fine, thanks, Joe.' Ellie wished she didn't feel quite so downbeat. 'I hope you haven't spoiled Jacko with too many presents.'

She winced as she said this. She didn't really mind how many presents Joe had bought. This was one of his few chances to play the role of a father. She'd been trying for a light-hearted comment and had totally missed the mark.

Now, Joe's cold, hollow laugh chilled her to the bone.

His face seemed to be carved from stone as he turned to leave. 'Well, all the best, Ellie.'

'Hang on. I'll wake Jacko so you can say goodbye to him, too.'

'Don't disturb him.'

'You've got to say goodbye.' Ellie was close to tears. 'Actually, we'll come out to the river crossing with you. We can follow you in the ute. Just in case there's a problem.'

'There won't be a problem.'

To her dismay, her tears were threatening to fall. 'Joe, humour me. I want to see you safely off this property.'

For the first time, a faint smile glimmered. 'Of course you do.'

Ellie parked on a ridge above the concrete causeway that crossed the river and peered through the rain at the frothing, muddy flood rushing below.

She could see the bright blue of Joe's hire car parked just above the waterline and his dark-coated figure standing on the bank, hands on hips as he studied the river.

'I think it's already too high,' she said glumly to Jacko. The river level was much, much higher than she'd expected. Clearly, the waters from the north had already reached them overnight.

She felt a flurry of panic. Did this mean that Joe would have to stay with them for Christmas after all? How on earth would they cope with the strain?

Even as she wondered this, Joe took off his coat, tossed it back into his vehicle, then began to walk back to the swirling current.

He wasn't going in there, surely?

'Joe!' Ellie yelled, leaping out of the ute. 'Don't be mad. You can't go in there.'

He showed no sign that he'd heard her. No doubt he was as keen to leave her as she was to see him go, but marching into a racing torrent was madness.

Ellie rushed down the track. 'Joe, stop!' The river was mud-brown and seething. 'You can't go in there,' she panted as she reached him.

He scowled and shook his head. 'It's OK. I just need to check the condition of the crossing and the depth. It's too risky to drive straight in there, but I can at least test it on foot. I'll be careful. I think it's still shallow enough to get the car across.'

'But look how fast the water's running. I know you're keen to get away, but you don't have to play the tough hero now, Joe.' Knowing how stubborn he could be, she tried for a joke. 'I don't want to have to tell Jacko that his father was a moron who was washed away trying to cross a flooded river.'

Joe's blue eyes flashed through the sheeting rain. 'I've been trained to stay alive, not to take senseless risks.' He jerked his head towards the ute. 'If you're worried about Jacko, you should get back up there and stay with him.'

Ellie threw up her hands in despair. She'd more or less encouraged, or rather *urged*, Joe to leave. But as she stood there debating how to stop her ex from risking his neck, she heard her little son calling to her.

'Go to him,' ordered Joe.

Utterly wretched, she began to walk back up the slope, turning every step to look over her shoulder as Joe approached the river. By the time she reached the ute, Joe was already in the water and in no time he was up to his knees.

Anxiously, she watched as he carefully felt the ground in front of him with one foot. He edged forward but, despite the obvious care he was taking, a sudden swift surge in the current buffeted him, making him sidestep to regain his balance.

'Joe!' she yelled, sticking her head out into the rain. 'That's enough! Get out!'

'Joe, that's 'nuff!' parroted Jacko.

A tree branch hurtled past Joe, almost sweeping him with it.

Turn back. Ellie was urging him, under her breath now, so she didn't alarm Jacko.

To her relief, Joe must have realised his venture was useless. At last he turned and began to make his way back to the bank.

But Ellie's relief was short-lived, of course. Sure, she was grateful that Joe hadn't drowned himself, but she had no idea how they could live together amicably till the river levels dropped. It would take days, possibly weeks, and the strain would be intolerable.

She was so busy worrying about the challenge of sharing Christmas with her ex that she didn't actually see what happened next.

It seemed that Joe was standing perfectly upright one moment, and then he suddenly toppled sideways and his dark head disappeared beneath the ugly brown water.

Joe had no warning.

He had a firm footing on the causeway, but with the

next step there was no concrete beneath him and he was struggling to regain his balance. Before he could adjust his weight, he slid off the edge.

He felt a sudden jarring scrape against his leg as he was pulled down into the bowels of the dark, angry river.

He couldn't see, couldn't breathe.

Scorching pain shot up his calf, and now he discovered that he also couldn't move. His foot was jammed between the broken section of the concrete causeway and a rock.

Hell. This was it. He'd survived four years of war and now he was going to die here. In front of Ellie and Jacko.

He was a brainless idiot. What had Ellie called him? A moron. She was dead right. No question.

And now… As his lungs strained for air, frantic memories flashed. The first time he'd seen Ellie in the outback café. The first time they'd kissed.

Last night and the chubby, sweet weight of Jacko in his arms.

His signature, acknowledging their divorce.

Don't freaking panic, man.

This was a major stuff-up, but he'd been trained to think.

He had to forget about the pain in his leg and his dire need for air and he had to work out a plan. Fast.

Clearly, his first priority was to get his head above water, but he was anchored by his trapped leg and the massive force of the rushing river. There was only one possible course of action. He had to brace against the current and use every ounce of his upper body strength, especially his stomach muscles, to pull himself upright.

Almost certainly, he couldn't have done it without

his years in the Army and its daily routine of rugged physical training.

As he fought his way upright, his arm bumped a steel rod sticking out of the concrete. As soon as he grabbed it, he had the leverage to finally lift his head above the surface.

He dragged a great, gasping gulp of air. And immediately he heard Ellie's cry.

'Joe! Oh, God, Joe!'

She was in the river, making her way towards him through the seething, perilous water. Her dark hair was plastered to her head, framing her very white, frightened face, and she looked too slender and too fragile and too totally vulnerable.

At any moment, she would be whipped away downstream and Joe knew he wouldn't have a chance in hell of saving her. In the same moment, he thought of trusting little Jacko strapped in his car seat, needing Ellie.

'Get back,' he roared to her. 'Stay on the bank. I'm OK.'

'You're not. Let me help you.'

'No,' he bellowed angrily. '*Get back!*'

He, at least, had something to hang on to, which was more than Ellie had. 'There's no point in both of us getting into trouble. If you're washed away, I won't be able to help you. For God's sake, Ellie, stay there. Think of Jacko. What happens to him, if neither of us gets out?'

This seemed to get through to her at last. She stood there with the river seething about her ankles, clearly tormented by difficult choices, but at least she'd stopped stubbornly coming towards him.

Joe knew he had to get moving. His foot was still

jammed and his only hope was to ignore the pain and to haul his foot out of the trapped boot.

Clenching his teeth, he kept a death grip on the steel rod as he concentrated every sinew in his body into getting his foot free. The force of the river threatened to push him off balance. Slicing pain sheared up his leg as if it was once again sliced by something rough and hard, but somehow, miraculously, his foot was finally out.

Now he just had to stay upright as he fought his way back. He was limping and he stumbled twice, his bare foot slipping on rocks, but he didn't fall and, as he reached the shallows, Ellie was there beside him.

'Don't argue, Joe. Just give me your arm.'

He was happy to let her help him to the bank.

At last…

'Thanks,' he said. And then, with difficulty, 'I'm sorry.'

'Yeah, well, thank God it's over.' Ellie seemed to be suddenly self-conscious. She quickly let go of him and stepped away. Her hair was sleek and straight from the rain and her clothes were plastered to her slender body. And, now that they were safe, Joe probably looked at her for longer than he should have as they stood on the muddy bank, catching their breath.

'You're bleeding!' Ellie cried suddenly, her eyes widening with horror as she pointed to his injured leg.

Joe looked down. Blood was running from beneath his ripped jeans and spreading in bright red rivulets over his bare foot.

'I think it's just a cut,' he said.

'But we need to attend to it. I hope it won't need stitches.'

'I'm sure it's not urgent. Go to Jacko.'

As if backing up Joe's suggestion, a tiny voice in the

distance screamed, 'Mama!' The poor little kid was wailing.

'He needs you,' Joe said, shuddering at the imagined scenario of poor Jacko abandoned in the car while both his parents were swept away.

At least Ellie was already on her way to him. 'You'd better come too,' she called over her shoulder.

There was only one option. While Ellie comforted Jacko, Joe found a towel to wrap around his bleeding leg and, after that, they drove their respective vehicles back to the homestead.

'Nuisance, I know,' Joe said as he set his luggage on the veranda again. 'This totally stuffs up your plans.'

Ellie shrugged. She'd morphed from the bravely stubborn warrior woman who'd rescued him from the river back to a tight-faced, wary hostess.

'We should take a closer look at your leg,' was all she said.

'I don't want to bleed all over the house.' Joe's leg was stinging like crazy and he'd already left bloody footprints on the veranda.

'Let me take a look at it.' Ellie dropped to her knees beside him, frowning as she carefully parted the torn denim to examine his leg more closely.

This was the first time Ellie had touched him in years, and now she was kneeling at his feet and looking so worried. He felt momentarily deprived of air, as if he was back in the river.

Ellie felt incredibly flustered about patching up Joe's leg.

She'd been hoping for distance from her ex, and here

she was instead, tending to his wounds. And the task felt impossibly, disturbingly intimate. She knew she had to get a grip. It was only a matter of swabbing Joe's leg, for heaven's sake. What was wrong with her?

Of course, she was still shaken from the shock of seeing him almost drown in front of her. She kept reliving that horrifying moment when his dark head had disappeared beneath the swirling flood water.

She'd believed it was the end—Joe was gone for ever—and she'd been swamped by an agonising sense of loss. A slug of the darkest possible despair.

Even now, after they were both safely home and showered and changed, she felt shaky as she gathered bottles of antiseptic, tubes of cream and cotton wool swabs and bandages and anything else she thought she might need.

Now she could see the contrariness of their situation. She and Joe had made every attempt to split, finally and for ever, and yet fate had a strange sense of humour and had deemed it necessary to push them together again.

Here was Joe in her kitchen, dressed in shorts, with his long brown leg propped on a chair.

It wasn't fair, Ellie decided, that despite an angry red gash, a single limb could look so spectacularly masculine, so strongly muscled and large.

'Blood,' little Jacko announced solemnly, stepping closer to inspect the bright wound on Joe's calf.

'Jacko's always seriously impressed by blood,' she explained.

Jacko looked up at Joe with round worried eyes, blue gaze meeting blue. 'Band-Aid,' he pronounced solemnly.

'Thanks, mate.' Joe smiled at the boy. 'Your mum's looking after me, so I know I'm in good hands.'

To Ellie's dismay, she felt a bright blush heat her face. 'I'm afraid Joe will need more than a Band-Aid,' she said tightly as she drew a chair close. 'Jacko, why don't you go and find Teddy? I'll give him a Band-Aid, too.' With luck, she would get most of this task done while the boy was away, looking for his favourite stuffed toy.

But, to her annoyance, she couldn't quite meet Joe's eyes as she bent forward to examine his torn flesh. 'It looks like a very bad graze—and it's right down your shin.' She couldn't help wincing in sympathy. 'It must have hurt.'

'It's not too bad. I don't think it's too deep, do you?'

'Perhaps not, but it's had all that filthy river mud in it. I'd hate you to get infected.' Gently, conscientiously, Ellie washed the wound with warm water and antiseptic, then dabbed at the ragged edges with a cotton wool swab and extra antiseptic. 'I hope this doesn't sting too much.'

'Just slosh it on. I'll be fine.'

Of course. He was a tough guy.

Ellie wished she was tougher. She most definitely wished that being around her ex-husband didn't make her feel so breathless and trembling. And overheated.

She forced herself to be businesslike. 'Are you up-to-date with your tetanus shots?'

'No worries there. The Army made sure of it.'

'Of course. OK. I think I should put sterile dressings on these deeper patches.'

'I'm damn lucky you have such a well stocked first aid kit.'

'The Flying Doctors provided it. There are antibiotics, too, if you need them.'

'You're an angel, Ellie.'

Joe said this with such apparent sincerity she was terrified to look him in the eye, too worried he'd read her emotions, that he'd guess how upset she'd been by his accident, that he'd sense how his proximity set her pulses hammering.

Carefully, she tore the protective packaging from a dressing patch and placed it on his leg, gently pressing the adhesive edges to seal it to his skin. Then, without looking up, she dressed another section, working as swiftly and efficiently, and as gently, as she could.

'The Florence Nightingale touch suits you.'

Ellie's head snapped up and suddenly she was looking straight into Joe's eyes. His bright blue gorgeous eyes that had robbed her of common sense and stolen her heart at their very first meeting.

Joe responded with a slow shimmering smile, as if he liked looking at her, too. Her face flamed brightly. Dismayed, she clambered to her feet.

'Teddy!' hollered Jacko, suddenly running into the room with his fluffy golden bear.

Excessively grateful for the distraction, Ellie found a fluorescent green child-pleasing Band-Aid and ceremoniously applied it to the bear's furry leg. Jacko was suitably delighted and he showed the bear to Joe, who inspected the toy's injury with commendable attention for a man not used to children.

'OK,' Ellie told Joe brusquely as Jacko trotted off again, happily satisfied. 'You can throw your things into Nina's room. You should be comfortable enough sleeping in there.'

This time she was ready when a blush threatened at the mere mention of his sleeping arrangements. A deep breath and the sheer force of willpower kept it at bay, but she didn't miss the flash of tension in Joe's eyes.

Almost immediately, however, Joe recovered, and he gave her an easy shrug. 'I'm fine with sleeping in the swag.'

'Don't be silly. You can't sleep on the study floor with an injured leg.'

His shoulders lifted in a shrug. 'OK. I'm not fussy. I'll sleep wherever's most convenient for you.'

Their gazes locked and Ellie's pulses drummed. She knew Joe must have been thinking, as she was, of the big double bed where she slept. Alone. The bed they'd once shared so passionately.

Hastily she blocked out the dangerously stirring memories of their intimacy, but, as she put the first aid kit away, she wondered again how she was going to survive several days of Joe's presence in her house. She felt quite sure she'd already stumbled at the first hurdle.

CHAPTER FIVE

JOE'S BROTHER, HEATH, answered when Joe rang home with the news that he couldn't make it for Christmas.

'Jeez, mate, that's bad luck.'

'I know. I'm sorry, but with all this rain it's impossible to get through.'

'Mum will be upset.'

'Yeah.' Joe grimaced. It was way too long since he'd been home. 'So, how are Mum and Dad?'

'Both fighting fit.' Heath laughed. 'Excuse the pun. Should remember I'm talking to a soldier.'

'Former soldier.'

'Yeah. Anyway, they were really excited about seeing you.'

Joe suppressed a sigh. 'I suppose Dad's busy?'

'He and Dean are out in the paddock helping a heifer that's having twins. But Mum's around.'

'I'd like to speak to her.'

'Sure. She's just in the kitchen, up to her elbows in her usual Christmas frenzy. Making shortbread today, I think. I'll get her in a sec—but first, tell me, mate— if you're stuck at Karinya, does that mean you'll have to spend Christmas with Ellie?'

'Looks that way.' Joe tried hard to keep his voice neutral.

'But you're still going ahead with the divorce, aren't you?'

'Sure. Everything's signed, but I can't deliver the final paperwork till the rivers go down. As far as we're both concerned, though, it's a done deal. All over, red rover.'

'Hell. And now you're stuck there together. That's tough.'

'Well, at least I get to spend more time with Jacko.'

'That's true, I guess,' Heath said slowly, making no attempt to hide his doubts. 'Just the same, you have my sympathy, Joe.'

'Thanks, but I don't really need it. Ellie and I are OK. We're being perfectly civil.'

'Civil? Sounds like a load of laughs.'

'You were going to get Mum?' Joe reminded his brother.

'Yeah, sure. Well, Happy Christmas.'

'Thanks. Same to you, and give my love to Laura and the girls.'

'Will do. And good luck with you know who!'

Joe didn't have long to ponder his brother's final remark. In no time he heard his mother's voice.

'Darling, how lovely to hear from you. But Heath's just told me the terrible news. I can't believe you're stranded! What a dreadful shame, Joe. Are you sure there's no way you can get across that darned river?'

'I nearly drowned myself trying.' Joe wouldn't normally have shared this detail with his mother, but today it was important she understood there was no point in holding out hope.

'Oh, good heavens,' she said. 'Well, I guess there's no hope of seeing you for Christmas.'

'Impossible, I'm afraid.'

'That's *such* a pity.'

In the awkward silence, Joe tried to think of something reassuring to tell her. He'd felt OK before talking to his family but, now that he'd heard their voices, he felt a tug of unanticipated emotion. And nostalgia. He was remembering the happy Christmases of his past.

'So, how are you?' his mother asked after she'd digested his news.

'I'm fine, thanks. Copped a bit of a scrape on the leg, trying to cross the river, but nothing to worry about.'

'And how's Jacko?' His mother's voice softened, taking on a wistful quality.

His parents had never met Jacko, their grandson, and now the sadness in her voice was a stinging jolt, like a fish hook in Joe's heart. He'd told himself that his parents probably didn't mind—after all, they had six other grandkids—but there was no denying the regret in his mother's voice.

'Jacko's a great little bloke,' he told her. 'I'll email photos.'

'That would be lovely. I'm sure he's a dear little boy, just like you were.'

It was hard to know how to respond to this, especially as his throat had tightened painfully. 'He's a cute kid, all right. Gets up to mischief.'

'Oh, the little sweetheart. I can just imagine. Joe, we'll still get to meet Jacko, won't we? Even though you're divorced?'

'Yes. I'll make sure of it.' *Somehow. Some time.* Joe added silently. He wasn't sure when. But it hit him now that it was important for Jacko to meet his side of the family.

He imagined the boy meeting the raft of Madden uncles and cousins—meeting Joe's parents. It hadn't occurred to him till now, but he wanted the boy to know the whole picture. It was important in shaping his sense of identity.

Hell. He'd been so busy carving out a new life for himself that he hadn't given his responsibilities as a father nearly enough thought.

Now, he thought about Christmas at Ridgelands. He could picture it clearly, with the long table on the homestead veranda groaning beneath the weight of food. There'd be balloons and bright Christmas decorations hanging from posts and railings. All his family around the table. His parents, his brothers and their wives and their kids…

They would have a cold seafood salad as a starter, followed by roast turkey and roast beef, all the vegetables and trimmings. Then his mother's Christmas pudding, filled with the silver sixpences she'd saved from decades ago. Any lucky grandchild who scored a sixpence in their pudding could exchange it for a dollar.

There would be bonbons and silly hats and streamers. Corny jokes, family news and tall stories.

When Joe had first arrived back from Afghanistan, he'd been too distanced from his old life to feel homesick. Now, he was seized by an unexpected longing.

'Oh, well,' his mother was saying, 'for the time being, you'll have to give Jacko an extra hug from me.'

'Will do.' Joe swallowed. 'And I'll make sure I come to see you before I leave for the new job.'

'Oh, yes, Joe. Please do come. It's been so long. Too long.'

'I know. I'll be there. I promise. Give my love to Dad, and everyone.'

'Yes, darling. We'll speak again. Can we call you on this number?'

'Sure.'

'And you give my love to—' His mother paused and ever so slightly sighed. 'Perhaps I should say—give my *regards* to Ellie.'

'You can send Ellie your love.' Joe's throat was extra-sore now, as if he'd swallowed gravel. 'She's always liked *you*, Mum. *I'm* her problem.'

'Oh, darling,' An unhappy silence lapsed. 'I just hope you and Ellie manage to have a stress-free Christmas together.'

'We'll be fine. Don't worry. We're on our best behaviour.'

Joe felt a little shaken as he hung up. While he'd been a soldier on active duty, his focus had been on a foreign enemy. With the added problem of an impending divorce hanging over him, he'd found it all too easy to detach himself from home.

Now, for the first time, he began to suspect that avoiding his family had been a mistake. And yet, here he was, about to run away again.

He'd barely put down the receiver when the phone rang almost immediately. He supposed it was his mother ringing back with one last 'thought'.

He answered quickly. 'Hello?'

'Is that Joe?' It was a completely different woman's voice.

'Yes, Joe speaking.'

'Oh.' The caller managed to sound disappointed and put out, as if she was wrinkling her nose at a very unpleasant smell. 'I was hoping to speak to Ellie.'

'Is that you, Angela?' Joe recognised the icy tones of his ex mother-in-law.

'Yes, of course.'

'Ellie's out in the shed, hunting for Christmas decorations. I'll get her to call you as soon as she gets in.'

'So where's Jacko?' Angela Fowler's voice indicated all too clearly that she didn't trust Joe to be alone with her grandson.

'He's taking a nap.'

'I see,' Angela said doubtfully and then she let out a heavy sigh. 'I rang, actually, because I heard about all the rain up there in Queensland on the news. There was talk of rivers flooding.'

'Yes, that's right, I'm afraid. Our local creeks and rivers are up and Karinya's already cut off.'

'Oh, Joe! And you're still there? Oh, how dreadful for poor Ellie.' Ellie's mother had always managed to imply that any unfortunate event in their marriage was entirely Joe's fault. 'Don't tell me this means… It doesn't mean you'll be up there with Ellie and Jacko for Christmas, does it?'

'I'm afraid we don't have a choice, Angela.'

There was a horrified gasp on the end of the line and then a longish bristling pause.

'I'll tell Ellie you called,' Joe said with excessive politeness.

'I suppose, if she's busy, that will have to do.' Reluctantly, Angela added, 'Thanks, I guess.' And then… 'Joe?'

'Yes?'

'I hope you'll be sensitive.'

Joe scowled and refused to respond.

'You've made life hard enough for my daughter.'

His grip on the phone receiver tightened and he was tempted to hurl the bloody phone through the kitchen window. Somehow he reined in his temper.

'You can rest easy, Ange. Ellie has served me with the divorce papers and I've signed on the dotted line. I'll be out of your daughter's hair just as soon as these rivers go down. In the meantime, I'll be on my best behaviour. And I hope you and Harold have a very happy Christmas.'

He was about to hang up when he heard Ellie's footsteps in the hall.

'Hang on. You're in luck. Here's Ellie now.'

Setting down the phone with immense relief, he went down the hallway. Ellie was on the veranda. She'd taken off her rain jacket and was hanging it on the wall hook, and beside her were two large rain-streaked cardboard cartons.

'Your mother's on the phone,' Joe told her.

A frown drew her finely arched eyebrows together. 'OK, thanks.' She was still frowning as she set off down the hall. 'I think Jacko's awake,' she called back to Joe. 'Can you check?'

'Can do.'

Even before Joe reached the boy's room, he heard soft, happy little chuckles. The lively baby talk was such a bright, cheerful contrast to his recent phone conversation.

In fact, Joe couldn't remember ever hearing a baby's laughter before. It was truly an incredible sound.

He slowed his pace as he approached the room and

opened the door slowly, carefully, and he found Jacko, with tousled golden hair and sleep-flushed cheeks, standing in his cot. The little boy was walking his teddy bear, complete with its fluoro Band-Aid, along the railing. He was talking to the bear in indecipherable gibberish. Giggling.

So cute.

So damn cute.

Joe felt a slam, like a fist to his innards. The last time he'd seen his son, he'd been a helpless baby, and now he was a proper little person—walking and talking and learning to play, beginning to imagine.

He'd missed so many milestones.

What will he be like next time I see him?

It was difficult enough that Joe had to spend this extra time with Ellie, while trying to ignore the old tug of an attraction that had never really died. But now, here was his son jerking his heart-strings as well.

As soon as Jacko saw Joe, he dropped the teddy bear and held up round little arms. 'Up!' he demanded.

Joe crossed to the cot and his son looked up at him with a huge, happy grin. It might even have been an admiring grin. A loving grin?

Whatever it was, it hefted a raw punch.

'Up, Joe!'

'OK, mate. Up you come.'

Jacko squealed with delight as Joe swung him high, over the side of the cot. Then, for a heady moment, Joe held the boy in his arms, marvelling at his softness, at his pink and gold perfection.

Hell. He could remember when this healthy, bouncing kid had been nothing more than a cluster of frozen invisible cells in a laboratory—one of the *sproglets* that had caused him and Ellie so much hope and heartbreak.

Now the collection of cells was Jacko, their miraculous solo survivor.

And, after everything they'd been through, Joe found himself in awe.

'Wee-wee!' announced Jacko, wriggling with a need to be out of Joe's arms.

He quickly set the kid down. 'Do you want the toilet?'

Jacko nodded and clutched at the front of his shorts, pulling a face that made the matter look urgent.

'Let's go.' With a hand on his shoulder, Joe guided him quickly down the hallway to the bathroom, realising as he did so that, despite having several young nieces and nephews, *this* was a brand new experience.

'I think you have to stand on this fellow,' he said, grabbing a plastic turtle with a flat, step-like back and positioning it in front of the toilet bowl.

Jacko was red-faced as he climbed onto the step and tugged helplessly at the elastic waistband on his shorts. It was a moment before Joe realised he was needed to help the boy free of his clothing, which included pulling down a miniature pair of underpants printed with cartoon animals.

'OK. There you go. You're all set now.'

And then, out of nowhere, a fleeting memory from his own childhood flashed. Tearing a corner of paper from the roll on the wall, Joe dropped it into the bowl.

'See if you can pee on the paper,' he said.

Jacko looked up at him with open-mouthed surprise, but then he turned back and, with commendable concentration, did exactly as Joe suggested.

The kid was smart.

And right on target.

'Bingo!' Joe grinned. 'You did it. Good for you, Jacko!'

Jacko beamed up at him. 'Bingo, Joe!'

'You've earned a high five!' Joe held out his hand.

'What are you two up to?'

They both turned to find Ellie in the hallway behind them, hands on hips. Beautiful but frowning.

'I did Bingo, Mummy,' Jacko announced with obvious pride as he stood on the turtle with his shorts around his ankles.

'Bingo? What are you talking about?' She directed her frown at Joe.

He pointed into the bowl. 'Jacko hit the piece of paper. I thought it would help him to aim.'

'Aim?' Ellie stared at him, stared at both of them, her dark eyes frowning with disbelief. As comprehension dawned, her mouth twisted into the faintest glimmer of a smile—a smile that didn't quite make it.

'He's not in the Army *yet*,' she said tightly. 'And don't forget to wash your hands, Jacko. It's time for your afternoon tea.'

'So, do you have a job for me?' Joe asked once Jacko was perched on a stool at the kitchen bench and tucking into a cup of juice and a plate of diced cheese and fruit.

Ellie looked pained—an expression Joe was used to seeing after a phone call from her mother. No doubt Angela Fowler had once again piled on the sympathy for her poor daughter's terrible fate—this time, being forced to spend Christmas with her dropkick ex.

In the past, that pained look had irritated Joe. Today, he was determined to let it wash over him.

'Perhaps I could assemble the Christmas tree?' he suggested.

'That would be helpful.' Ellie didn't follow through with a smile. 'The tree's in one of the boxes on the veranda.'

'You'd like it in the lounge room?'

'Yes, please.'

Ellie took a deep breath as she watched Joe head off to the veranda.

Conversations with her mother had always been heavily laced with anti-Joe sentiments and today had been a doozy.

This is a dangerous time for you, Ellie. I don't like the idea of the two of you alone up there. You'll have to be very careful, especially if Joe tries anything.

Tries what, Mum?

Tries to...to win you back.

Of course, Ellie had assured her mother there was no chance of that. Absolutely. No. Chance. But she wished this certainty hadn't left her feeling quite so desolate.

These next few days were going to be hard enough with the two of them stuck in the house while the rain continued pelting down outside. It would be so much easier if she could carry on with the outside work, but the cattle were safe and until the rain stopped there wasn't a lot more she could do.

Unfortunately, she couldn't even give Joe a decent book to read. Since Jacko's birth, she'd only had time for cattle-breeding journals, women's magazines and children's picture books.

Ellie decided to let Joe get on with the tree while she cooled her heels in the kitchen with Jacko, for once letting him dawdle over his food, but as soon as he'd finally downed his afternoon tea, he was keen to be off.

'Where's Joe?' was the first thing he asked.

So they went back to the lounge room and, to Ellie's surprise, Joe had almost finished assembling the six-foot tree. He made it look dead easy, of course.

Jacko stared up at the tree, looking puzzled, as if he couldn't understand why adults would set up a tree inside the house. As an outback boy, he hadn't seen any of the city shops with brightly lit trees and Santa Clauses, although he had vague ideas about Christmas from books and TV.

'This is our *Christmas* tree,' Ellie explained to him. 'Mummy's going to make it pretty with lights and decorations, and soon there'll be lots of presents underneath it.'

At the mention of presents Jacko clapped his hands and took off, running in circles.

'Well, that got a reaction,' said Joe, amused.

'He can still remember the pile of presents he scored for his second birthday.'

Too late, Ellie remembered that Joe hadn't sent the boy anything. Lordy, today there seemed to be pitfalls in even the simplest conversation.

Joe was grim-faced as he fitted the final top branches in place.

Ellie went to the CD player and made a selection—a jaunty version of *Jingle Bells*. She hoped it would lift the dark mood that had lingered since her mum's annoying dire warnings on the phone.

Determined to shake off the grouchiness, she went

to the second carton and took out boxes of exquisite tree ornaments. Decorating the tree had always been her favourite Christmas tradition. Today it was sure to lift her spirits.

'Ooh! Pretty!' Jacko squealed, coming close to inspect.

'Yes, these ornaments are very pretty, but they're made of glass, Jacko, so you mustn't touch. They can break. I'm going to put them on the tree, and they'll be safe there. They'll make the tree beautiful.'

Jacko watched, entranced, as Ellie hooked bright, delicate balls onto the branches. She knew it was too much to expect him not to touch but, before she could warn him to be *very* gentle, he batted with his hand at a bright red and silver ball.

Ellie dived to stop him and Joe dived too, but they were both too late. The ball fell to the floor and smashed.

Ellie cried out—an instinctive response, but probably a mistake. Immediately, Jacko began to wail.

It was Joe who swept the boy into his arms and began to soothe him.

Ellie was left watching them, feeling strangely left out. She waited for Jacko to turn to her, to reach out his arms for her as he always did when he was upset. But he remained clinging to Joe.

Joe. Her son's new, big strong hero.

She refused to feel jealous. If she was honest, she could totally understand the appeal of those muscular, manly arms.

Once upon a time Joe was my hero, too. My tower of strength.

Now, she would never feel his arms around her again.

Yikes, where had that thought sprung from? *What's the matter with me?*

She hurried out of the room to get a dustpan and broom and, by the time she returned, Jacko had stopped crying.

Joe set him down and the boy stood, sniffling, as he watched Ellie sweep up the glittering broken pieces.

'I told you to be careful,' she felt compelled to remind him as she worked. 'You mustn't touch these pretty ornaments, or they'll break.'

'He's too little to understand,' said Joe.

Ellie glared up at him. 'No, he's not.' *What would Joe know about little kids?*

Joe shrugged and looked around the room. 'Perhaps we can find something more suitable for him to play with. Something like paper chains? They might distract him.'

Ellie had actually been thinking along the same lines and it annoyed her that Joe had made the suggestion first. 'So you're suddenly an expert on raising children?'

'Ellie, don't be like that.'

'Like what?'

Joe simply stared at her, his blue eyes coolly assessing.

Oh, help. It was happening already. All the old tensions were sparking between them—electricity of the worst kind. Dangerous. Lethal.

All she'd wanted was a simple, relaxing afternoon decorating the tree.

'There are paper chains in those shopping bags,' she said, pointing to one of the cartons. Then, summoning her dignity, she rose and took the dustpan back to the kitchen.

By the time she returned, Jacko and Joe had trailed bright paper chains along the shelves of the bookcase and they were now looping them around a tall lamp stand.

The CD was still playing. The singer had moved on to *Deck the Halls*, and Ellie set about decorating the tree again, hoping for peace on Earth and goodwill towards one particular man.

She couldn't deny that Joe was great at playing with their son. Every time Jacko became too curious about the tree, Joe would deflect him. They played hide and seek behind the sofa, and Joe taught Jacko how to crawl on his belly, Commando style. Watching this, Ellie winced, sure that Joe's injured leg must have hurt.

She almost said something about his leg, but held her tongue. He was a big, tough soldier, after all.

Joe hid Jacko's teddy bear behind a cushion and the boy squealed with delight every time he rediscovered the toy. After that, Jacko played the game again and again, over and over.

Ellie tried really hard not to feel left out of their games. She knew that the nanny, Nina, played games like this all the time with Jacko, while she was out attending to chores around the property. But she'd never imagined macho Joe being quite so good with the boy.

It shouldn't have bothered her. It *didn't* bother her. If Joe was proving to be an entertaining father, she was pleased. She was even grateful.

She was. Truly.

Meanwhile, the Christmas tree became a thing of beauty, with delicate ornaments and shiny stars, and trailing lines of lights and silver pine cones.

After Jacko's umpteenth game of hiding the toy bear

behind the cushion, Joe strolled over to inspect Ellie's progress.

'It's looking great,' he said. 'Really beautiful.'

His smile was genuine. Gorgeous? It sent unwanted warmth rippling through her. 'At least it helps to make the house look more festive.'

Joe nodded and touched a pretty pink and purple glass spiral with his fingertips. 'I remember these. We bought them for our very first Christmas.'

To Ellie's dismay, her eyes pricked with the threat of tears. Joe shouldn't be remembering those long ago times when they were still happy and hopeful and so blissfully in love.

'I'd rather not rehash old memories, Joe. I don't think it's helpful.'

She saw a flash of emotion in his eyes. Pain? Her comment hadn't hurt him, surely? Not Joe. He had no regrets. Not about them. He'd gone off to war without a backward glance.

And yet he definitely looked upset.

Ellie wondered if she should elaborate. Try to explain her caution.

But what could she explain? That she hadn't meant to hurt him? That, deep down, she still cared about him? That the memories were painful *because* she cared?

How could those sorts of revelations help them now? They couldn't go back.

Confused, Ellie felt more uptight than ever. She spun away from Joe and began to gather up the empty boxes and tissue paper that had housed the decorations, working with jerky, angry movements.

To her annoyance, Joe simply stayed where he was by the tree, watching her with a thoughtful, searching gaze.

'You could always help to clean up this mess,' she said tightly.

'Yes, ma'am.' He moved without haste, picking up the shopping bags that had housed the paper chains. Crossing the room, he dropped them into one of the cartons and, when he looked at her again, his eyes were as hard and cool as ice. 'You can't let up, can you, Ellie?'

'What do you mean?'

'You're determined to make this hard for both of us.'

'I'm not *trying* to make it hard,' she snapped defensively. 'It *is* hard.'

'Yeah? Well, you're not the only one finding it hard. And it doesn't help when you make it so damn obvious that you can't stand the sight of me.'

Ellie smarted. 'How can you say that?'

'How?' Joe looked at her strangely, as if he thought she'd lost her marbles. 'Because it's the truth. It's why I left four years ago.'

No! The protest burst on her lips, but she was aware that Jacko had stopped playing. He was standing very still, clutching his teddy bear, watching them, his little eyes round with worry.

They were fighting in front of him, which was terrible—the very last thing she wanted.

'If we're going to survive this Christmas,' Joe said tightly, 'you're going to have to try harder.'

Ellie felt her teeth clench. 'I know how to behave. I don't need a lecture.'

'Well, you certainly need something. You need to calm down. And you need to think about Jacko.'

'Are you serious?'

'This atmosphere can't be good for him.'

How dare you? Of course she was thinking about Jacko.

Ellie was stung to the core. Who did Joe think he was, telling her off about her parenting? Was he suggesting she was insensitive to Jacko's needs? Joe, who hardly knew the boy?

She was Jacko's *mother.* She knew *everything* about her son—his favourite food, his favourite toy and favourite picture books. She knew Jacko's fears, the times he liked to sleep, the way he liked to be cuddled.

She'd been through his pregnancy on her own, and she'd given birth to him alone. She'd raised Jacko from day one, nursing him through colic and croup and teething. Later, chickenpox. Jacko's first smile had been for Ellie alone. She'd watched him learn to roll over, to sit up and to crawl, to stand, to walk.

Around the clock, she'd cared for him, admittedly with Nina's help, but primarily on her own.

She and Jacko were incredibly close. Their bond was special. Incredibly special.

How dare Joe arrive here out of the blue and start questioning her mothering skills?

Without warning, her eyes filled with tears. Tears of hurt and anger. Scared she might start yelling and say things she'd regret, she turned and fled from the room.

Damn. What a stuff-up.

As Ellie hurried away, Jacko stared up at Joe with big, sad blue eyes. 'Mummy crying.'

Joe swallowed the boulder that jammed his throat. Why the hell had he started a verbal attack on Ellie? This was *so* not the way he'd wanted to behave.

How do I tell my two-year-old son that I'm the reason his mother's crying?

Anxiety and regret warred in Joe's gut as he crossed the room to the boy and squatted so they were at eye level. 'Listen, little mate. I'm going to go and talk to your mum. To…ah…cheer her up.'

Joe had to try at least. It took two to fight. Two to make peace. He had to pull in his horns, had to make an effort to see this situation from Ellie's point of view.

'I need you to be a good boy and stay here with Ted.' Joe dredged up a grin as he tickled Jacko's tummy.

Obligingly, Jacko giggled.

The kid was so cute. Already Joe knew it was going to be hard to say goodbye.

'How about we hide your bear behind the curtain over there?' he suggested, pointing to the floor-length curtains hanging either end of the deep sash windows that opened onto the veranda. He showed Jacko how to hide the bear behind them, just as they had with the cushions, and the little boy was thrilled.

'Ted!' he squealed, astonished by the big discovery when they lifted the curtain. 'Do it again, Joe!' At least he was all smiles again.

'You have a go at hiding him,' said Joe.

Jacko tried, frowning carefully as he placed the bear behind the curtain. Once again, he lifted the fabric and saw the bear, and he was as excited as a scientist discovering the Higgs boson particle.

'OK, you can play with him here,' Joe said. 'And I'll be back in a tick.'

'OK.'

Reassured that Jacko would be happy for a few minutes at least, Joe went in search of Ellie.

CHAPTER SIX

ELLIE STOOD AT one end of the long front veranda, elbows resting on the railings, staring out at the waterlogged paddocks. The rain had actually stopped for now, but the sky was still heavy with thick, grey clouds, so no doubt the downpour would start again soon.

She wasn't crying. She'd dried her tears almost as soon as she left the lounge room and she was determined that no more would fall. She was angry, not sad. Angry with herself, with her stupid behaviour.

She'd been determined to handle Joe's return calmly and maturely, and when he'd been forced to stay here she'd promised herself she would face that with dignity as well. Instead she'd been as tense and sharp-tongued as a cornered taipan.

She was so disappointed with herself, so annoyed. Why couldn't her behaviour ever live up to her good intentions?

You make it so damn obvious that you can't stand the sight of me.

Did Joe really think that? How could he?

It seemed impossible to Ellie. The sad truth was—the sight of Joe stirred her in ways she didn't want to be stirred. She found herself thinking too often about the way they used to make love.

Really, despite their troubles, there'd been so many happy times, some of them incredibly spontaneous and exciting.

Even now, *irrationally*, she found herself remembering one of the happiest nights of her life—a night that had originally started out very badly.

It had happened one Easter. She and Joe were driving down the highway on their way to visit her mum, but they'd been so busy before they left that they hadn't booked ahead, and all the motels down the highway were full.

'Perhaps we should just keep driving,' Joe had said grimly when they reached yet another town with no spare rooms.

'Driving all night?' she'd asked. 'Isn't that dangerous, Joe? We're both pretty tired.'

He'd reluctantly agreed. 'We'll have to find a picnic ground then and sleep in the car.'

It wasn't a cheering prospect, but Ellie knew they didn't have much choice. While Joe went off to find hamburgers for their dinner, she tried to set the car up as best she could, hoping they'd be comfortable.

She'd shifted their luggage and adjusted their seats to lie back and she'd just finished making pillows out of bundles of their clothing when Joe returned. He was empty-handed and Ellie, who'd been ravenous, felt her spirits sink even lower.

'Don't tell me this town's also sold out of hamburgers?'

'I don't know,' he said simply.

Her stomach rumbled hungrily. 'Are all the shops closed?'

'Don't know that either. It doesn't matter.' Joe's sudden cheeky smile was unforgettably gorgeous. He held up a fancy gold ring, dangling keys. 'I've booked us into the honeymoon suite in the best hotel in town.'

Ellie gasped. 'You're joking.'

Still smiling broadly, Joe shook his head. 'Ridgy-didge.'

'Can…can we afford a honeymoon suite?'

He shrugged, then slipped his arm around her shoulders, pressed a warm kiss to her ear. 'We deserve a bit of comfort. We never had a proper honeymoon.'

It was the best of nights. Amazing, and so worth the extravagance.

All thoughts of tiredness vanished when they walked into their suite and saw the champagne in an ice bucket, a huge vase of long-stemmed white roses and chocolate hearts wrapped in gold foil on their pillows.

Like excited kids, they bounced on the enormous king-sized bed and then jumped into the spa bath until their room service dinner arrived. And they felt like film stars as they ate gourmet cuisine dressed in luxurious white fluffy bathrobes.

And, just for one night, they'd put their worries aside and they'd made love like honeymooners.

I shouldn't be thinking about that now…

Ellie was devastated to realise that she was still as physically attracted to her ex as she'd been on that night. The realisation made her panic.

What a mess.

With a despairing sigh, she sagged against a veranda post. How had she and Joe sunk to this? She'd thought about their problems so many times, but she'd never pin-pointed a particular event that had killed their marriage. It had been much the same as today. Ongoing bicker-ing and building resentments had worn them down and eroded their love.

Death by a thousand cuts.

But why? How? How could she be so tense and angry with a man she still fancied? It wasn't as if she actively disliked Joe.

She supposed they should have seen a marriage guid-ance counsellor years ago.

Joe had been too proud, of course, and Ellie had been too scared—scared that she'd be psychoanalysed and found lacking in some vital way. But if she'd been braver, would it have helped?

She probably would have had to tell the counsellor about her father's death and how unhappy she'd been after that. Worse, she would have had to talk about her stepfather and how she'd run away from him.

Ellie didn't actually believe there was a connection between Harold Fowler and her marriage breakdown, but heaven knew what a counsellor might have made of it. Even now, she still shuddered when she thought about Harold.

And here was the thing: it was the sight of *Harold* that Ellie couldn't stand. Not Joe.

Never Joe.

Her mum had married Harold Fowler eighteen months after her father died, after they'd sold the farm and moved into town. Harold owned the town's main hardware store—he was loud and showy and popu-lar, a big fish in a small country pond. And a couple of years later he was elected mayor. Ellie's mum was thrilled. She loved being the mayor's wife and feeling like a celebrity.

Harold, however, had given Ellie the creeps. Right from the start, just the way he looked at her had made her squirm and feel uncomfortable, and that was before he touched her.

She'd been fifteen when he first patted her on the bum. Over the following months, it had happened a few more times, which was bad enough, but then he came into the bathroom one night when she was in the shower.

He was full of apologies, of course, and he backed out quickly, claiming that he'd knocked and no one had answered. But Ellie had seen the horrible glint in his eyes and she was quite sure he hadn't knocked. Her mother hadn't been home that night, which had made the event extra-scary.

And Harold certainly hadn't knocked the second time he barged in. Again, it had happened on a night when Ellie's mum was away at her bridge club. Ellie was seventeen, and she'd just stepped out of the bath and was reaching for her towel when, without warning, Harold had simply opened her bathroom door.

'Oh, my darling girl,' he said with the most ghastly slimy smile.

Whipping the towel about her, Ellie managed to get rid of him with a few scathing, shrilly screamed words, but she'd been sickened, horrified.

Desperate.

And the worst of it was she couldn't get her mother to understand.

'Harold's lived alone for years,' her mum had said, excusing him. 'He's not used to sharing a house with others. And he hasn't done or said anything improper,

Ellie. You're just at that age where you're sensitive about your body. It's easy to misread these things.'

Her mother had believed what she wanted to, what she needed to.

Ellie, however, had left home for good as soon as she finished school, despite her mother's protests and tears, giving up all thought of university. University students had long, long holidays and she would have been expected to spend too much of that time at home.

She had realised it was futile to press her mother about Harold's creepiness—mainly because she knew how desperate her mother was to believe he was perfect. Harold was such a hotshot in their regional town. He was the mayor, for heaven's sake, and Ellie was afraid that, if she pushed her case, she might cause the whole thing to blow up somehow and become a horrible public scandal.

So she'd headed north to Queensland, where she'd scored a job as a jillaroo on a cattle property. Over the next few years, she'd worked on several properties—a mustering season here, a calving season there. Gradually she'd acquired more and more skills.

On one property she'd joined a droving team and she'd helped to move a big mob of cattle hundreds of kilometres. She was given her own horses to ride every day. And, finally, she was living the country life she'd dreamed of, the life she'd anticipated when she was almost thirteen. Before her father died.

Whenever she phoned home or returned home for the shortest possible visits, she was barely civil to Harold. He got the message. Fortunately, he'd never stepped out of line again, but Ellie would never trust him again either.

Trust…

Thinking about all of this now, Ellie was struck by a thought so suffocating she could scarcely breathe.

Oh, my God. Is that my problem? Trust issues?

That was it, wasn't it?

She clung to the railing, struggling for air. Her problems with Joe had nothing to do with whether or not she was attracted to him. The day they met remained the stand-alone most significant moment of her life.

She'd taken one look at Joe Madden, with his sexy blue eyes, his ruggedly cute looks, his wide-shouldered lean perfection and nicest possible smile, and she'd fallen like a stone.

But I couldn't trust Joe.

When it came to coping with the ups and downs of a long-term marriage, she hadn't been strong enough to deal with her disappointments. She'd lost faith in herself, lost faith in the power of love.

Ellie thought again about her father climbing a windmill and dying before he could keep his promise to her. She thought about her creepy stepfather, who'd broken her trust in a completely different way. By the time she'd married Joe…

I never really expected to be happy. Not for ever. I couldn't trust our marriage to work. It was almost as if I expected something to go wrong.

It was such a shock to realise this now.

Too late.

Way too late.

She'd never even told Joe about her stepfather. She'd left it as a creepy, shuddery, embarrassing part of her past that she'd worked hard to bury.

But that hadn't affected how she'd truly felt about him.

She'd loved Joe.

Despite the mixed-up and messy emotional tornado that had accompanied her fertility issues and ultimately destroyed their marriage, she'd *truly* loved him—even when he'd proposed their divorce and he'd told her he was leaving for the Army.

And now?

Now, she was terribly afraid that she'd never really stopped loving him. But how crazy was that when their divorce was a fait accompli?

No wonder she was tense.

Ellie thumped the railing with a frustrated fist. At the same moment, from down the veranda she heard the squeaky hinge of the French windows that led from the lounge room. Then footsteps. She stiffened, turned to see Joe. He was alone.

She drew a deep breath and braced herself. *Don't screw this up again. Behave.*

'Are you OK?' Joe asked quietly.

'Yes, thanks.'

He came closer and stood beside her at the railing, looking out at the soggy paddocks. 'I'm sorry, Ellie. I'm sorry for getting stuck into you. My timing's been lousy, coming back here at Christmas.'

She shook her head. 'I'm making too big a deal about the whole Christmas thing.'

'But that's fair enough. It's the first Christmas Jacko's been old enough to understand.'

She sighed, felt emotionally drained. Exhausted. 'Where's Jacko now?'

'In the lounge room. Still hiding the bear, I hope. Persistent little guy, isn't he?' Joe slid her a tentative sideways smile.

She sent a shy smile back.

Oh, if only they could continue to smile—or, at the very least, to be civilised. Joe was right. For Jacko's sake, they had to try. For the next couple of days—actually, for the next couple of *decades* till Jacko was an adult, they had to keep up a semblance of friendship.

Friendship, when once they'd been lovers, husband and wife.

'I got my knickers in a twist when you suggested I wasn't sensitive about Jacko,' Ellie admitted. 'It felt unfair. He's always been my first concern.'

'You've done an amazing job with the boy. He's a great little guy. A credit to you.'

The praise surprised her. Warmed her.

'I don't know how you've done it out here on your own,' Joe added.

'The nanny's been great. But I'll admit it hasn't always been easy.' She stole another quick glance at him, saw his deep brow, his wide cheekbones, his slightly crooked nose and strong shadowed jaw. She felt her breathing catch. 'I guess this can't be easy for you now. Coming back from the war and everything.'

When he didn't answer, she tried again, 'Was it bad over there?'

A telltale muscle jerked. 'Sometimes.'

Ellie knew he'd lost soldier mates, knew he must have seen things that haunted him. But Special Forces guys hardly ever talked about where they'd been or what they'd done—certainly not with ex-wives.

'I was one of the lucky ones,' he said. 'I got out of it unscathed.'

Unscathed emotionally? Ellie knew that the Army had changed its tactics, sending soldiers like Joe on shorter but more frequent tours of duty in an effort to minimise post-traumatic stress, but she was quite sure that no soldier returned from any war without some kind of damage.

I haven't helped. This hasn't been a very good home-coming for him.

Quickly, bravely, she said, 'For the record, Joe, it isn't true.'

He turned, looking at her intently. 'What do you mean?' His blue eyes seemed to penetrate all the way to her soul.

Her heart began to gallop. She couldn't back down now that she'd begun. 'What you said before—that I can't bear the sight of you—it's not true.' *So not true.*

'That's the way it comes across.'

'I know. I'm sorry. Really sorry.'

She could feel the sudden stillness in him, almost as if she'd shot him. He was staring at her, his eyes burning. With doubt?

Ellie's eyes were stinging. She didn't want to cry, but she could no longer see the paddocks. Her heart was racing.

She almost told Joe that she actually *fancied* the sight of him. Very much. Too much. *That* was her problem. That was why she was tense.

But it was too late for personal confessions. Way too late. Years and years too late.

Instead she said, 'I know I've been stupidly tense about *everything*, but it's certainly not because I can't stand the sight of you.' *Quite the opposite.*

She blinked hard, wishing her tears could air-dry.

Joe's knuckles were white as he gripped the veranda railing and she wondered what he was thinking. Feeling. Was he going over her words?

It's certainly not because I can't stand the sight of you.

Could he read between the lines? Could he guess she was still attracted? Was he angry?

It felt like an age before he spoke.

Eventually, he let go of the railing. Stepped away and drew a deep breath, unconsciously drawing her attention to his height and the breadth of his shoulders. Then he rested his hands lightly on his hips, as if he was deliberately relaxing.

'OK, here's a suggestion,' he said quietly. 'It's Christmas Eve tomorrow. Why don't we declare a truce?'

'A truce? For Christmas?'

'Why not? Even in World War One there were Germans and our blokes who stopped fighting in the trenches for Christmas. So, what do you reckon?'

Ellie almost smiled. She really liked the idea of a Christmas truce. She'd always liked to have a goal. And a short-term goal was even better. Doable.

'I reckon we should give it a shot,' she said. If soldiers could halt a world war for a little peace and goodwill at Christmas, she and Joe should at least make an effort.

He was watching her with a cautious smile. 'Can we shake on it?'

'Sure.'

His handclasp was warm and strong and, for Ellie, just touching him sparked all sorts of flashpoints. But now she had to find a way to stay calm. Unexcited. Neutral.

Her goal was peace and goodwill. For Christmas.

Their smiles were uncertain but hopeful.

But then, in almost the same breath, they both remembered.

'Jacko,' they exclaimed together and together they hurried down the veranda to the lounge room.

There was no sign of their son, just his teddy bear lying abandoned on the floor near the empty cartons.

Ellie hurried across the room and down the hallway to the kitchen. 'Jacko?' she called, but he wasn't there either.

Joe was close behind her. 'He can't have gone far.'

'No.' She went back along the hallway to the bedrooms, calling, 'Jacko, where are you?' Any minute she would hear his giggle.

But he wasn't in his room. Or in her bedroom. Or in the study, or Nina's room. The bathroom was empty. A wild, hot fluttering unfurled in Ellie's chest. It was only a small house. There wasn't anywhere else to look.

She rushed back to the lounge room as Joe came through the front door.

'I've checked the veranda,' he said.

'He's not here.' Ellie's voice squeaked.

'He must be here. Don't panic, Ellie.'

She almost fell back into her old pattern, hurling defensive accusations. *How could you have left him?*

But she was silenced by the quiet command in Joe's voice, and by the knowledge that she'd been the one who stormed out.

'What was Jacko doing before you came outside to talk to me?' she asked with a calmness that surprised her.

'He was playing hide and seek with the bear. Here.'
Joe swished aside the long curtain beside the door.

Ellie gasped.

Jacko was sitting against the wall, perfectly still and
quiet, peeping out from beneath his blond fringe, hugging his grubby knees.

'Boo!' he said with a proud grin. 'I hided, Mummy.'

They fell on him together, crouching to hug him,
laughing shakily. United by their mutual relief.

It wasn't a bad way to start a truce.

Dinner that night was leftover Spanish chicken. For
Joe and Ellie the atmosphere was, thankfully, more relaxed than the night before, and afterwards, while Ellie
read Jacko bedtime stories, Joe did kitchen duty, rins-
ing the plates, stacking the dishwasher and wiping the
bench tops.

By the time he came back from checking the station's working dogs and making sure the chicken coop
was locked safely from dingoes, Ellie was at the kitchen
table, looking businesslike with notepaper and pen, and
surrounded by recipe books.

'I need to plan our Christmas dinner menu,' she said,
flipping pages filled with lavish and brightly coloured
Christmas fare.

'I don't suppose I can help?'

She looked up at him, her smile doubtful but curious.
'How are your cooking skills these days?'

'About the same as they were last time I cooked for
you.'

'Steak and eggs.' Her nose wrinkled. 'I was hoping
for something a little more celebratory for Christmas.'

'Well, if you insist on being fussy...' He pretended

to be offended, but he was smiling as he switched on the kettle. 'I'm making tea. Want some?'

'Thanks.'

At least the truce seemed to be working. So far.

While Joe hunted for mugs and tea bags, Ellie returned to her recipe books, frowning and looking pensive as she turned endless pages. As far as Joe could tell, she didn't seem to be having much luck. Every so often she made notes and chewed on her pen and then, a few pages later, she scratched the notes out again.

'Our Christmas dinner doesn't have to be lavish,' he suggested as he set a mug of tea with milk and one sugar in front of her. 'I'm fine with low-key.'

'I'm afraid it'll have to be low-key. We don't have much choice.'

With an annoyed frown, Ellie pushed the books away, picked up the tea mug and sipped. 'Nice tea, thanks.' She let out a heavy sigh. 'The problem is, I didn't order a lot of things in for Christmas. Jacko and I were supposed to be spending the day with Chip and Sara Anderson on Lucky Downs. All they wanted me to bring was homemade shortbread and wine and cheese. But now, with the creeks up, we won't be able to get there.'

She waved her hand at the array of books. 'Some people spend weeks planning their Christmas menus and here am I, just starting. Yikes, it's Christmas Eve tomorrow.'

Joe helped himself to a chair and picked up the nearest book: *Elegant and Easy Christmas*.

'Those recipes are gorgeous,' Ellie said. 'But they all need fancy ingredients that I don't have.'

He flicked through pages filled with tempting pictures—a crab cocktail starter, turkey breast stuffed with pears and chestnut and rosemary, a herb-crusted standing rib roast, pumpkin and caramel tiramisu.

'I see what you mean,' he said. 'These are certainly fancy. Would it help if we make a list of the things you have in store?'

'Well, yes, I guess that's sensible.' Ellie rolled her eyes. 'I've a pretty good range of meat, but my problem is the trimmings. I don't have the sauces and spices and fancy herbs and that sort of thing. So I'm afraid we're stuck with ordinary, boring stuff. For Christmas!'

'Hmm.'

She looked up, eyeing Joe suspiciously. 'You're frowning and muttering. What does that mean?'

'It means I'm thinking.' Truth was—an exciting idea had flashed into his head. Crazy. Probably impossible.

But it was worth a try.

'Excuse me,' he said, jumping to his feet. 'I need to make a phone call.'

'There's a phone here.' Ellie nodded to the wall phone.

'It's OK. I've bought a sat phone, and I have the numbers stored.'

She looked understandably puzzled.

Adorably puzzled, Joe thought as he left the room.

By the light of the single bulb on the veranda, he found the number he wanted. Steve Hansen was an ex-Army mate and, to Joe's relief, Steve answered the call quickly.

'Steve, Joe Madden here. How are you?'

'I'm fine, Joe, heard you were back. How are you, mate? More importantly, where are you? Any chance of having a Christmas drink with us?'

'That's why I'm ringing,' Joe said. 'I've a huge favour to ask.'

'Well, ask away, mate. We both know how much I owe you. If it wasn't for you, I would have flown home from Afghanistan in a wooden box. So, what is it?'

CHAPTER SEVEN

MIDAFTERNOON ON CHRISTMAS Eve and the Karinya kitchen was a hive of activity.

At one end of the table, Ellie and Jacko were cutting shortbread dough into star shapes—with loads of patience on Ellie's part. At the other end, Joe, having consulted an elderly everyday cookbook, was stuffing a chicken with a mix of onion, soft breadcrumbs and dried herbs. To Ellie's amusement, he was tackling the task with the serious concentration of a heart surgeon.

By now the rain had stopped and the air was super-hot and sticky—too hot and sticky for the ceiling fan to make much difference. Flies buzzed at the window screens and from outside came the smell of once parched earth now turned to mud.

With the back of her hand, Ellie wiped a strand of damp hair from her eyes. She was used to hot Christmases and she'd come to terms with the ordinariness of this year's Christmas fare so, despite the conditions, she was actually feeling surprisingly upbeat.

She was certainly enjoying her truce with Joe.

And yet she was nervous about this situation. Playing happy families with her ex *had* to be risky. It was highly possible that she was enjoying Joe's company far too much. Already, today they'd caught themselves laughing a couple of times.

Surely that had to be dangerous?

Could laughter lead to second thoughts? Could she find herself weakening and becoming susceptible to Joe's charms, just as her mother had warned?

Then again, she knew these happy vibes couldn't last. By Boxing Day, she and Joe would be back to normal.

Normal and divorced and leading separate *peaceful* lives.

'OK,' she said briskly, whipping her attention from her broken marriage to her neat sheets of shortbread stars and her small son's not-so-neat efforts. 'I think it's time to pop these gourmet masterpieces into the—'

She stopped in mid-sentence as an approaching sound caught her attention.

Thump-thump-thump-thump-thump-thump-thump...

Jacko squealed. 'Heli-chopper!'

Joe looked up from his task of stitching the chicken and grinned. 'That's probably Steve.'

'Steve?' Ellie frowned as the roar of the chopper blades grew louder. Closer.

'Steve Hansen. A mate of mine from the Army. He got out last year.'

'Oh.'

In a heartbeat Ellie guessed exactly what this meant. Joe was no longer stranded here. She went cold all over. Joe had found an escape route. A friend with a helicopter was coming to his rescue. He was about to leave her again.

Ridiculously, she began to shiver in spite of the heat. *This* was the reason for last night's mysterious and secretive phone call. Joe had never explained, and all morning she'd been wondering.

Now, with an effort, she dredged up a smile. 'Well, that's *your* Christmas sorted.'

Joe looked at her strangely, but anything he might have said was drowned by the helicopter's noisy arrival directly above the homestead roof.

There'd been helicopters at Karinya before. They'd come to help with the mustering, so little Jacko wasn't frightened by the roaring noise. In fact he was squealing with delight as he dashed to the window.

The chopper was landing on the track beside the home paddock and, with a whoop of excitement, Joe picked the boy up and flipped him high onto his broad shoulders.

Ellie gulped. The sight of her son up on his father's big shoulders was...

Breathtaking...

'Are you coming to say hello to Steve?' Joe called to her before he hurried outside, leaving her with her arms akimbo and a table covered with raw chicken and unbaked cookies.

Ellie had no idea how long this interruption would take, so she found space for the uncooked food in the fridge.

By then, the helicopter had landed and Joe and Jacko were waiting at the bottom of the front steps until the blades stopped whirring. Jacko was jigging with excitement. Ellie's stomach felt hollow as she joined them.

It's OK. I'll be fine. Joe has to leave some time, and it's probably easier to say goodbye now, without going through the whole business of Christmas first.

Joe was grinning at her, his rugged face relaxed and

almost boyish with excitement. He looked a bit like Jacko. Or Jacko looked like him.

It wasn't a cheering thought now, when he was about to leave them. Ellie's heart did a sad little back-flip.

The rotor blades slowed. A door in the helicopter opened and a beefy red-haired pilot with a wide friendly grin appeared.

'Ho! Ho! Ho!' he called jauntily as he climbed down.

'Merry Christmas!' responded Joe and the two men greeted each other with handshakes and hearty back slaps. Joe's smile was wide as he turned back to Ellie and Jacko. 'Come and meet Steve. He was in Afghanistan with me, but he's set up in Townsville now and he's started his own chopper charter business.'

Pinning on her brightest smile, Ellie took Jacko's hand and encouraged him forward. 'Hi, Steve. Nice to meet you.'

'You, too,' Steve said warmly. 'Merry Christmas.' He shook hands with Ellie, then bent to ruffle Jacko's hair. 'Hello, young fella. You're a chip off the old block if ever I saw one.'

'This is Jacko,' Joe said proudly, adding a bright-eyed smile that included Ellie.

'Hi, Jacko.' Steve waggled his eyebrows comically, making the little boy giggle.

To Ellie, he said, 'I remember how excited Joe was when this little bloke was born. The news came through when we were all in the mess. You should have seen this man.' He slapped a big hand on Joe's shoulder. 'He was so damn proud, handing around his phone with a photo of his son.'

'How…how nice.' Ellie was somewhat stunned. She

glanced at Joe, saw the quick guarded look in his eyes, which he quickly covered with an elaborate smile.

'And now Jacko's a whole two years old,' Joe said.

'You're a lucky little bloke, Jacko,' announced Steve and then he nodded to the helicopter. 'And you're certainly in for an exciting Christmas.'

An exciting Christmas? Ellie frowned. What was this about?

She was struck by a ghastly thought. Surely Joe wasn't planning to take Jacko with him? 'What's going on?' she demanded.

Now it was Steve who frowned.

'Everything's fine, Ellie,' Joe intercepted quickly in his most soothing tone. 'Steve's brought out extra things for Christmas.' Turning to Steve, he said, 'I haven't told Ellie about this. I was keeping it as a surprise.'

'Ah!' Steve's furrowed brow cleared and was replaced by another grin. He winked at Ellie. 'Romantic devil, isn't he?'

Clearly Joe's Army mates didn't know about their divorce. Ellie found it difficult to hold her smile.

'Stand back then, Mrs Madden, while we get this crate unloaded.'

Dazed, she watched as Steve Hansen climbed back into the helicopter and began to hand down boxes and packages, which Joe retrieved and stacked on the ground.

There was an amazing array. Boxes, supermarket bags, wrapped parcels. A snowy-white Styrofoam box with *Townsville Cold Stores* stamped on the side.

As the last carton came out, Joe turned to Ellie with a complicated lopsided grin. 'I thought you deserved a proper Christmas. You know, some of the fancy things you were missing.'

She gave a bewildered shake of her head. 'You mean this is all fancy Christmas food? For me?'

'North Queensland's freshest and best,' responded Steve from the cockpit doorway. 'I set my wife Lauren on the hunt and she's one hell of a shopper.'

Ellie was stunned. 'Thank you. And please thank Lauren.' Again she was shaking her head. 'I can't believe you and your wife have gone to so much trouble, especially on Christmas Eve. It's such a busy time.'

Steve shrugged. 'Joe knew exactly what he wanted, and bringing it out here has been my pleasure.' He gave another of his face-splitting smiles. 'Besides, I'd do anything for your husband. You know Joe saved my life?'

'No,' Ellie said faintly. 'I didn't know that.' She hardly knew anything about Joe's time in the Army.

'Out in Oruzgan Province. Your crazy husband here broke cover to draw enemy fire. I was literally pinned between a rock and a hard place and—'

'Steve,' Joe interrupted, raising his hand for silence, 'Ellie doesn't need to hear your war stories.'

But Steve was only silenced momentarily. 'He's way too modest,' he said, cocking his thumb towards Joe. 'They're saying we're all heroes, but take it from me— your husband is a *true* hero, Ellie. I guess he's never told you. He risked his life to save mine. He was mentioned in despatches, you know, and the Army doesn't hand those out every day.'

'Wow,' Ellie said softly.

Wow was about all she could manage. The admiration and gratitude in Steve's eyes was so very genuine and sincere. She had difficulty breathing.

He risked his life to save mine.

But Joe obviously hadn't told Steve that he was now divorced, which made this moment rather confusing and embarrassing for Ellie, not to mention overwhelming. Her throat was too choked for speech. Her lips were trembling. She pressed a hand to her mouth, willing herself not to lose it in front of these guys.

'Thanks for sharing that, Steve,' she managed to say eventually. 'Joe never tells me anything about Afghanistan.' To keep up the charade, she tried to make this sound light and teasing—a loving wife gently chiding her over-protective husband.

'Well, it's been a pleasure to finally meet you and Jacko,' Steve said. 'But I'm afraid I have to head back. We're throwing a Christmas party at our place tonight. Pity you guys can't join us, but Lozza will have my guts for garters if I'm late.'

Already, he was climbing back into the cockpit.

Without Joe.

'You'd better hurry and get your things,' Ellie told Joe.

'My things?'

'You're not leaving without your luggage, surely?'

His blue eyes shimmered with puzzled amusement as he stepped towards her. Touched her lightly on the elbow. 'I'm not leaving now, Ellie,' he said quietly. 'I'm not going anywhere till the floods go down.'

'But—'

He cupped her jaw with a broad hand. 'Relax. It's cool.' His smile was warm, possibly teasing. His touch was lighting all kinds of fires. 'I couldn't let you eat all this stuff on your own.'

And then his thumb, ever so softly, brushed over her lips. 'Let's wave Steve off, and get these things inside. And then we can really start planning our Christmas.'

Our Christmas.

Joe was free to leave. Steve Hansen would have taken him back to the coast in a heartbeat—no questions asked. Instead Joe had *chosen* to stay.

And the way he'd looked at her just now was like the Joe of old.

But that was crazy. He couldn't... They couldn't...

She mustn't read too much into this. It was Christmas and Joe wanted to spend more time with Jacko. It was the only logical, believable explanation—certainly, the only one Ellie's conscience could accept.

But as Steve took off with the downdraught from his chopper flattening the grass and sending the cattle in the next paddock scampering, she had to ask, 'So, if you knew Steve could fly out here, why didn't you get him to rescue you?'

Joe shrugged. 'It would have been difficult, leaving the hire car stranded here.'

It was a pretty weak excuse and Ellie didn't try to hide her scepticism.

'Besides,' Joe added smoothly, 'you and I decided on a truce, and how can you have a truce between two people if one of the combatants simply walks away?'

As excuses went, this was on the shaky side too, but Ellie wasn't going to argue. Not if Joe was determined to uphold their truce. And not when he'd gone to so much trouble and expense to celebrate Christmas with her and Jacko.

'Come on,' he said, hefting the white box of cold stores. 'Let's see what Steve's managed to find.'

* * *

The packages were piled into the kitchen and it was just like opening Christmas presents a day early.

In the box from the cold stores, nestling in a bed of ice, they found the most fantastic array of seafood—export quality banana prawns, bright red lobsters, a slab of Tasmanian smoked salmon, even a mud crab.

'I may have slightly over-catered,' Joe said with a wry grin. 'But seafood always looks a lot bigger in the shell.'

In another cold bag there was a lovely heritage Berkshire ham from the Tablelands. This brought yet another grin from Joe. 'If the wet closes in again, we'll be OK for ham sandwiches.'

The rest of the produce was just as amazing—rosy old-fashioned tomatoes that actually smelled the way tomatoes were supposed to smell; bright green fresh asparagus, crispy butter-crunch lettuce, further packets of salad greens, a big striped watermelon. There were even Californian cherries, all the way from the USA.

In yet another box there were jars of mustard, mayonnaise and marmalade. Pickles and quince paste from the Barossa Valley. Boxes of party fun—bonbons and sparklers, whistles and glow sticks.

And there was a plum pudding and brandy cream, and a bottle of classic French champagne, and another whole case of wine of a much classier vintage than the wines Ellie had bought.

She thanked Joe profusely. In fact, on more than one occasion, she almost hugged him, but somehow she managed to restrain herself. Joe might have been incredibly, over-the-top generous, but Ellie was quite sure a newly ex-wife should *not* hug the ex-husband she'd so recently served with divorce papers.

It was important to remember that their Christmas truce was nothing more than a temporary cessation of hostilities—*temporary* being the operative word.

Ellie forced her mind to safer practical matters—like what they were going to do with the stuffed chicken and shortbread dough sitting in the fridge.

'We'll have them tonight,' suggested Joe. 'They'll be perfect for Christmas Eve.'

So the chicken and assorted roast vegetables, followed by shortbread cookies for dessert, became indeed the perfect Christmas Eve fare.

A cool breeze arrived in the late afternoon, whisking away the muddy aroma, so Ellie set a small table on the veranda where they ate in the gathering dusk, sharing their meal with Jacko.

Joe stuck coloured glow sticks into the pot plants along the verandah, lending a touch of magic to the warm summer's night.

Jacko was enchanted.

Ellie was enchanted too, as she sipped a glass of chilled New Zealand white wine, one of Joe's selections.

She had spent the past four years working so hard on Karinya—getting up at dawn, spending long days out in the paddocks overseeing the needs of her cattle, and then, after Jacko was born, fitting in as much time as possible to be with him as well.

Most nights, she'd fallen into bed exhausted. She'd almost forgotten what it was like to take time out to party.

Putting Jacko to bed on Christmas Eve was fun, even though he didn't really understand her explanation about the pillowslip at the end of his cot. He would soon work it out in the morning, and Ellie's sense of bubbling anticipation was enough enthusiasm for both of them.

When she tiptoed out of Jacko's room, she found Joe on the veranda, leaning on the railing again and looking out at the few brave stars that peeked between the lingering clouds.

He turned to her. 'So when do you fill Jacko's stocking?'

She smiled. 'I've never played Santa before, so I'm not exactly an expert, but I guess I should wait till I'm sure he's well and truly asleep. Maybe I'll do the deed just before I go to bed.'

'I'd like to make a contribution,' Joe said, sounding just a shade uncertain. 'I asked Steve to collect something for Jacko.'

'OK. That's nice. But you can put it under the tree and give it to him in the morning.'

'I'd like to show it to you now. You might want to throw it in with the Father Christmas booty.'

'Oh, there's no need—'

But already Joe was beckoning Ellie to follow him inside, into the study, where he promptly shut the door behind them.

'This makes a bit of a noise and I don't want to wake him.' He was trying to sound casual, but he couldn't quite hide the excitement in his eyes.

Intrigued, Ellie watched as he pulled a box from beneath the desk and proceeded to open it.

'Oh, wow!' she breathed as Joe drew out the world's cutest toy puppy. 'A Border Collie. How gorgeous. It looks so real.' She touched the soft, furry, black and white coat. 'It almost feels real and it's so cuddly. Jacko will love it!'

'Watch this.' Joe pressed a button in the puppy's stomach and set it on the ground. Immediately, it sat up and barked, then dropped back to all fours and began to scamper across the floor.

'Oh, my goodness.' Ellie laughed. 'It's amazing.'

The puppy bumped into the desk, backed away and then proceeded to run around in circles.

'I knew Jacko was too little for a real dog,' Joe said. 'But I thought this might be the next best thing.'

'It is. It's gorgeous. He'll be over the moon.' *The presents I bought won't be half as exciting.*

Joe was clearly pleased with her reaction. 'One of the guys in our unit bought a toy like this for his kid's birthday, and his wife put a movie of the boy and the puppy on the Internet. It was so damn cute it more or less went viral at the base.'

'I can imagine.' Ellie was touched by how pleased Joe looked, as if it was really important to find the right gift for his son.

'The other present I brought back with me was totally unsuitable,' he said. 'A kite. What was I thinking?'

'A kite from Afghanistan?'

Joe rolled his eyes to the ceiling. 'Yeah.'

'But their kites are supposed to be beautiful, aren't they?'

'Well, yes, that's true, and it's a national pastime for the kids over there, but a kite's not really suitable for a two-year-old. I just didn't think. I'll keep it for later.'

The puppy had wound down now and Joe scooped it up, unselfconsciously cradling it in his arms.

It wasn't only *little* boys who looked cute with toy dogs, Ellie decided.

'So you might like to put this in with the Santa stash,' he said.

'But then Jacko won't know *you* bought it for him.'

'That's not important.'

Ellie frowned. 'I think it is important, Joe. If you're going to go away again for ages at a time, a lovely gift like this will help Jacko to remember you.'

Perhaps this was the wrong thing to say. Joe's face turned granite-hard—hard cheekbones, hard eyes, hard jaw.

Silence stretched uncomfortably between them.

Ellie wished she knew what he was thinking. Was he regretting his decision to work so far away? Perhaps he felt differently about leaving Jacko now that he'd met the boy and so clearly liked him?

It was more than likely that Joe loved Jacko. For Ellie, just thinking about Joe heading off there to that freezing, lonely, big ocean made her arms ache strangely. They felt so empty and she felt sad for Joe, sad for Jacko too—for the tough, complicated father and his sweet, uncomplicated son.

Maybe she even felt sad for herself?

No. I've made my choices.

It seemed like an age before Joe spoke. 'I'd rather my son remembered *me*, not the toys I've given him.'

Ellie swallowed. It was hard to know whether he was taking the high moral ground or simply being stubborn. But he was sticking to his decision.

She held out her hand. 'In that case, I'd love to add this puppy to the Santa bag. Jacko will adore it. He'll be stoked.'

'You want to keep it in this box?'

'No. It looks more true-to-life out of the box.' Ellie hugged the puppy to her stomach. 'Joe, you haven't bought a Christmas present for me, have you?'

The hard look in his eyes lightened. 'There might be a little something. Why? Does that bother you?'

'Yes. I don't have anything for you. I never dreamed—'

He smiled crookedly. 'Chill, Ellie. It's no big deal. I know you haven't been anywhere near shops.'

Just the same, she was going to worry about this and it would probably keep her awake.

This is damn hard, Joe thought as Ellie left with the dog. Coming home was *so* hard. So much harder than he'd expected.

Of course, he'd always known he would have to make big adjustments. Soldiers heard plenty of talk about the challenges they would face as they transitioned from the huge responsibilities and constant danger of military life to the relative monotony and possible boredom of civilian life.

But Joe had been convinced that his adjustments would be different, easier than the other men's. To begin with, he wasn't coming home to a wife and family.

Or at least he hadn't planned to come home to a wife and family.

And yet here he was—on Christmas Eve—divorced on paper, but up to his ears in family life and getting in deeper by the minute.

He had to face up to the inescapable truth. No matter how much distance he put between himself and his family, there would always be ties to Ellie and Jacko.

It was so obvious now. He couldn't believe he hadn't seen it before.

And here was another thing. By coming back to Karinya, he was forced to see his absence in Afghanistan from Ellie's point of view, and he didn't like the picture he discovered.

While he'd played the war hero, earning his fellow soldiers' high regard, his wife—she'd still been his wife, after all—had slogged for long, hard days on this property, and she'd done it alone for the most part. As well, with no support whatsoever from him, she'd weathered the long awaited pregnancy and birth of their son.

On her own.

After the years of heartbreak and invasive procedures that had eroded their marriage, Joe knew damn well that the nine months of pregnancy must have been a huge emotional roller coaster for Ellie.

And what had he done? He'd tried to block out all thoughts of her pregnancy. And he'd let her soldier on. Yes, Ellie had most definitely *soldiered* on. Alone. Courageously.

Just thinking about it made Joe tremble now. During that whole time, Ellie must have believed he didn't care.

Hell. No wonder she had trouble trusting his motives today. No wonder she'd expected him to escape in Steve's chopper as soon as he had the chance.

And yet, strangely, escape had been the last thing on his mind. Shouldn't he be worried about that?

CHAPTER EIGHT

When Ellie woke early next morning, she felt an immediate riff of excitement, a thrill straight from childhood.

Christmas morning!

She went to her bedroom window and looked out. It was raining again, but not too heavily. She didn't mind about the rain—at least it would cool things down.

'Happy Christmas,' she whispered to the pale pink glimmer in the clouds on the eastern horizon, and then she gave a little skip. Rain, hail or shine, she was more excited about this Christmas than she had been in years.

Having a child to share the fun made such a difference. And this year they had all Joe's bounty to enjoy, as well as his pleasant company during their day-long truce.

The truce was a big part of the difference.

Don't think about tomorrow. Just make the most of today.

On the strength of that, Ellie dressed festively in red jeans and a white sleeveless blouse with a little frill around the neckline. When she brushed her hair, she was about to tie it back into its usual ponytail when she changed her mind and left it to swing free about her shoulders.

Why not? They might be in the isolated outback, but it *was* Christmas, so she threaded gold hoops in her ears as well, and sprayed on a little scent.

On her way to the kitchen she passed Jacko's room, but he was still asleep, still unaware of the exciting bundle at the end of his cot. He normally wouldn't wake for at least another hour.

As Ellie passed the open door of Joe's room, she glanced in and saw that his bed was made, so he was already up, too. She felt pleased. It would be nice to share an early morning cuppa while they planned their day together.

Maybe they could start with a breakfast of scrambled eggs and smoked salmon with croissants? And they could brew proper coffee and have an extra croissant with that new, expensive marmalade.

Joe might have other ideas, of course. He wasn't in the kitchen, however.

Ellie turned on the kettle and went to the doorway while she waited for it to come to the boil. Almost immediately, she saw movement out in a paddock.

Joe?

She crossed the veranda to get a better view through the misty rain. It was definitely Joe out there and he was bending over a cow that seemed to be on the ground.

Ellie frowned. Most of her pregnant cows had calved, but one or two had been late to drop. She hoped this one wasn't in trouble.

Grabbing a coat and Akubra from the pegs by the back door, she shoved her feet into gumboots and hurried down the steps and over the wet, slippery grass, dodging puddles in the track that ran beside the barbed wire fence.

'Is everything OK?' she called as she reached Joe.

He'd been crouching beside the cow, but when Ellie called he straightened. He was dressed as she was in a dark oilskin coat and broad-brimmed hat. In the dull grey morning light, his eyes were very bright blue.

Ellie had always had a thing for Joe's eyes. This morning they seemed to glow. They set her pulses dancing.

'Everything's fine,' he said. 'You have a new calf.'

And now she dragged her attention to the cow and saw that she had indeed delivered her calf. It was huddled on the ground beside her, dark red and still damp, receiving a motherly lick.

'Her bellowing woke me up,' Joe said. 'So I came out to investigate, but she's managed fine without any help.'

'That's great. And now we have a little Christmas calf,' Ellie said, smiling.

'Yes.' Joe smiled too and his gaze rested on her. 'Happy Christmas, Ellie.'

'Happy Christmas.' Impulsively, she stepped forward and kissed him lightly on the cheek.

He kissed her in reply—just a simple little kiss on her cheek, but, to her embarrassment, bright heat bloomed where his lips touched her skin.

Awkwardly, she stepped away and paid studious attention to the little calf as it staggered to its feet. It was incredibly cute, all big eyes and long spindly legs.

'It's a boy,' Joe said, and almost immediately the little fellow gave a skip and tried to headbutt its tired mum.

Ellie laughed, but the laugh died when she saw Joe's suddenly serious expression.

'I've been thinking about you,' he said. 'I never asked what it was like—when Jacko was born.'

She felt winded, caught out. 'Oh, God, don't ask.'

He was frowning. 'Why? Was it bad?'

You shouldn't be bothering with this now. Not after all this time.

'I know I should have asked you long ago, Ellie.' Joe's throat worked. 'I'm sorry, but I'd like to know. Was…was it OK?'

Even now, memories of her prolonged labour made her wince. She'd been alone and frightened in a big Townsville hospital, and she'd been unlucky. Rather than having the assistance of a nice, sensitive and understanding midwife, the nurse designated to look after her had been brusque and businesslike. Unsympathetic.

So many times during her twenty plus hours of labour, Ellie could have benefited from a little hand-holding. A comforting companion. But she wouldn't tell Joe that. Not now.

Especially not today.

She dismissed his concern with a wave of her hand. 'Most women have a hard time with their first.'

A haunted look crept into his eyes. 'So it was tough?'

OK, so he probably wouldn't give up without details. She told him as casually as she could. 'Almost twenty-four hours and a forceps delivery.'

She wouldn't tell him about the stitches. That would totally gross him out. 'It was all perfectly normal in the end, thank heavens, but it had its scary moments.'

Joe looked away. She saw the rise of his chest as he drew a deep breath.

'But it was worth it,' Ellie said softly. 'It was so worth every minute of those long hours to see Jacko.' And suddenly she had to tell Joe more, had to help him to see the joy. 'He was the most beautiful baby ever born, Joe. He had this little scrunched up face and dark hair. And he was waving his little arms. Kicking his legs. He had long feet, just like yours, and he was so amazingly perfect. It was the biggest moment of my life.'

You should have been there.

Oh, help. She was going to cry if she kept talking about this. Joe looked as if he was already battling tears.

It was Christmas Day. They should *not* be having this conversation.

Forcing herself to be practical, Ellie nodded to the new calf and its mother. 'I'll bring them some supplements later but, right now, I'm hanging out for breakfast. Are you coming?'

It took a moment for the furrows in Joe's brow to smooth. He flashed a scant, uncertain smile. 'Sure.'

'Let's hurry then. I'm starving.'

On the homestead's back veranda, Ellie pulled off her gumboots and removed her hat and coat. Joe shouldn't have been paying close attention. But, beneath the outdoor gear, she was dressed for Christmas in skinny red jeans and a frilly white top. Winking gold earrings swung from her ears and her dark glossy hair hung loose.

'So I was thinking scrambled eggs and smoked salmon?'

Breakfast? With his emotions running high, Joe's thoughts were on tasting Ellie's soft pink lips and hauling her red and white deliciousness close. He wanted to peel her frilly neckline down and press kisses along the delicate line of her collarbone. Wanted to trace the teasing seams of her jaunty red jeans.

Yeah, right, Brainless. Clever strategy. You'd land right back where you started with this woman. Ruining her life.

'Joe?'

He blinked. 'Sorry?'

With evident patience, Ellie repeated her question. 'Are you OK with scrambled eggs and smoked salmon?'

'Sure. It sounds—'

'Mummy!' cried a high-pitched voice from inside the house. 'Look, Mummy, look! A puppy!'

Ellie grinned. 'Guess we'll deal with breakfast in a little while.'

For Joe, most of Christmas Day ran pretty much to plan. Jacko loved his gifts—especially the little dog, and the colourful interlocking building set that Ellie had bought for him. The three of them enjoyed Ellie's leisurely breakfast menu, and Joe and Ellie took their second cups of coffee through to the lounge room where they opened more presents from under the tree—mostly presents for Jacko from their respective families.

Ellie loved the fancy box of lotions and bath oils and creams that Steve Hansen's wife had selected for her. And, to Joe's surprise, she handed him a gift.

'From Jacko and me,' she said shyly.

It was very small. Tiny, to be accurate. Wrapped in shiny red paper with a gold ribbon tied in an intricate bow.

'I know I said I didn't have anything for you, Joe. I meant I hadn't *bought* anything. This…this is homemade.'

Puzzled, he opened it and found a USB stick, a simple storage device for computers.

'I've put all Jacko's photos on there,' Ellie said. 'Everything from when he was born. I...um...thought you might like to—'

She couldn't go on. Her mouth pulled out of shape and, as her face crumpled, she gave a helpless shake of her head.

Dismayed, Joe dropped his gaze and stared fiercely at the tiny device in his hand.

'It'll help you to catch up on Jacko's first two years,' Ellie said more calmly.

But Joe was far from calm as he thought about all the images this gift contained. Two whole years of his son's life that he'd virtually ignored.

He saw that his hand was trembling. 'Thanks,' he said gruffly. 'That's—'

Hell, he couldn't make his voice work properly. 'I...I really appreciate this.'

It wasn't enough, but it was the best he could do.

They phoned their families.

'It's bedlam here,' Joe's mother laughed. 'Wall to wall grandchildren.'

'Jacko loves the picture books you sent, Mum. And the train set from his cousins. They were a huge hit.' The phone line was bad after all the rain and he had to almost yell.

'We miss you, Joe. And we're dying to meet Jacko, of course. Everyone sends their love. I hope you're having a nice day, darling.'

'We are, thanks. It's been great so far. Everything's fine.'

He and Jacko went into the lounge room and built a tall tower with the new blocks while Ellie phoned her mother. Joe had no intention of listening in, but she also had to speak loudly, so he couldn't help but hear.

'Harold gave you a diamond bracelet? How…how thoughtful. Yes, lovely. Yes, Mum, yes, Joe's still here. No, no. No problems…No, Mum. Honestly, you didn't have to say that. All right. Apology accepted. No, it doesn't mean I'm giving in. Yes, we're having beautiful seafood. One of Joe's Army mates brought it out in a helicopter. Yes, I thought so. *Very* nice. And Happy Christmas to you, too!'

Ellie came back into the lounge room and pulled a heaven-help-me face. 'I think I need a drink.'

'Right on time.' Joe grinned. 'The sun's well over the yardarm.'

They opened a bottle of chilled champagne and chose a CD by a singer they'd both loved years and years ago. And the music was light and breezy and the day rolled pleasantly on.

Jacko romped with his toy dog and played the new game of hide and seek, putting the dog behind cushions and then the curtains. Joe and Ellie made a salad with avocado, three kinds of lettuce and herbs. They set the dining table for lunch with the seafood platter taking pride of place. They added bowls for the crab shells and finger bowls floating with lemon slices.

They pulled bonbons that spilled rolled-up paper hats and corny, groan-worthy jokes. Jacko blew whistles and pulled crackers that popped streamers. The adults ate seafood and drank more champagne, while Jacko had orange juice and chicken. They laughed.

They laughed plenty.

Over plum pudding with brandy cream, while Jacko enjoyed ice cream with chocolate sprinkles, Joe told some of the funnier stories from Afghanistan. Ellie re-called the bush yarns the ringers had told around the campfire during last winter's cattle muster.

Joe couldn't drag his eyes from Ellie. She was glow-ing—and not from the wine. Her smiles were genuinely happy. Her dark eyes shone and danced with laughter. Even in an unflattering green paper hat, she looked enchanting.

And sexy. Dangerously so.

Seafood in the outback was a rare treat and she ate with special enthusiasm, sometimes closing her eyes and giving little groans of pleasure.

One time she caught Joe watching her. She went still and a pretty pink blush rose from the white frill on her blouse, over her neck and into her cheeks.

Watching that blush, Joe was tormented.

This truce was perilous. It was setting up an illusion. Messing with his head. Encouraging him to imagine the impossible.

After their long leisurely lunch, Ellie bundled a sleepy Jacko into his cot. The new black and white puppy, now named Woof, took pride of place next to his much-loved teddy bear. He was one very happy little boy.

On leaving his room, she found, to her surprise, that the dining table had already been cleared. Joe was in the kitchen and he'd cleared away the rubbish. He'd also rinsed their plates and glasses, and had almost finished stacking the dishwasher.

'Goodness, Joe. The Army's turned you into a do-mestic goddess.' *And a sex god*, she thought ruefully. *Or is it just too long since I've had a man in my kitchen?*

Grabbing the champagne bottle from the fridge, Joe

held it up with a grin. 'Want to finish this? There are a couple of glasses left.'

Ellie smiled. She was loving everything about this Christmas. 'It would be a crime to let those bubbles go flat.'

They took their glasses back to the lounge room. Outside, it was still drizzling and grey, but it was cosy inside with the coloured lights on the Christmas tree and a jazz singer softly crooning, and with Joe sprawled in an armchair, long legs stretched in close-fitting jeans and a white open-necked shirt that showed off his tan.

Ellie thought, *I'm almost happy. I'm so close to feeling happy that I can almost taste it.*

She *might* have been completely, unquestionably happy if this truce were real and not a charade.

It was scary—*super*-scary—to be having second thoughts, to wish that she and Joe could somehow time-travel back into their past and right a few wrongs. OK, right a *mountain* of wrongs.

It wasn't going to happen, of course. This pleasant and charming interlude was nothing more than time out. Time out for Christmas. From reality.

It was important to remember that. Ellie planned to make sure she remembered it. She hadn't needed her mother's phone call to remind her.

Joe hoped he looked relaxed, but it was getting harder and harder to stay cool and collected while Ellie kicked off her shoes and made herself comfortable on the sofa.

She arched and stretched like a sleepy cat and then sank against the cushions, offering him an incredibly attractive view of her long legs in slinky red jeans. She wriggled her bare toes and sipped champagne with a smile of pure bliss.

The urge to join her on the sofa was a major problem.

And here was an inconvenient truth.

Ellie was the only woman Joe had ever truly wanted and, despite the bitterness and sorrow that had blown apart their marriage, the wanting was still there. Had never really left. It was an involuntary, visceral, inoperable part of him. And right now it was—

Driving him crazy.

Ellie took another sip of her champagne and held the glass up to the light, admiring the pale bubbles. Then she looked at Joe and her gaze was thoughtful, almost...

Wistful?

He held his breath. It was so hard to sit still when all he wanted was to be there on the sofa with her, helping her out of that frilly blouse.

Almost as if she could read his thoughts, Ellie's smile turned wary. Colour warmed her cheeks again and her eyes took on a new heightened glow. She shifted her position, and Joe wondered if she was feeling the same fidgety restlessness that gripped him.

His head was crammed with memories of making love to her. He could remember it all—the sweet taste of her kisses, the silky softness of her skin, the eager wildness of her surrender—

'So,' Ellie said with an awkward little smile, 'how would you like to spend the afternoon?'

She was joking, right?

'Are you interested in watching a DVD?'

'Might be dangerous,' Joe muttered.

'A DVD? Dangerous?'

He pointed to the positioning of the TV screen. 'We'd have to share that couch.'

Ellie looked startled, as well she might. She tried to cover it with a laugh. 'And that's a problem?'

'When you're wearing those tempting red jeans—yes, a big problem.'

Her expression switched from startled to stunned. And who could blame her? It had probably never occurred to her that her ex still had the hots. For her.

Joe grimaced.

Ellie simply sat very still, clutching her champagne flute in two hands, staring at him with a hard to read frown.

To his surprise, she didn't look angry. Or sad. Merely bemused and thoughtful.

His heart pounded. What was she thinking? If she showed the slightest hint that she was on the same wavelength, he would be out of this chair...

Then Ellie dropped her gaze to her glass and ran a fingertip around its rim. 'That's part of our problem, isn't it?'

Joe waited, unsure where this was heading.

'There's always been an attraction.' Ellie swallowed, gave a self-conscious shrug. Kept staring at her glass. 'But perhaps we would have been better off if we'd spent more time talking. I know you hate getting too deep and meaningful, Joe, but I don't think we ever spent enough time just talking, did we?'

'Not without arguing, no.'

'Have you thought about it very often?' She looked away and swallowed nervously. 'Have you given much headspace to what went wrong for us?'

'Some.' Joe's throat was so tight he could barely speak. 'Yes.'

Ellie drained her champagne and set the glass on the coffee table. 'I must admit I don't like failing or giving up, so I've given quite a bit of thought to our problems since you left. Too much, I guess.'

'What conclusions have you come to?'

Ellie regarded him with a narrowed, doubtful gaze. 'I can't imagine you'd really want to talk about this now.'

'No, it's OK. Go on. I'm listening. I'd actually like to hear your point of view.'

She seemed to think about this for a moment and then suddenly dived in. 'Well, I've always thought we were like that old song. Married in a fever. One minute we were the world's hottest lovers. Next, we were trying to set up a cattle business and start, or I should say restart, our family.'

'And then it all got so hard.'

'Too hard,' Ellie agreed with a frown. 'And that's when we didn't talk enough. Or when we tried to talk we just ended up yelling.'

Joe nodded, recalling the distressing scenes he'd tried so hard to forget.

'But there's one thing I'm very grateful for, Joe. Even in the heat of it, you never raised a finger to hurt me.'

'I wouldn't. I couldn't.'

Ellie had tears in her eyes now. 'But I think, in the middle of it all, we somehow lost sight of each other.'

'Or maybe we never really took the time to know each other properly.'

'Yes, that too.' She looked down at her hands and rubbed at a graze on her knuckle. She sighed heavily.

'But, as I said the other day—it's probably not helpful to dredge up the past.'

Joe wasn't so sure. Already he could see evidence of how they'd both changed. When they were married, a conversation like this would have landed them square in the middle of another argument.

He had to admit he'd avoided over-thinking their past. It was easy in the Army to be completely distracted by the demands of an ever present, very real and life-threatening enemy. He'd lived from day to day, from task to task. It was simple—and necessary—to focus on the present and to block out his emotions, including any guilt regarding Ellie.

Now, it was hard to believe he'd been so single-minded. Some would call it pig-headed.

Selfish.

But had he anything more to offer Ellie now? He'd like to think that time and distance had honed the raw edges and given him maturity.

Watching him, Ellie gave an uneasy sigh, then pushed out of the couch and got to her feet. She walked to the window and peered out. 'It's stopped raining,' she said dully.

A kind of desperation touched Joe. She was walking away, changing the subject. And yet he had the feeling they'd been drawing close to something important. He'd even wondered if it was something they both wanted, but were too afraid to reach for.

He edged forward in his seat, his mind racing, trying to balance his gut instincts with cool reason.

At the same moment, Ellie spun away from the window. 'Oh, stuff it! I think I *do* need to talk about this. I mean, it's our only chance. Once you're gone—'

She lifted her hands as if she felt lost. Helpless.

Joe's chest tightened. This was a *huge* moment and he suddenly knew that he wanted to grab it with both hands. Even so, he felt nervous—as nervous as he had in Afghanistan crossing a field laced with landmines.

'I'm happy to talk,' he said carefully. 'I mean—we're in a kind of now-or-never limbo at the moment, so perhaps we should make the most of it.' He chanced a smile. 'And we do have the protection of a truce.'

Slowly, cautiously, Ellie returned his smile, and then she walked back to the sofa and sat at one end, straight-backed, lovely, but clearly nervous. 'Where should we start?'

Good question. 'I'm open.'

Ellie squinted her dark eyes as she gave this some thought. 'Maybe we could start with the whole Army thing. There's so much I don't really know about you, Joe. Not just what you've done as a soldier since we split. I never really understood why you wanted to join the Army in the first place—apart from a chance to escape.'

'Well, I was planning to join the Army before I met you.'

'Yes, I knew that. But why, when your family own a cattle property? Don't you like cattle work?'

'Sure. I like working on the land.' Joe knew he could say this honestly. He loved the physical demands, loved being at one with the elements, loved the toughness and practicality required of people in the bush. 'But with four older brothers, I had very little say in how things were run at home. So the idea of the Army was more an act of rebellion than anything.'

Ellie looked surprised.

'I was fed up with being bossed around by those brothers of mine. They were always giving me orders. Not just on the property either. They loved telling me what I should and shouldn't do with my life. I decided, if I was going to be bossed around, it may as well be for a damn good reason and not simply because I was the runt of the litter.'

'Some runt,' she said with a smile.

'That's how I felt.'

Her smile was sympathetic. 'There was an age gap between you and the rest of your brothers, wasn't there? What was it? Six years?'

'Almost seven. I think they hoped I'd stay at the homestead and be a mummy's boy, but I wasn't staying home when they were off having adventures. So I was always trailing after them like a bad smell, trying to keep up. Annoyed the hell out of them, of course.'

'Not great for the self-esteem.'

Joe gave a shrug. 'I eventually came into my own, but not until boarding school. By then, all my brothers had left and, as far as my classmates were concerned, I wasn't anyone's little brother. I was just Joe Madden.'

'Football star.'

'For a few years, yeah.'

'And the Army was a bigger and more exciting version of boarding school?'

This time Joe chuckled. 'You missed your calling. You should have been a shrink.'

But Ellie was frowning again, as if she was lost in thought. 'I *still* think the Army provided an excellent excuse to escape when our marriage got too rough.'

'You're probably right.' He fingered a loose thread

in the upholstery on his chair. 'Maybe it was something I had to get out of my system.'

'Is it out of your system now?'

That was a damn good question. 'I think so. I've certainly no ambition to become an old soldier.' Joe looked up and met her gaze. 'So what about you, Ellie?'

To his surprise, she looked suddenly trapped. 'How do you mean?'

'If we're spilling our guts, I thought you might have something about you and your family that we've never outed.'

'I was an only child,' she said quickly. Almost too quickly. 'No sibling issues for me.'

But the shutters had come down. Everything about her was instantly defensive.

Joe waited. Ellie had never really explained why she'd left home straight after high school and moved to Queensland. He knew her dad had died when she was young and her relationship with her mum was OK, but not close, certainly not as close as Angela would have liked. There were issues, he was sure.

'I thought we were talking about you and the Army,' she said stiffly.

Ohhh-kaaay. Closed door.

Joe wasn't prepared to push Ellie on this. Not today. 'So we're back to me.' He shrugged. 'So, what else would you like to know?'

'Are you glad you joined up?'

The question was loaded, and Joe did his best to skirt it. 'The Army has its good points and I've certainly gained new skills.' He smiled. 'And not all of them involve blowing things up.'

More relaxed again now, Ellie picked up a cushion

and hugged it to her chest. Joe told himself he could not possibly be jealous of a cushion.

'So do you feel OK after everything you've seen and done over there?'

'Are you asking if I have post-traumatic stress?'

'Well, you seem fine, but there's so much talk about it. I wondered.'

'Well, I certainly feel OK, and I came out with a clean psych test. Perhaps I was lucky.'

'I guess you were due some good luck.' Her expression was a little sad. 'Just the same, do you think being a soldier has changed you at all?'

Joe hesitated, remembering the rockiest days of their marriage and the times he'd retreated when he'd known Ellie needed him. He'd watched his wife sink deeper into despair and it had felt like a knife in his heart, but he'd had no idea how to help her. At the time, he'd been completely inadequate.

'I'd like to think I've changed,' he said. 'I've certainly had to shoulder some hefty responsibilities.'

Ellie nodded slowly. 'It shows. I think it's given you confidence. You seem much surer of yourself now.'

This assessment caught him by surprise, especially as the smile that accompanied it was warm and tender.

Careful, Ellie.

When she looked at him like that, he was back to thinking about rolling with her on that couch.

CHAPTER NINE

JOE HAD THAT look again.

The look stole Ellie's breath and sent heat licking low, making her uncross and recross her legs, making her think too much about his powerful body, hidden by that snowy white shirt and blue jeans. He had that look in his eyes that made her forget all the warnings she'd given herself and wish for things she had no right to wish for.

She sat up straighter, and Joe watched with an attentiveness that did nothing to ease the edgy distractedness of her thoughts.

Talk, Ellie. This conversation's been going well. Don't lose it now.

'So,' she said quickly before she lost her nerve, 'I guess we agree that our relationship might have been more successful if we'd taken things more slowly at the start. We might have understood each other better if we'd talked more. Been a bit more tolerant.'

Joe nodded, but then his eyes took on a wicked teasing gleam. 'Then again, I'm not sure it was possible for us to go slow.'

She felt her cheeks glow.

'The way I remember it, we were pretty damn impatient,' Joe went on, clearly ignoring her discomfort.

This was *not* a helpful contribution, even though it was true. Right from the start, they hadn't been able to keep their hands off each other.

'At least we're managing to behave ourselves now,' she said tightly.

'We're divorced, Ellie.'

Clunk.

'Yes. Of course.' But she felt winded, as if he'd carelessly tossed her high and then left her to fall.

She slumped back against the cushions and closed her eyes while she waited for her heartbeats to recede from a frantic gallop to an only slightly less frantic canter. When she opened her eyes again, Joe was still watching her, but his expression was serious now.

'Just so I'm clear,' he said quietly. 'You're not having second thoughts, are you? About the divorce? About us?'

Second thoughts?

No, surely not. The very idea made her panic. She had her future planned. Joe had his future planned. They had their separate lives planned.

She couldn't have regrets. There was no point in trying to turn the train wreck of their marriage into a fairy tale.

And yet…

Had Joe really opened a door?

Was *he* having second thoughts about their marriage? And their divorce?

He was looking a tad winded, and Ellie could well believe that he'd shocked himself with his question.

It was too much to take in, sitting down. She launched

off the sofa and onto her feet again, and began to pace while her mind spun like a crazy merry-go-round.

'Second thoughts?' she repeated shakily. 'I don't think so, Joe.'

And yet…

And yet…

Her sense of loss was a dull ache inside her, and every time she looked at Joe now the pain grew sharper.

'But I…I don't know for sure.' She shot him a quick, searching glance. 'What about you?'

His throat worked and he tried for a smile and missed. 'I was good with our settlement. But…but if you wanted to reconsider it—'

Ellie stopped pacing. *Oh, God. This was not supposed to happen.*

'It was all decided,' she whispered. 'I've filed for divorce. I've served you with the papers. You've signed them.'

'I know. I know. And don't panic, Ellie. Nothing has to change.'

'No.' She took a deep breath, and then another.

'Unless…' Joe added slowly, carefully. 'Unless we want it to change.'

Whoa!

He was opening up a choice.

He was actually making her an offer. A second chance to right their wrongs.

Ellie's heart soared high with hope, then hovered, trembling with fear, terrified of failure. How could they possibly make this work?

'It can't be wise, can it?'

'Does it feel unwise?'

'No.' She stared at him anxiously. 'I don't know.'

'I guess we can only trust our own judgement.'

'Trust. That's a biggie. And…and now there's Jacko to consider as well. I'd hate to stuff things up for him.'

'It's the last thing I'd want, Ellie.'

She was swamped by an urge to simply rush into Joe's arms, to have done with the what-ifs and the wherefores and to simply give in to her burning need to have his arms about her, his lips working the magic she could so well remember.

I have to be sensible.

More than any other time in her life, she had to be cautious and unimpulsive and prudent.

'How can we be sure we won't just make the same mistakes?' But, even as she asked this, she knew the answer. After everything she'd been through, there were no guarantees. From the point of conception, every stage of life was a calculated risk.

After four years in the Army, Joe would know this, too.

'I guess we could avoid our first mistake,' he said. 'We could try taking things slowly, spending time together, getting to know each other again.'

'Just talking? Just friends?'

'It's only a suggestion.' Joe was out of his chair now and he was pacing too, as if he was as restless as she was.

It wasn't a sitting-down kind of conversation.

'What about this job you have lined up?' Ellie challenged. 'Chasing pirates or poachers or whatever?'

'The agency probably wouldn't be thrilled if I pulled out at the last minute, but I'd be prepared to.'

Ellie reached the bookcase and turned. Half a room separated them now. 'So if we tried this, how would it work? Would you be living here, at Karinya, and helping me with the cattle?'

'Yes, just as I was before, I guess.' He smiled at her. 'But hopefully without the arguments.'

'Or the sex.' Ellie's pacing came to an abrupt halt.

Her gaze met Joe's and she saw his eyes blaze with a look of such fierce intensity that her breathing snagged.

It wasn't possible, was it?

She and Joe couldn't live together and simply be friends. She was practically climbing the walls after just a few days of having him here, touching close and yet out of reach. And now they were planning to extend this condition indefinitely.

As if they were both frozen by the prospect, they stood, poised like opponents at Wimbledon, both as tense as tripwires, both breathing unevenly, with the stretch of carpet an unpassable gulf between them. Their no-go zone…

Help.

All Ellie could think about was crossing that space, rushing into Joe's arms and sealing her lips to his. Winding her limbs around his tree trunk body. Kissing him senseless.

Say something, Joe. Break the spell.

He didn't move, didn't speak, and something inside Ellie—most probably her willpower—snapped.

She flew across the carpet.

'I'm sorry,' she murmured half a second before her lips locked with Joe's.

But Joe wasn't looking for an apology, not if the hungry way he returned her kiss was any guide. He pulled her close, held her close, keeping her exactly where he wanted her, hard against him in all the right places, while his lips and tongue worked his dazzling, dizzying magic.

He tasted of Christmas and champagne and all kinds of happiness, and Ellie was swooning at the long-remembered taste and smell and intensely masculine feel of him.

Her knees gave way, but fortunately her hands linked behind his neck provided a timely, but necessary anchor.

If there were warning voices shouting in her head, she didn't hear them. She was drowning in a whirlpool whipped to urgency by years of loneliness and heart-break and a longing she could no longer deny.

I'm sorry, Joe. I've been trying so hard to forget you, but I can't. I've missed you so much.

So, so much.

The hunger in his kisses was reassuring. Wrapped in his arms with their wild hearts beating together, she could feel the passion in him…both thrilling and com-forting, as if they'd both arrived at the same place and knew it was where they were meant to be.

Everything about Joe felt familiar yet even more ex-citing than before. Especially now when, in the smooth-est of manoeuvres that Ellie didn't stop to analyse, he swung her off her feet and onto the sofa.

Cushions tumbled as their bodies tangled, urgency ruling the day. Joe kissed her chin, her earlobe, her throat, and her skin leapt to life wherever he touched. In no time he was peeling down the neckline of her blouse, trailing downward kisses that grew hotter and hotter.

Ellie helped him with the buttons. The blouse fell away and Joe released a soft groan. In a haze of need, she might have groaned too. She wanted his touch. Wanted it more than air.

'Mum! Mamma!'

Oh, help.

They stilled as if they'd been shot. Hearts racing, they stared at each other in disbelief.

'Mummy!' came another imperious summons from the little bedroom down the hallway.

Ellie was panting slightly. She was straddling Joe, flushed and half-dressed.

Joe looked into her eyes and smiled, his eyes hinting at dismay warring with amusement. 'His master's voice,' he said softly.

A shaky sigh broke from Ellie.

'Mummee!' Jacko called again and the cot was rattling now.

Joe reached for her, a hand at her nape, easing her down towards him. He kissed her gently, taking his time to sip at her lower lip. 'Saved by our son,' he murmured.

Our son. Not the kid or the boy. *Our* son.

'I don't feel saved.'

'No, you feel damn sexy.' He skimmed broad hands over bare skin at her waist, inducing a delicious shiver. 'At least we've made interesting progress.'

Indeed. Already, as they eased apart, Ellie sensed a new light-heartedness in Joe.

But that wasn't supposed to happen.

'I'll get Jacko,' he offered, rising to his feet while she began to re-button her blouse.

'Thanks.'

A moment later, Ellie heard his cheerful greeting and Jacko's delighted crow in response. She went to the bathroom and found a hairbrush, studied her reflection in the mirror. Her skin was flushed and glowing, her hair a messy tangle.

They'd come so close…

So close.

But had they been taking an important step, as Joe hinted, or had they teetered on the brink of a huge mistake?

And, more to the point, if they went ahead with their plan for a second chance, could she make it work? Could she be a better partner now?

When she thought about the woman she used to be, too anxious and heartbroken and self-absorbed to see beyond her own problems, she cringed.

She wanted to be so much better.

Was fate pushing her to grab this new chance?

A freak of nature, a flooded river, had brought Joe back into her life, but, just now on the sofa, they'd been gripped by a passion that revealed a deeper truth. They couldn't deny the attraction was still there. Stronger than ever.

It was still hard to believe that they might retrieve their marriage. For so long Ellie had thought of herself as already divorced. It wouldn't be easy to start again. They'd both have to make big adjustments. Huge. But if Joe was willing…

She wanted to give it her very best shot.

Joe lifted Jacko from the cot and took him to the bathroom and then to the kitchen for a drink and a snack, but he was working on autopilot. His mind was on Ellie and the big step they'd just taken. The choice they'd made.

The choice *he'd* made.

Sure, impulsive physical need had played a part, just as it had when he'd first met Ellie. But when he'd married her he hadn't really had a choice. He'd made his girlfriend pregnant and he'd felt a strong obligation to 'do the right thing' by her.

Again, four years ago, when he was so clearly making Ellie unhappy, he'd felt obliged to set her free. He hadn't known any other way to handle their problems and at the time, he'd convinced himself he had no other choice, although, as Ellie had correctly pointed out, he'd also been escaping.

Today, however, he'd had choices.

He had a signed legal document setting him free and he had a job to go to, a safe escape route. He had plenty of options.

But he'd also learned, after only a few days here, that he and Ellie had both changed during their years apart. Sure, they'd been on vastly different journeys—there couldn't be two experiences more different than war and motherhood—but they'd both matured as a result.

And, of course, they now had Jacko. Within a matter of days Joe loved the boy with a depth that he'd never dreamed possible. As for Ellie...

He knew now that he'd never stopped loving Ellie. He'd walked away from her when it all got too difficult and he'd buried his pain beneath the façade of a hardened soldier, but the bare truth was—his feelings for her were still as tender and loving as they'd been at the start.

So, yeah, he had loads of choices now.

And today he'd chosen to stay.

With Jacko between them, they spent the afternoon taking a tour of inspection around Karinya. Ellie carted nutritional supplements to the new mothers and calves, and she showed off her investments to Joe—two new dams and a windmill pump—as well as her successful experiments with improved pastures.

'You've done an amazing job,' he kept saying over and over.

They visited his favourite haunts, including the old weathered timber stockyards and the horse paddock. Together, they leaned on the railings, feeding carrots and sugar cubes to the horses that came to greet them, while Jacko played at their feet with a toy dump truck, filling its tray back with small rocks and then tipping them out.

'I think I should apologise,' Ellie said, needing to give voice to the issue at the forefront of her thoughts. 'I can't believe we decided on a set of rules and I immediately went crazy and broke them.'

'Have you heard me complaining?' Joe asked with a smile.

'But we didn't stick to the plan we'd made five minutes earlier.'

'Maybe it wasn't a very good plan. Not very realistic, at any rate.' Covering her hand with his, Joe rubbed his thumb over her knuckles. 'Don't start worrying, OK?'

Ellie smiled. 'OK.' There was something so very reassuring about this new confidence of Joe's. And, if she wanted this to work, she had to learn to trust him, didn't she?

Back in the ute, they drove on. They checked the river height and found that it was going down. In another day or two it would be crossable. But there was no more talk of Joe leaving.

Instead, happy vibes arced between them. A delicious anticipation whispered in the afternoon air. As they drove back to the homestead, they shared smiles and gazes over the top of their son's snowy head, gazes that shimmered with hope and excited expectation.

For their evening meal, Joe carved the Christmas ham with great ceremony and they ate thick, delicious pink slices piled on sourdough bread and topped with spicy mango chutney. Dessert was a cheese platter, plus extra helpings of Christmas pudding, and there was another bottle of Joe's delicious wine.

After dinner, to Jacko's squealing delight, the three of them played hide and seek together in the lounge room. Then they piled onto the sofa, with Jacko on Joe's knee, and together they read his new picture books. Ellie and Joe made the appropriate animal noises—Joe was the lion, the cow and the bear, while Ellie was the monkey, the duck and the sheep—and Jacko copied them, of course, amidst giggles and gales of laughter.

While Joe supervised Jacko's bath time—a rather noisy affair involving submarines and dive-bombing planes—Ellie took care of the dishes and tidied the kitchen. They put Jacko to bed.

And then, at last, they were alone.

Ellie was a tad self-conscious as they settled in the lounge room, enjoying the last of the wine. She was on the sofa and Joe was in the armchair again, but she knew they shared expectations about the night ahead. She was plucking up the courage to raise the question of sleeping arrangements. Surely Joe wouldn't stay in Nina's room tonight? Was it up to her as his hostess to mention this?

Despite this minor tension, their mood was relaxed. Music played, low and mellow. The tree lights glowed. They talked about their little boy—about the miracle that he was and how cute and clever—even which boarding school he might attend in the distant future.

Then, almost as if he could hear them, a little voice called, 'Drink o' water, Mummy.'

With a roll of her eyes, Ellie put down her glass and went to the kitchen to fill Jacko's cup. When she took it in to him, he only wanted two sips.

'Nuff,' he said, shaking his head.

'This is just a try-on,' Ellie scolded gently. 'Now snuggle down.' She kissed him. 'Time for sleep. Night, night.'

Jacko snuggled, closed his eyes and looked angelic. Satisfied and pleased, Ellie returned to the lounge room.

'Where were we?' she said to Joe.

'I believe we were congratulating ourselves on our wonderful son.'

They laughed together softly, so as not to disturb him.

Then Jacko wailed again. Ellie waited for a bit, but the wailing grew louder and, when she went to his room, she saw that he'd thrown his teddy bear out of the cot. Of course, she picked it up and gave it back to him. 'No more nonsense. It's bedtime,' she said more sternly.

Back in the lounge room, Joe was flicking through a magazine. Ellie settled on the sofa once more, picked up her glass.

'Joe!' came an imperious summons from the bedroom. 'Joe! Joe!'

Ellie sighed. 'He's overexcited.'

'Too much hide and seek after dinner?'

'Possibly. This happens from time to time.'

'So how do you usually handle it?'

'Depends. Sometimes Nina—'

'Nina?'

'The nanny.'

'Oh, yes, I forgot about her. When's she due back?'

'After New Year. Anyway, sometimes we let Jacko cry and he just gives up after a bit.'

Joe frowned at this.

'It's acceptable parenting, Joe. It's called controlled crying. We've never let him cry for *very* long.'

He still looked disapproving. 'Perhaps I should go in there and try speaking to him sternly?'

'Like a sergeant major?' Ellie sent him an *as if* look.

'A little fatherly discipline.'

'Are you sure you know how to reprimand a two-year-old?'

'I can only try.'

She shrugged. 'At this time of night, anything's worth a try.' But, suddenly unsure, she added quickly, 'Don't be too hard on him, Joe.'

Despite her last minute doubts, Ellie's gaze, as she watched Joe leave the room, was one of pure lust and feminine admiration. She was prepared to admit it now—Joe Madden had always been the most attractive guy she'd ever met, and now he was hotter than ever.

It wasn't just the extra muscle power. There was a new confidence and inner strength in him that showed in the way he held himself. And it was there in his gorgeous smile. In his attitude, too. He'd certainly taken fatherhood in his stride.

Actually, this last surprised her. Back in the bad old days when they were having so much trouble starting their family, Ellie had always been worried that Joe's heart wasn't really in the project—that parenthood was more her goal than his. Heaven knew she'd accused him of this often enough in the past.

Now, she heard Jacko's delighted greeting as Joe reached him, and she listened with keen interest for the 'stern message' he planned to deliver.

She was steeled for the gruff voice, followed by Jacko's whimpering cry. Telling Jacko off wouldn't work, of course. Almost certainly, she would have to go in there and soothe her little boy.

The house remained hushed, however, and all Ellie heard was the low rumble of Joe speaking so quietly that she couldn't hear the words. And then silence.

The silence continued.

Ellie finished her wine and the CD came to an end. She didn't bother to replace it. She was too absorbed and curious about the lack of sound down the hallway.

Eventually, it got the better of her and she tiptoed to the door of Jacko's room.

In the glow of the night light, she saw Joe by the cot and Jacko lying on his tummy, eyes closed, his long lashes curling against his plump cheeks. Joe was patting his back gently and patiently.

Ellie smiled. So much for the firm fatherly reprimand.

Sensing her presence, Joe looked up and lifted his free hand to halt her. Then he touched a finger to his lips and the message was clear. *I'm in charge here and everything's under control.*

Fascinated, she propped a shoulder against the doorjamb and waited, while Joe continued his gentle patting regime with surprising tenderness and patience. It was hard to believe this big tough man had just returned from a war that involved blowing things up and quite probably killing his enemy.

After another minute or so, Joe lifted his hand carefully from Jacko's back. Ellie waited for the boy to do his usual trick of wriggling and squirming till the patting resumed.

But Jacko remained peaceful and still and, a moment or two later, Joe came out of the room.

His smile was just a tad smug.

Safely back in the lounge room, Ellie narrowed her eyes at him. 'So that was your stern father act, huh?'

Joe grinned. 'Worked a treat.'

'You old softie.'

'That's one thing I'm not.' He touched her elbow. 'Come here and I'll prove it.'

Heat rose through Ellie like a flame through paper. Without hesitation, Joe drew her in.

And just like that she was in his arms and he was kissing her, hauling her closer still. And, of course, his boast was accurate. There was nothing soft about this guy, apart from his lips. The rest was hard-packed manly muscle and bone from head to toe.

The house was silent as they kissed.

And the silence continued. The only sound was the far-off call of a curlew in the trees along the river.

Joe took Ellie by the hand and led her to the darkened doorway on the far side of the lounge room, and the question about the night's sleeping arrangements became irrelevant.

This was the bedroom he knew well, the room they'd once shared.

They didn't bother with lights. The glow of the

Christmas tree reached where they stood at the foot of the bed, as they shared another kiss, another embrace.

Now their kisses were long and leisurely and sweet. They'd been denied this for so long, never believing it could happen. But despite the four years' separation, they lingered now on the brink, confident and trusting, savouring the exquisite anticipation.

Joe kissed Ellie's neck and she kissed his rough jaw. His lips brushed over her lips, once, twice in teasing, tantalising, unhurried caresses.

He lifted her chin to trace her jaw line with his lips. 'I've missed you, Ellie.'

'Me too. I've missed you so much.' She hadn't admitted it before, but she wanted him to know. 'The whole time you were away, I was terrified you'd be killed. There'd be stories about Afghanistan on the news, and I always had to turn them off.'

Tears threatened, but she didn't want to cry. Instead she sought pleasure, easing his shirt from his jeans and slipping her hands beneath, rediscovering the texture of his skin, the hair on his chest.

Her hands dipped lower and a soft sound broke from Joe, and next moment he was undressing her and she was loosening his clothes as best she could.

She had a brief moment of panic. 'I'm not the same, Joe. Since the pregnancy and everything, things have—'

'Shh.' He silenced her with his kiss as his hands cupped her less than perky breasts. 'You're lovely, Ellie,' he murmured against her lips. 'Beautiful. I'm still crazy about every little part of you.'

He melted the last of her fears as he guided her to the bed—the bed they'd shared till four years ago. And now, still, they took their time, making love slowly, tenderly, with whispered endearments and heartbreaking thoroughness.

They knew each other so well, knew all the ways they longed to be touched and kissed and roused—a knowledge they alone shared—intimate truths that lay at the heart of their marriage.

This night wasn't just about sex and wanting—it was a time-honoured act of love, where past hurts could begin to heal and glimmers of hope for their future dawned.

Afterwards they lay close together, talking softly in the moon-silvered dark.

'Welcome home,' Ellie said.

She felt Joe's smile against her neck. 'It's good to be back.'

'We have to make it work this time.'

Gently he lifted a strand of hair from her cheek. 'We will, Ellie.'

She turned, admiring his strong profile limned by moonlight. 'I love the way you're so confident now.'

'Older and wiser perhaps…'

'That should apply to me too then.'

'I'm sure it does.'

Ellie suspected that she'd changed, too. She was also more confident, more willing to believe in a happy future. But was she prepared to trust?

I must. It's important…

'At least we no longer have the whole baby thing hanging over us.'

Joe shifted away slightly, as if he needed to see her face. 'I assume with everything you've been through that you're content with just one?'

'Oh heavens, yes. Aren't you?'

'Absolutely. I'm perfectly content with the three of us.' He chuckled. 'Anyway, I doubt we could improve on Jacko.'

Ellie smiled at the obvious pride in his voice, but of course she agreed. They couldn't hope for more than their cute little guy, even if they were able to, which they weren't.

'So we're OK not using precautions?' Joe asked.

'Well, yes, we must be, surely. Look how hard it was to get Jacko.' Ellie frowned. 'But I will check with the doctor next time I'm in town. Another pregnancy is the last thing I'd want now when we're starting over. I'm more than happy to close that chapter in my life.'

'That's fine by me.'

Unexpected relief flowed through Ellie. That particular ordeal was behind them. They'd been tested in the fire and were stronger now. 'So we should be OK, shouldn't we?'

'I reckon we should be very OK.'

As if to prove it, Joe kissed her again, deep and hard and long.

Melting fast, she wound her arms around him, and they made love again with a new sense of giddy freedom and joyful abandon.

CHAPTER TEN

BOXING DAY MORNING dawned. As always, Ellie woke early, and the first thing she saw was Joe lying beside her. She indulged in a few secret moments to drink in the sight of him, so dark and manly and downright hot, and her heart performed a little joyful jig.

She went to the kitchen and made tea and when she brought two steaming mugs back to bed Joe was awake.

'I can't lie around having tea in bed,' he protested. 'I've a cattle property to run.'

'Humour me, Joe. Just for today. It's a public holiday. I know that doesn't mean much out here, but let's pretend.'

Ellie opened the French windows onto the verandah and plumped up the pillows and they sat in bed together, looking out over Karinya's paddocks, where bright new tinges of green were already showing after the recent rains.

She clinked her tea mug against his. 'Here's to us.'

'To us,' he agreed, dropping a kiss on her brow.

'That's assuming you're still happy to stay.'

'Of course I am, Ellie.'

Joe shot her a wary sideways glance. 'You've got to trust me, you know. This won't work if you don't.'

'I know.' She was surprised he'd pinpointed the heart of her problem. She was learning to trust—to trust not just Joe, but herself, even to trust in their ability to face the unknown future. 'I'm sorry,' she said.

'And no more apologies. We could spend a lifetime apologising to each other, but we've got to put the past behind us.'

Ellie nodded and sipped at her tea. 'We're going to have to tell Jacko that you're his daddy.'

Joe looked so happy at this he brought tears to her eyes. She was quite sure he would have hugged her, if they hadn't been holding mugs of scalding tea.

After a while, she said, 'It wasn't all bad before, was it?'

Joe shook his head. 'To be honest, I have more good memories than bad ones.'

She settled deeper into the pillows, pleased. 'Do you have a favourite memory?'

'Sure,' he said with gratifying promptness. 'It would have to be that day you brought dinner out to the Lowmead paddock.'

'Really?'

'Yeah. I'd had a hell of a time, trying to fix that bore. It took me hours and hours in the blazing heat. And, just as I finally got on top of it, you turned up with a big smile and all this fabulous food.'

Ellie felt a little glow inside, just watching the way Joe smiled at the memory.

'You brought me soap and a towel,' he said. 'And, while I was cleaning up, you set up the picnic table and chairs under a tree. There was a red checked tablecloth and you'd cooked up this fabulous curry, and we had chilled wine, and caramel rum pie for dessert.'

'So it's true, after all?' She gave him a playful dig with her elbow.

'What's that?'

'The way to a man's heart is through his stomach.'

Joe chuckled. 'Guess it must be.' He picked up her hand, threaded his fingers with hers. 'That day's a standout because it was so spontaneous.'

'Spontaneous for you. I'd had it all planned for days.'

'A brilliant surprise. We were so relaxed and happy.'

'We were,' she agreed.

'So what's your favourite good memory?'

'Oh, I think it has to be the night we almost slept in the car park.'

'But ended up in the bridal suite?'

'Yes. It was just such fabulous fun.'

'Especially as we'd never had a proper honeymoon. We'll have to go there again some time.'

Ellie lifted a sceptical eyebrow. 'Do you think they'd welcome Jacko?'

'My mother would babysit.'

'Well, yes, that would be nice.' But Ellie's chest tightened at the mention of Joe's mother. She was reminded of her mother. She drew a quick calming breath. 'I suppose we're going to have to tell our families, aren't we?'

'About us?'

'Yes.'

'My folks will be delighted.'

'Mine won't.'

For the first time that morning, Joe frowned.

'It's OK.' She kissed his lovely stubbled jaw. 'Mum's going to have to cop it sweet. If she doesn't, I'm not going to let it bother me.'

'Promise?'

'Promise.'

* * *

The transition into their new lifestyle was surprisingly smooth. The river levels went down and neighbours who were travelling to Charters Towers offered to drive Joe's hire car.

Joe rang to resign from his new position patrolling the Southern Ocean. At New Year, Joe and Ellie both rang their families with their news and, as they'd predicted, Joe's parents were delighted.

'Joe, darling, I'm so relieved,' his mother cried. 'I've been praying for this.' She was tearful on the phone, but she was laughing and excited through her tears. 'Just wait till I tell your father. He'll be thrilled. As you know, we're dying to meet Jacko. And to see Ellie again. Do you think you'll be able to visit us soon? But if it's too difficult, perhaps we could visit you? We have so many extra hands to help here. It would be easier for us to get away.'

Before Ellie could ring her mother, there was a call from Nina, the nanny.

'Ellie, I'm so sorry to leave you in the lurch, but I've just had the most amazing job offer. It's my dream—a position at the Cairns Post.'

Ellie knew Nina had studied journalism and that the nanny job had only ever been a fill-in. 'Don't worry,' she said with a serenity that surprised her. 'My husband's back from the Army, so we'll manage between us.'

She hadn't told Nina about her plans to divorce Joe, so the girl accepted his return as a perfectly normal and lovely surprise.

Of course, Ellie had been looking forward to having a nanny so that she could be free to join Joe in the outdoor work that she enjoyed so much, but Joe was much keener to share both the housework and the yard work than he'd been in the past, so she knew that she'd spoken the truth. They'd sort something out between them.

They'd arrived at a new calmness, a new sense of closeness and solidarity. It truly did feel as if they'd been through a long and painful trial and come out the other side stronger. And, as a reward, it seemed they'd been granted their fairy tale ending, and Ellie was beginning to trust that it really could last this time.

Although her phone call to her mother tested her newfound confidence.

'Oh, Ellie, I knew it! You're as weak as water when it comes to that man.' Her mother's voice was shrill with dismay. 'I don't expect it will be very long before he leaves you again.'

Ellie made an effort to argue in Joe's defence, but her mother showed no signs of relenting.

'Do you really think you're helping me, Mum, by getting stuck into Joe every chance you have?'

Her mother spluttered. 'I'm only thinking of you, dear.'

'I don't think so.'

'But Ellie—'

'You've been down on Joe ever since you met him.' Actually, that wasn't quite true. Her mum had been suitably charmed by Joe the first time she'd met him. It was only later, around the time of their wedding, that her attitude seemed to have soured. Ellie had never understood why.

'It's not just my opinion, Ellie. Harold warned me about Joe.'

'Harold?'

'Yes. He's learned so much from local politics and he's a very astute judge of human character. But you've always been so sure you know better. I don't suppose you'll visit us now, will you?'

'Well, I—'

'We'll just have to come and visit you then.' This was announced snappily before her mother hung up.

Ellie wasn't given an option. Her mother and Harold were coming, steamrollering their way into her home.

The very thought made her feel fragile and nervous. She tried to shrug it off. She told herself that, with Joe on her side now, she was strong enough for anything.

She almost believed this until the morning she re- alised that her period was two weeks late.

CHAPTER ELEVEN

SHE COULDN'T BE pregnant, surely?

The sudden fear that gripped Ellie was all too familiar. She was remembering the miscarriage that had started the downhill spiral and had ultimately wrecked their marriage.

Even the memories of Jacko's safe delivery couldn't calm her. Everything from Jacko's conception to his birth had been carefully controlled under strict clinical supervision. Ellie had spent most of the nine months of her pregnancy in Townsville while a manager took care of the cattle and Karinya.

An unplanned pregnancy now would bring to the surface all her old anxieties, all the tension and worry about another possible miscarriage or ongoing complications.

The last thing she wanted was to go through that again. Not now she had Jacko, and she and Joe were so happily reconciled.

Everything was going so well. Joe was genuinely pleased to be back here, to be with her and to be working Karinya. Only last night he'd told her this again.

'After growing up on a cattle property, I can't help feeling attached to the land—to the red dirt and the mulga. I'm scratching my head now, wondering how on earth I thought I'd be happy floating around in the Southern Ocean without you and Jacko.'

But would Joe still be happy if their old problems surfaced?

Ellie was aware of the irony of her new dilemma—she'd spent so many years longing for a baby, and now she was dismayed by the prospect. She and Joe had negotiated their new future together based on the understanding that their fertility and pregnancy issues were behind them.

They were starting a new life—just the three of them.

I can't be pregnant. Not with my record. It must be just out of kilter cycles.

She hunted around at the back of the medicine cabinet and found a pregnancy testing kit—years old, but never opened. Fingers crossed, it would still work.

She was so nervous she thought she might throw up as she waited for the result to show. She closed her eyes, not brave enough to watch what was happening to the stick, and she prayed that two coloured lines would *not* appear.

I can't be pregnant. I can't.

She allowed longer than the allotted time, just to be sure, and then she opened her eyes the tiniest crack, and peeked nervously at the tiny screen.

Two lines.

Oh, my God. Two strong, thick, no-doubt-about-it lines.

This couldn't be happening. Sweat broke out on her forehead, her arms, her back.

She stared at the lines in a disbelieving daze. She knew she *should* feel happy about this, but she could only feel shocked and scared. And foolish.

Pregnancy would land her right back where she and Joe fell off the rails. They would be reliving that horror stretch. They'd have to go through all that uncertainty again.

Why on earth had she been so confident that this couldn't happen?

How could I have been such a fool?

Her hands were shaking as she wrapped the testing stick in a tissue and hid it in the rubbish bin. She put the second stick back in its box in the cupboard. She might try again in a few days' time, just to double-check, to make sure this wasn't a crazy mistake. Until then, she wouldn't tell Joe. She *couldn't* tell Joe.

There was no need to upset him unnecessarily, especially when his parents were due to visit them at the end of the week.

Stay Zen, Ellie.

She nailed on a smile, knowing that her major challenge now was to make sure that neither Joe nor Jacko could sense how tense she was.

Over the next few days, Ellie thought she managed quite well, but there was still no sign of her period. She tried again, and the second testing stick showed another pair of very strong lines.

Her tension mounted. Joe's parents would be arriving at the weekend and she'd been looking forward to their visit. She hoped they would see for themselves how happy she and Joe were now, and she'd been in a frenzy of preparations, setting up an extra bed in the spare room, cleaning and polishing, baking cakes and slices.

Now, she was going to have to tell Joe about the pregnancy before they arrived, and she really had no idea how he'd react. In the near future, she would need to see a doctor, too. That thought made her even more anxious.

On the night before the Maddens were due, Ellie's stomach was churning as she went to say goodnight to Jacko. Joe was reading him his favourite picture books—they'd been taking it in turns lately—but she'd spent longer than usual in the kitchen tonight, putting the final touches to her baking.

It was time to call a halt to the reading or Jacko would be over-excited.

She'd thought Joe was reading the books on the sofa, but the lounge room was empty. There was a light in the bedroom—no voices though, no growling lions or gibbering monkeys. Surprised, Ellie crossed quickly to the bedroom doorway.

The sight she found there stole her breath.

Her husband and son were sound asleep, lying together on top of the quilt. Joe had one arm stretched out and Jacko was huddled close, sheltered by his shoulder.

They looked so peaceful, so close. Father and son...

There was something so silently strong and protective about this simple scene. It touched a chord deep within her.

In the past few weeks she'd been growing more and more confident that, whatever happened, Joe was here to stay. Now, watching him sleeping beside his son, she felt a strong new soul-deep level of certainty.

With Joe she could face the future. They had everything they'd ever wanted right now, and they could cope with this pregnancy together, whatever the outcome.

I'll definitely tell him about the baby tonight, she decided. She would run a nice relaxing bath and, when she came to bed, she would wake Joe gently and tell him about the pregnancy. She would tell him so calmly that he'd know she was OK, that their marriage—no matter what happened—was going to be OK…

Ellie was smiling as she tiptoed away. The only dark cloud on her horizon was the prospect of Harold arriving with her mother in a fortnight's time. But she wouldn't think about him tonight, wouldn't let him spoil her calm and upbeat mood.

She ran a lovely warm bath, lit a rose-scented candle and placed it on a stool in the corner of the bathroom. She turned out the main light and the room was pretty in the soft glow of candlelight. Deliberately, she made herself relax and lie back, eyes closed, breathing slowly, deeply and evenly, in and out.

She pictured herself serenely and confidently telling Joe her news—not too excited and not at all anxious. She would be positive and optimistic, taking this new pregnancy in her stride.

The candle scents and the soft light were soothing. She sank a little lower into the warm, welcoming water. No matter what happened in the next few weeks, she would do everything to remain calm. For Joe. She would—

The phone rang in the kitchen.

Ellie sat up quickly. Joe was asleep. She wondered if it had woken him, or whether she should clamber out of the bath and run, dripping, through the house.

Then she heard Joe's footsteps crossing the lounge room and going down the hall. Heard his voice.

'Hello, Angela.'

Her mother.

Whoosh. Ellie sank beneath the water, incredibly relieved that Joe was dealing with this call. She couldn't handle a conversation with her mum tonight. It would only wind her up again, wiping out the Zen.

She certainly didn't want to think about two weeks of Harold in her house—and with only one bathroom. How many times might he accidentally open the door?

This ghastly thought wouldn't go away. It wrecked Ellie's peace and brought her sitting up so abruptly that water sloshed over the side of the bath. How on earth could she kid herself that baths were relaxing?

Without warning and totally against her will, she was reliving those nights when Harold came in. The images were still disgustingly vivid in her memory.

Harold's leer. His teeth flashing in his red face as he grinned at her. His eyes bulging as he stared at her breasts.

Ellie shuddered and squirmed, her skin crept and her relaxation was obliterated in a flash. It was useless to continue lying in the bath with memories of her stepfather intruding. She stood quickly and scrambled over the side, not caring about the dripping water. She pulled the plug and the bathwater began to gurgle noisily down the plughole and along the old-fashioned plumbing.

As she reached for a towel, she thought she heard another sound beyond the gush of the disappearing water—the faint creak of the bathroom door opening. *Creepy Harold.*

She spun around.

Irrational fear exploded in her chest.

A shadowy male figure hovered in the doorway.

'Get out!' she screamed in a hot streak of panic. '*Get out!*' Her reaction was visceral, erupting from a place beyond logic. Eyes tightly shut, she screamed again. 'You monster. Leave me alone!'

'For God's sake, Ellie.'

She was so gripped by blinding panic it took a moment to come to her senses.

Joe?

Joe was standing at the door?

Of course it was Joe.

And he was staring at her in horror, as if she'd turned into a multi-headed, fire-breathing monster.

I'm sorry.

Ellie was panting and too breathless to get the words out at first. She tried again. 'I'm sorry, Joe, I—'

But he didn't wait for her apology. He took another glaring look at her, gave a furious shake of his head, then whirled around and left her, slamming the door behind him.

Appalled, shaken, Ellie sank onto the edge of the bath.

She couldn't believe she'd reacted like a maniac in front of Joe, as if she was terrified of her husband, the man she loved. It wasn't as if they hadn't shared the bathroom before. Only last week they'd had all kinds of steamy fun making love in the shower.

And she couldn't believe this had happened tonight of all nights, when she'd been trying her hardest to remain calm.

Clearly, she was as tense as a loaded mouse trap.

The look on Joe's face had said it all. She'd seen his stark despair, his disappointment and disgust.

She wanted to rush after him, but common sense prevailed. She would have a much better chance of offering a calm, rational explanation if she wasn't dripping wet and wrapped in a towel. Hastily she dried her body, her arms and legs and roughly towel-dried her hair.

Her silk kimono was hanging on a hook behind the door and she grabbed it quickly, thrusting her arms into the loose sleeves and tying the knot at the waist. As she dragged a comb through her wet hair, her reflection looked pale, almost haggard.

Too bad. She didn't have time to fuss about her appearance. She had to find Joe. The way he'd looked at her just now had frightened her badly.

It was as if he'd wanted to put as much distance between them as possible, as if he was certain their marriage was doomed, as if he'd already left her.

She didn't find him in the lounge room, or the kitchen, or the study, or their bedroom.

Had he left already? Taken off into the night?

Fearing the worst, Ellie hurried out onto the dark front veranda. Joe wasn't standing at the railing as she'd hoped.

Then she saw a shape on the front steps. She felt a brief flutter of relief until she realised that Joe was sitting slumped forward, as if defeated, with his head in his hands.

He looked shattered.

Her tough, highly trained, Special Forces soldier was sunk in total despair.

I've done this to him.

Ellie could feel her heart breaking.

She pressed her hand against the agonising ache in her chest. Now, more clearly than ever, she was aware of the depth of her love for Joe. These past few weeks had been the happiest in her life. The two of them were conscious of how close they'd come to losing each other and each new day together had felt precious. They'd even been laughing again, the way they had when they first met. And with Jacko joining in the fun, their lives had been so joyous. So complete.

Or had it all been a fragile mirage?

Had this bitter end always been waiting for them, hovering just around the corner?

After her hysterics in the bathroom, how could she possibly tell Joe about the pregnancy? How could she expect him to believe she'd cope with it calmly?

How could he have any faith in her?

Ellie was almost afraid to disturb him now, but she knew she had no choice. She had to try to apologise and to explain. Perhaps she even had to finally tell him about Harold.

Wasn't it time for courage at last?

Speaking to Joe was the first step.

Her legs were unsteady as she moved forward, her bare feet silent on the veranda floorboards.

'Joe?' she said softly.

His head jerked up. Instantly, he glared at her. 'What the hell's going on, Ellie?'

'Joe, I'm so sorry.'

Already he'd sprung to his feet, as agile as a panther. But his face was white in the moonlight. 'What's got into you?' He threw up his hands. 'What was that all about in there?'

'I'm sorry. It wasn't a reaction to you, Joe. Please believe me. I didn't know it was you.'

His scowl was derisive. 'Who else would it be, for God's sake? You saw me. I was standing right in front of you and you kept screaming. I'm your husband, damn it, not an axe-murderer. I thought—'

He shook his head and his lip curled in disgust. 'I

thought we were going to be OK, and then you go and pull a crazy stunt like that.'

'It wasn't a stunt.'

'What was it, then?' His eyes were fierce. 'You must have been truly terrified. Of what? Me? Am I supposed to find that reassuring?'

'I thought… For a moment, I thought…' Ellie swallowed the rising lump of fear that filled her throat. 'I can't explain unless I tell you…' The fear was stifling. 'There's…there's something I should have told you years ago.'

Joe stared at her, his blue eyes narrowed now—puzzled and mistrustful.

Ellie knew he must be wondering why she still had an apparently important issue that she hadn't shared with him. It probably made no sense at all after the soul-searching depth of their recent conversations.

'So, what is it?' he asked cautiously.

Despite the trembling in her stomach, Ellie came down the steps till she was next to him.

'It's Harold,' she said.

'Your stepfather?'

Ellie nodded.

Joe was frowning. '*He* freaks you out?'

'Yes.' It was all she could manage.

For long, nerve-racking seconds, Joe stared at her. She could see a muscle jerking in his jaw, betraying his tension, and she could see his thoughts whirring as he put two and two together. She saw the moment when understanding dawned.

He swore softly. 'That's why you left home so young?'

'I had to get away.'

Joe swore again with extra venom. He stood, glaring off into the black silent night, and when he turned to Ellie again, his eyes were still harsh, still uncertain.

'You've never breathed a word of this.'

'I know. I always meant to.'

'Why? Why couldn't you tell me?'

'I tried, but it was unbelievably hard. I felt so ashamed. And I'd already tried to tell my mother and she wouldn't believe me, so I thought I should just try to forget it, to put it all behind me.'

'Oh, Ellie.' Joe reached for her then. He took her hands, folded them in his, and then he slipped his arm around her shoulders and drew her close and his warm lips brushed her forehead. He sighed, and she felt his breath feather gently against her cheek.

It was the most wonderfully comforting sensation. Ellie dropped her head against his shoulder, savouring his strength. It felt so good to have offloaded this at last. And Joe understood. She should have known he would. She should have trusted him…

Then Joe said, 'Tell me now.'

Instinctively, she flinched. 'But you've already guessed.'

'My imagination's working overtime. I want to know the real story.'

'You might think I'm making a whole lot of fuss about nothing.'

'Nothing? After you almost clawed my eyes out tonight?'

She gave a defensive little shrug. 'I wasn't that bad.'

'Bad enough. And, whatever happened, I know it's affected you—it still affects you after all these years.' He gave her shoulder an encouraging rub. 'I'm not going to doubt you, Ellie.'

She knew this was true. Joe wasn't like her mother; she'd been blinkered and so impressed with her new role as the mayor's wife that she hadn't wanted to hear anything bad about Harold.

Joe, on the other hand, was genuinely worried—about her.

And so she told him.

They sat together on the wooden step, looking out over the dark, silent Karinya paddocks, where the only sound was the occasional soft lowing of a cow. Ellie's kimono fell open, exposing her knees, but she didn't worry about covering them, and she told Joe her story, starting with some of the things he already knew, like her father's death just before her thirteenth birthday, and how her mum had sold their farm and moved into town, marrying Harold Fowler eighteen months later.

'But, right from the start, Harold gave me the creeps,' she admitted.

She went on to explain how he'd just patted her at first, but over the next couple of years his attention had become more and more leering and suggestive, and then he'd come into the bathroom without knocking, choosing nights when her mother wasn't home.

She explained how she'd tried unsuccessfully to tell her mother.

'I knew then that if I stayed at home, the situation would have only got worse.' Ellie shuddered. 'And tonight I was thinking about Harold coming to stay here for two whole weeks. I don't suppose he'd dare to do anything stupid out here, but I was lying in the bath tonight, remembering, and wondering how on earth I would cope, and then the bathroom door opened and… and I freaked.'

Joe had listened to everything without interrupting, but now he said, 'Actually, he's not.'

Ellie frowned. 'Pardon?'

'Harold's not coming here. That's what I was coming in to tell you. Your mother phoned. She sounded a bit upset, but she usually does when she's talking to me. She was ringing to tell you that she's coming out here on her own. Harold's too busy to get away, tied up with council meetings or something.'

Ellie let out a loud huff of disbelief.

'And it's just as well he's not coming,' Joe said, clenching his fists on his knees. 'I might have felt obliged to take him outside and read him his horoscope.'

She almost smiled at this. 'I wonder if he guessed.'

'I reckon he knows I'm not his biggest fan. I haven't liked to say too much to you, but I've never taken to that guy.'

'And I should have told you about this long ago.'

Joe shrugged, then he looked at her for long thoughtful seconds before he spoke. 'It's interesting that you're not hung up about sex.'

Ellie gave him a shy smile. 'Not with you, at any rate.'

'Thank God.'

'But I think I probably have trust issues. I'm always expecting to be disappointed.'

'You've had your share of disappointments.'

'But I've reacted badly too. It probably sounds crazy, but I'm wondering if my father dying had an effect as well as Harold. I was always scared you were going to leave me.'

'And then I did leave.'

'And who could blame you?' Ellie's throat ached

as she looked away, remembering all the times she'd lashed out at Joe, blaming him unfairly, even though he couldn't possibly have been responsible for all her disappointments. She'd never really known where that unreasonable anger had sprung from. 'I guess I should have had some kind of counselling.'

'It's not too late.'

'No, but I already feel better, just having told you.'

Joe drew her in for another hug and, with her head against his shoulder, she closed her eyes, absorbing his warmth, his strength, his love.

Quietly, almost gently, he asked, 'So, while we're here, I guess I should ask if there's anything else you need to get off your chest?'

Oh.

Of course there was.

Ellie's nervousness shot to the surface again and she sat up straight, pulling away from him. She drew a deep breath. 'Actually, yes, I'm afraid there's something else quite important.' Her throat tightened and she swallowed, trying to ease her nervousness. 'There's another reason I've been tense, although I'm sure I'm going to be OK.'

Of course he looked worried, but he was trying to hide it. 'You're not sick, are you?'

'No, no. I'm fine. But—' Ellie dragged a quick steadying breath '—according to *two* home tests, I'm…I mean *we*…are…'

His face was in shadow so she couldn't see his expression, but she knew he was staring at her. Staring hard.

'You're *pregnant*?' he asked so softly it was almost a whisper, an incredulous whisper.

'I'm afraid it looks that way, if the home tests are accurate. They're a bit out of date, but the lines were very clear.'

This confession was met by a troubling silence. Ellie hugged her knees, not daring to guess what Joe might be thinking.

At last she had to ask, 'Are you OK, Joe?'

'Yeah, I'm OK, but I'm worried about you. How do *you* feel about this?'

It was a much better response than she'd feared.

'I'm getting used to it. Slowly. It was a horrible shock at first. I was so sure I was safe.'

'You had me convinced it couldn't happen.'

'I know. I'd convinced myself.' She hugged her knees more tightly still.

'How long have you known?'

'A few days. Since Monday. I hope you don't mind that I kept it to myself. I didn't want to bother you if it was a false alarm.'

Joe was staring at her again, and it was some time before he spoke. 'Wow.'

'Wow?'

'Yeah. I'm seriously impressed, Ellie.'

This was the last—the very last—reaction she'd expected.

'You've been worrying,' he said. 'I know you must have been. I know what a big deal another pregnancy is for you, and yet all week I had no idea you were worried about a thing. You've just carried on calmly, getting ready for my parents' visit as if nothing was the matter.'

'Well, I made a decision, you see. I'm going to stay calm about this pregnancy, whatever happens.'

Joe was smiling as he slipped his arm around her again. 'Good for you.'

Relieved beyond belief, Ellie leaned in and pressed a kiss to the underside of his jaw. 'I'll be upset if I lose another baby, of course I will, but you're the most important thing in my life now. You and Jacko. I've learned my lesson. I'm not going to let anything spoil what I already have.'

Reaching for Joe's hand, she pressed her lips to his knuckles. She still couldn't get enough of touching and kissing him.

'I love you, Ellie Madden,' he murmured against her hair.

'I know it's hard to believe from the way I behaved, but I've never really stopped loving you.'

'I can't believe I nearly let you go.'

'I can't believe I pushed you away.'

A hush fell over them and Ellie guessed they were both thinking how close they'd come to losing each other permanently.

'But we're going to be fine now,' Joe said.

'We are,' she agreed with absolute certainty.

'And I hope, for your sake, that this pregnancy's a breeze, Ellie, but, whatever happens, I promise I'll be there for you.'

Joe touched her cheek, turning her face to his. 'This time, and for ever, I'll be with you every step of the way.'

He sealed his promise with a kiss and it was, without doubt, their happiest, most heartfelt kiss ever.

EPILOGUE

SUNLIGHT STREAMED THROUGH stained glass windows onto massive urns of white lilies and gladioli and carnations, the legacy of a big Townsville society wedding that had been held in the church on the previous day.

This morning, after the main service, a smaller group gathered around the font. Most of the Madden family were present, including Joe's parents. One of his brothers had been required to stay back to look after the property, but the other three were present, plus their wives and a flock of Joe's nephews and nieces.

Ellie's mother, Angela, was there too, smiling and looking genuinely happy for the first time in many months.

The past year had been an extremely distressing and difficult ordeal for Angela, but her separation from Harold and their subsequent divorce were finally behind her.

Now she was already settled in Townsville in a beautifully appointed penthouse apartment with stunning views of Cleveland Bay and Magnetic Island. After the christening, all the gathered friends and family were going back there today for a celebratory barbecue lunch on the rooftop terrace.

The new apartment was in Angela's name, but the mortgage was her ex-husband's responsibility. Of course, she'd taken him to the cleaners. After suffering unbearable public humiliation when gossip about his harassment of several young women had spread like wildfire through their country town, it was the least Angela could do—especially when she'd realised, to her horror, that the accusations her daughter had made all those years ago were true.

But all that was history now and today's gathering was an extremely happy occasion. Ellie looked radiant in a rose-pink linen dress that showed off her newly slim figure. In her arms, plump baby Will slept like a dream, blissfully unaware that he was wearing a long, intricately smocked christening gown edged with handmade lace that had been worn by members of the Madden family for over a century.

Will's older brother Jacko couldn't understand why a boy had been dressed in girl's clothes, although Jacko had learned quite quickly that babies were strange creatures who slept too much and cried a lot and demanded far more than their fair share of attention.

Today, however, Jacko was also in the limelight, as he was being christened alongside baby Will. Ellie had been too busy when Jacko was a baby to think of such things as christenings. These days, however, she was taking every aspect of motherhood in her stride.

There had only been one scary incident during the early months of this pregnancy when Joe had rushed her in to the hospital in Charters Towers, but, fortunately, it had been a false alarm. After a few days, she'd been allowed home again and, after that, everything had gone smoothly.

Will was an easy baby, who liked to sleep and eat and smile. His birth had not caused any dramas. He'd arrived just before dawn on a beautiful September morning, and Joe was with Ellie for every precious, amazing moment.

And now Joe's mother held Jacko's hand as the minister stepped forward.

Joe caught Ellie's eye and they both smiled. They'd taken a very roundabout way to reach this point, but the rough and rugged journey had been worth it. They knew there'd be more bends in the road ahead, but that was OK as they'd be travelling together. Always.

* * * * *

Noelle was small, but pink and perfect, with just a smattering of hair the color of Nina's. And gazing down at her made him smile.

"You're a beauty like your mama," he told her in that same almost inaudible whisper. "But you must be tired, too, so why don't you go back to sleep for a little while?"

As if obeying, the newborn balled up her fists under her chin, closed her eyes and did just that.

Making Dallas smile all over again.

You're not mine…

*You're neither one mine…*he reminded himself.

But somehow it felt as if they were. Or at least as if they should be. And the thought of walking away from either of them was something he just couldn't find it in himself to do.

**MONTANA MAVERICKS:
RUST CREEK COWBOYS
Better saddle up.
It's going to be a bumpy ride!**

THE MAVERICK'S CHRISTMAS BABY

BY
VICTORIA PADE

MILLS & BOON

First published in Great Britain 2013
by Mills & Boon, an imprint of Harlequin (UK) Limited,
Eton House, 18-24 Paradise Road, Richmond, Surrey TW9 1SR

© Harlequin Books S.A. 2013

Special thanks and acknowledgement to Victoria Pade for her contribution to the Montana Mavericks: Rust Creek Cowboys miniseries.

ISBN: 978 0 263 90165 8

23-1213

Harlequin (UK) policy is to use papers that are natural, renewable and recyclable products and made from wood grown in sustainable forests. The logging and manufacturing processes conform to the legal environmental regulations of the country of origin.

Printed and bound in Spain
by Blackprint CPI, Barcelona

Victoria Pade is a *USA TODAY* bestselling author of numerous romance novels. She has two beautiful and talented daughters—Cori and Erin—and is a native of Colorado, where she lives and writes. A devoted chocolate lover, she's in search of the perfect chocolate-chip-cookie recipe.

For information about her latest and upcoming releases, and to find recipes for some of the decadent desserts her characters enjoy, log on to www.vikkipade.com.

Chapter One

"Oh, this is not good…" Nina Crawford said to herself as she cautiously pulled her SUV to a stop at the sign on the isolated country road outside her hometown.

Mother Nature had not been kind to Rust Creek Falls this year. First a summer flood had devastated the small Montana town, and now—still in the midst of trying to recover from that—it was being hit by a December blizzard.

The weather report had predicted only a moderate storm that would arrive later tonight. Nina ran her family's general store in town and, trusting that weather report, when an elderly, arthritic customer on an outlying farm had called in and asked that a heating pad be delivered to her, Nina hadn't hesitated to leave the store in the hands of her staff and grant that request. And even when that lonely elderly woman had offered Christmas cookies and chamomile tea, Nina still hadn't had any worries about spending an hour visiting.

But the sky had grown increasingly ominous and dark with storm clouds, and when the first few flakes began to fall much earlier than they were supposed to, Nina had left.

Only to find herself miles from home when the howling winds had whipped that snow into a blinding frenzy.

Temperatures had plummeted rapidly, and already the snow was freezing to the windows of Nina's SUV, adding to the limitations of her vision. She rolled down her window, hoping to be able to better see if another vehicle was coming from her left.

It didn't help much. Visibility was low. Very, very low.

She studied the crossroads, searching for anything that might give her an indication that another car was coming. But she didn't see any approaching headlights in the whiteout conditions, and all she could hear was the screaming wind. So, hoping the coast was clear, she rolled up her window and ventured into her right turn.

But the moment she got out onto the road she did see headlights. Coming straight for her.

Trying to avoid a collision she swerved sharply, and so did the other vehicle.

The next thing Nina knew her SUV was nose-down in a ditch and she'd fallen pregnant-belly-first into the steering wheel.

Which was when she felt the first pain.

"No, no, no, no…"

Fighting the rise of panic, she did what she could to push herself back from the steering wheel—which at that angle was no easy task.

Her due date was January 13. It was currently two

weeks before Christmas. If her baby was born now it would be a month early.

She *couldn't* deliver a month early.

She couldn't....

A pounding on her side window startled her and the fright didn't help matters.

"Are you all right?" a man's voice shouted in to her.

Her SUV hadn't hit anything so her airbag hadn't activated and the engine was still running. But dazed and scared, she didn't know if she was all right. She just couldn't think straight.

Then the door was opened from the outside. And standing there was Dallas Traub!

It wasn't exactly encouraging to see a member of the family that had been at odds with her own for generations.

"Are you all right?" he repeated.

"I don't know. I may be going into labor. I think I need help...."

"Okay, stay calm. My truck is stuck, too, on the other side of the road. But at least it isn't nearly up on end the way you are. If we can get you out of here you can lie down in my backseat."

Fear and the dull ache in her abdomen robbed Nina of the ability to argue. Traub or not, he was all there was and she was going to have to accept his aid.

"Can you turn off the engine?" he asked.

That made sense but it hadn't occurred to Nina. And, yes, she could do that, so she did, leaving the keys in the ignition.

"I'm glad to see that you can move your arms. Do you have feeling everywhere—arms, legs, hands, feet?"

"Yes."

"Did you hit your head? Do you have any neck pain?"

"No, I didn't hit my head and I don't have any neck pain. I just hit the steering wheel."

"Are you bleeding from anywhere? Did your water break?"

As odd as it seemed, not even a question that personal sounded out of place at that point.

"I don't think I'm bleeding, no. And I'm perfectly dry…."

"Good. All good," he judged. "Would it be okay if I lifted you out of there?"

"I think so…."

"Let me do all the work," he advised. Sliding one arm under her legs, the other behind her back, he gently but forcefully pulled her toward him until she found herself extracted from behind the wheel and cradled against his big, masculine chest.

"Maybe I can walk…." Nina said.

"We're not going to take any chances," he responded, wasting no time heading across the road.

The man was dressed in a heavy fleece-lined suede jacket, but Nina had to assume that he was all muscle underneath it because he carried her as if she weighed nothing. And when he reached the white truck that was nearly invisible in the snow blowing all around it, he even managed to open the rear door on the double cab.

Another cramp struck Nina as he eased her onto the backseat and her panic must have been obvious to him because he said, "It's okay. Just breathe through it. It'll pass and we'll get someone out here before you know it."

"And if my baby doesn't wait for that?" Nina nearly shouted over the wind.

"I've been in a delivery room for three of my own kids

and birthed more animals than I can count—if it comes to that, I can take care of it. We'll be fine."

It crossed her mind to call him a liar because nothing about this was at all fine. But there was actually something soothing in his composure, in his take-charge attitude, and Traub or not, Nina had to hope that he really could get her through this if need be.

Just please don't let there be the need....

"We should conserve fuel, so I'll turn on the engine long enough to get it warm in here, then we'll turn it off again," he explained, closing the rear door and getting into the front of the cab from the passenger seat to slide across and turn the key in the ignition. "But I'm going to leave my hazards flashing, to make sure anyone approaching can see us in the snow."

Warm air instantly drifted back to Nina but she was feeling more uncomfortable lying down, and she pushed herself to sit up to see if that helped.

It actually did and she explained that. "Just see if you can get someone out here to us," she instructed.

That was when he tried his cell phone and found that he had no reception.

"Try mine," Nina said, taking it out of the pocket of her wool winter coat to hand to him, fighting renewed panic.

But her phone was as useless as his was.

"Oh, God…" Nina lamented as every muscle in her body tensed.

"Another contraction?" he asked.

"No, I don't think so," she answered, so scared she wasn't sure what she was feeling beyond that.

He angled sideways in the front seat. "We're gonna be

fine. I promise," he said in a way that made her believe it and relax a little again.

Until he said, "There are pockets out here where you can get cell reception if you just hit one. I'll walk out a ways and see if maybe—"

"No! You can't leave!" Nina said in full-out panic once again. "You know the stories about farmers getting lost in storms like this just trying to find their way between their house and barn. You can't go!"

"I do know the stories," he said.

Then he slid to the passenger side again and got out of the truck.

A moment later he climbed into the backseat with her, carrying a thick coil of rope she'd heard him drag out of the truck bed. He rolled down the rear passenger window, held one end of the rope and tossed the rest of the coil through the window. Then he rolled the window up again, catching the rope in a small gap at the top of it.

"Okay..." he said then, handing her the end of the rope that he'd retained. "Hang on to this, I'll hang on to the other end and I won't go any farther than the length of it. If you need me, just yank and I'll come right back. Otherwise, I'll use it to make sure I *can* get back."

"You'll be careful?"

"I will be. And I'll leave the engine running to keep you warm in the meantime. All right?"

"I suppose," Nina agreed reluctantly, holding on to that rope with a tight fist.

Dallas Traub wrapped his hand around hers and squeezed. "Everything is going to be okay," he said confidently.

Her own hand wasn't cold, and yet his around it felt even warmer. It was also slightly rough and callused, and the size and strength of it along with those signs of hard ranch work all infused her with more of a sense of calm and a renewed belief that he could and would take care of her. Traub or not. Regardless of what happened.

Nina even managed to smile weakly. "Be careful," she said, thinking of his safety, too.

"I will."

He let go of her hand and Nina was surprised to find herself sorry to lose his touch. Which was what she was thinking when he opened the door, ducked under the rope and got out, leaving her alone. And sorry to lose his company, too. His comforting presence.

The touch, the company, the presence of a Traub.

She closed her eyes and breathed deeply again, willing herself to settle down for the sake of her baby, willing her baby to rest, to stay put, not to be born today....

Then another cramp struck.

"Please, no, not yet," she begged her unborn child and the fates, as if that could stop things if she really was going into labor.

How long had Dallas Traub been gone? It seemed like forever and Nina looked across the front seat through the windshield, hoping to spot him. But all she could see was snow.

She caught sight of herself in the rearview mirror then and realized that the stocking cap she had on was askew. For some odd reason she regretted that Dallas had seen her looking so disheveled, so she straightened the cap. She also gave in to the urge to fluff her hair a bit where the long brown locks cascaded from beneath the cap past her shoulders.

Her ordinarily pink cheeks were quite pale and she reached up and pinched them to add some color. Her mascara had survived the accident and all that followed it without smudging beneath her very dark brown eyes, but unfortunately her thin, straight nose had a bit of a shine that she didn't like to see.

She tried to blot that with the back of her hand, regretting that she'd left her purse in her SUV with her compact in it. And with her lip gloss in it, too.

Not that, in the midst of possible peril, she was actually thinking about putting on lipstick to accentuate lips she sometimes thought were not full enough. She merely wanted to moisten those lips to keep them from chapping, she told herself. Certainly it wasn't that she cared at all what she looked like at that moment. Especially to a Traub. When she'd just had a car accident. When she could potentially be going into labor.

But, oh, she wished this particular Traub would come back....

She considered yanking on the rope just to get him to, but she didn't let herself. They needed help and if there was any chance that he might find cell reception she couldn't cut that short.

But soon, come back soon....

Then, as if in answer to her silent plea, the rear passenger door opened and there he was.

She also didn't understand why the way he looked registered in that instant, but she was struck by how tall and capable-looking he was. She guessed him to be about six foot three inches of broad-shouldered, Western masculinity.

But it wasn't merely his size that impressed her. He was remarkably handsome—something else that she'd never noticed in all the times they must have crossed paths around Rust Creek Falls.

Nina knew all the Traubs in general, but she'd never really noted much about them in any kind of detail. Now it struck her that Dallas really did have rugged good looks with a squarish forehead, a nose that was a bit hooked, but in a dashing sort of way, lips that were full and almost lush, and striking blue eyes that had enough of a hint of gray to add more depth than she'd ever have attributed to a Traub.

"Did you get a call out?" she asked as he extracted the end of the rope through the window, tossed the recoiled mass into the truck bed again and then climbed into the backseat with her, closing the door and the window after himself.

"No," he said. "We're really in a dead zone out here. But don't worry about it. Somebody will come looking for us. My folks are stuck at home with my three boys— believe me, before too long they'll start to wonder where I am." Then he switched gears and asked, "How are you doing?"

"I'm okay...." Nina answered uncertainly.

"Any more pains?"

"One," she admitted.

"And how about heat? Think we can turn it off for a little while?"

"Sure. If you're warm enough."

He stood to lean over the front seat to reach the key, and Nina found herself sneaking a glance at him from that angle.

He was wearing jeans that hugged an impressive derriere and thick thighs, and she knew she had no business taking note of any of that.

Then the engine went off and he sat back down, turning toward her and perching on the very edge of the seat so he could pull down the rear cushion as he said, "There should be a blanket in here…"

He produced a heavy plaid blanket from the compartment hidden behind the seat.

"You're probably not going to like this, but we'll both stay warmer if we share the blanket and some body heat," he said then.

"It's okay," Nina agreed, knowing he was right.

And not totally hating the idea of having him close beside her or of sharing the blanket with him. But she didn't analyze that.

Opening the heavy emergency blanket, he set it over Nina and reached across her to tuck it in on her other side.

Then he sat near enough to share the warmth he exuded and laid it across himself, too.

"You're sure you feel better sitting up?" he asked.

"I am."

"If something changes and you need to lie down just let me know…."

"I will," Nina said.

She did slump a little more into the blanket, though. And somehow that brought her a bit closer to him, too. But he didn't seem to mind that she was slightly tucked to his side and it seemed as though it might be insulting if she moved away again, so she pretended that she didn't notice.

"So…" he said when she was settled, turning his head toward her and looking down at her. "You're *Nina* Crawford, right? You run the General Store in town?"

Apparently Dallas Traub wasn't any clearer about the details of his Crawford rivals than Nina was about the Traubs. And since they'd never had any one-on-one, face-to-face contact before this, Nina was even surprised that he knew her name.

"I'm Nina, right. And yes, I run the store." The store that the Traubs rarely frequented, making it well-known that they chose to do their shopping in nearby Kalispell rather than give business to the Crawfords.

"I'm Dallas—in case you didn't know…."

"You live on your family's ranch—the Triple T, right?"

"I do work on the ranch, but I have my own house on the property. I'm divorced, and with three boys—Ryder, who's ten, Jake, eight, and Robbie, who just turned six a couple of weeks ago."

"And you have custody of them?" Nina asked, recalling that no one was too sure what had happened to his marriage, but that it had ended about this time last year. Gossip had been rampant and she remembered thinking that, since he was a Traub, his wife had probably just wised up. Nina hadn't found it so easy to understand why his ex-wife had left her kids behind, though.

Now, appreciating the way Dallas had been caring for her, appreciating the effort he was putting into distracting her by making conversation, how just plain kind and friendly he was being toward her, she had less understanding of his wife's leaving him, too.

"Yep, it's all me, all the time…" he said somewhat forlornly and without any of the confidence he'd shown in every other way since he'd opened her car door. "Not that my family isn't good about helping out—they are. But still—"

"You're the Number One in Charge. Of *three* kids."

"And there's nothing easy about being a single parent," he said, clearly feeling the weight of it. His gaze went for a split second in the direction of her middle. "I guess

I don't know many specifics about the Crawfords," he said then. "I probably know the most about your brother Nate now, just from the election for mayor—"

"Since he was running against your brother Collin and lost," Nina pointed out.

"But I don't think I knew you were married or pregnant…."

"Pregnant, not married. Never have been."

"But you were with someone weren't you? Leo Steadler? He did some work for us a couple of years back and—"

"I was with Leo for four years." Four years that had led only to disappointment.

"But he left town, didn't he?"

Nina could hear the confusion and suspicions that were mounting. "He did."

"Rather than stepping up?"

There was outrage in that that made Nina smile. "The baby isn't Leo's."

"Oh."

She smiled again, having a pretty good idea what he was filling in the blanks with. The same things her own family had assumed—first that the baby was Leo's, then that she'd had some kind of rebound fling that had resulted in an unwanted pregnancy.

But they were all wrong. And since she wasn't ashamed of the choice she'd made and had been perfectly honest with everyone else, she decided to be perfectly honest now, even with Dallas Traub.

"After four wasted years with Leo, when it ended I decided I wasn't going to wait for another man to come along." And make more empty promises of *someday*.

"There was no telling how long it might take to meet someone—"

"If ever," he muttered as if he held absolutely no optimism when it came to finding a soul mate.

"And then what?" Nina went on. "What if I used up another year or two or three or *four* and found myself right where I was after Leo? I'd just be older and I still wouldn't have the baby I've always wanted. The family. And sometimes you just have to go after what you want, regardless of what anyone else thinks. So I took some time off, went to a sperm bank in Denver without telling my family—"

"You just did that on your own?"

"I did," Nina said with all the conviction she'd felt then still in her voice. "I didn't see the point in sitting through people trying to talk me out of it, so I just did it. And, voilà! The magic of modern medicine—I'm having the baby I want, on my own."

Looking up at him, Nina watched him nod slowly, ruminatively, his well-shaped eyebrows arching over those gray-tinged blue eyes. "Wow," he said, as if he didn't quite know what to make of her. "My family is very big on marriage and would freak out over something like that. How did yours take it?"

"They freaked out," Nina confirmed. "But when the dust settled…" She shrugged. "I've always been my own person and strong-willed and…well, hard to stop once I put my mind to something. My family has just sort of gotten used to that. And a baby? That's a good thing. So after the initial shock, they got on board."

"I'd say *that* was a good thing, otherwise having a baby on your own might be kind of an overwhelming proposition."

"But I just didn't want to wait anymore."

"You seem kind of young for the clock to be ticking loud enough to go that route."

"That was something my family said. I'm twenty-five, so sure, my age isn't an issue. Except that I've always wanted to have kids fairly young, in my twenties. I don't know how old you are, but if you have a ten-year-old, that's probably about when you got started, isn't it?"

"I'm thirty-four, so yeah. Ryder was born when I was twenty-four."

"And that means that you have the chance to be around to see your kids at forty, at fifty or sixty. To know your grandchildren and maybe even your great-grandchildren. That's how I want it, too. Family is the most important thing to me. As far as I'm concerned, that's what life is about."

"But isn't it about doing all that with a partner?" he asked, still sounding baffled.

"Ideally. But look at you—there are no guarantees that even if you start out with a partner you'll end up with one."

"Yeah…" he conceded a bit dourly. "It's just…single-parenthood is a tough road. I'm never sure whether or not I might be dropping the ball in some way. Especially lately…"

Nina was curious about that, but out of the blue a pain more severe than any she'd felt yet hit her, pulling her away from the back of the seat.

Dallas sat up just as quickly, angled toward her and put an arm around her from behind.

"It's okay," he said in that deep masculine voice that she was finding tremendously soothing. "Just ride it out. Don't fight it. Breathe…"

She tried to do all of that, but this pain was sharp. She closed her eyes against it and the renewed fear that came with it.

"It's okay," he repeated. "It'll all be okay."

Then she felt him press his lips to her temple in a sweet, tender, bolstering kiss that she knew had to have been a purely involuntary reaction of his own when he didn't know what else to say to her.

The pain disappeared as fast as it had come on, and Nina wilted.

The fact that she wilted against Dallas Traub was also not something she thought about before it just seemed to happen.

But he held her as if it were something he'd done a million times before, and it seemed perfectly natural for her head to rest against his chest.

"There was a long time between pains," Nina said when she was able. "I thought they'd stopped."

"It's good that they aren't coming with any kind of regularity. Real labor is like clockwork. Maybe these are just muscle spasms."

The baby had been moving and kicking normally as they were talking so it didn't seem as if it was in distress, but still, there was nothing heartening about the situation.

"But you know," Dallas said in a lighter vein. "If I end up delivering this guy you'll have to name him after me—Dallas Traub Crawford."

That did make Nina laugh. "Both of our families would freak out over *that*," she said. "And I haven't let them tell me if the baby is a boy or a girl—I want to be surprised."

"The name still works even if it's a girl."

"Dallas Crawford." Nina tried it on for size and then

laughed again. "Let's see…first I had to convince everyone that Leo isn't the father, that I actually had artificial insemination. Then we'll throw you into the mix? I can just imagine the rumors."

"Rust Creek'd be talking about it for years."

"And both of our families would probably stop speaking to us for consorting with the enemy."

"Seems possible," Dallas agreed with a laugh of his own.

Headlights suddenly appeared through the snow, coming from the direction of town, and within moments a vehicle pulled up beside them.

"What did I tell you? Help has arrived," Dallas said.

Nina sat up and away from him, regretting the loss of his arm around her when he let go of her and turned to open the door.

Gage Christensen, the local sheriff, was standing just outside.

"You out here joyriding?" Dallas joked, but Nina heard the relief in his tone.

"When the storm hit your mother called the farm where you were delivering hay to find out if you'd left there. They said you had, and since you hadn't gotten home, she called me."

Dallas glanced over his shoulder at Nina. "What did I tell you? The thought of being stuck for too long with my three boys got the troops sent out to find me in a hurry."

Then, back to Gage Christensen, he said. "I have Nina Crawford in here and I think she needs to get to the hospital in Kalispell—the sooner the better…."

So he was clearly more worried about her condition than he'd originally let on.

"Looks to me like I can pull around behind you and

push you forward enough to get you going. Then I'll do the hospital run," Gage Christensen said.

"Why don't you get me out of this ditch and just follow us? It's probably not a great idea to move Nina but I'd like to know we have some backup. And maybe after the storm someone can come out here and get her SUV."

Nina was surprised that Dallas hadn't jumped at the opportunity to be off the hook. But she appreciated that he hadn't, that he still seemed concerned for her.

"Let's see what we can do," the sheriff said, returning to his own vehicle.

Turning back to Nina, Dallas grasped her upper arm in one of those big hands and squeezed. "Just relax, we'll be on the way before you know it," he said, once more sounding confident.

Nina nodded, relieved that they were going to get out of there.

Then Dallas left, closed the rear door, and came in from the passenger side of the front seat to slide across and restart the engine, turning on the heat again.

It wasn't long before there was a slight bump to the rear of Dallas's truck. Then there was the sound of spinning tires and the feel of the truck inching forward until Dallas's wheels caught enough traction to move onto the road.

"Now we're cooking," he said victoriously.

"My purse—I should have my insurance card," Nina said as it became clear that they actually were going to be able to travel.

"I'll get it," he said, coming to a slow stop, then rushing out of the truck's cab into the storm again to return with her oversize hobo bag and her keys.

"Thank you," she said when he handed everything to

her over the front seat. Then, a bit emotionally, she added, "Thank you for everything today...."

"Let's just get you to the hospital," he said, putting the truck into gear and setting off cautiously into the still-blinding blizzard.

Watching the back of his head as he drove, Nina couldn't help marveling at the fact that she was continuing to be looked after by none other than Dallas Traub.

Personable, kind, caring, strong, reassuring and more handsome than she'd ever realized before, he couldn't know how glad she was that he hadn't merely handed her off to the sheriff.

And in that moment she couldn't help wondering why it was that she was supposed to hate him.

Chapter Two

"Is anyone here for Nina Crawford?"

Dallas got to his feet the moment he heard that. He was in the waiting area for the emergency room of the hospital in Kalispell, where he'd been since arriving with Nina and having her whisked away.

"I'm Dr. Axel," the woman introduced herself.

Dallas wasn't sure whether or not to admit he wasn't family but before he could say anything the woman continued.

"Nina and the baby are doing fine. The pains she was having were the result of hitting the steering wheel, not labor. There's no indication that she's about to deliver. We've done an ultrasound and the baby looks good, plus Nina is hooked up to a fetal monitor and there are no signs of any kind of distress."

"Great!" Dallas said, relief ringing clear.

"As I'm sure you know," the doctor went on, "Nina is at thirty-five weeks so birth at this stage—while inadvisable—would still likely not pose unusual problems for mom or baby should something change suddenly. But with the storm and the difficulties on the roads, getting her back here in a hurry might pose a problem and I'd rather err on the side of safety. So we're keeping her overnight. That way we can continue to monitor things and watch them both, just in case."

"Sure."

"She's being taken to a room now—if you check with one of the people at the desk they'll be able to tell you the number."

Dallas thanked the doctor, then he went to the reception desk, gave Nina's name and learned what room she'd been taken to.

It was only after he had that information that he wondered if he *should* stay.

After all, he *wasn't* family.

But while Gage Christensen had promised to notify the Crawfords of the accident and tell them Nina's whereabouts, none of them had arrived yet. Despite the fact that the blizzard had stopped and only a light snow was falling, the roads still weren't great, so there was no surprise there. And Dallas didn't like the thought of Nina being alone, even if everything was okay.

So he opted to stay. Just the way he'd opted to stay after getting Nina here, despite the sheriff pointing out that he'd done enough, that there was nothing more he could do now that she was in the hands of the professionals, and that he might as well go home to his own family.

His family—his boys—were being well taken care of by his parents, all of whom he'd talked to while he was in the waiting room. Everything was going on as usual. But for now, without him, Nina had no one.

And he just couldn't bring himself to leave her.

So he went to the elevator, got in and hit the button for her floor.

The maternity floor.

He knew it well. He'd been there for the birth of each of his three sons. With Laurel...

That memory wrenched his gut. The way countless other memories had during the past year.

The past year of hell...

It just wasn't easy.

Not waking up to find his wife had left him.

Not raising three kids on his own.

Not dealing with his own anger and grief and sometimes rage and despair.

Not dealing with his sons' emotions, which were sometimes right on the surface and other times came out so subtly he missed them until it was too late.

Not going on, living in the same town where they'd both grown up, being where almost everything in their life had happened, revisiting places like this hospital, where events had come about that were apparently not as meaningful to his ex-wife as they were to him....

Yeah, *hell* pretty much described it. And he was just trying to work his way through the emotional muck, in much the same way that Rust Creek Falls was still working its way through the muck left from the flood.

But he had confidence that Rust Creek Falls would get through its reconstruction and come out on the other end. He still wasn't altogether sure about himself. Or about Ryder or Jake or Robbie.

When the elevator arrived on the maternity floor, he

found Nina's room without a problem and breathed a sigh of relief. It was a private room on a different corridor than where new mothers were located.

If he'd had to walk into one of the same rooms Laurel had been in with any of the boys he didn't know if he could have done it. He could only push himself so far, even though he was doing his damnedest to get out of this hell he'd been in since Laurel had left.

Just pretend you're okay even if you aren't—that was what he'd decided he had to do. And maybe if he pretended he wasn't buried under the blues, he'd finally start to actually see daylight again.

But one way or another, he'd already made an early New Year's resolution—he was determined to spare his family and friends any more of what he'd been wallowing in for the past twelve months. No more telling everyone to beware of love, to avoid relationships. No more being the naysayer as he watched people couple up. He'd at least keep his mouth shut.

The door from the corridor was open and the curtain around the bed was only partially drawn so he could see that Nina was asleep, and he reconsidered staying once again. After the day they'd had she was probably exhausted and she could well sleep until her family got there, or even until morning.

But he really, really didn't want to go yet. Just in case.

So he went silently to the visitor's chair and sat down, settling in to study Nina rather than thinking more about the other times he'd been on the maternity floor or about the misery of this past year.

Nina Crawford...

Jeez, she was beautiful.

Her long, shiny hair was the color of chestnuts and it fanned out like silk on the pillow.

Her skin was pure porcelain.

Her nose was perfect, thin and sleek, and just slightly pointed at the end.

Her mouth was petal-pink, her lips just lush enough to make a man want to kiss them.

Her face was finely boned with a chin that was well-defined, cheekbones that were high and sculpted, and a brow that was straight and not too high, not too narrow.

And even though her eyes were closed and her long, thick lashes dusted her cheeks, he had a vivid recollection of just how big and brown they were—doelike and sparkling, they were the dark, rich color of coffee.

Yep, beautiful. Exquisitely, delicately beautiful.

Without the doctor telling him, he would have never guessed that she was as far along as she was. By now, with all three of the boys, Laurel had not looked the way Nina did. Not that he hadn't thought Laurel was beautiful, because he had.

He was a man of nature, and he'd genuinely thought the entire process had that feel to it—natural and as beautiful as a sunrise evolving out of the dark of night.

But the more weight his ex-wife had gained, the more unhappy she'd become. Even more unhappy than she'd been during the rest of the marriage she'd never really been happy in….

Laurel was the last thing he wanted to think about, though, so he sealed off the memory and focused on Nina, who honestly did make true the adage about pregnant women glowing.

Or maybe that was just the way she looked all the time….

Since he'd never noticed her before, he couldn't actually be the judge.

Although sitting there now, studying her, he wondered *why* he'd never noticed her before. How could anyone who looked the way she did have gone *un*noticed?

She was only twenty-five—that was probably a factor because she was too young for him to have paid attention to. Plus he'd been so involved with his marriage—first in the early throes of love, and then trying to save it—that he hadn't really paid attention to any other females. And even as an adult, Nina's being a Crawford just automatically clumped her together with the rest of her family, who had all been cast under the shadow of contempt. Put it all together and he supposed that he'd just been blind to her.

But he wasn't blind to her anymore.

At that moment he was sorry he wasn't sitting as close to her as he'd been in the backseat of his truck. With the blanket over the two of them. With his arm around her—the way it had been when he'd put it there without even thinking about it.

The same way he'd kissed her without even thinking about it....

A Crawford. He'd kissed a Crawford.

A pregnant Crawford.

This had been a very strange day....

But still, thinking about it, here he was wishing he was back there. Stuck in a blizzard. At risk of having to deliver that baby.

Because it had somehow been nice there like that. With her.

It had been the best time he'd had in a very, very long while....

Okay, maybe he'd lost it. The best time he'd had in a long time, and it had been in that situation, with a Crawford?

That was crazy.

And yet, true…

Because she was something, this Nina Crawford.

Even under the worst circumstances, out there stuck in the snow, there had still been something positive and affirming about her. Strong. He'd known she was worried and scared, and even in the face of that she hadn't bemoaned anything, she'd held her head high about making the choice she'd made to have that baby on her own, and she was just…

Something.

Something a whole lot better than he'd been for the past year since his divorce.

Something a whole lot better than the cranky naysayer he sometimes felt as though he'd turned into.

She was a positive force. He was a negative one.

Figured. The Crawfords and the Traubs—oil and water. That was how they'd always been. How they always would be. Except that he and Nina hadn't been oil and water today.

Not that that meant anything. Or mattered.

Even if she wasn't a Crawford, he thought, she was still only twenty-five and pregnant, while he was thirty-four and had three kids. Nothing about any of that put them on the same page. And people who weren't on the same page couldn't—or at least shouldn't—come together. He'd learned that the hard way with Laurel.

Not that what had gone on today was anything like he and Nina Crawford *coming together,* he told himself when his own thoughts alarmed him a little.

He just felt responsible for her for the moment. Because he was the other party involved in the near-collision that had put her in the hospital.

There wasn't any more to it than that.

If he could just stop recalling every minute of being alone with her in his backseat.

"*Dallas Traub?* What are you doing here?"

Now *that* was a Crawford that Dallas recognized.

"Nate," Dallas answered in a whisper, glancing up to find Nina's brother Nathan Crawford in the doorway with their parents—Todd and Laura, who had also been front and center through the recent mayoral election in support of their son—who had lost the race to Dallas's brother, Collin.

Dallas stood instantly to face them. "Didn't Gage tell you what happened?" he whispered, both in response and as a signal to keep voices low.

"He said Nina went off the road and had to be brought here. He didn't say anything about you," the matriarch of the Crawford family whispered back harshly, obviously having taken the cue.

But the attempt to keep things quiet was already too late because from the bed Nina said, "Stop. Dallas isn't to blame. It was all my fault. I couldn't see him coming until it was too late and I'd pulled out in front of him. We both swerved to keep from crashing."

"Still bad enough. What are you doing here now?" Todd Crawford demanded.

"Daddy, Dallas has been great!" Nina informed her father. "He took care of me until the sheriff got there and even then he didn't let Gage move me, and he had Gage follow us to make sure we got here all right. And here he is, even now!"

Dr. Axel joined the group then and Nina seemed to seize the sudden presence of the obstetrician as help in mediating, because she said, "Hi, Dr. Axel. Could you maybe take my family out in the hallway and let them know what's going on with the baby?"

The doctor did as requested, herding the other Crawfords from the room.

"Thought I needed to be rescued, did you?" Dallas said with a laugh, moving to stand directly at the foot of the bed.

"Three against one—bad odds," she answered, sounding groggy and worn-out.

"I didn't want to leave you by yourself," Dallas explained his continuing presence.

"That was thoughtful." She gestured in the direction her family had gone. "I'm sorry that was your reward for being so nice."

"No big deal," he assured her, finding that what *was* feeling like a big deal to him was the idea that he was going to have to leave her now....

"Everything with you and the baby is fine, you know that, right?" he said then.

"I do. I'm giving you credit for that."

"Nah. I didn't do anything."

"You did—"

"I'm just glad you and the baby are okay."

"And that you didn't have to deliver it," Nina said with a smile that let him know she was teasing him.

"That, too," he agreed, laughing in return and basking in the warmth of that smile that he liked more than seemed possible.

"Is it still snowing?" she asked then.

"It is, but the wind stopped so it isn't as bad out there."

"You should get home, then. To your boys."

Dallas nodded. He did need to get home. He just couldn't figure out why he was so reluctant to leave Nina. Nina *Crawford,* he reminded himself, as if that would help. "I suppose your family can take over from here."

"They will. And everything is okay anyway, so there isn't really anything to take over. I'll lie in this bed and get waited on tonight, then go home tomorrow."

Again Dallas nodded, lingering. "I'm sorry for all of this. That it happened," he said, although that wasn't strictly the case. He *was* sorry for what had happened. Just not for the time he'd had with her *after* it had happened.

"I'm sorry, too," Nina said. "I'm sure you had better plans today than to end up stuck on the side of a road in a blizzard thinking you might have to turn your backseat into a delivery room, and then sitting at this hospital for the past four hours."

"Believe it or not, I've had worse days," he declared with a laugh.

The reappearance of her family and the doctor at the door made it clear that he had to go whether he liked it or not. "Anyway, since you're in good hands, I'll head for home."

"Thank you," Nina said in a tone that had some intimacy to it.

"Anytime," he answered with humor.

"Be careful going back."

"I will be," he promised.

And that was that.

But for another moment Dallas stayed there, still finding it oddly difficult to leave. To walk out and put this day behind him. To sever the connection that somehow seemed to have formed between them through the adversity they'd shared. To return to the way things had been before—to barely being aware that Nina Crawford existed.

He had to go, though. What else was he going to do? Especially when her family and doctor all came to stand around her bed, the Crawfords' scorn for him thick in the air as they pretended he was invisible.

He stole one last glance at Nina, whose big brown eyes met his, who gave him a smile that spoke of the connection they'd made, if only for a little while today. Then he raised a palm to her in a goodbye wave and finally did manage to leave.

Wishing—for no reason he understood—that a lot of things might be different.

And realizing only as he got back on the elevator to go down to the lobby that for just a little while with her he hadn't felt so bad....

By Friday, Nina was home in her small apartment above the General Store and feeling good again. Better than ever, in fact. But she was still following doctor's orders not to return to work until Saturday.

Her mother had been hovering. Laura Crawford had even spent Thursday night with Nina. But over lunch Friday afternoon, when Laura was still there and giving no indication of leaving, Nina had convinced her that everything was back to normal, and that Laura should go home.

Once she had and Nina was alone, her thoughts turned to Dallas Traub.

Since Wednesday's near-collision she'd been finding

it nearly impossible *not* to think about him and had used the presence of family to distract herself. But, finally left to her own devices, she couldn't seem to think about anything but the swaggeringly sexy, blue-eyed Traub with the great head of hair who had taken such kind and tender care of her.

She wanted to thank him again for everything he'd done on Wednesday.

That was all there was to her constant thoughts of him, she told herself. And it was reasonable to want to express her gratitude.

After all, not only had he put aside whatever petty differences their families had, but he'd gone out of his way for her at every juncture.

Until her family had arrived and been rude to him.

And even then he'd been calm and courteous. He'd absorbed their scorn and contempt with aplomb and without dishing out any of his own before he'd gone on his way.

She owed him more than gratitude, she decided.

But thanking him again was a start, in order to let him know just how much she appreciated everything.

And if she also felt the need to hear his voice again and make some kind—*any* kind—of contact with him?

Maybe it was an odd phenomenon where a person developed a sense of kinship with their rescuer.

That seemed possible.

It seemed more possible than any kind of alternative. Like wanting contact with him because she was attracted to him....

How crazy would that *be?* she asked herself.

Attracted to someone when she was eight months pregnant?

Attracted to a Traub?

Completely crazy, that's how crazy it would be.

And even more crazy still when she factored in his age. *That* was the frosting on the cake.

Dallas was nine years older than she was, so even if she wasn't pregnant, and even if he wasn't a Traub, his age alone was enough for her to steer completely clear of him.

Leo had been ten years older than she was, and Nina had had enough of the disadvantages that came with a relationship with a wide gap in ages. Enough of accommodating and adapting and making all the adjustments because that age seemed to bring with it the privilege of some kind of seniority.

And Leo hadn't had kids.

Dallas Traub did. *Three* of them.

Kids only increased the need for any woman who got involved with him to be accommodating.

Involved?

She didn't know why Dallas Traub and involvement had even come in the same thought. Of course she wasn't and would never get *involved* with him!

She just wanted to talk to him, for crying out loud. And then maybe find a way to show her appreciation. Like with a fruit basket or something.

To reiterate her thanks. To apologize for the way her family had treated him.

It was all just the right thing, given what he'd done for her. Nothing more to it. Dallas had done her a huge kindness and service, and she owed him her gratitude.

And, hey, maybe if the two of them could treat each other courteously it could be the beginning of some kind of bridge between the two families, so that her child and his sons might not have to hate each other for no reason anyone could actually explain.

That was probably a stretch. The bad blood between the Traubs and the Crawfords had been going on for generations, and the mere act of reiterating her thanks to him wasn't likely to cure that.

But still, she felt compelled to make the phone call.

It required a few other calls to friends to get Dallas's cell phone number, but she finally did. When she dialed it he answered right away.

The sound of that deep, deep voice filled her with something she couldn't explain. Something warm and satisfying.

But she ignored the response and said, "Dallas? This is Nina Crawford."

He laughed. "You're the only Nina I know. Hi!" he added, sounding happy to hear from her. Which was somewhat of a relief because it *had* crossed her mind that, now that they weren't in dire straits, things between them might return to the normal state of affairs. At least, normal for *their* families.

"I've been thinking and thinking about you—how are you?" he asked immediately and in a tone that held only friendliness.

"I'm really good," she said. "I got home yesterday and can't work until tomorrow. But I feel fine and I would be downstairs doing everything I usually do right now if not for doctor's orders."

"Downstairs? In your store?"

"That's where I work," she answered with a laugh.

"I'm there now."

He was just downstairs?

Knowing he was that nearby sent a sense of elation through her. Strange as it seemed…

"I live in the apartment above the store," she informed him. "Want to come and see for yourself that—thanks to you—I'm faring very well?"

Nina had no idea where that had come from. It was nothing but impulse.

But Dallas didn't hesitate before he said, "I'd like that! How do I get there?"

"Go to the back of the store. There's a staircase behind Women's Sleepwear and Intimates—"

"The boys will love that," he said facetiously. Then he added, "Oh, I didn't think about that. My boys are with me. Maybe we shouldn't come up—"

"I'm kid-friendly," she assured. Then she laughed again. "I'd better be."

"You're sure you don't mind? And that you're well enough?"

"I'm sure. Come on up."

That was all the convincing it took for him to say eagerly, "Be right there."

Hanging up, Nina knew that it was absurd to be as excited as she was by the fact that she was about to get to see Dallas again right now.

But that's the way it was.

She was excited enough to make a quick detour to the nearest mirror to make sure her hair didn't need brushing and to hurriedly apply a little mascara and blush.

She was wearing jeans and a red turtleneck sweater that was long enough and just loose enough to accommodate her not-too-large belly. And while she was shoeless, her socks were red-and-green argyle for the holiday so she stayed in her stocking feet to open the door.

Dallas was there when she did, his fisted hand ready to knock.

"Whoa," he said, stopping short so she didn't get the knock in the face.

Nina couldn't help grinning at that first glimpse of him. Tall, broad-shouldered, wearing boots, jeans and that same suede coat over a plaid flannel shirt with the collar button open to expose a white T-shirt underneath it.

Rugged, masculine, rock-solid and drop-dead gorgeous—so her mind hadn't built him up to be more than he actually was, she thought. She'd been wondering if that might be the case.

"Come in! Take off your coats," she invited, stepping aside.

Dallas crossed the threshold, trailed by three boys of varying heights, all of them younger versions of him, with the same blue eyes hazed with gray, the same heads of thick brown hair, the same bone structure.

"This is Ryder." He began the introductions with a hand on the head of the tallest as they all removed their coats. "And Jake." Clearly the middle child. "And Robbie—"

"I just got to be six and I go to kinnergarten," Robbie announced.

"Then I'll bet your teacher is Willa Christensen," Nina said.

"No. It's my aunt Willa but in school I need to call her Mrs. Traub. Like me, Robbie Traub. But she's not my mom, she's my aunt since she married my Uncle Collin."

"Ah, that's right. I guess I sort of forgot that Willa married your brother," Nina said to Dallas.

"Lookit all this Christmas stuff! Lookit that tree!"

Robbie said then, wasting no time moving into Nina's apartment to survey her many Christmas decorations.

"It is pretty festive in here," Dallas agreed.

"I love Christmas," Nina said before focusing on the other two boys, who were staying near to their father. "So Robbie is six. You're eight, Jake? And Ryder, you're ten, right?"

"Yeah," Jake confirmed while Ryder said nothing at all.

"Well, come on in. You can have a look around, too, if you want. There's a dish of candy canes and taffy—if it's all right with your dad you can help yourselves. And how would you all like some hot chocolate and Christmas cookies?"

"I would!" Robbie answered first.

"Me, too," Jake seconded.

Ryder merely shrugged his concession just before Dallas said, "What do you say?"

"I would, please," Robbie amended.

"Me, too, *please*." Jake added some attitude while a simple "Please" was muttered by Ryder as the older boys joined the younger in looking around and ultimately being drawn to the train that circled the tree skirt.

"Does this work?" Jake asked.

"It does. The switch is on the side of the station house," Nina answered, closing the door behind them all.

"Watch what you're doing," Dallas warned his sons.

"It's okay," Nina told him. "They can't hurt anything. Like I said, kid-friendly."

She led the way into the kitchen portion of the big open room that included a fair-sized kitchen and dining area separated from the large living room by an island counter.

"This is a nice place. I didn't even know it was up here," Dallas said as Nina set about heating milk and adding cocoa and broken chocolate bars.

"It's where the first Crawfords in Rust Creek Falls lived when they started the store. A lot of us have taken advantage of it over the years. You can't beat the commute to work," she joked.

"You'll bring your baby home here?"

"I will. There are two bedrooms—the nursery is almost ready, I just have a few finishing touches to put on it. And living up here after the baby is born—even before I've actually gone back to work—will let me still oversee some things. Then when I *can* get back to business as usual, I'll have a nanny or a sitter here with the baby, but I'll be able to carry a baby monitor with me to listen in and I'll also be able to come up as many times a day as I want or need to."

"Handy," he agreed.

"I think it will be."

"And is this still going to be a house of sugar when you have your own kid?" he asked as she set iced cookies out on a plate and then brought the pan of hot chocolate from the stove.

He was teasing her again and it struck her that there was already some familiarity in it. Familiarity she liked...

"It's Christmas," she defended. "And the middle of the afternoon—I'm sure they had lunch and dinner is far enough away that this won't spoil their appetites."

"And they'll be so wired they won't have to ride home in the truck, they'll be able to run behind it," he joked before advising, "Give them all half cups of hot chocolate."

"Killjoy," Nina accused playfully. And slightly flirtatiously, though she didn't know where that had come from....

"Oh, so you've heard about how glum I've been the past year," he joked back, smiling that crooked smile that lifted one side of his agile-looking mouth higher than the other.

His eyes were intent on her, and the humor allowed them to share a moment that told Nina she wasn't alone in whatever it was she'd been feeling about him as her rescuer. That, regardless of the old feud between their families, things between the two of them were different now even if they were no longer in dire straits.

It pleased her. A lot.

Dallas took two mugs of hot chocolate in each of his big, capable hands, leaving Nina to carry the fifth and the plate of cookies into the living room. They set everything on her oval oak coffee table and the boys gathered around it, sitting on the floor while Nina and Dallas sat on her overstuffed black-and-gray buffalo-checked sofa.

After the boys tasted their hot chocolate and each took a cookie, Robbie looked to his father and said, "When are we gonna put up our tree?"

"You don't have a tree yet?" Nina asked, surprised.

"Dad's been too busy," Jake answered, disappointment and complaint ringing in his tone as the three boys carried their cookies and hot chocolate with them and went back to playing with the train.

"Busy and not much in the mood," Dallas confessed, quietly enough for the boys not to be able to hear.

"Scrooge," she teased him the same way.

"I'm not usually," he admitted, his voice still low and echoing with sorrow. "But this year...I don't know. It's felt all year like this family has been left sort of in shreds and I'm not quite sure how to sew it back together again. Or if I'm even up to it."

"Kids need their holidays kept, no matter what," Nina insisted.

But she couldn't be too hard on him, considering that this was the anniversary of the end of his marriage and it couldn't be an easy time for him.

So rather than criticizing any more, she decided to fall back on the reason she'd contacted him in the first place.

"I called because I wanted to thank you again for helping me on Wednesday," she said, setting her own cup of hot chocolate on the coffee table and breaking off a section of a bell-shaped cookie. "I also wanted to apologize for the way my family treated you at the hospital."

"I'm sure they were worried and upset about you and the baby—"

Robbie overheard that and perked up to look at them over his shoulder. "You're gonna have a baby? I thought you just liked beer."

Confused, Nina looked from the youngest Traub to Dallas and found Dallas grimacing. "We met an old friend of mine earlier today. He was a lot heavier than the last time I saw him and I razzed him about his beer belly."

"Ah…" Nina said.

"But you," Dallas went on in a hurry, obviously doing damage control. "It doesn't seem like you've gained an ounce anywhere but baby—you really look…well, beautiful…"

It sounded as if he genuinely meant that—not like the gratuitous things that often came with people talking about her pregnancy. And that, too, pleased Nina. And when their eyes met once again, when she really could see that he didn't find anything about her condition off-putting at all, and when Nina had the feeling that there was suddenly no one else in the world but the two of them, it made her all warm inside.

But there were other people in the world, in the room, in fact. His kids.

And just then Ryder said, "I need to get to Tyler's."

Dallas seemed to draw up short, as if he, too, had been lost in that moment between them and was jolted out of it by his eldest son's reminder.

"His friend Tyler is having a sleepover," Dallas explained. "And I still need to pick up a few things downstairs—our houses and the main barns were spared by the flood but some of the outbuildings and lean-tos had some damage. I thought we'd fixed everything but the blizzard showed us more weak spots, and I came for some lumber and some nails." He paused, smiled slyly, then said, "And I figured if I came here rather than going to Kalispell I'd get the chance to ask how you're doing…"

"I'm doing fabulously," she answered as if he'd asked her.

The sly smile widened to a grin that lit up his handsome face.

"I told Tyler I'd be at his house by now," Ryder persisted.

Dallas rolled his eyes but allowed his attention to be dragged away. "Okay, cups to the kitchen," he ordered in a tone that sounded reluctant.

"I'll take care of it," Nina said.

"Not a chance." Dallas overruled her, even cleaning up after her by taking her hot chocolate mug, too, and leaving her to merely follow behind them all with the cookie plate.

Once the cups were rinsed and in the sink, and coats were replaced, Nina went with them to the apartment door, opening it for them.

The boys immediately went out and headed for the stairs.

"Wait for me right there," Dallas warned as he lingered with Nina.

Then he glanced at her again with the same look in his blue eyes that had been there when he'd told her she was beautiful. "I'm really glad to see that you're okay. Better than okay."

"It's all thanks to you," she told him.

He flashed that one-sided smile again. "All me, huh? Doctors, the hospital—none of that had anything to do with it?"

"They just did the checkup. It was you who got me through the worst. And then took heat from my family for it."

"Just happy to help," he said as if he meant that, too.

"I owe you...."

"Nah. You don't owe me anything."

Nina merely smiled. "I'm glad you came up today."

"Me, too."

"Dad!" Ryder chastised from the top of the stairs.

"In a minute," Dallas said without taking his eyes off Nina. He was clearly reluctant to leave. "Guess I better go. Take care of yourself. And that baby," he advised.

"I will," she agreed.

Then he had no choice but to go, and Nina leaned out of her apartment door so she could watch him join his sons, so she could watch the four of them descend the steps.

And all the while she was still smiling to herself.

VICTORIA PADE 47

Because she'd thought of a much, much better thank-you gift than a fruit basket.

A gift that would put her in the company of Dallas Traub one more time.

Chapter Three

"You have to be kidding. You want me to tie a Christmas tree to the top of your SUV so you can surprise some *Traubs* with it?"

It was after five on Sunday. Nate had dropped by the store just before closing and Nina had asked her brother to do her a favor so the teenager who was running the Christmas tree lot didn't have to stay late to do it.

"Dallas needs a tree," she told Nate matter-of-factly. "And it's the least I can do after Wednesday. It's a thank-you Christmas tree."

"Thanks for running you off the road and nearly killing you?"

"*I* pulled out in front of *him,*" Nina repeated what she'd said to her family numerous times since the near-collision. "I don't know what I would have done without him."

"You wouldn't have ended up in a ditch."

"Nathan!" Nina said in a louder voice, attempting to get through to her brother. "Dallas Traub saved me and my baby!"

Okay, maybe that was somewhat of an exaggeration, but in the thick of things on Wednesday, Dallas *had* felt like a lifesaver.

"I want to repay him with this Christmas tree," she insisted.

"We don't owe any Traub anything," Nate said, scowling at her.

"I owe Dallas," Nina said firmly and succinctly.

She'd always been a strong, independent person who acted on her own instincts and answered whatever beliefs, desires or drives she might have, even if they went against popular opinion. Like having this baby on her own. And like giving Dallas and his boys a Christmas tree whether anyone in her stubborn family approved or not.

"If you're bound and determined to give a Traub a tree then have it delivered," her brother reasoned. "Why do you have to take it out to him yourself?"

"I *want* to take it out to him myself," she said defensively, trying not to think about just how much she wanted to do this herself. "He inconvenienced *him*self and even put himself in danger by taking me into Kalispell during a blizzard when he could have just let the sheriff do it and gone home to his own family. Delivering my gift in person is only right."

Which she believed.

But she also couldn't stop thinking about Dallas and wanting to see him again—that was a strong part of her determination to do the delivery herself, too.

Of course, she told herself that now that she'd met Dallas's kids, now that she knew Dallas was having trouble getting into the holiday spirit those kids deserved—the holiday spirit that every kid deserved—it just seemed appropriate that she step up and provide it. In her time of need, Dallas had come to the rescue. Now, in this small way, maybe she could come to his.

And getting to spend a little time with him in the process was inconsequential and meaningless—that was what she kept telling herself.

"Some Traub will probably shoot you on sight when you drive onto their property," Nate said.

Nina rolled her eyes. "This isn't the Wild West anymore. Besides, I've been asking around at the store yesterday and today to get an idea of the actual arrangement of the houses at the Triple T ranch. Dallas and his boys have their own place that sits on one of the borders of the ranch. I can get to it from a side road without going any farther onto the property."

"He's still likely to shoot you," Nathan muttered. Her brother's grumblings about angry Traubs were so ridiculous they made Nina laugh. Regardless of the conflicts between the Crawford family and the Traub family, her own current feelings about Dallas—and his sons—didn't hold any animosity. And she was reasonably certain that Dallas didn't bear her ill will at this point, either.

Certain enough that she had no compunctions about showing up at his doorstep unannounced to surprise him with the tree. And some ornaments and some lights and just a bit of Christmas cheer that her brother didn't know she already had loaded into the rear of her SUV.

"Yes, I'm sure Dallas went to all the trouble of saving me only to turn around and shoot me today," she said facetiously in answer to her brother's comment.

"I don't like it, Nina," Nate said then, seriously, solemnly, showing genuine concern. "You know how things are with the Traubs—they're the enemy."

"In what?" Nina challenged. "Some stupid generations-old family feud? They're the Hatfields and we're the McCoys? Or vice versa? I'm beginning to think that that's just plain dumb."

"You might not think it was so *dumb* if it was you who just lost that race for mayor to a *Traub*."

Nathan couldn't seem to say the name without rancor—actually no one in her family ever could—but still Nina thought maybe she was being insensitive to her brother. Nate had poured his heart and soul into the campaign for the office of Rust Creek's mayor and then lost. To Collin Traub.

"I understand, and I don't blame you for having hard feelings about losing the run for mayor," she assured Nathan. "But this is something just between Dallas and me. Separate from any family squabbles or defeats or any of the rest of it. After all, he did *me* a great kindness separate from everything. Or would you have rather *he* had looked at the situation on Wednesday and left me to fend for myself because I'm a Crawford?"

"No…" Nate admitted with clear reluctance. "I just don't think you owe him anything for it."

"If it had been someone else who did what he did, would you feel the same way?" Nina reasoned.

Her brother scowled again but refused to answer.

Nina knew why and said, "No, you wouldn't feel the same way. You and Mom and Dad would have rushed into the hospital room and fallen all over yourselves thanking him. And right now you'd have that tree tied to my luggage rack and you'd probably be telling me to tell whoever how grateful you all are that he helped me out."

Nate didn't respond to that but he did hoist the tall pine tree up onto her luggage rack and reach down for the bungee cords to hold it there.

After securing the cords and yanking on the tree to make sure it was held tight, Nate got down off her running board and returned to her, still frowning his disapproval.

"It's a good thing we've had nothing but sunshine since Wednesday and the roads are clear or I wouldn't let you do this," he said.

As if he could stop her.

Nina refrained from saying that and instead said, "But the roads are clear, there isn't another storm in sight and thanks for that." She nodded toward the tree now fastened to the roof of her SUV.

Nate would only accept her gratitude with a shrug, letting her know he still didn't approve of what she was doing or of her having contact with any Traub.

But Nina merely kissed her brother on the cheek and sent him on his way.

So that she could be on her way, too.

Even as she tried to contain the wave of excitement that flooded through her at the thought that she was on her way to seeing Dallas again....

Dallas's house was a large two-story that sat not too far back from the side road that bordered the Traub's Triple T ranch.

Nina was glad to see the glow of lights on behind the curtained windows when she pulled up in front of it. On the drive from Rust Creek Falls proper it had occurred to her that he might be having Sunday dinner with his parents, who lived in the main house on the property. But if the lights were on, he was probably there. Which meant she was going to get to see him again after all, and that made her happier than she wanted to admit.

Turning off her engine, she got out of her SUV and went up the four steps onto the porch, crossing it to get to the front door.

There were butterflies in her stomach suddenly, as the thought flitted through her mind that Dallas might not be happy to see her. What if she'd merely been enjoying a temporary truce?

Or what if his parents or his brothers were *here* for Sunday dinner?

Even if things were still okay between her and Dallas, Nina had no doubt that his family's response to her would be as bad as her family's response to him had been. And the thought of that put a damper on what she had planned.

But she'd come to do this and she couldn't let these last-minute concerns stop her. She had to at least find out what was going on inside that house. She couldn't just turn tail and run because things might be different than what she'd envisioned. So she raised a finger to the doorbell and rang it.

Holding her breath.

Then the door opened, and Dallas was standing there—somehow looking even taller, more broad-shouldered and even more handsome, too, despite the fact that he was obviously in stay-at-home clothes that included faded, ages-old jeans and a gray sweatshirt with the sleeves pushed to midforearms.

He also had a kitchen towel slung over one of those broad shoulders and a shadow of beard on the lower half of his face that gave him an extra-rugged appeal Nina tried not to notice. Instead, she focused on the fact that his expression showed shock, then pleased shock as his eyebrows arched and he gave her a glimpse of that lop-sided smile of his.

"Nina!"

"Hi. I hope this isn't a bad time."

His eyebrows arched higher, as if to ask, "A bad time for what?"

She nodded over her shoulder at her car. "I was going to get you a fruit basket or something to say thanks, but after Friday I thought a Christmas tree, some decorations and a few other holiday things were a better idea. And if you're up for it, I'd like to help you trim the tree and get some cheer going for your boys."

The arched eyebrows dipped into an almost-frown. "I can't let you do all that," he said.

"You can't let me say thank you?"

"You've said thank you. A couple of times."

He seemed kind of down tonight and that only made Nina more determined to do this.

"Still, what you did was huge to me, and I want to do this for you to show you how much I appreciated it. For you and the boys…" She added the boys at the end because for some reason there seemed to be an undertone of intimacy in her voice that she wanted to dispel.

"Are you even supposed to be out? Let alone carting Christmas trees around and decorating them for people?" Dallas asked then.

"I was back at work yesterday and today without any limitations, and I feel great. I don't know if it's supposed to be this way this close to the end, but I have a ton of energy—some to spare—and I'd really like to do this."

"Decorate a tree for me?"

"For you and the boys," she said, qualifying this time because there was a hint of intimacy in *his* voice now, and regardless of how excited she was to be looking up into his oh-so-handsome face she was also warning herself to keep things in perspective.

After a brief moment of seeming to consider what she was offering, Dallas shrugged in a way that made her think he was shrugging off some of his low spirits. Then he laughed a little and said, "Well, okay, I guess. If you're up for it."

"I am. If you'll get the tree off the car, I'll get the stuff out of the back—I brought a tree stand so you can just plunk it into that and we can get going."

"Yes, ma'am," he said with a wider smile at the take-charge attitude she was showing, the take-charge attitude that wasn't too different than what he'd shown on Wednesday in the blizzard.

Then he called over his shoulders for his sons to come and put on their coats while he removed the dish towel from his shoulder, slung it over the banister on the staircase behind him and thrust his arms into the largest of the four coats hanging on hooks beside the door.

"Lead the way…" he suggested to Nina as the boys came to the door like a tiny herd of elephants, their curiosity piqued, as well.

"Coats!" Dallas ordered a second time, explaining what was happening as the boys put them on and they all joined Nina on the porch.

"You brought us a Christmas tree?" Robbie exclaimed as they went out to the SUV.

"I did," Nina confirmed. "And a few other things that

you can help me carry in while your dad and your brothers get the tree down."

"I been wantin' a tree!" Robbie said as if it were a revelation.

"Now you'll have one," Nina said with a laugh.

Even the oldest boy—Ryder, who had been so solemn on Friday when they'd met—seemed to perk up at the prospect of decorating for Christmas. And the more childish side of middle-son, Jake—who Nina had already realized liked to play it tough—was revealed as the two older boys aided their father in getting the tree unlashed from the roof of the SUV.

"Go on in and get out of the cold," Dallas commanded Nina when she and Robbie had taken the sacks from her rear cargo compartment. "The family room is to the left—that's where we put the tree."

Thinking more of the little boy than of herself, Nina did as she'd been told.

Inside the house, Nina took off her coat and so did Robbie—dropping his on the floor in his excitement to take the sacks into the other room and see what was in them.

Still in the entry, Nina picked up the child's coat and replaced it on the hook it had come from. Then she draped her own jacket over the newel post at the foot of the wide staircase that led to the second level of the house rather than taking someone else's hook.

She was wearing a turtleneck fisherman's-knit cable sweater that reached to midthigh of the skinny jeans she had on with her fur-lined, calf-high boots. After making sure the sweater wasn't bunched up over her rear end, she took the dish towel from where Dallas had set it over the banister and went in the direction Robbie had gone—to the left of the staircase.

The family room was a wide-open space paneled in a rustic wood, with man-sized leather furniture arranged around the entertainment center and the stone fireplace beside it.

Nina took the dish towel into the kitchen that was in the rear portion of the same area, separated from it only by a big round table surrounded by eight ladder-backed chairs.

On the counter beside the sink were four TV dinners with most of their contents left uneaten, and Nina wondered how often Dallas served frozen meals like that, hoping it wasn't too often. And hoping, too, that the whole household hadn't been feeling so sad tonight that none of them had felt like eating.

She left the dish towel folded neatly on the other side of the double sink and went to Robbie to help unload the bags she'd brought, explaining as she took things out what they were intended for.

"Dad! We have lights and tinsel and ornaments and these sparkly balls and candy canes, and Nina's gonna make us apple cider to drink while we put the tree up!" Robbie announced when his father and brothers carried the evergreen into the family room.

"I can see that," Dallas answered as he leaned the tree against a wall.

When the other boys were following Dallas's instructions to take his coat and theirs to hang up, and Robbie was still engrossed in emptying the bags, Nina said in an aside to Dallas, "I brought a bunch of new ornaments in case you didn't want memories raised with ones you used before...."

"Good idea. We can decide later what we might want to add and what we might not."

The older boys returned then. At Nina's suggestion Christmas music was turned on as she heated the cider and put it into mugs, and everyone got busy putting up the tree and decorating Dallas's house.

Nina half expected Dallas to merely sit on the sofa and watch her and the boys do the decorating, because in the four years she'd been with Leo, that was what he'd done. Christmas spirit seemed to have been something he'd outgrown, and while he'd assured her that he enjoyed the sight of a well-lit tree, he'd refused to exert the energy to actually decorate it.

But Dallas pitched in and did every bit as much as she did until the room was decorated—not quite as elaborately as Nina's apartment, but enough so that it looked very festive.

When all the work was done, Robbie demanded that all the lights be turned off except for the tree lights, and that they all stand back to see how the tree looked in the dark. It looked beautiful, and Nina had the sense that the activity and the addition of the holiday cheer had lifted some of the cloud from the household. If not permanently, then at least for the time being.

Then Dallas said, "Tomorrow is a school day and you guys are late getting to sleep. Tell Nina thank-you for all of this and then upstairs to showers and pajamas and bed."

Ryder and Jake thanked her perfunctorily, but Robbie gave her an impromptu hug around the middle to accompany his expression of gratitude. Then the boys went up the stairs in a thunderous retreat that seemed louder than a mere three kids could cause, and Nina and Dallas were suddenly alone.

"This was a really, really nice thing you did," Dallas said when the noise had dwindled to thumps and bumps overhead. He seemed inordinately grateful. As grateful as she'd been for his help during the blizzard. As grateful as if she'd done something for him that he just hadn't had it in him to do on his own.

"I wanted to do it," Nina assured him.

"Now sit and catch your breath," he insisted. "I'll reheat the cider and have another cup with you."

Better judgment told Nina to decline, to just head for home. She'd done what she'd come to do and she should just leave.

But she couldn't deny herself a few minutes alone with Dallas now that the work was finished and the boys were elsewhere.

So she sat on the big overstuffed leather sofa across from the Christmas tree that they'd set beside the fireplace.

She enjoyed the view of her handiwork and how much more cheerful the room looked while Dallas microwaved refills of cider for just the two of them. Then he brought the mugs and joined her.

Nina was at one end of the long couch, and after handing her the mug he sat on the opposite end. Far, far away.

Or, at least, that was how it seemed.

But it was good, Nina told herself. Because even if she was liking that scruff of beard on his face a little too much and thinking that it was sooo sexy, sitting at a distance from each other proved that there was nothing more to this than two relatively new acquaintances sharing a friendly evening together topped off by a cup of cider.

She took a sip of hers and said, "I wasn't exactly sure what I'd find when I came out here. You know, a Crawford setting foot on the Traub's Triple T ranch..."

"You thought you might be shot on sight?" Dallas joked, gazing at her over his own mug just before he took a drink, too.

"That's what Nate thought—he loaded the tree onto the car for me. I gave him grief for saying such a dumb thing, but I have to admit that I was glad when I found someone at the store today who could tell me which place out here was yours so I didn't have to go to the main house and ask. I sort of figured if I did I'd run into the same kind of wrath from your family that you got from mine."

"At least the hospital was a public place—that probably made it a little safer."

"But obviously not much," Nina said.

"I can't imagine Nathan was any too happy to load up a Christmas tree for you to bring to me," Dallas said then.

Nina shrugged her concession to that. "Losing the election to your brother *has* riled up my family all over again. I'm sure you know how that goes."

"Oh, I know. The slightest thing that happens with a Crawford and everyone on my side is up in arms."

"But it's gotten me to thinking..." Nina mused. "And it occurred to me that I don't even know for sure what started the Crawfords and the Traubs hating each other in the first place. Do you know?" she asked, having wondered a great deal about that since Wednesday when she'd discovered that she couldn't find a single thing wrong with Dallas. When, in fact, she could only find things more right than she wanted them to be.

"I've been thinking a lot about that, too," Dallas admitted. "Here you are, a nice person, great to be around—" and if the warmth in his gaze meant anything, he didn't hate the way she looked, either "—and I keep wondering why I'm supposed to think you're the devil incarnate just because you're a Crawford. But to tell you the truth, I don't know, either."

"I know there's been a history of Crawfords and Traubs competing for the same public positions—like this last election for mayor," Nina said.

"Right. There have been Traubs and Crawfords vying for the sheriff's job and city council seats along the way—I remember our fathers both running for an empty seat on the city council when I was a teenager."

"And that time my dad won—I'd forgotten that he sat on the city council for a while back then," Nina said.

"But there's always a winner and a loser in those things—sometimes in favor of a Traub, sometimes in favor of a Crawford—"

"And then there are hard feelings on the part of whichever side loses," Nina finished for him.

"Sure," Dallas agreed. "Plus I think I remember hearing something about a romance—a long, *long* time ago, when Rust Creek was nothing but cowboys and farmers. I think there was a story about a Traub and a Crawford both wanting the same woman, or something. And when neither of them got her they blamed each other...."

"I hadn't even heard that one," Nina said, laughing again. "I did hear one once about a business deal gone wrong, but all I know for sure is that whenever I've asked *why* the Crawfords and the Traubs hate each other it's started a tirade against the Traubs without any real answer. But it sounds like it's a matter of the Traubs and the

Crawfords being *too* much alike and wanting the same things over and over again."

"It does, doesn't it?" Dallas agreed, laughing with her. "But at this point it just seems silly to me."

Nina was so glad to hear him say that. Probably because it was how she felt, as well, she told herself. It probably didn't have anything to do with the fact that she was enjoying being there with him so much, or the fact that she kept remembering how he'd taken care of her during the blizzard and the feel of him carrying her to his truck, the comforting feel of his arm around her when she'd had pain.

The feel of that kiss he'd placed on her temple…

"It seems silly to me, too," she told him in a voice she wished hadn't come out sounding so breathy.

"So maybe you and I can just have our own little peace treaty," Dallas suggested.

"And who knows? Maybe it will have a ripple effect and our families will stop doing what they've always done."

"Oh, you really are an optimist, aren't you?" Dallas teased her.

Nina smiled but before she could say more a voice from the top of the stairs hollered, "Ready for inspection."

The challenging tone told Nina that it was Jake alerting Dallas that showers were finished, pajamas were on and whatever bedtime routine followed from there was ready to begin.

"I'll be up in a minute," Dallas called back. Then to Nina he said, "I don't make them line up and stand at attention or anything—I know that's how that sounds. But if I don't check, they've been known to turn on the

shower, sit on the floor and look at a comic book, then
turn the water off and figure I'll never know that they
didn't bother to actually get in. And don't even get me
started on the tooth brushing—"

"I understand," she said.

"It will only take me a minute, though, and I'll be
right back."

He wanted her to wait, he wanted this evening to go
on.

And so did Nina.

But it just didn't seem wise. She'd done what she'd intended to do—maybe more because there was a cheerier
atmosphere to the house now that didn't have anything to
do with the decorations—and having this little while on
their own had just been a bonus. So she knew this was
the moment it all had to come to an end.

"I should get going," she told him resolutely, setting
her mug on the scarred coffee table and standing without any difficulty—something she was suddenly grateful
that pregnancy hadn't robbed her of the way it did other
women she'd seen at this stage.

"Let me at least walk you out, then," he said, sounding disappointed.

At the door, he helped her on with her coat then slipped
into his on the way outside.

"I can't tell you how grateful I am for all this tonight,"
he said as they reached her SUV and he opened her door
for her.

"It was my thanks to you," Nina reminded.

"But doing the work was enough. Total up the cost of
the tree and all that stuff and I'll come in and pay you."

Just the idea that he would come in to the store, that

she would get to see him again, made that offer tempting to Nina.

But she shook her head. "Absolutely not. I just hope maybe this, tonight, helped you get more in the mood."

She meant in the *Christmas* mood but the way she'd said it had somehow managed to sound racy. And it made Dallas grin.

He had a great smile and an even greater grin.

And seeing it was payment enough for Nina.

Payment that sent goose bumps of delight up and down her arms...

How had any woman left a man like him behind? she wondered suddenly.

But merely having that thought jolted her slightly, and in response she got in behind the steering wheel, turning on the ignition to warm the engine before she glanced back at Dallas.

He was standing with his hand on the door, studying her, his grin now a small, thoughtful smile. And he was looking at her in a way that caused her to feel that same connection to him that she'd felt before. The connection that was personal and private, solely between them.

"This was really...good," he said as if labeling the evening *good* was an understatement but he couldn't think of how else to put it. "I enjoyed it," he added as if that surprised him.

"Me, too," Nina answered softly, unable to keep from admitting it herself.

Another moment passed while they stayed like that, as if Dallas couldn't quite let her go.

But then he took a step that put him out of the way of the door closing and said, "Drive safe."

"As a rule, I do," she joked in reference to the events of Wednesday.

That made his smile widen, but he didn't say anything else. He just closed her door, waved through the window and returned to his house as Nina made a U-turn and headed out the way she'd come in.

It was only as she drove back to Rust Creek Falls that she reminded herself that she was in no way on the market or in the market—or in the position or the shape—to be starting anything with any man.

Let alone Dallas Traub.

Chapter Four

By Wednesday evening it felt to Nina as if it had been decades since she'd seen Dallas, and she wondered what on earth was going on with her.

She couldn't stop thinking about the guy. She daydreamed about him. She dreamed about him in her sleep. She looked at every man who walked into the store, hoping it would be him. She found herself trying to come up with "accidental" ways to meet—as if driving out to the Triple T ranch and pretending her car engine had died right in front of his house would in any way appear to be an accident.

She was a little afraid that she'd lost her mind.

Before they were stranded together in that blizzard she had only been vaguely aware that he existed. And even then only as one of the group of hated Traubs. Individually he'd meant nothing to her. And now she woke up in the middle of the night vividly reliving being carried in his arms across that country road. Wishing he were there with her in her bed so he could put those same arms around her again, and convinced that she was truly going crazy.

She told herself that it was the flood of pregnancy hormones. That even though this was the worst time ever for her to be attracted to someone, maybe a sort of biological imperative had kicked in and caused it anyway, to tempt her to mate.

Or maybe she couldn't stop thinking about him as some sort of involuntary distraction mechanism to keep her from worrying about labor and delivery. Because she was definitely thinking more about Dallas than she was about going into labor.

About his gray-blue eyes and his distinctive nose and his crooked smile and his great hair and that body that just didn't quit…

But whatever was causing it, it was all torture. This was a man she had no reason to ever see again. A man she wasn't even very likely to run into, despite the size of Rust Creek Falls, because the conflict between their families had made it so that they occupied completely different parts of the town in order for their paths *not* to cross.

And yet he was the one man she was just dying *to* see.

It was crazy.

But she was hoping for some diversion, at least for tonight.

The flood that had hit Rust Creek Falls early in the summer had wreaked widespread havoc and destruction on much of the small town and the surrounding farms and ranches. It had cost the previous mayor his life and resulted in the election that had increased the animosity between the Crawfords and the Traubs. The damage to the elementary school had required it to be closed for repairs and classes so far this year to be held in the homes of the teachers of each grade.

Aid and relief efforts had helped. People in neighboring Thunder Canyon had done all they could. A New York–based organization called Bootstraps had become involved, and one of their volunteers, Lissa Roarke, had been particularly instrumental in bringing the needs of Rust Creek Falls to the attention of the rest of the country by appearing on a network talk show, as well as starting a charity website and blog that had brought in funds.

But many people were still struggling. And while the situation had improved and rebuilding was ongoing, full recovery would take time.

Many of the natives of Rust Creek Falls who had left the area to pursue careers and lives beyond the confines of a small town had returned to help, and the current residents who were lucky enough to have their homes and businesses spared—like the Crawfords—were determined to do all they could for the less fortunate among them.

One of those efforts on Nina's part was sponsoring and overseeing Santa's Workshop. She'd instigated the Tree of Hope—a Christmas tree in Crawford's General Store that had gone up in November. It was decorated with wish-list tags filled out by local children and families in need.

Donations of food, clothing and toys had been coming in to supply the "wishes" written on those tags, with the Crawfords committed to filling any gaps to make sure that everyone in Rust Creek Falls had gifts and a complete Christmas dinner this year, no matter what it took.

Organization of the donations had been ongoing, but with Christmas a week away, Nina had put signs in the store windows and all around town asking for volunteers to come to the store tonight to wrap packages and put food baskets together so that they could be delivered over the coming weekend. And that was what she was hoping would keep her mind off Dallas Traub for at least a few hours—gift wrapping and filling Christmas dinner baskets alongside any number of the good people of Rust Creek Falls whom she had faith would show up.

She'd asked her parents to take over the running of the store for the evening, and at six o'clock she opened the back door of the stockroom, where the necessary tasks were to be performed.

Already there were folks waiting to be let in, to get to the tables Nina had set up in the stockroom for work.

And when one of the volunteers proved to be Dallas, there was no containing her exhilaration, even though she tried.

"Hi!" she greeted him more brightly and enthusiastically than she had anyone else. "I can't believe you came…"

He seemed slightly reserved and somewhat tentative but he still managed a joke.

"Was there fine print on the fliers that I missed that said 'No Traubs'?"

"No. I just… I'm so glad to see you. We can use all the help we can get," she said, stumbling over her words and settling on something she hoped hid what she was really thinking and feeling.

"Does my being here cause problems?" he asked, misinterpreting her nervousness. "Will it upset your family too much?"

"No, it's okay. My parents are out front, running the store. Nate is back here to keep things organized for easy loading on delivery day, but I have one table that's kind of back in a nook—you and I can wrap packages there and that shouldn't bother anyone."

"You're sure?" Dallas asked, more of that reserve showing than facing her family seemed to warrant.

"Absolutely positive. Come on, I'll show you," she encouraged, taking him to the very rear of the stockroom, where they could be secluded. "This was going to be my station, anyway. Unless you'd rather be somewhere else…"

"No! I mean, we've already established that you and I work well together. Why shouldn't we do it again? And it's probably better if I'm not right under your brother's nose," he said, doing some verbal tap dancing himself.

"Okay then," Nina concluded. "I put some of the smaller toys back here to wrap, since this space is limited. How are you as a gift wrapper?"

"Fair with paper, lousy with ribbons or bows."

"Then you do the paper, I'll do the ribbons and bows."

"Works for me," he said, with a little more excitement at what was in store for him.

He was wearing his heavy suede coat again and he took it off then. It had been on over jeans that were much nicer than what he'd worn Sunday night and a navy blue V-neck sweater with a white crew-necked T-shirt underneath.

A sweater that made his shoulders look even bigger and stronger…

Nina chastised herself for thinking that. It was just the sort of image that stayed in her mind to haunt her later and make it all the more difficult not to think about him.

"Paper station. Ribbons-and-bows station," she decreed, pointing to one end of the fold-out card table for him to go to and taking the opposite end herself to face him while she worked.

She had on maternity skinny jeans, this time with her most comfortable flat shoes and a boatneck, dark purple sweater long enough to fall well past her stomach.

"I can't say that I expected you to do this tonight," she said as they got busy.

"After Sunday? You earned a little payback," he said. "My brother Sutter wasn't busy, so he could babysit, and I get a night out—seemed like a win all the way around."

"This is a night out for you?" Nina laughed.

He grinned at her as if being with her was what mattered and said, "A good one."

Her brother came looking for her just then, and when he spotted Dallas his expression went from sweet to sour before he seemed to decide against whatever he'd been going to say and merely asked where she wanted the baskets stored.

"They can go into cold storage—I cleared enough space for them, and in there the turkeys and hams will stay cool," she informed him, wishing he could be more congenial but knowing she was hoping for too much.

"Sorry," she whispered to Dallas when her brother had left.

"Hey, he didn't physically throw me out—I count that as a win," he said as if not even her brother's rudeness could upset him at that moment.

Still, it embarrassed Nina. And reminded her of just how complicated it was for a Crawford to have anything to do with a Traub.

And yet, not even knowing that could change how she felt about being right there, right then, with Dallas...

"Ah, this is *great!*"

The first thing that went through Nina's mind when Dallas said that was that he was talking about what she was thinking about—being with her in spite of the difficulties.

Then she realized he was getting ready to wrap an action figure that had sparked his interest and admiration, and seemed to have made him relax a bit.

"He turns into a fighter jet—my boys would all love this," he added.

It sounded as if Dad would, as well, and as Nina cut some wrapping paper for him to use she said, "And maybe if you're good, Santa will bring you one, too."

He laughed at her goad and played along. "I'd *love* that! One of my favorite Christmas gifts was a robot that turned into a race car. When my younger brother Clay broke it there was war."

"Brother against brother?" Nina asked facetiously.

"Brother*s* against brother*s*—I had Forrest and Braden on my side—we were the oldest three and they had two of the other figures that went with mine so we were the Bad Guy Busters." He said it with dramatic effect before going on. "Clay had put a big dent in the game by breaking my guy. He enlisted Sutter and Collin—who I think might have been involved in breaking the toy in the first place because those three younger ones were always after our stuff—and it was all-out war. There were more toy casualties on both sides, a toilet head-dunking, rocks put in shoes as retaliation—"

Nina laughed. "How long did this particular civil war go on?"

"Oh, a full two days. Until Mom found sand in the younger boys' beds—that was the last straw. The Bad Guy Busters had its action figures confiscated, we all went without dessert for a week, the younger guys were sentenced to folding our socks that same week, and Braden, Forrest and I had to *nicely* play what we considered *baby* board games with Clay, Collin and Sutter as our punishment."

"And peace was restored?"

"Until the next time," he said, as if it had been a continuing saga. "We were six boys—there were more battles than I can remember. Weren't there in your house? You come from a big family, too."

"The same as yours—six kids. And yeah, there were plenty of fights. My sister, Natalie, and I would get into it. The boys would get into it. Sometimes it was the girls against the boys, or just Natalie or I would be fighting for some reason with Nate or Brad or Jesse or Justin. I've heard that only-children actually go into relationships at a disadvantage because they haven't had the experience of fighting with siblings."

Dallas laughed that deep barrel-chested laugh he had. "Well then, my kids have that advantage because they do their fair share of fighting, too."

He handed her the wrapped package and started on a baby doll while Nina tied the first gift with ribbon and chose a bow.

"How about you?" he asked as she did. "What was your favorite Christmas gift?"

"There was a doll the size of a real four-year-old that I wanted when I was about nine—I still have it tucked away to give to my own daughter if I have a girl, now or later. But I'd have to say that there was a tie between that as my favorite Christmas gift and a small television I lobbied for forever when I was thirteen. I wanted to be able to watch what *I* wanted to watch without having to negotiate with brothers or my sister or my parents, and I *loved* that."

"You wanted to do what you wanted to do whether anyone else liked it or not even then, huh?"

Nina laughed. "Pretty much."

"Yeah, having my own stereo was just as big a deal for me. My own stereo and a set of headphones so I could listen to what I wanted, as loud as I wanted."

"And what kind of music did you listen to?"

He told her and she couldn't resist giving him a hard time. "Oh, I get it—oldies."

"Hey!" he countered as if he was insulted. But his grin gave him away.

"To me, those were oldies," she said with a smile.

"I suppose they were," he conceded. "You're just a *baby* after all. A baby having a baby…"

Some goading of his own.

Nina laughed, enjoying herself. Enjoying him and this back-and-forth between them. "Well, at least the diapers *I'll* be buying won't be—"

"If you say for an adult I just might come across this table and—"

"Wave your cane at me?"

That made him laugh again. "It's a good thing I'm not sensitive. But be careful because I am a *spry* thirty-four and I could come over this table…"

He made that sound far more intriguing than threatening and she liked that he could poke fun at himself. Plus, for some reason what sprang into her mind was just how *spry* he'd been when he'd carried her across that country road in the blizzard. And as much as she wished their age difference produced something unattractive about him, it didn't. She couldn't deny that he was a very, very fine specimen of a man.

"So tell me what else you like besides controlling the television," he said then. "What toppings do you like on your pizza?"

"Is there a *bad* topping on a pizza?"

"Good answer!" he declared. "Sometimes you want it loaded with meat, sometimes peppers and onions and mushrooms and olives do just fine."

"Or just plain cheese or even white pizza—how can you go wrong with pizza?" Nina agreed. Then she said, "Ice cream—favorite flavor?"

"Again, no bad ice cream. I'm an ice cream guy...."

"Okay, let's narrow it down—chocolate or vanilla?"

"Chocolate. You?"

"Chocolate. The deepest, darkest, richest—"

"Chocolate," he finished for her with another grin. "Got it. How about movies? What's your favorite movie?"

They went on like that while they continued to work, and by the time all the packages were wrapped and the volunteers were beginning to leave, Nina had learned that she and Dallas Traub had a great deal in common. And that there still wasn't anything about him that she *didn't* like.

In fact, spending that time with him only made her like him more. Much to her dismay...

By ten-thirty the store had closed, Nate had left along with Nina's parents, and Nina was walking out the last of the volunteers. Except Dallas. She wasn't sure if she was misreading something, but it seemed as if he was hanging back, as if he wasn't eager to leave.

He was straightening up while she thanked her helpers. When she closed the stockroom's back door after they'd left she turned and leaned against it, weary from her fifteen-hour workday, but even so, not anxious to see Dallas go.

"Don't worry about taking the tables down. My stockers will do it in the morning when they come in," she said to Dallas as he finished folding one up.

"I don't mind," he said.

She shook her head. "No, you've done enough." As much as she didn't want this evening to end, she didn't have the heart to ask more of him.

Dallas checked the time on the wall clock above the time-stamp machine next to the door. "I suppose I should probably get going," he conceded. "Tomorrow is a school day, so I have to have the kids up at dawn."

He disappeared back into the alcove of shelves where they'd worked and reappeared with his coat, putting it on as he came to the door.

"It's nice that you just have to go upstairs and you're home," he observed.

"Really nice on days this long," she agreed. But she was still leaning against the closed door, essentially blocking his exit.

He didn't seem in any hurry, though, because when he joined her he sat gingerly on the table below the time-stamp machine where she kept new time cards and bulletins for her employees.

She also kept a bowl of buttermints there, just as a small treat for anyone who might want one coming or going. Dallas helped himself to a mint, squeezing it out of its packaging into his mouth.

"Thanks for coming tonight and all you did," Nina said as he ate it.

"The flood made this year rough. I was glad to see the names on those gifts—it's good to know that everyone, but especially the kids, won't be missing out on Christmas morning because of it. And you're doing food baskets, too?"

"There was a sign-up sheet. Some people put their own names on it, knowing they couldn't afford a real Christmas dinner this year. Some people put the names of friends or family or neighbors on it who they knew were too proud to do it themselves. I just hope everybody who needs it was brought to our attention one way or another. It's Christmas, after all. I want everybody to be able to sit down to a nice Christmas dinner."

He studied her, smiling, a warmth in his eyes that heated her to the core. "That's great…" he said softly, almost more to himself than to her. "And a lot of work," he added. "You must be tired."

Nina merely shrugged. "It's worth it."

"But you need some fun, too…." He hesitated, as if he wasn't sure what her response might be to what he was about to say. Then he came out with it anyway.

"Since you opened my eyes to my Scrooge-ness this year, I'm trying to be more conscious of making this a decent Christmas for the boys," he joked, making Nina laugh. "Friday night the snow castle opens and I promised I would take them. You wouldn't want to go with us, would you?"

The Montana town usually had enough snow by this time to inspire townsfolk to start using it for entertainment—there had been years when there were snowmen and snowwomen on every street corner; sometimes there was a snow-sculpting contest. One year there had been an entire snow fort. This December they'd erected a snow castle complete with a snow maze that led up to a cupola where Santa was to make an appearance on Friday night.

"I know the store is on Christmas hours, and maybe you have to work or something," he added into the miniscule pause left when Nina didn't answer immediately.

But she hadn't answered yet because her immediate desire was to say yes, and she'd forced herself not to jump in, to think about the complications and the reasons she should say no.

Unfortunately, when it came down to it, those complications and reasons just didn't carry enough weight against the drive to say yes.

"I actually don't have myself scheduled for the evening hours so I'm free…" she said, even though those complications and reasons didn't make that exactly true.

But everyone—including Nina—had been watching the castle being built in the past few days, and she wanted to go.

And she especially wanted to go with Dallas now that the opportunity had arisen, so she couldn't make herself turn him down.

Despite everything else…

"I'd love to go," she finished.

Dallas grinned at her answer. "Robbie is clinging to the last belief in Santa Claus, and this year, for some reason, he's really determined to talk to him."

"I think as long as kids believe you should let them."

"Me, too. I've warned his brothers not to bust his bubble, and they're being pretty good about it. Kids in his class have told him Santa isn't real, but he's just telling them they're wrong."

"Yeah, this is probably his last year," Nina said with a laugh. "But let him have it while he can."

"So you'll go?"

"I will," Nina said without any hesitation this time. "Unless the boys might object…?"

"Hey, after Sunday night they think *you're* Santa Claus. I've been fielding questions since then about when we're going to see you again, so they'll be thrilled."

"That's nice," Nina said, touched.

"You put the spirit in Christmas this year when I dropped the ball," he admitted. "And I have to say that it's helped to have a little cheer in the house…. It's helped me and the lousy mood I've been in for this last year—and I'm not even just keeping up appearances, I'm actually feeling it. So, what do you say? Maybe around seven Friday night? We'll come by here and get you?"

What harm could come of it? Nina asked herself. She was pregnant and couldn't let anything romantic develop between them. And the three kids he already had would be there as chaperones.

It was just something to do. Something she wanted to do and otherwise probably wouldn't since she didn't yet have a child to take to see Santa.

"Seven works for me," she confirmed.

"Great!" he said with that slow, one-sided grin as he got up from the table.

Nina knew she couldn't go on holding him hostage by blocking the door, so she stepped away from it. But not so far away from it that she wasn't still standing there, facing him, when he reached for the handle.

"Thanks again for the help," she repeated.

"My pleasure," he assured her, his blue eyes holding her gaze.

And what flitted through her mind in that instant was the kiss he'd placed on her temple when they'd been stranded.

It was something she'd thought of more often than she wanted to admit since it happened, but there it was again—just a vague recollection of what it had felt like.

Accompanied by the inexplicable wish that he would kiss her again…

Though not on the temple.

On the lips.

And that it wouldn't be a kiss meant only to comfort her. It would be a real kiss….

Then she caught herself.

Thoughts—feelings—such as these weren't so harmless. And she shouldn't be having them.

She took a step away from Dallas, knowing that in the shadow of those thoughts of kissing, the wish that he would, she should tell him she'd just remembered something else she had to do on Friday night, so she couldn't go to the snow castle with him, after all.

But then he smiled at her again—this time a small, thoughtful smile—just before he opened the stockroom's back door and said, "Go on, get up to your place and relax. I'll see you Friday night."

And the only thing she heard herself say was, "Friday night."

Then he left, and she was flooded with disappointment.

Disappointment that he was gone.

Disappointment that he hadn't kissed her.

Disappointment that she knew she had no business having.

After a fifteen-hour workday at eight months pregnant—she was just tired, she told herself. That's why she felt what she did.

She hadn't honestly wanted Dallas Traub to kiss her.

But regardless of how she tried to believe it as she turned off the stockroom lights and went up to her apartment, she still took with her that disappointment.

And an awful, niggling curiosity that other kiss just hadn't satisfied.

About what it might be like to have Dallas Traub kiss her full on the mouth, for real...

Chapter Five

"Our snow guys went all out with this, didn't they?" Dallas marveled to Nina as they followed his three boys through the maze on Friday evening.

"It's beautiful, isn't it?" Nina agreed.

Dallas enjoyed the sight of her peeking through a cut-out in the maze's wall to view one of many Christmas dioramas along the path of the maze.

There were also decorative carvings in the walls themselves, glittering with life from the glow of the tiny white Christmas lights overhead.

The castle at the end of the maze had been carved from a wall of snow, and after crossing the drawbridge into it, Santa came into view. He was sitting on a red-velvet throne positioned on an ornately sculpted wooden platform.

"There he is!" Robbie exclaimed at first glimpse. "Are we in line?"

"I think we are, buddy," Dallas assured his son, since once they crossed the drawbridge there was a choice of going straight ahead to Santa or turning off and following what appeared to be portions of the maze that led back out.

"Are you gonna sit on Santa's lap?" Jake goaded him, nudging Ryder with an elbow.

"Jake…" Dallas said in a warning tone.

"Sure I am. That's how you talk to Santa," Robbie answered his brother, as if Jake were ignorant.

"You already wrote him a letter," Ryder said.

"This is different," Robbie insisted.

"Well, don't take too long. My nose is cold," Ryder grumbled, ducking his stocking-capped head deeper into the collar of his coat. His gloved hands were in his pockets and his posture was sulky now that they were at a standstill.

"Do this," Nina said, demonstrating by cupping her hands over her own mouth and nose and blowing warm breath into them.

Much to Dallas's relief, Ryder complied rather than answering her with more of his sullenness.

Dallas leaned over enough to say quietly into her ear, "I'm glad he spares you the preview of adolescence he gives me."

"You've taught him good manners," she whispered back, making him wonder how she always managed to make him feel better.

A moment later they reached Santa, just as the child on Santa's lap finished.

"Okay, Robbie, you're up," Dallas said. The smallest Traub marched purposefully to Santa and climbed onto his lap without hesitation. Nina and Dallas followed close behind, and the other boys stood off to the side.

Needing to know exactly what his son would be expecting from Santa, Dallas listened intently.

"I a'ready wrote down what I want on that letter I sent you," Robbie informed Santa matter-of-factly as he took a small photograph from his pocket. "But I need to give you this."

Dallas had no idea what Robbie was up to and paid even closer attention.

The little boy handed Santa the photograph. "It's my school picture. I don't know where my mom is but when you bring her presents this year, would you give her this, too? I think she might want it."

Boom! Dallas felt as if something had hit him. Hard. Just one more blow this year had to dish out to him when he least expected it....

He didn't know why, but he looked to Nina.

Only, she had tears in her eyes, and seeing that put him too close to panic, so he looked back to Robbie.

It just hadn't occurred to him that his son might have been so determined to see Santa because he was desperate to connect with the mother who wasn't around anymore, and for the life of him, Dallas wasn't sure what to do.

Should he break in and stop this? Should he let it go on?

Santa was equally at a loss, and looked to Dallas for guidance, so Dallas knew he had to figure something out fast.

Going on instinct, he went nearer and patted Robbie on the back. "I'm sure your mom will want it and be really glad you thought to get Santa to bring it to her." Then he nodded at Santa to take the picture.

"You think Santa knows where she is?" Ryder demanded bitterly.

Dallas heard the pain that went with that bitterness and it was another punch that he could only absorb before he cast his other son a warning look. It was Robbie who answered Ryder. "Santa knows where everybody is. How do you think he gives 'em presents?"

Ryder rolled his eyes, but Jake's eight-year-old tough-guy image seemed to have been shaken, and he looked as though he might be wondering whether his younger brother had come up with something he should have gotten in on.

Then Robbie hopped down off of Santa's lap and said, "Thank you, Santa. Tell my mom I've been a good boy this year, and I miss her."

"Merry Christmas!" Santa said, as he handed Robbie a candy cane—and two more for his brothers.

"Was that okay?" Robbie asked his father as they headed through the exit portion of the maze.

Dallas had to swallow a lump in his own throat before he could say, "Sure it was okay. It was nice. I'm proud of you for thinking of it."

Then he palmed Jake's head in one hand, leaned over and said, "We can get your school picture and Ryder's, too, to Santa for the same thing, if you guys want."

"She can't have my picture," Ryder said angrily.

"Yeah, mine, either," Jake chimed in, the tough guy back in place, but not securely, and clearly to disguise his own hurt feelings.

Dallas glanced at Nina again, this time feeling the

urge to rescue her, and apologized. "Sorry you had to get in on this...."

"It's okay. I know you all have to be struggling."

Her compassion and understanding caused him to like her even more, and he realized that somehow just having her there with him made this whole thing easier to bear.

They exited the maze just in time for the puppet show being done not far away, so they watched that. It seemed to help everyone recover because by the end of it the boys were all laughing, and that let Dallas relax again.

Then they moved on to watch a juggler being harassed by a mime before the boys all picked out Christmas ornaments to have their names engraved on and played various games that involved snowballs in one way or another.

Just when everyone was getting too cold to be out much longer, they encountered Dallas's brother Braden.

"Mom said this is where you were tonight, so I came looking for you." Braden greeted Dallas and gave a curious, confused glance at Nina, whom he obviously had not expected to find on the excursion.

Much to Dallas's further dismay, Braden ignored her and spoke only to him. "I want to get an early start in the morning, so I thought I'd take the boys to spend the night."

"Yeah!" Robbie agreed enthusiastically.

"Whenever you're done here," Braden added.

"I'm done. It's cold," Ryder contributed.

"Sure," Dallas agreed with a shrug.

Braden glanced at Nina again, his expression confused and disapproving. He still didn't acknowledge her, but he did seem to make a reluctant concession by saying to Dallas, "You don't have to end your night. I can just take the boys. I have my key, so we can swing by your place to get their stuff."

"Okay," Dallas answered, going on to sort through the details of what was going to be an ice-fishing trip for Braden and the boys the next day.

Then, after Dallas reminded the boys to say good-night to Nina and they complied, they left with their uncle. Without their uncle ever having said a word to Nina.

Dallas closed his eyes, letting his head drop forward and just hang for a moment as he dealt with the remnants of what had been dredged up in him tonight.

But as he told himself yet again to put a good face on things, even if he was still recovering from the body blows of the evening, it occurred to him that knowing he was going to open his eyes to Nina, knowing that he was about to have more time with her, left him genuinely feeling better. More than better, actually. It left him feeling glad to go on, despite everything else.

Then he took a deep breath and looked at her again, and smiled a smile that felt as if it was for her alone.

"Okay. Sometimes things just take a turn on you," he said. "First the deal with Santa and then my brother being rude—"

Nina laughed. "No more rude than my brother was to you the other night at the store," Nina pointed out.

Dallas shook his head. "Yeah. Wow. Coming at us from all directions. So, how about we salvage what we can of tonight, get out of this cold and get some hot wings?"

"Comfort food?" Nina said with a warm smile that had a power all on its own to raise him out of despair.

"Comfort food," he confirmed.

Then he linked his arm through hers and led her away from the event that had started out fun, hit a few snags but seemed as if it just might be salvageable after all.

"Will you be up all night with heartburn now?"

Nina laughed at Dallas's concern. She'd suggested they take their hot wings back to her apartment to eat because the restaurant had been so crowded. They'd finished the spicy snack and were throwing away the containers.

"I actually don't have a problem with heartburn, no matter what I eat. Or even what time of day I eat it," she answered, as they took their glasses of herbal iced tea with them into her living room.

"You're amazing—are you *sure* you're pregnant?"

She laughed again, glancing down at the long sweater she was wearing over leggings and boots. "I'd be dressed a little differently if I wasn't."

"Still hard to tell," he said.

"Take a drink of the herbal tea and think about the wine I would ordinarily have opened. Then tell me you aren't convinced."

He grinned at her, set his glass on the coffee table and pushed up the sleeves of the heavy crewneck T-shirt he was wearing.

His wrists were thick above those massive workman's hands, his forearms were impressively muscled and there was something so masculine about it all that it struck Nina as incredibly sexy.

She instantly chastised herself for that, also taking herself to task for liking what she saw as much as she did.

But she *did* like it. There was no denying it.

Pulling her eyes away, she decided to finally venture a question of her own. "Are you doing okay? I mean, it ripped my heart out to hear what Robbie said to Santa. I can't imagine that it was easy for you."

"Yeah, it pretty much ripped my heart out, too," he admitted. "I had no idea that was the reason he was so determined to talk to Santa this year. I guess it also explains why he still needed to hang on to believing Santa was real—he's been coming up with more reasons than you can imagine to convince us all, but I suppose he was really just trying to keep himself convinced."

"Do you think he feels like Santa is his only hope of reaching his mother?"

"I'm never too sure what's going on in any of the boys' heads. Sometimes they talk a little about what they're feeling, sometimes it comes out like this. But Laurel's family is all gone, her friends don't know where she is, so sure, I guess Robbie has to feel like Santa is his only hope," Dallas confided grimly. "And not only is that the sad truth, it's even sadder that Santa is no hope at all."

That fact, and the injury that showed in Dallas's expression, broke Nina's heart all over again. And even though she knew she was prying, her curiosity got the better of her so she did it anyway.

"You were married to Laurel Hanes, weren't you?"

Dallas grimaced, bent his head forward and rubbed the back of his neck as if to ease some stress there. "Yeah," he acknowledged as he raised it back up again. "For nine years. But we were together for twenty—from the time we were both thirteen."

So he'd spent most of his life with the woman, and whittling it down to only the marriage seemed to diminish it somehow.

"Childhood sweethearts," Nina said to validate the

time he'd spent with his ex. "But you didn't get married until you were twenty-four?"

"Not because of me. I would have married her right after high school. But Laurel dragged her feet. 'Marriage is forever, why rush it?' That's what she'd say. She wanted to stretch her wings a little. To travel some with her friends. To just have fun before we settled down. I didn't have any doubt that we'd get there—no one did, it just always seemed like a given that Laurel and I would be together forever—so I didn't push it. I just weathered my mom pressuring me for a wedding and grandchildren—the sooner the better, in her point of view—and waited for Laurel to be ready."

"I'm sure Laurel appreciated your patience," Nina said when his tone let her know he now considered that somehow foolhardy.

"That sounds good but I just think I was too dumb to see the forest for the trees," he muttered.

"But she was eventually ready," Nina pointed out.

Dallas made a face at that. "Not exactly. Laurel got pregnant with Ryder."

And his expression told her that hadn't been such a joyous surprise.

"It was an accident," he added. "Laurel had the flu, missed a couple of birth control pills, and I guess we didn't take that seriously enough."

"Were you both unhappy about it?"

"I wasn't unhappy about it at all. By then it seemed like Laurel had had plenty of fun, plenty of wing-stretching. She'd done her traveling—her friends were actually all married and settled down themselves—so it seemed like our time to tie the knot. I just figured the baby was a sign for us to finally do it."

"And what did Laurel think?"

"It still took some convincing," he admitted. "But she came around."

"No enthusiasm? No running into your arms and saying 'Yes! I'd love to marry you and have this baby'?" Nina asked, thinking that that was the kind of response he'd deserved. The kind of response the coming of Ryder had deserved.

He chuckled wryly, humorlessly. "No, there was none of that. It was more like, 'Okay, I guess we have to....'"

"But once you actually got her to take the leap?" Nina was hoping for anything positive, for his sake.

"She didn't get any happier about it," he said reluctantly. "There were some times that were better than others," he claimed, as if to make it sound better. "She liked all the attention and parties and showers that came with the wedding and then with being pregnant, too. But after Ryder was born, the day-to-day got her down, and she just wasn't happy. She was restless and she complained that she was bored. Well, she pretty much complained about everything."

"But she didn't want out...." Nina said, because it was the most encouraging thing she could come up with.

"Like a divorce? No, she didn't talk about that. And if she thought about it...I don't know if she did, but *if* she did the idea probably got further and further away when her dad died, and then her mother a year later. That left her without any family, other than us."

"And I'm sure she loved you and the boys," Nina insisted, wanting to believe it herself.

"I suppose. In her own way. And she knew how it was with me, with my family—we believe in marriage. In marriage being for life. She knew that to me—to my family—divorce would be a disappointment, so I would have fought tooth and nail to keep that from happening."

There was such sadness, such shame in his tone that it was obvious the end of his marriage *had* left him feeling like a failure, seeing himself as a failure. Nina could only hope his family hadn't added to that, but her own lifelong prejudice against the Traubs left her thinking they might have.

"So, no talk of divorce and you had two more kids…." Nina said to prompt him to go on, wanting to understand.

"I talked her into Jake. I thought since she'd liked being pregnant, liked all the attention, maybe that might perk her up."

"And she agreed."

"Yeah. Plus…" He shrugged. "You know, she grew up the same way I did—probably the same way you did—believing that that's what people do, they get married, they have a family. I guess then she was sort of resigned to her lot in life."

"But having Jake didn't help?"

"No. And Robbie was another accident. She didn't actually want to go through with having him."

"She didn't want Robbie?" Nina asked defensively. It was painful to hear that the little boy who loved his mother so much hadn't been wanted by that mother.

Dallas confirmed it with another shrug. "I had to promise her a trip to Europe to get her to have him, and Laurel spent the whole nine months planning the holiday rather than planning anything for the new baby. Rather than even talking about the new baby. I think if we hadn't already had a crib and bottles and blankets and all the gear, she might have wrapped him in a bath towel, stuck him in a dresser drawer and called it good."

"So she probably wasn't any happier once her European vacation was over." Nina knew the minute she said the words that she shouldn't have let so much of her disapproval into her voice.

Dallas didn't seem to take offense, though. He merely shook his head. "Nope, no happier. In fact, I think the trip only made things worse. Coming back to her life here, to the day-to-day grind of just being a wife and mother, was a letdown."

Nina hadn't known Laurel Hanes, but she was growing to dislike her. "Did she consider a career? Hobbies? If her friends had kids, didn't she like doing things with them? She actually sounds depressed—did you think about going with her for counseling?"

"She didn't want to work, and since we didn't need the money I didn't push that. She tried hobbies—hated them all. When it came to her friends, she started saying that all they could talk about was their kids and cooking and this town, and she hated that, too. Yes, I did try to get her to talk to a doctor or a counselor—to *somebody*— but she wouldn't do it. She said *she* wasn't depressed, that everything around her was just depressing—if that makes any sense. It didn't to me."

"So there was, what? Five more years after Robbie was born?"

"Yep. Five more years. Then, the day after Christmas last year I woke up alone in bed. There was a letter from Laurel on her pillow. She said I'd been a good husband— better than her friends' husbands—that I'd made a good home for her, that I was a good father, but that she'd been sleeping with one of our itinerant ranch hands—"

"Oh, no…" Nina muttered, seeing the lines of tension in his handsome face and knowing how hard that had struck him. How hard it would strike anyone. "Did you have any idea?"

"None. The ranch is a big place and I'm out on it from dawn till dusk most days. Robbie was in preschool, Ryder and Jake were at school, she was alone in the house, and the house isn't within sight of neighbors. I don't know for sure, because she didn't say in her note, but I give my ranch hands their jobs for the day and send them out to do them—I'm not watching them all the time. There's no way I could. I suppose that gave the guy free rein to drop by my place while I was out and…"

Seeing his anguish, his embarrassment, broke Nina's heart for the third time that night.

"I hauled that bed out to the middle of nowhere and set it on fire, I'll tell you that," he said under his breath. "I'd have set the whole damn house on fire if I could have, but about all I could do was gut the master bedroom and bath and redo it all with a vengeance."

Nina nodded. She could appreciate that he wouldn't have wanted the room where his wife had likely cheated on him to hold any reminders.

"Did the letter say anything else? Anything about the kids she was leaving behind?" Nina asked.

"It said that by the time I read it, Laurel and Jeff would be long gone from Rust Creek Falls. That, to her, living here was barely existing and that she needed to go out and live life. That there were divorce papers on the bureau that she'd had a lawyer draw up. That she didn't want anything but her freedom, she was giving me full and unconditional custody of the boys, and all I had to do was sign the papers and have them filed, and we could pretend none of it had ever happened."

Twenty years with someone, a marriage, a life, three

kids and the woman wanted to pretend none of it had ever happened? Nina tried to hide the outrage she felt on Dallas's behalf.

"There wasn't so much as a clue where she went from here," he went on. "Not another word about the boys or a message to them, and we haven't heard from her since. As if nothing here exists for her anymore."

"She hasn't even called to see if the boys are all right or anything?"

He shook his head once more. "Nothing."

"Oh, Dallas, I'm so sorry," Nina told him, sorry not only for what had happened but also for the unkind thoughts she'd had about him when she'd heard a Traub was getting divorced. And now she knew why there wasn't any general knowledge of what had actually happened to end his marriage, that his wife cheating on him and running out on him with a ranch hand wouldn't have been something he'd wanted spread around.

He shrugged yet again. "In some ways we're better off," he said. "Laurel just never grew up and settled down, so she was like living with a sourpuss teenager—to the boys, too. She didn't have any patience with them. They annoyed and irritated her and she let them know it. She was just generally hard on them and she never really seemed to enjoy anything about them or with them—not even holidays or birthdays—"

"But she was still their mom, and to them—"

"Yeah, they lost their mother—I see that. But I'm hoping that when they're grown and they look back on things, they might remember the fits and rants Laurel threw. The broken dishes when she was mad for no good reason. Her stomping on toys and breaking them if they weren't put away when she wanted them put away. All her griping and complaining and screaming that she hated her life and all of us along with it. Her saying that Rust Creek Falls was worse than living in hell…"

Nina also took offense to that opinion of her hometown, the hometown that everyone was working so hard to rebuild. But she didn't say it. Instead she said, "I guess not everyone is cut out for living in a place like Rust Creek—I know I've seen my share of people who can't wait to get out."

"Yeah. Sure," he agreed. "But for me…I love it here— even though it does hold way too many memories of Laurel."

"I love it here, too," Nina chimed in. "I can't imagine ever living anywhere else. Or a better place to raise kids."

"If we can just get it back on its feet…"

"It's coming along," Nina said, knowing he was changing the subject.

She could tell he thought he might have said too much about his ex-wife and the problems they'd had, and that he wanted to rein that in some. And since getting off the subject softened his expression, Nina also thought it better to put the conversation to rest.

Besides, he was looking at her with eyes that were no longer clouded by anger or frustration or hurt when they stopped talking about his marriage, and that was nice. Eyes that were warm and full of something else entirely, and it made her melt a little inside…

Then he seemed to snap out of that, too, and maybe remember himself because all of a sudden he said, "Could the Traubs and their sordid history have dragged this night down any worse?"

Oddly enough, Nina realized that she wouldn't have traded a moment of it for anything. But she didn't quite know how to say that when her time with him and his boys had seen some pain for them all.

So she just said, "It wasn't so bad. It was better than a lot of Friday nights I've spent."

"Now you're just being nice," he said as if he appreciated it nonetheless. "But I should probably get going— I've boo-hooed us right into a late night."

He stood then. "Speaking of getting Rust Creek Falls back on its feet, though—you're delivering the toys and food baskets tomorrow, right?"

There had been talk of that on Wednesday night during the compiling of the baskets and the wrapping of the gifts, so it came as no surprise that he knew it.

"I am," Nina confirmed, standing, too.

"Well, the boys will be ice fishing all morning and then my folks are taking them into Kalispell to do some shopping, to have dinner and see a Christmas movie, so I'm on my own and I'd like to help."

"Deliver toys and baskets?"

"You. I'd like to help *you* deliver toys and baskets."

As much as it heated her up a few more degrees to hear that, it also set off an alarm in her. She liked this guy more and more with every minute they spent together, and that just shouldn't be happening. Now, of all times, she should be totally focused on the coming of her baby, on preparing for bringing her baby home, on her own future as a single parent. She should not be focusing on a man.

But it would be nice to have help tomorrow...

"I was thinking," he went on, "that my going along would also give me a chance to see what's happening with some of the still-struggling folks around here. I'd like to make sure they aren't being overlooked by the reconstruction teams."

She could hardly say no to that, could she?

Instead she said, "Okay…"

"Just tell me when you were planning to start, I'll come over and load the back of my truck, and we'll do some early Christmas giving."

Nina told him the time as he put his coat back on and they headed for her apartment door.

When they'd reached it, Dallas turned that lopsided smile to her and said, "Still no heartburn?"

Nina laughed. "None. You?"

"Threatening," he admitted, making her laugh even more.

"You know what they say about your thirties—your digestion slows down," she teased him.

He laughed. "I don't think anybody says that. And it's more likely caused by you getting the damned hottest wings that place sells."

She pointed to herself. "Not thirty, no heartburn." Then to him. "Over thirty, heartburn." Then she shrugged as if she'd proven her point.

He laughed again. "You know, you're just a little bit evil."

"As long as it's just a little bit…"

"Yeah, I wouldn't have it any other way," he confessed.

Then there it was—Nina was thinking about him kissing her again. Out of the blue. For no rational reason. Involuntarily.

Ahh, this is crazy, she lamented.

But it was still there.

Enough so that she felt her chin tip up to him, her eyes look more deeply into his, her lips part…

Stop, stop, a voice in her head shouted.

But he was coming closer. Bending slightly. Aiming…

He was going to do it. He was going to kiss her! And, oh, but she wanted him to!

Then he kissed her all right.

But he detoured and landed one on the tip of her nose.

And it wasn't enough.

It just wasn't.

She tilted her chin higher still and she kissed him.

Barely.

Briefly.

A mere brush of her lips to his. Not actually enough to give her more than a hint of what a real kiss from him might be, but still, she kissed him.

And then she looked into those blue eyes and noticed that his eyebrows were not arched high.

But he didn't say anything. He just smiled a very slow smile as he straightened up and said, "I'll see you around eight tomorrow morning to load up and we'll get on the road by nine."

Nina could only nod and say good-night before he left.

Before he left her to the voice in her head shrieking, *I kissed him! I kissed him!*

Then she told herself in no uncertain terms that a person who was eight-plus months pregnant had no business going around kissing men. Especially not Traubs.

But despite that, she was having trouble regretting it.

And she couldn't help wishing she'd done a better job of it when she'd had the chance…

Chapter Six

"Is this perfect timing or what? Breakfast!" Dallas said when he went in the back door of his parents' house at seven o'clock on Saturday morning.

"Ellie Traub, you're a saint," he added, setting the bag he'd brought in on the floor and taking off his coat to hang on a hook behind the door before leaning over to give his mother a peck on the cheek.

She was standing at the counter, coffeepot in hand. That greeting and the impromptu kiss he didn't ordinarily bestow had stalled her midpour. "Aren't you chipper this morning," she marveled.

"Suns out melting the snow, the sky is as clear a blue as you could want, the air is crisp—it's a beautiful day."

His father's head pivoted slowly in his direction. Bob Traub took off his reading glasses, set down his newspaper and stared at his son.

"And I'm starving and that bacon smells fantastic!" Dallas announced.

His mother finished pouring coffee and reached into the cupboard for another cup for Dallas.

"There's not only bacon, there's sausage, scrambled eggs, hash browns, and toast and jam, too," she informed him, listing what was already prepared and piled on platters in the center of the kitchen table. "You're lucky there's anything left—Braden and your boys were already here to eat before they went out to the lake."

There was still plenty left. Having raised six sons, Ellie Traub had long ago gotten into the habit of cooking enough to feed an army.

Dallas took the chair he'd sat in at every meal growing up, joining his father while his mother got him a plate, napkin and silverware, and served him that steaming cup of coffee.

"There's cheese and peppers in the eggs, and hot sauce if you want it," his mother said as she sat down across from him, watching him.

The mention of hot sauce reminded him of Nina and the hot wings and the night before. And the fact that she'd kissed him...

"Eggs and hot sauce make you happy?" his mom asked, sounding puzzled.

Dallas hadn't realized that he was smiling until that moment. But he couldn't seem to stop it. Not with the thought that in an hour he was going to be with Nina again. All day long.

"It's nothing," he answered, heaping food on his plate.

He ate heartily, complimenting his mother's cooking and his father's new choice of chicken feed for producing an improvement in the flavor of the eggs.

"And this coffee," he said after a sip of it. "Is there something different about it? It's great!"

"Same coffee, made the same way," his mother informed him, watching him even more intently.

"Jam's your mother's, though," his father said. "Delicious even though we had to use Colorado peaches because the flood did so much damage to the fruit trees around here."

Taking his father's comment as a recommendation, Dallas slathered the homemade peach jam on his toast, nodding as he did at the grocery sack near the door. "There's that change of clothes you wanted for the boys, Mom. Shoes, too. You're thinking that they'll be back from fishing around noon and you'll head for Kalispell?"

"If they make it until noon," his father piped up. "Last time I took those boys out on the ice the cold got to them after a couple of hours, and we had to come back. I'm betting they'll be here by ten and we'll be having lunch in Kalispell."

"The drive should be good, though. No bad weather on the horizon. A really, really beautiful day!" Dallas said.

"Chipper," his mother said to his father. "He's chipper."

Bob Traub shrugged. "He's in a good mood."

"For the first time in a year. He's been down-in-the-mouth and mopey, and none of us could get him out of it, and now, all of a sudden—"

"I'm sitting right here and the two of you are talking about me as if I'm invisible," Dallas said with a laugh.

Neither of his parents commented. Instead, his mother looked at him again and said, "What are your plans for today and tonight, with the boys off your hands?"

A dicey question. He considered lying. But he was a

grown man, and it was his own business how he spent his time.

Besides, it was likely that word would get back to them about what he was actually going to do today, and he'd just get caught.

"Thought I'd help deliver the Christmas gifts and food baskets going out from that Santa's Workshop deal," he said as if there wasn't any Crawford connection.

But both of his parents paused their breakfasts to look at him as if he'd just grown gills.

"That's that thing coming from Crawford's General Store," his mother said. "Where you went the other night to help wrap presents…"

"Yep."

Then from his father, "Braden said that Crawford girl was with you and the boys last night."

"*Nina*—the boys knew her by name. Said they've been to her house…" his mother added.

"They've been to her *apartment*—she lives over the store. She wanted to thank me for that whole blizzard mishap."

Dallas saw one of his mother's eyebrows raise. "She's the pregnant Crawford, isn't she?" Ellie Traub said with a note of alarm in her voice.

Dallas had finished eating and sat back with his hand around his coffee cup. He knew all the negatives. Nina was a Crawford. She was pregnant. She was only twenty-five. Top all of that off with the fact that he had three kids, was still stinging some from Laurel leaving him and that he'd spent the past year just about as down on marriage and relationships and women in general as anyone could be, and there was nothing about what was happening with Nina that made any sense.

And yet...

He just couldn't seem to help himself. He couldn't seem to force himself to stay away from her. She made him feel good. And it was such a relief after the past year of feeling rotten....

"Yes, Nina is the pregnant Crawford," he answered his mother's question belatedly. And more somberly than anything he'd said since coming in the back door.

"Is she the reason you're in a better mood?" his mother persisted, sounding even more alarmed.

"The boys were cheerier, too, now that I think about it," his father observed before Dallas had a chance to answer.

"Because of *her?*" Ellie Traub demanded.

Dallas understood where the outrage in his mother's tone was coming from. She'd gone to great lengths to make things as normal and upbeat as possible for her grandsons since Laurel had disappeared, to do everything she could to make them happy. Of course it would hurt Ellie's feelings if she thought someone else had been more successful at it, let alone a Crawford.

And addressing that gave Dallas a way of avoiding the subject of whether or not Nina was responsible for his own lighter spirits.

"The boys are just looking forward to Christmas and being out of school for winter break after this week. And you're doing things like taking them to Kalispell today— that's what's making them cheerier."

"But you? Is that Crawford girl the reason you're in a better mood?" his mother demanded.

"Maybe it's just time passing," Bob Traub suggested to his wife.

But Dallas decided in that moment that he wasn't going to mislead them so he said, "I know Nina is a Crawford and around here the Crawfords are the enemy. But…I don't know…there's nothing wrong with her that I can see. She's a decent, kind, warm—"

"You like her," his mother accused him.

But, Dallas noted, with shock rather than rancor suddenly.

And so he admitted more than he even wanted to admit to himself.

"I do like her. She's a nice person."

"That's it? That's all there is to it?" his father asked hopefully.

"That's it," Dallas said because that *needed* to be all that was going on with Nina. "And she's doing a good thing with this Santa's Workshop deal, so I wanted to help out. Her friends and neighbors are our friends and neighbors, too, and making sure they have Christmas this year is important, no matter what."

He knew his parents agreed, and that was why they had nothing to say to it.

But after a moment his father said, "That girl *is* a Crawford though…"

"And an unwed mother," Ellie Traub cautioned.

Dallas sighed. "And if I don't take off I'm going to be late," he said, standing and taking his dishes to the sink.

As he got into his coat, he thanked them in advance for the boys' outing to Kalispell and told them to drive safely, that he'd be waiting when they got home this evening.

But it was really the time between now and then that he was thinking about. That he was looking forward to. The time he was about to spend with Nina.

* * *

Nina had not been excited by the prospect of delivering the food baskets and Santa's Workshop gifts. She hated that the flood had left so much need for the community and she was dreading seeing people she knew and liked still struggling in the aftermath. Especially at this time of year.

But sharing the chore with Dallas made all the difference. And not just because he did all the heavy work.

He approached each household like a friend making any ordinary Christmas visit to say hello and drop off a holiday token of that friendship. There was no air of charity to any of it—that was something Nina had set out to do, and she appreciated that Dallas offered that same attitude. But in the process he still managed to glean important information about how people were faring.

While Nina mostly chatted with the women of the households to learn their viewpoints and continuing difficulties, Dallas ended up on many tours that exhibited what progress—or lack of progress—had been made on houses or outlying properties. And several times Nina heard him make promises of his own services or resources after the holidays.

Together they came away with a lengthy list to pass along to the reconstruction crews and the other recovery efforts for special attention to things that were being overlooked or for additional needs that should be met. They made a good team—that was what occurred to Nina as the day progressed.

A good team. A twosome.

But not a couple—that was something that she had to keep reminding herself. They were *not* a couple.

Even though that was how it felt as they spent the

day driving around together, chatting, comparing notes, sharing snacks—some that Nina hand-fed to Dallas as he drove—and then stopping to pay their joint visits.

It also struck her that in her entire four years with Leo she'd never had a day quite like that one and never felt as connected and as couplish as she did with Dallas.

But regardless of how it seemed—or felt—to her, they were not a couple.

A good team, yes—something else she'd never experienced with Leo.

A twosome—only for the day.

But not a couple.

Even if she had kissed him the night before.

Which she was determined should—and would—never happen again.

It was after seven that evening before the last of the baskets and gifts were delivered. As they headed back to the General Store and Nina's apartment, Dallas said, "That was a long day."

"It was," Nina agreed, sounding as weary as she felt. Ordinarily she had energy to spare, but she'd spent most of the previous night awake, worrying about that kiss even as she relived it again and again. So she was running on about four hours of sleep.

"I'm not much of a cook," he said conversationally, making her think of the TV dinners she'd seen at his place when she'd brought the Christmas tree. "But I do have one specialty—chicken in a butter and lemon sauce that I serve over linguine. Could I interest you in that for dinner tonight?"

"You want to cook me dinner?" Nina asked tentatively, unsure if he was serious.

"I do," he said firmly. "I'd like to fix you dinner, share

it with you, then clean up the mess—all while you sit with your feet up, a beverage of your choice in hand and watch without lifting a finger."

"You'd *like* to do all that," she said dubiously, ignoring how wonderful it sounded to her. "Why, when you've just had as long a day as I've had?"

"Because all I've seen you do since the blizzard is work your little tail off, and today topped everything. I keep wondering when you get to be pampered. You do so much for everyone else, despite being pregnant—even though you don't look it—and it seems to me that there should be someone else doing something for you every now and then. And tonight I'd like it if you'd let it be me."

"Really?" Had her worries overnight that he might have hated her kissing him been for naught?

"Really. Play Cleopatra on the Throne and let me pamper you tonight."

"I don't have anything in gold lamé," she warned, telling herself to say no to this, to let today end now, but incapable of finding one whit of willpower to actually do that.

"I just want you comfortable. You can wear your bathrobe if you want."

"To a fancy dinner made just for me? Never!"

He cast her a half grin. "I didn't promise fancy, just chicken and linguine."

Nina laughed at him. "Okay. It sounds good," she conceded.

He pulled into a parking spot behind the store, near the back stairs to the outside entrance of her apartment, and turned off the truck engine.

"Then you go upstairs while I go shopping downstairs, and we'll do this," he instructed.

But that's all they'd be doing, Nina silently told herself. A simple dinner. Between people who were maybe becoming friends instead of enemies.

But nothing more than friends.

Friends who didn't kiss each other good-night…

"Okay, enough! Your dinner was delicious, my kitchen is spotless, now come and sit down—you're making me feel guilty," Nina insisted an hour and a half later when Dallas had accomplished all he'd set out to do for her.

He put one final touch into polishing her faucet then folded the dish towel he'd used, set it on the counter and swept an arm in the direction of her living room so she would lead the way.

Nina did, going to sit on one end of her couch, facing the center of it with her feet tucked under her.

Dallas sat more toward the center, angled in her direction and stretching a long arm across the top of the back cushion to more or less face her. "I can't believe I forgot dessert," he lamented for the third time since he'd realized his oversight.

"I'm glad you did—I'm stuffed and you've already spoiled me rotten."

"Someone should," he said.

"Oh, absolutely. I'm all for it," she joked.

"I'm serious."

She could tell that he was, too—it was reflected in his expression. But he was so ruggedly gorgeous; the stern, stoic lines on his face only accentuated it and made Nina smile.

Undaunted, he went on anyway. "You should have some help this late in the game and then a lot more once you bring the baby home. Aren't there parts of doing this on your own that are a little tough on you?"

Nina shrugged. "My family helps where they can, and I know I can always call if I need more."

"That's not the same as having a husband or the father of the baby to lean on day-to-day."

"Having a husband or the father of the baby around wouldn't guarantee that I'd have someone to help," Nina insisted. "I know for a fact that Leo wouldn't have, even if the baby was his."

The lines on Dallas's face deepened into a frown. "Like I said during the blizzard, I knew Leo, but just as a guy who worked for us here and there. I didn't really *know* him. You thought he was a waste of time..."

"My time *with* him was wasted," she amended. "After four years of *somedays* that never came."

"Somedays?"

"Whenever I'd ask if we were headed for marriage, for having a family, he'd say, 'Sure, someday...'"

"But he was just leading you on?"

"I don't know. I'd like to believe that he at least thought he meant it when he said it. Otherwise it sort of makes me a dumb sap for having believed him, and it's bad enough that I came away from that whole time with him feeling like...I don't know, like his minion..."

That made Dallas smile. "His *minion?*"

"Well, I did pretty much do his bidding."

"Ohh, that doesn't sound good."

"Leo was ten years older and that put me at a disadvantage. Especially the longer we were together. Leo was a creature of habit... I guess maybe we all tend toward that, but he loved to say he was set in his ways, that he needed his *routines,* that he'd been doing things the way he'd been doing them for years and years and couldn't change, that because I was so much younger I could be more flexible—"

"He's about the same age I am," Dallas said defensively, as if the other man's point of view didn't make sense to him.

But to Nina the fact that Dallas and Leo were about the same age was still noteworthy and she reminded herself not to lose sight of that.

"I have never said I'm set in my ways," Dallas claimed.

"But I'm sure you have habits, routines, things you've been doing the way you want to do them for years and years," Nina pushed.

"Sure, but like *you* just said, everybody does," Dallas countered.

"And everybody wants them to be adapted to, and with Leo, our age difference meant that—"

"He got his way and you didn't."

"Yes," Nina confirmed because that *was* what it had boiled down to.

"And you attribute that to him being a lot older than you are…"

"I loved him, and it just did seem easier for me to adapt to him. To him it was a big deal if we ate where and what and when he wanted to eat because if we didn't he didn't feel well. If I pushed him to do something I wanted to do, and he didn't enjoy it, he was cranky, he complained, and I didn't end up enjoying it, either. If he wanted to stay in and I made him go out there was yawning and moaning, and there was no telling where he might fall asleep—he actually did that in his chair at the table during a dinner party with one of my friends—"

"Wow. He really made sure it was all on his terms. So

you just, what? Put whatever you wanted—or needed—on the back burner?"

"For the most part it wasn't a big deal to me—*for me*—to adapt. Especially when he just…couldn't. And I kept telling myself that it was all only small stuff, anyway. If he came home from work tired and I didn't…well, I was a lot younger, I had more energy, more stamina, I figured when I was ten years older I'd probably feel the same way—"

"So you took care of him."

"And I tried not to pressure him. It wasn't as if I could *force* him to be younger and have more energy or stamina. Or if he had to eat what and when he had to eat, so what? But I made it clear that I wanted to get married, to have kids—"

"And that was where the *somedays* came in."

"Right."

"And when you pushed for that? Is that what ended the relationship?"

"I suppose you could say that was when *my* age became an issue. When I reached the time when I'd planned to start a family I told him so—"

"But *someday* still hadn't come for him?"

"No, he finally didn't just put me off—I suppose I should give him credit for that. He said that the more he thought about, the more he thought he just wasn't cut out for marriage and kids. He loved me and all—that's what he said—and it wasn't me. He said that he was perfectly happy going on the way we had been. But marriage and family just weren't for him."

"Did he think you might accept that?" Dallas asked, as if he thought the other guy was deluded.

"There was a part of him that seemed to…I don't

know…hold out hope for it, maybe. Because he tried to talk me into going on the way we had been. But I wouldn't." Nina stated the simple fact. "It was one thing to eat a hamburger at five when I might have wanted pizza at seven, or to watch an action movie when I would rather have seen the romantic comedy. But when it came to getting married, to having a baby… Well, that was my life we were talking about."

"It was time to draw the line," Dallas concluded, his tone compassionate and sympathetic, making it clear that he understood that it hadn't been as easy for her as it might sound.

"Yes," Nina confirmed quietly, more emotion creeping into her voice than she'd allowed before. But it *hadn't* been easy to accept that *someday* was never going to come with Leo. That she could either have Leo or the life she'd always wanted, but that she couldn't have them both. That those four years had been squandered with him.

It hadn't been easy to open her eyes and realize that she had to make a choice between postponing the family she wanted until she found someone else—all the while running the risk that she might not find someone else—or having that family on her own. Without anyone to help out with the day-to-day or to pamper her the way Dallas had tonight…

"So, that was it?" Dallas asked, interrupting her thoughts both with his words and by raising his hand from the top of the sofa back and using an index finger to gently follow the curve of the side of her face. "You ended it with Leo?"

"I did."

"I'm thinking that he might not have taken it too well,

since he left town—which is a really big change for someone *set in his ways*."

"My ending things actually did seem to shock him."

Dallas's smile was lazy and kind. "Well, you had set
a precedent of giving him his way."

"I know. I had. I guess I just thought that we'd eventually end up on the same page—"

"That *someday* would come."

"Right. That, given time, he'd *want* to marry me. He'd
want to have kids with me. Instead, the longer things
went on and the older he'd gotten, the further he'd also
gotten away from marriage and wanting to become a
father." She shrugged again. "I didn't really see until
then just how much the age difference put us at different places in our lives, which was a much bigger thing
than just not being on the same page. For Leo, the ship
had just sailed on a time to get married and start having
kids, and I couldn't change that—"

"Any more than you could give him more energy or
stamina."

Nina shrugged yet again. "Age *does* make a difference.
Look at you and me—you have *three* kids. You're done
with the baby stuff, you're on to the kids-in-school stuff. I
haven't even changed my first diaper and you're probably
thinking that you're glad never to change another one."

Dallas chuckled but didn't deny it.

Which cemented Nina's feelings that she had to be
very careful not to get in too deep with yet another man
at a stage of life different than her own.

"So no. If this was Leo's baby? I'd still be having
to adapt to Leo," Nina concluded, ending where they'd
begun this conversation.

"Yeah, but I'm still not sure that, with Leo, that wasn't

as much an age issue as a personality issue," Dallas postulated.

"Sure, that had to be a part of it, too—lots of people, men and women, don't get married or start families until they're in their thirties. Or later. But still…"

But still she also knew that a big age difference couldn't be discounted, that more years brought with them more baggage and deeper roots—like Dallas's own long-term history with his ex-wife and the scars left by the end of it, and the children who also now had to be a factor. Or her own child who would become a consideration she hadn't had before.

"But still, age is an issue," Dallas finished for her when she stalled. "Getting married and having kids at her age made Laurel feel as if she'd missed out on too much. Age plays a role, in one way or another, with us all, whether we like it or not."

"It just does…"

"And so for you and Leo, that was it? You ended things with him at a time when you wanted to start your family and you just went for it." He nodded in the direction of her bulging middle.

"Yep," she confirmed.

"On your own…"

"Yep."

He nodded his head slowly, acceptingly, without any indication of disapproval that she could see.

Then he said, "That takes a lot of courage. I gotta say, I admire it. And you're one hell of a lesson to me."

Nina laughed. "Are you telling me that the young pup is teaching the old dog new tricks?" she teased good-naturedly.

"Yeah," he said, laughing, too. "Watching you has

been like a kick in the pants. I've been wallowing for the past year and here you are—you had your own disappointment and disillusionment, and you picked yourself up and went right on. Seeing it is letting me know that it's time for me to walk off my own disappointments and disillusionments. To stop letting them hold me back. To move on."

He was still running his index finger along the side of her face in a featherlight stroke that was soothing and arousing at once, sending something glittery all through her to make talking about Leo less depressing.

Then that finger reached the corner of her jawbone and slipped around it to come under her chin and tip it up.

And it wasn't only his life he was moving on with, because he moved on to kissing her...

At first Nina was taken off guard, and she thought again that he must not have hated the fact that she'd kissed him the night before.

Then all she could think about was the kiss that was happening at that moment.

A genuine kiss that lingered long enough for her to relish it.

And, oh, did she...

His lips were wonderful—soft and warm and lush. They were parted just slightly and his head swayed like a palm frond in a tropical breeze. The whole thing seemed to pick her up and carry her away to something so much nicer than what they'd been talking about, answering the yearning in her that she'd felt since he'd first kissed her during the blizzard. The yearning that had only been worse since the night before. The yearning that she didn't want to have but couldn't seem to stop no matter how hard she tried.

The yearning that wasn't at all stifled when that kiss came to an end a moment later.

She opened her eyes to Dallas's handsome face hovering just above hers, those same lips in one of his single-sided smiles, his gray-blue eyes studying her as if he liked what he saw.

"To moving on," he toasted in a deep, gravelly voice.

"To moving on," Nina seconded, feeling dazed and just wanting him to kiss her again.

But he didn't. He took a deep breath that expanded his barrel chest and sighed with what sounded like resignation.

Then he said, "I'd better go. I have to be home when my folks bring the boys back."

Nina raised her chin higher in concession to that.

"But tomorrow night is the Candlelight Walk," he continued. "I'm gonna make sure that the boys experience every bit of Christmas festivity there is from now until the big day, so I told them we could go. I'd like it if you'd come with us—and I have a plan for getting you down Main Street since I wouldn't make you walk it."

All of Rust Creek Falls was invited to light a candle at one end of Main Street and parade with those candles to the opposite end where a bonfire was to be lit, carols were to be sung and refreshments would be served. It seemed as if the community had grown so much closer since the flood, and the city council had organized the walk as a method of bringing everyone together as the family of Rust Creek Falls before each separate family began their own private celebrations.

"You have a plan to get me down Main Street," Nina reiterated. "You don't think I can walk? You think I need a crane?"

He grinned, standing and making a show of helping her to her feet.

"It's a surprise," he said, rather than answering her accusation and affront.

"What if I say no?" she challenged as he put on his coat and they headed for her back door.

"Then you'll ruin the surprise."

There was that little bit of cockiness about him that was too delicious for her to resist.

"So don't say no," he added at the door with a challenge of his own.

Nina considered that his kiss and the continuing yearning for another one might be clouding her judgment.

But he had her intrigued.

And her own family had already decided to forego the walk because her parents and two of her brothers were helping out in the store all day tomorrow and wanted to just go home after closing, so she hadn't planned to go, either.

Only now she could.

With Dallas...

"Well, I wouldn't want to ruin a surprise," she finally conceded.

"Great! The candle lighting is at seven, so I'll be here about fifteen minutes before that."

"Crane and all?"

"Crane and all," he said, taking his turn at teasing her.

Then, with his hands in his coat pockets he leaned forward and kissed her again—a kiss as good as the earlier one had been—before he said, "Thanks for today."

Nina laughed. "*You* did me the favor by driving and helping out with the deliveries, then *you* made me dinner and cleaned the whole mess. Thank *you!*"

"I'm just glad I got to spend today and tonight with you. You're my inspiration, remember?" he added.

"Ah, that's right. Because I'm so *inspirational*," she joked.

His smoky-blue eyes delved deeply into hers. "More than you know," he seemed to confide.

Then he kissed her once more—barely, the way she'd kissed him the previous night—and went out into the cold.

And once Nina had closed the door behind him she stayed where she was, wrapping her arms around her pregnant belly, basking in the warm feelings that Dallas Traub had left her with.

Chapter Seven

With only three days until Christmas, and Sunday the last weekend day before the holiday, Nina knew the store would be swamped. She and all of her staff and extra holiday personnel were scheduled, and she'd also asked her parents to come in.

Todd and Laura Crawford were semiretired, handling primarily behind-the-scenes business for the store now—ordering merchandise and doing the bookkeeping. But for Nina and the holiday they'd agreed to work the floor.

Nina expected them to arrive just before the store opened. She didn't expect them to arrive just as she was sitting down to breakfast.

"Have you eaten? I can scramble a few more eggs and make extra toast," she offered as they took off their coats.

"We ate," her mother answered, but both of her parents accepted glasses of orange juice as they sat at her small kitchen table and encouraged her to eat while her food was hot.

"We came early because we wanted to talk to you," her mother added as Nina put butter and jelly on her toast. "We've been hearing a lot about you and Dallas Traub."

"What's going on with that?" her father demanded.

"I've seen him a few times since the blizzard. He's helped out with the Santa's Workshop things—"

"From what we're hearing it sounds more like you're dating him," her mother accused, clearly not happy with the idea.

"I wouldn't say we were *dating.*" Nina balked at that term herself, despite the fact that the evening at the snow castle and the plan for the Candlelight Walk couldn't really be called anything else. "But we are—" she wasn't sure how to describe what they were and settled on "—friends, I guess."

"You're *friends* with a Traub?" her mother said as if even that was repugnant.

"I don't know why that's so awful to you," Nina responded, thinking that maybe she could reason with them. "After everything that Dallas did for me during the blizzard—"

"He ran you off the road." Her father again.

"I ran myself off the road. And him, too. And since then he's not only wanted to know how I'm doing, he's volunteered—"

"To get next to you," her mother insisted. "The Traubs are probably angling for something—"

"What could they possibly be *angling* for?"

"That's the problem," her father picked up where her mother had left off. "You don't *know* what they're angling for until they stab you in the back."

"Dallas is not positioning himself to stab me in the back," Nina asserted, unable to even imagine that.

"Maybe you don't know the Traubs like we do," her father suggested.

"Maybe you don't know them the way you think you do. I haven't heard anything that makes them sound any different than we are," Nina informed her parents firmly.

"No different than we are?" Her mother nearly shrieked as if that was inconceivable. "Have you forgotten the election?"

"I haven't forgotten that, like all politics, there was mudslinging from both sides," Nina reminded them pointedly.

"She's siding with the enemy," her father said to her mother.

Nina closed her eyes in frustration and shook her head. "*Why* are we enemies?" she demanded. "What do we really have to be enemies about? They run a ranch, we have a store—we're not business competitors. Yes, I'm sorry that Nate lost the election for mayor, but there have been other elections where a Crawford won and a Traub lost. And losing didn't ruin Nate's life. Nothing that I can think of about the Traubs has ruined any Crawford's life unless it was so long ago no one can even remember. So what's the big deal? They're regular people just like us—"

"Oh, my God, are you getting *involved* with Dallas Traub?" Laura Crawford said in horror.

Involved...

Did kissing count as that? Or wanting to kiss him again? Or finding herself beginning to crave more than kissing...?

No, she couldn't be getting *involved* with Dallas, Nina told herself. Becoming friends was one thing. Making any sort of headway in ending this ridiculous feud would be a good thing. But involved?

"No, I'm not getting *involved* with Dallas," she answered her mother's question in no uncertain terms because it needed not to be true.

He was too old for her. He might not think he was set in his ways but he had responsibilities that made it impossible for him *not* to be rooted in any number of obligations. A woman coming into his life would have to do plenty of adapting. Adapting that Nina wasn't willing to do yet again.

Especially not now, when she had her own baby to look forward to, to be responsible for, to become set in her own ways with without dragging that baby into a situation where it would have to adapt, too.

"But we also aren't enemies," Nina went on, deciding to be honest with her parents about that. "If you all want to go on hating a whole group of people just because somewhere a million years ago other Crawfords got into it with the Traubs, that's your business. But I can't for the life of me see why our families should be *feuding*. Just saying the word seems silly."

Todd looked at his wife and said, "She won't think it's silly when this Traub or another one does something spiteful or vengeful or just plain down-and-dirty to her."

"And one or another of them will," Laura agreed with her husband but aimed her comment at Nina. "And what worries me is that this time it's getting personal and you could get hurt. You and the baby…"

Nina sighed. "Dallas *saved* me and the baby. You think he would turn around and do something to hurt us now?"

"I think if you're having some kind of feelings for him it could very well happen, yes," Laura said direly. "Maybe that's his game—to suck you in with false charms and then kick you in the teeth and laugh about it."

Dallas was definitely charming. But there was nothing false about it. And as for the thought that he might be playing her, luring her in so he could do something to hurt her later? That was just ridiculous, and if her mother had been on the other side of those kisses the previous evening the way Nina had, Laura would know just how ludicrous it was.

"Why would he do something like that?" Nina asked, her tone reflecting the absurdity of it. "That doesn't even make sense. You think anyone would spend time *luring* one of us in just to be mean and then laugh about it later?"

"A Traub would," her father contended firmly and without the slightest doubt.

Nina could only roll her eyes. She had reasons enough not to get involved with Dallas, they just weren't the reasons her parents clung to. But since she *did* have reasons of her own, and since she could see that her parents weren't going to budge in their hatred of the Traubs— yet another reason why she knew she couldn't let things with Dallas go too far—she decided to stop arguing it.

"You don't have to worry," she told her parents as she took her breakfast dishes to the sink. "My path and Dallas's have crossed a few times, we are *not* enemies and I won't let you talk me into being enemies with him. But there isn't anything going on between us."

If kissing didn't count.

Except that it had counted.

A whole lot...

But she tried not to think about that. And vowed that it wouldn't happen again, telling herself that—for her reasons if not for her family's—she should probably start keeping some distance from him after tonight's Candle-light Walk.

Because she'd already agreed to that. And she really wanted to go. And to see what kind of surprise he had for her.

But after that? Separate corners. She swore it.

For now, though, all Nina could do was announce that it was time they went down to the store and open up.

Thinking that no matter what it was that had the Craw-fords and the Traubs hating each other, it seemed insur-mountable.

As promised, Dallas arrived to pick up Nina for the Candlelight Walk just before seven that night. When she heard the knock on her back door she called for him to come in while she put on her final layer—a calf-length, double-breasted wool coat that she was wearing over her warmest knee-high boots, navy blue wool leggings, and a matching heavyweight turtleneck tunic.

As Dallas opened her unlocked door and stepped over the threshold she said, "Hi. Almost ready," and pulled a navy blue and white tweed knit cap over her free-falling hair before putting on the matching scarf and gloves.

"Good—you're dressed nice and warm," he said, giv-ing her the once-over and a smile that said he approved. And liked what he saw.

"You look warm, too." And she liked what she saw just as much—he was wearing boots, jeans and a brown henley sweater over a tan turtleneck T-shirt that were all barely visible underneath his shearling-lined suede coat.

"My truck is parked in front of the store but I had some help bringing your surprise, and that's out back," he said with a grin.

"Then let's go," Nina said.

Her surprise was waiting for them at the foot of her back steps—a horse-drawn sleigh.

"She's a two-seater bobsleigh," Dallas informed her as he followed Nina down the stairs. "The swan body shape makes her an Albany."

Polished bronze sides and a swooping back surrounded two fairly narrow rows of tufted black velvet seats, front and back. The three Traub boys were sitting close together in the rear to fit, and Robbie was bouncing up and down in his excitement.

"Lookit this," he commanded Nina. "I din't even know we had it! It's like Santa's sleigh!"

"It's beautiful, isn't it?" she answered the smallest boy's enthusiasm with some of her own, taking in the sight of the red ribbon–wrapped pine boughs attached to the gracefully curved top edge, and more red ribbons braided into the reins.

"That's Toad and Trina pullin' us." Robbie introduced the horses, whose harnesses bore bells and more red ribbons.

"Hi, Ryder. Hi, Jake. Hi, Toad and Trina," Nina greeted them.

"Hi," the other boys responded in unison, both of them sitting up straight enough to make it clear they were excited, too. Particularly Ryder, who held the reins as if he'd been given a very important responsibility.

"Come on, let's go!" Jake urged.

"Okay, okay, hold your horses," Dallas said, making an obvious joke as he offered a leather-gloved hand for Nina to take so he could help her into the sleigh.

"We'll have the candlelight ride rather than the candlelight walk?" Nina took that hand, and regretted his glove and hers keeping her from too much sensation.

"We will," he confirmed as she sat on the plush seat.

Dallas went around the rear to get into the other side. Because the sleigh wasn't wide they were arm to arm, and Nina had to resist the urge to snuggle in even closer.

Then Dallas turned to get the reins from Ryder and Nina said, "There's no snowpack left on Main Street—is this going to work?"

"I won't say it's good for the runners but I waxed them pretty heavily and we won't be going far, so it should be okay."

A tap of the reins on the horses' backs and the animals took them from behind Crawford's General Store onto Sawmill Street and around to Main.

The store was at the high end of Main—which was what had spared it from the flood damage—and most of the town was gathering there, lighting candles and getting ready to start the walk.

Dallas pulled up behind the crowd and sent Ryder for two of the candles that were being given out by the city council. When Ryder returned with them, Dallas lit them and set them in holders nestled amid the ribbon-wrapped boughs on the front corners of the sleigh.

"Isn't that pretty?" Nina asked, angling her comment and her own enthusiasm toward the boys in back and making sure they could see.

Minutes later the walk began, and again Dallas urged the horses to move, setting them to a very slow pace. Up ahead the parade of people, all carrying candles, lit the way with the tiny flickers of so many flames casting a beautiful golden glow.

"Oh, this is so nice," Nina breathed, putting her family's feelings about the Traubs to rest for the time being so she could just enjoy the festivities.

The procession down Main Street didn't take long, and when the first of the walkers reached the park where the bonfire was laid in a contained area, Nina craned to watch and said to the boys, "Stand up so you can see—they're lighting the bonfire!"

The sleigh was moving so slowly there was no danger to the boys in standing for the remainder of the ride that took them alongside the park where those of the community who hadn't been inclined to walk down Main Street had parked in advance.

One big *whoosh* and the entire area was alight with flames, causing the crowd to gasp before they cheered and clapped.

After that an announcement was made that there were marshmallows to be toasted, as well as one table where hot chocolate or cider could be had and another that held Christmas goodies of all kinds.

Then the church choir began to sing carols and the crowd started to mingle.

While Nina was the only one of the Crawfords to come, the Traubs had made a good showing. Dallas's parents and brothers Collin, Braden and Sutter were all there. Tense but polite greetings were exchanged with Nina before Dallas allowed the boys to have their way and drag them to roast marshmallows, cutting the encounter blissfully short.

Collin's wife, Willa, and Sutter's fiancée, Paige Dalton, were also with that group and had greeted Nina more warmly. Then, on their way to the beverage table, they made a second stop with Dallas and Nina and the boys. Paige was Ryder's fifth-grade teacher, Willa had Robbie in kindergarten, and they both wanted to wish all three boys a personal Merry Christmas.

As Nina, Dallas and the boys roasted marshmallows in one of many little fires that were lit in small flame-safe boxes around the bonfire, Nina and Dallas exchanged hellos and small talk with local veterinarian Brooks Smith and his new wife, Jazzy.

"Oh, look," Jazzy said after a few minutes of that, "Dean Pritchett and Shelby are here!"

She waved the couple over. Dean Pritchett was a carpenter who had come from Thunder Canyon to help with some of the rebuilding after the flood and fallen in love with substitute teacher and single mom Shelby Jenkins. They joined the group, along with Shelby's daughter, Caitlin, whom Nina shared her marshmallows with.

"And Sheriff!" Dallas said as Gage Christensen and his fiancée, Lissa Roarke, walked up to them, hand in hand.

Gage told Nina he was glad to see that she was doing all right after the blizzard scare, and Nina thanked him again for his help that day.

During Lissa's volunteer work in Rust Creek Falls, she and the sheriff had become involved—and eventually engaged—and now that they were part of the small group, talk just naturally turned to the ongoing flood projects. At least, it did until Shane Roarke brought his marshmallow to their little roasting station.

Shane Roarke was Dallas's cousin and had only recently learned that his father was Thunder Canyon's notorious ex-mayor Arthur Swinton. The notorious Swinton was currently in prison for embezzling funds from Thunder Canyon.

It was common knowledge that Shane and his adopted

siblings, Los Angeles attorneys Maggie and Ryan Roarke, were attempting to get Arthur's prison sentence commuted, so conversation turned to questions about how things were going with that.

Nina only heard, "We're making headway," as the answer to those questions before the three Traub boys, tired of listening to adult conversation, urged Dallas and Nina to take them to the cookie table.

Telling everyone they had to go and exchanging more wishes for a Merry Christmas, Nina and Dallas moved on to the table that held not only cookies but brownies, cakes, cupcakes and fudge.

Each boy was allotted only one choice—and complained about it—before Collin came to tell Dallas that the family had had enough of the cold and was leaving.

"Can we go with 'em? I'm cold, too," Robbie piped up when he heard that.

"Me, too," Jake chimed in.

"Yeah, my feet are freezing," Ryder added.

"Mom!" Dallas called across the distance that his parents were keeping from them. "Can you take the boys home for me? I'll pick them up in a while."

"Sure. Come on," she urged her grandsons. "I want to get going."

Dallas prompted his sons to say good-night to Nina, and then Nina and Dallas both watched as Collin herded them off with the rest of the Traubs.

"It *is* cold," Nina said.

It was the truth. But it was also the truth that she'd had a very long, hard day and was longing to just sit in front of her own fireplace.

"You know, we *could* go back and light a fire at my place, and I could mull us a little cider…"

"You're cold, too," Dallas guessed.

"A little bit."

"Yeah, I'm feeling it myself," he confessed. "So you don't have to ask me twice. Just give me a minute…"

He left Nina standing there while he went to talk to a teenage boy Nina didn't recognize, and then he and the teenager came back.

"Okay, let's go," Dallas said, only mentioning after the fact, on the way to the sleigh, that the teenager who was following them was Tyson, the son of one of his ranch hands.

"Tyson brought the sleigh out for me and he's going to take us to your place in it, then get it home for me." Leaning close to Nina's ear he whispered, "I'm paying him well for his services."

For the trip back to her apartment, Dallas and Nina sat in the rear row while Tyson took the front and the reins.

There was a blanket that the boys had apparently been sitting on, and Dallas opened it over their laps. When he tucked it in around them Nina had a flashback to the blizzard and being alone with him in his truck.

Although it seemed strange that an experience such as a near collision and fearing she was going into premature labor in the middle of nowhere could become a fond memory, it somehow had. And she read that as another sign that things between them might be stretching the boundaries.

But then he settled back with her shoulder cozily against his and told the teenager they were ready, and all Nina could think about was how much she liked being there like that with him.

The return trip to her apartment was much quicker than the procession to the bonfire had been. Then Dallas helped her out of the sleigh, dispatching Tyson to get it home.

Nina led the way up her back steps and into her apartment, the heat there feeling blissful after being out in the cold for so long.

"How are *you* at building a fire?" Nina asked as they took off their outerwear.

"Fires in fireplaces, campfires, bonfires, burning off weeds—seems like I've been building them all my life. Want me to do this one?" he asked, pointing his chin in the direction of her hearth.

"If you would. Kindling and logs are in the bucket right beside it. I'll do the cider and meet you there."

"Sounds like a deal."

Nina left him to it. But because this portion of her apartment was basically one big room, she could steal glimpses of him while she heated and spiced the cider. Hunkered down in front of her fireplace, his thick thighs stretching the denim of his jeans, and his very, very fine derriere resting on the heels of his boots, he was a sexy sight that she cautioned herself against appreciating as much as she was.

But she still couldn't help it. He was just all man— big and brawny and muscular and masculine—and she thought she would have had to be dead not to recognize that fact.

And she definitely wasn't dead. In fact, she knew she was awash in extra hormones that made it especially difficult for the woman in her not to be extraordinarily aware of him.

Still, she tried to tamp down on it as she brought two mugs of steaming cider into the living room, where he had, indeed, built a beautiful fire.

"Oh, that feels good," Nina said as she joined him. "Why don't we move the coffee table and sit on the floor in front of the couch so we can be closer to the fire?"

Agreeing, Dallas held both cups while she eased herself down, tucking her feet to one side and watching as he sat beside her and tasted his cider.

"Mmm, that's perfect," he judged.

Nina took a sip of hers, too, then said, "So, Arthur Swinton..." referring to the man who had become the subject of conversation just before they'd left the marshmallow-toasting station earlier. "I've never been too clear about him. Seems like he was a big shot in Thunder Canyon, then a bad guy who went to jail, then I thought I heard he was dead, then he wasn't, and now people seem to be saying positive things about him again."

"Yeah, that all sounds about right," Dallas answered. "You know we just learned that Shane Roarke—who is Arthur Swinton's biological son—is actually our cousin?"

"I think I did hear something about that," Nina said vaguely.

"Yeah, Shane was raised by adoptive parents, with a brother and a sister who were also adopted. Then he found out that Arthur Swinton was his biological father and that Grace Traub—one of our Thunder Canyon relations—was his biological mother. Grace died a long time ago, but apparently, when she was in her late teens, she was involved with Swinton and got pregnant, then gave the baby up."

"There are Traubs in Thunder Canyon, and here—you guys are all over the place."

"In Texas, too," he said. "But Thunder Canyon was where Swinton was."

Somewhat larger than Rust Creek Falls—and only three hundred or so miles south—Thunder Canyon had prospered in recent years, and because there were many connections between the two towns a number of its residents had gone to great lengths to assist their neighbors in Rust Creek Falls since the flood.

"He was on Thunder Canyon's town council for years and he even ran for mayor a while back. Then somebody figured out that he'd been embezzling funds from Thunder Canyon—"

"Oh, that's right—*that's* why he was in jail," Nina said.

"Swinton wouldn't say what happened to the money or where it was hidden—if it was hidden—"

"And it was rumored that he'd died in jail…"

"Uh-huh. Except that he really just escaped. Then he was recaptured—"

"So, not dead," Nina said, making Dallas laugh.

"No, not dead. And at that point he was pretty widely considered Thunder Canyon's villain. Then folks found out about him having a son—"

"Shane Roarke."

"Right. Shane. But Grace never told Swinton she was pregnant. She went out of town to have Shane and put him up for adoption. When Shane found out Swinton was his father he came from California to Thunder Canyon and let Swinton know. When word got around, public opinion softened for Swinton. There's been some sympathy for him not getting to see his son grow up. Now Shane and his adopted siblings, Ryan and Maggie—who are both attorneys—are working on getting him out of jail."

"I heard some talk about Arthur Swinton raising money for Rust Creek Falls."

"Yeah, Shane claims that he's somehow managed to do that, even from prison. We haven't seen the money yet, but Shane believes that it's a legitimate campaign and that something is going to come of it. As a symbol of Swinton's goodwill."

"I hope for your cousin's sake that that's true. And for Rust Creek Falls' sake, too—we could certainly use the money to help with the reconstruction."

"But the school is about finished. I heard today that it'll be reopening after winter break, which is great. It's getting to be a pain to take all three kids to three different places for their classes."

"I'm sure!" Nina commiserated.

For a moment they sat quietly, enjoying the fire and the cider until their cups were empty and set aside on the floor.

Then Dallas said, "Speaking of school, tomorrow night is the Christmas program. It's always kind of a hoot and makes me feel like Christmas is really here. They're having to do it in the social hall at the church this year, but the boys and I wondered if you might like to see it? It'll give you a preview of Christmases to come," he said with a nod in the direction of her middle.

"I'd love that!" Nina heard herself answer before she'd considered what she was agreeing to, acting solely on impulse. Then she remembered that she'd told herself to start keeping her distance from Dallas and realized this wouldn't aid *that* cause.

"But won't your family be there?" she asked, seizing one of the multiple reasons she'd told herself to keep that distance in the first place.

"Yep," he confirmed with a note of defiance underlying his tone. "But the boys asked me to invite you, so everyone else will just have to deal with it."

The boys had asked her. It wasn't Dallas's idea.

No sooner had that thought crossed Nina's mind than Dallas seemed to read it. He turned to face her, peering into her eyes. Using his index and middle fingers he brushed her hair over her shoulder and confided in a quieter voice, "And how could I deny them when it's what I want, too?"

Looking into that handsome face of his, those gray-blue eyes staring into hers—it was a lethal combination that sank all of Nina's better judgment.

All of it.

Because when he kissed her, she was right there with him, kissing him back. And unable to think about anything except that kiss and that it was what she'd been wanting since the minute he'd stopped kissing her the night before.

And, oh, what a kiss…

Saturday's kiss had been good, but this one was even better. Deeper right from the start.

His mouth was pressed more insistently to hers. His lips were parted farther and more sensuously, and she only realized after the fact that hers were, too.

And then there was his tongue…talented, enticing, tempting hers into a coy fencing match, upping the level of intimacy.

And Nina gave as good as she got, still thinking about nothing but that kiss and him, and how much she just wanted to go on and on kissing him.

Which was what she did. What they did. For a long while. Making out there in front of the fire, things heating up between them that the fire had nothing to do with.

His arms had come around her, her hands were in his hair and he was holding her tightly against him. So tightly that her breasts, fuller these days, were smooshed to his unyielding chest, blissfully pressing into him, her nipples turning to insistent little peaks that she wondered if he could feel. That were beginning to cause her to think about more than the mere pressure of even his rock-solid pectorals.

Oh, yeah, kissing this way was only making her want more!

So much more that it gave Nina pause.

She wasn't even supposed to kiss him again. Let alone for the entire past half hour. And the way they'd been kissing.

Distance, she reminded herself. Separate corners...

Less, not more...

Whether she liked it or not... She drew her hands down, her shoulders back and pushed on Dallas's shoulders. Pushed him away.

And he got the idea.

Reluctantly tongues retreated, leaving mouths to linger for another moment before they parted, too. Before the kissing that Nina wanted never to end, ended anyway.

Dallas took a deep breath and raised his head high enough to tuck hers under his chin, staying that way as he exhaled.

Then he said a musing, "Huh...how'd that happen?" As if he wasn't quite sure what had just carried them away.

"The cider was not hard or spiked," Nina joked in a soft voice, her face burrowed into his neck.

"Let's blame—"

"The spices?" Nina suggested.

"Or just the damn smell of your hair that goes right to my head…"

"The shampoo, then." Nina went on joking because she knew at that point that she had to lighten the mood. Or give in to it…

And she couldn't give in to it.

"Yeah, the shampoo," he agreed reluctantly, taking another deep breath and sitting back as he took her by the shoulders and repositioned her several inches away from him.

Then he said, "I believe we were talking about an innocent elementary school Christmas program…"

"We were," she confirmed, knowing without a doubt now that she shouldn't go.

"The program starts at seven, the boys have to be there at six, so what if I take them to the church, get them situated, then sneak over here and pick you up?"

Say no…

But out loud she said, "I'll be ready."

Dallas smiled as if he'd known she'd been thinking about turning him down after all and he was relieved that she hadn't.

Then he got to his feet, held out both hands to help her to her feet, as well, and they went to her door. He took his coat from where he'd hung it on the doorknob and put it on.

He looked at her the entire time, studying her, and then he shook his head and said more to himself than to her, "Nina *Crawford*…"

And this time she knew what he was thinking—that of all the people for whatever was happening to be happening, it was happening between a Crawford and a Traub.

Then he breathed deeply, sighed it out as if in some

kind of concession and leaned forward to kiss her again—
a long, sweet, sexy kiss that could well have started everything all over again had he not pulled away quickly.

Another deep breath, a sigh, a last lingering look into
her eyes, and he opened the door and left.

And Nina wilted against it once it was shut.

Knowing that distance and separate corners were not
at all what she wanted, in spite of what she'd sworn to
herself earlier.

What she really wanted was Dallas.

Any way.

Any time.

Anywhere.

Chapter Eight

The school Christmas program on Monday evening was funny and endearing and full of foibles. There were heartfelt, off-key Christmas songs—one per grade that advanced from the timid singing of the kindergarteners—who forgot some of the words—to the far more polished sixth graders. There were skits. There was a sixth-grade girl band with an overly loud drummer doing a rendition of "Rockin' Around the Christmas Tree." And the diamond in the crown was the production of "'Twas the Night Before Christmas."

The students enacted the poem while one of the older girls read it. A kindergartner in a mouse costume pretended to sleep, but couldn't keep her eyes closed.

A fourth grader played Santa in a costume stuffed with a pillow that was sticking out from under his cottonball-edged red jacket. He was also wearing a beard that was askew in one direction while his hat was off-kilter in the other, and his boots were black galoshes.

The sleigh was a red wagon with cardboard sides resembling Dallas's bobsleigh—not surprisingly, since Ryder had worked on the scenery and staging. But one of the sides fell off midplay.

The reindeer wore brown construction-paper antlers, with Jake in the lead wearing a red clown nose.

Some license was taken. The father was at the cardboard cutout window, but so was Mama in her kerchief as well as the two children who rose from their visions of sugarplums to witness Santa's ride.

Robbie was the youngest child of the pajama-clad family, although rather than watching Santa, Robbie scanned the audience for his father and waved when he spotted Dallas and Nina.

In the process of that, Robbie didn't see it coming when the nightgown-clad mother of the group tripped on her hem and fell into him, causing them to tumble and barely avoid falling off the stage.

Robbie's loud "Jeez, Janey," was answered by Janey's "It's this dumb nightgown," interrupting the performance and making the audience laugh.

By the time Mama in her kerchief got back to her feet and Robbie did, too, the narrator had lost her place and reread a few lines before getting to the only other dialogue in the play—Santa calling "Happy Christmas to all, and to all a good-night!"

Clapping and cheers and whistles rewarded the performance along with a standing ovation as everyone who had participated in the rest of the program, too, returned to the stage to take their final bows.

Robbie was at the very front, and he dramatically hid

one arm behind his back, crossed the other over his stomach and took a very deep bow as if the accolades were all for him.

Then the announcement came that refreshments were being set out at the back of the social hall, the kids got down from the stage to find their families and the mingling began—the portion of the evening that Nina had been dreading.

Dallas's parents had arrived before Dallas and Nina, and Dallas had urged Nina into the two free seats directly in front of them. Restrained hellos had been exchanged with Nina from there, just moments before the lights were dimmed so no more had had to be said.

But now Nina knew there was bound to be more of an encounter and she wasn't sure what would happen. Although she had been with Dallas and the boys at the bonfire, and the Traubs had been sort of civil, it hadn't seemed quite as couple-ish as sitting beside him through the program, and she wasn't sure how that would be viewed.

Especially when she had no doubt that every time Dallas had leaned over to whisper some comment into her ear, every time they'd cast each other a smile, the older Traubs had been watching.

She was right that there was no avoiding Dallas's parents. By the time all three boys found them, the four adults had met at the end of the row of seats to stand together.

At first the focus of the adults was on the boys, complimenting them for their parts in the various portions of the program. But then the boys wanted refreshments and their grandfather volunteered to take them, leaving Nina and Dallas alone with Ellie Traub.

Who was staring pointedly at her son.

But just when Nina was afraid the other woman was going to say something negative, she instead said to Dallas, "It's nice to see you like this."

"Mom. I saw you three times today at home and we're together at all these school things—are you losing it or what?" Dallas said, clearly perplexed by the comment that made it sound as if this encounter was out of the ordinary.

"It's nice to see you not down in the dumps," his mother amended, glancing at Nina.

Nina barely knew the woman. When any Traub did come into the store they were always curt and civil, and they got out again as quickly as they could.

But tonight something was different. And Nina thought what she was seeing in Ellie Traub's expression was acceptance. Reluctant acceptance, but acceptance just the same.

Then, in a more friendly, conversational tone, Ellie Traub said, "How do you spend the holidays, Nina? With your family, I expect."

"Usually. At my parents' house," Nina answered. "Christmas Eve *and* Christmas Day. But between yesterday and today, everyone except my mom and me came down with the flu, so my mom is playing nurse. She called just before I left tonight to tell me I've been banned from getting anywhere near them."

"So, no Christmas?" Dallas asked, alarmed.

Nina shrugged. "Mom said we'll just have a belated one when this passes—we'll exchange our gifts, have the same foods we planned, do it all the way we always do, but in a week or so."

"We have a big dinner Christmas Eve—friends and

family—why don't you come?" Ellie Traub invited her instantly.

Nina wasn't the only one shocked by that. She saw Dallas's eyebrows arch, and for a moment he looked as if he wasn't sure he'd heard correctly.

But his mother ignored both of their reactions and went on as if she hadn't just extended a major olive branch to the enemy. "We have tons of food—I always cook for an army, don't I, Dallas? And this year we're doing even more, making it even bigger. I saw the way the boys were with you—I'm sure they'd like it if you'd come." She cast a glance at her son, making Nina think that Ellie Traub was including Dallas as one of the *boys*.

"We'd *all* like it if you'd come," the older woman added.

It was on the tip of Nina's tongue to say: you *would?* And she couldn't quite think of anything else to say.

Then Dallas chimed in. "Come. We can't have you spending it alone."

"Oh, it's all right. No big deal. I'll be fine…"

"I insist, Nina! It's against our house policy to let anyone be alone at Christmas," Ellie Traub informed her. "Dallas will pick you up at six. Won't you, Dallas?"

The older woman looked at her son and smiled a loving, knowing smile.

"I will," he confirmed.

Then Bob Traub brought the boys back, delivering cookies to his wife and son while Robbie handed a frosting-decorated wreath to Nina.

"I called it first so I got to bring yours," he announced, as if it were a coup.

Nina thanked him, and after they'd all eaten their cookies Ellie Traub suggested that she and Bob take the boys home and get them to bed while Dallas took Nina. That seemed like the second seal of approval for them to be together.

Which they weren't, Nina reminded herself. They weren't *together*. But if his mother was conceding that they might be friends, that was okay. So that was how she chose to view it.

Then the boys followed Dallas's instructions to put on their coats, to mind their grandparents and go right to bed when they got home, and goodbyes were said.

"We'll see you tomorrow night," Ellie Traub told Nina as she left, drawing a surprised glance from Bob.

Then, in the process of urging their grandsons to the door, Nina heard Ellie Traub answer that surprise. "He's better, Bob, and I'm glad for whatever or whoever did it."

"Sooo…I'm thinking that a perk of hanging out with the owner is that maybe I could do a little last-minute Christmas shopping even though the store is closed…" Dallas suggested hopefully, as he opened his truck's passenger door for Nina to get out.

Conversation on the drive from the church to Nina's apartment had been about the funny points of the Christmas program, so this was a change of subject.

"Oh, really…" Nina responded.

"Not that the biggest perk isn't just getting to hang out with you," he claimed. "But tomorrow is Christmas Eve and I have a million things to do, and I still need a few stocking stuffers for the boys. I was just thinking that here we are—"

"Right above all those things in the store," Nina finished for him as she unlocked the outside door to her apartment and went in, turning on lights as she did.

"Unless going down there after hours will trigger an alarm system or security cameras will record it and alert the sheriff to come running or something…"

"I can bypass the security system, and we don't have cameras. Maybe next year, but not yet," Nina told him as they took off their coats.

Tonight she was wearing a longish wraparound gray sweater over slim-leg jeans with knee-high black boots whose three-inch heels she knew her obstetrician wouldn't have approved of. But, pregnant or not, she had no intention of looking dowdy—a fact that seemed to be more and more of an issue whenever she was dressing to see Dallas.

Dallas, who looked fabulous in a heavyweight tan field sweater and jeans that showed off a great rear end.

Something she knew she shouldn't have noticed.

"So, if we can bypass the security system and there aren't any cameras to record my special treatment…" he said, as if he were proposing being cat burglars, wiggling his eyebrows provocatively at the same time. "What do you say?"

"I suppose that, since I really liked getting a taste of what it will be like to be a parent at my kid's school Christmas program, I can reciprocate with a little extra store access." Nina conceded what she would have agreed to, in any event, just because it was Dallas asking.

"Then fire up a cash register and let's do it!" he said enthusiastically, making Nina laugh at him.

The panel that controlled the alarm system was on the second floor at the top of the steps that led down to the store. She punched in the code and then turned on half of the store lights. "We don't want to make it look like I'm open for business or, believe me, we'll have people knocking on the door and wanting to come in," she explained.

"Okay, then. You keep a lookout while I shop and I'll keep a lookout while you ring me up. Anyone comes to the door or the windows and we both go down," he said, again in cat-burglar mode.

"Deal," Nina agreed as they went into the dimly lit store.

While Dallas browsed, Nina lurked behind a partition, peeking out periodically to watch the front of the store and at the same time taking cans of pumpkin from a box to stack for the next day.

"Have you had any word from Laurel?" Nina asked, while Dallas picked out three yoyos and moved on to other small games intended to be stocking stuffers.

"My ex? No, not a peep," Dallas answered.

"Not a card or a letter? No gifts for the boys?"

"Nothing."

"I guess something could still come tomorrow. Mail will be delivered and so will packages," Nina said, hoping that the mother of Dallas's children wouldn't let this oh-so-important holiday go by without acknowledging those kids.

"I think, since each of their birthdays came and went this year without anything from her, they know better than to expect something now."

"Oh, that's right…" Nina said, recalling that he'd told her Laurel had let each of the boys' birthdays pass unacknowledged. Even so, it didn't seem any less awful for Ryder, Jake and Robbie's mother not to send them Christmas gifts.

"Still," she said, "they're little kids. There's got to be some tiny bit of hope, deep down, that she'll do something. And then when—if—she doesn't, it will put a damper on things for them."

"You're probably right," Dallas said, somewhat grimly, picking out three stocking-stuffer-size footballs. "I guess I like to think they've forgotten about her, that they don't care, and since they haven't said anything it makes it easier on me, but—"

"You know they *do* care."

"Yeah…" Dallas said reflectively. "Sure they do. Robbie trying to get her his school picture shows they haven't forgotten her—no matter how I'd like to delude myself."

"Have you thought of wrapping something up for them and putting her name on it so they *think* she sent them something?"

Dallas stopped sorting through tiny puzzle boxes to look at her. "Huh…" he mused. "No, that didn't occur to me. Do you think I should?"

Nina hadn't actually put any thought into it before she'd said it, but now she did. "I don't know…" she said. "I can't imagine that you want to do anything that makes her look good when she's done such awful things and hasn't bothered with those kids herself. But would it be good for them to believe she thought about them?"

"Or would it be raising false hopes?"

"Do you think they *don't* hope every day that she'll come back?" Nina asked, verbally tiptoeing.

Dallas had chosen three puzzles, but he paused before putting them into the basket he was carrying, clearly considering that question, too. "I suppose they might," he conceded. "I did for a while, at first. Even with the cheating and how tough things had been…there was probably about a month where I even thought I saw her just about everywhere I looked, as if she might show up around the next corner. I never talked about it, but, yeah, the boys probably did the same thing. Except where I came to grips with the fact that she wasn't coming back, it makes sense that they might just wish she *would* show up again."

That was such a sad thought. And Nina could tell by the frown etched into Dallas's square brow that he thought so, too.

Then he said, "I don't know if Ryder would actually believe it. Or even Jake."

"But they'd try because they'd want to…" Nina said in a voice barely above a whisper, wondering if she was pressuring him. Hoping not. "You could write on the tags that she still won't be coming back, but that she just wanted them to have something—maybe that would help keep their hopes from being raised. But at least they'd feel remembered—"

"Even if they aren't," Dallas muttered.

Nina thought she'd said enough. And since Dallas seemed to be thinking about the whole issue, she left him to that.

Then he said, "I'm not putting her name on anything so great they'll like it better than what I bought them."

Nina suppressed a smile at that hint of stubbornness. "You could get them shirts. Shirts are kind of a mom thing. But not exciting to little boys."

Dallas didn't say anything, but Nina saw him move from the part of the store where the stocking stuffers were displayed to a table of boys' wear.

"There's not a part of me that wants to make her look good," he confessed, even as he picked out three shirts in varying sizes and colors. "But she's their damn mother, and it's Christmas, and I don't want them feeling any worse than they probably already do because it was this time last year when she left. If the chance to believe their mother remembered them helps any…well, I guess it's worth it."

Nina joined him to take three boxes from the shelf below the display. "Let me wrap them in some of the paper we have here so they won't be wrapped in what their other presents are in—it would be a dead giveaway."

Dallas nodded. "Thanks," he said.

Nina knew what he was doing wasn't easy for him. That it wasn't something he could do wholeheartedly, but that for the sake of his sons he was burying his own resentments, and she admired that. *Him.* So much that she couldn't keep herself from reaching a hand to his arm for a squeeze of support for his selflessness. "I don't know if this is the right thing to do or not, but you're a good dad for doing it."

"It was you who came up with it," he said. "And thanks for that, too," he added with a genuine smile. "Thanks for thinking of my boys. Of what might help them get through this."

Nina almost said they just made a good team but stopped short, reminding herself that she and Dallas *weren't* a team. That they couldn't be. Even though she liked the feel of his arm in her hand so much she never wanted to let go…

"I'll scan these and wrap them while you finish shopping," she said instead, forcing herself to take her hand away from his bulging biceps.

"Thanks for everything you've done," he added. "I'm not sure I would have gotten through this holiday without you…"

"You'd have done fine," Nina demurred.

Still keeping an eye on the front windows and door,

she stayed as much out of sight as she could, and by the time she had three nicely wrapped shirt boxes, Dallas was finished with his shopping and ready for her to check him out.

Or, at least, to check out the items he was purchasing. She was trying *not* to check *him* out, despite the fact that her gaze kept drifting to him and getting stuck on him. Taking in every tiny detail. Liking it all...

The guy was just terrific-looking and it seemed impossible for her *not* to notice.

Terrific-looking and sooo sexy...

And that muscular arm she'd felt in his sweater sleeve had been big and rock-solid and—

And she'd decided this morning that it certainly must be pregnancy hormones that were putting her into overdrive when it came to Dallas, and that she wasn't going to be at the mercy of something like that.

So checking out his items was the only checking out she was going to do!

When she'd accomplished her task Dallas took his bag and they headed for the steps. But just as they reached them they heard voices from outside the front door.

"Are they open?" one voice asked.

"Some of the lights are on..."

Dallas dropped his bag, grabbed Nina and spun her around behind the wall that partitioned off a corridor to the employees' break room.

"Do you think they saw us?" Nina asked from where Dallas had her pinned to the wall.

"I don't know. They're trying the door. I didn't recognize them, though, did you?"

"No. Probably out-of-towners visiting somebody for the holidays."

"Let's just lay low for a few minutes," Dallas suggested. "Eventually they'll give up."

Nina laughed. "Or I could just holler out that we're closed…"

"And risk a story that will make us feel bad if we don't open up?" he asked, as if it were life or death. "Besides," he added with that lopsided smile of his, "this is so much more fun."

There was insinuation in his voice, making it clear that their position was the fun part. And certainly Nina couldn't find any fault in being backed up against a wall by him, the clean woodsy scent of his cologne going to her head and his superbly handsome face just inches above her…

"And since you're shielding me with your body I'm protected from grenade attacks, too," she joked in a feeble attempt to hint that he should move, at least trying to alter things.

But Dallas merely countered with, "Can't be too careful." And he didn't move. Instead he peered down into her eyes, grinning, making it clear that he liked it right where they were.

"You're so beautiful…" he whispered.

"Sure I am," she answered, making light of it. "Eight-and-a-half-months pregnant, and I've never looked better."

"I don't know about that, but I do know that little basketball belly you're sporting doesn't take anything away from those big brown eyes, or that peaches-and-cream skin, or that hair that's like…that's like heaven…" He brushed the tip of her nose with the tip of his. "And I also know that it doesn't take away from the fact that when I'm with you I feel like a new man."

He looked into her eyes again with pure warmth in his. And a glint that told her what was coming.

His arms were already around her, his head was already tilted in her direction and their mouths were mere inches apart. And when he closed those inches to kiss her, Nina just naturally tipped her chin up and met him halfway.

Somehow, it had come to seem as if being with him wasn't complete until he kissed her, and once he started, she couldn't make herself stop it. She just loved kissing him so much....

Mouths and tongues knew the dance well by then, and there was no hesitation, no inhibition, just really, really good kissing, and kissing and more kissing.

Nina's eyes were closed and it didn't matter to her where they were. It only mattered that Dallas was holding her, that her own hands were fanned out across his wide shoulders, that they dropped down to the biceps she wanted another feel of, massaging and gripping muscles that barely gave way beneath her strongest grasp.

The kissing grew more fevered, and breaths came deeper, heavier, thrusting Nina's breasts into contact with Dallas's chest.

Her nipples were taut little diamonds. And so, so sensitive. More now than they'd ever been before. More, at that moment, than she could ever have believed possible, so that just that much contact brought them alive.

She didn't know if it was the extra fullness that her breasts had now, too, but they felt as if they were ready to burst from her bra. The bra that—the same way she wouldn't concede to flat shoes—hadn't yet been replaced with maternity bras. A bigger size, yes. But still lacy and lovely, and suddenly feeling much too confining.

Dallas's hands were on her back, rubbing and massaging divinely, and doing there what she was doing to his arms. What she suddenly wanted desperately to feel on her breasts.

She sent her hands to travel to his neck, to his nape, then up to comb her fingers through his hair as kissing became even more sensual, as tongues chased each other, and darted and thrust with intent.

Nina pressed her front more firmly to his—and then she felt Dallas insinuate a hand under the back of her sweater...

It took everything she had not to cry out, *yes! Yes! Yes!*

But all she did was give a more sensual twist of her tongue, and ease back the tiniest bit to provide enough room for his hand, even as deep breaths brought her chest to his like ocean waves to the shore, receding and returning lest he forget...

His other hand, massive and strong, callused, joined the first under her sweater, on her bare back. A rancher's hands, they coursed upward, working her shoulders for a few minutes before one of them drifted down. To the outer side of her breast.

She moaned her encouragement, almost dying inside for want of having him just get there.

And then he finally did—he drew his hand around to take her breast in it.

A quiet purr of pleasure rumbled in her throat, but it wasn't complete. Because that stupid, stupid bra was there! Keeping her from having what she really wanted.

And she just couldn't stand it. Not a single minute longer.

Almost on their own, her hands dropped from the

back of Dallas's head, reached behind her and unhooked the bra...

A split second later she could hardly believe what she'd done.

But suddenly Dallas was kissing her in a way she'd never been kissed before, plundering her mouth with more sexual fervor than she thought a kiss could have. And both of his hands were on both of her breasts. His bare hands on her bare breasts. And that was all that mattered.

Never had she known anything to feel as fabulously intense. Every sensation, every tiny nuance was heightened. Every stroke, every knead, every tug, every caress, every squeeze. Every gentle pinch and roll of her nipples between his fingertips. Every feather-stroke brush against the very crest. Every supreme touch.

And the moan that answered it all came from depths she didn't even know she had.

As one hand shared time with each breast, his other hand returned to her back, splaying there to brace her for the full impact of what he was doing to breasts that couldn't get enough of him, and Nina began to wonder what it would be like to have his mouth on them instead...

Then Dallas pulled her in tighter, as if he just couldn't get enough of her. And that basketball-size belly he'd mentioned earlier came up against him...

Nothing about that gave him even the slightest pause.

But it was different for Nina.

It reminded her that she wasn't in a shape she'd ever been in before. And while she'd reveled in each change her baby had brought to her body, a jolt of self-consciousness hit her then, stopping her a little short.

Dallas sensed it instantly, and everything did pause then.

His hands stopped all movement. He ended their kissing. And concern was in his voice when he whispered, "Are you okay?"

This time her moan was bereft.

"I'm okay, but...I just...I just think maybe we'd better stop..."

She'd been staring into his throat when she said that, and now she tilted her head enough to look up into his face. His oh-so-handsome face that she'd come to adore, that held the expression of a man who'd been as lost in what they'd been sharing as she had been.

Before she'd thought about taking off her clothes.

He closed his eyes and arched his eyebrows high. Nina knew he was regrouping. Regaining some control. Even as the heat of his hand still on her flesh made her want him not to.

But then that hand slid away and joined his other one in refastening her bra before they both retreated and ended up flat to the wall on either side of her head.

He dipped down to kiss her again. A long, lingering, openmouthed, seductive kiss that made her have some very serious second thoughts.

Until he ended that kiss, too, and pushed away from her with a finality that said he was honoring her wishes, regardless of how difficult it might be for him.

Then he picked up the bag that held his purchases, took a deep breath and said, "I kind of need you to stay right where you are and let me go upstairs, put on my coat and get the hell out of here. Otherwise I'm not gonna to be able to go at all because there isn't a damn thing I've ever wanted *not* to do as much as leave you right now. Okay?"

"Okay," Nina agreed breathlessly.

"But I'll be back tomorrow night to pick you up for dinner."

Nina muttered another "Okay."

"And thanks," he added. "For the after-hours shopping, for thinking of the boys and for wrapping their shirts." He grinned at her—a grin that turned her knees to mush because he looked so good and sexy and mischievous, and just so Dallas. "And I'd say thanks for sending me home before we did something we might regret, except I just don't think I would have regretted it."

Then he turned and went up the stairs.

Nina watched him go, drinking in every bit of the sight of him climbing those steps, until he reached the top and she couldn't see him anymore.

Only then did she drop her head back to the wall and close her eyes, trying to tell her body that it was for the best that she hadn't let things go any further than they had.

But really, she didn't care what her reasons were.

She just wanted him back there.

She wanted his hands on her again.

And she wanted a whole lot more that she'd left herself only able to have in her imagination....

Chapter Nine

Nina was nervous about spending Christmas Eve with the Traubs and considered begging off at the last minute.

But such a big part of her wanted to be with Dallas that she couldn't make herself do that.

Then Dallas came to pick her up, and one look at him sent any idea of not going right out the window.

He looked terrific in charcoal-gray slacks and a lighter gray turtleneck sweater that hugged every well-honed inch of those broad shoulders, pectorals and biceps that she remembered so vividly having her hands all over the night before. And there was no way she could deny herself being with him.

"Wow! Look at you—you look fabulous!" he complimented her when he first set eyes on her.

She'd changed outfits four times, so she was gratified that he approved. She was wearing the simplest of sweaters—a soft black cocoon of cashmere with long sleeves.

It was the cut of it that made it special. It was tighter at the bottom, the hem reaching to midthigh, giving it a sexy swing. And the fact that the bateau neckline went from the very end of one shoulder to the very end of the other gave it a sexy allure that also kept the focus above the waist.

Under the sweater she wore black leather slim-leg pants with a pair of four-inch heel shoes that dipped enough in front to show just a hint of toe cleavage, so the pants and shoes were also hardly matronly.

But as happy as she was to see Dallas's genuine approval of how she looked—along with a glint of desire in his eyes—she continued to be nervous.

"Are you sure all of your family is going to be okay with having me there?" she fretted on the drive to the Triple T ranch.

"When Ellie Traub gives her stamp of approval to someone it goes a long way with the whole lot of us. And her personal invitation counts as that stamp of approval, so you don't have anything to worry about," Dallas assured her.

But somehow that didn't help as Nina thought about the years and years—actually the full decades and generations—that had gone into the feud between the Crawfords and the Traubs. About the ugly words and accusations that had been flung during the campaign for mayor.

And when she added to that her own inside knowledge of how the Crawfords thought and felt about the Traubs—and had to assume that the Traubs thought and felt the same way about her and the rest of her family—it wasn't easy to believe that a simple invitation was enough to override everything else.

Dallas must have seen her lingering doubts because he

cast her a supportive smile and said, "Plus, this Christmas Eve is a little different than usual. It's more of an open house tonight, and Mom is expecting a pretty big crowd. One way or another, though, I promise I'll be right by your side every minute. If at any point you want out, all you have to do is elbow me in the ribs and I'll get it done before you can blink twice. Okay?"

"Okay," Nina agreed, continuing to fret nonetheless.

But it was all for naught.

Dallas hadn't exaggerated when he'd said his mother was expecting a crowd. The large Traub family home was filled to the brim with people—many of whom Nina recognized as mutual friends and neighbors who continued to be in need this year, due to the flood.

It made the Traubs' Christmas Eve an elaborate party, and while Nina was glad for the opportunity to get lost in that sea of guests, she had to admit that the party itself was a nice thing to do for those whose Christmas Eve might not have been so festive otherwise.

And it proved what she'd begun to think about the Traubs before this—that the family she'd been taught to demonize was, instead, much like her own family— people who cared about the misfortune that had fallen on some Rust Creek Falls citizens worse than on others and who wanted to do whatever they could to make things better.

The house was decorated to the hilt, with the dining room table set buffet-style and laden with food. There were hams and turkeys and pork roasts and pasta dishes. There were green salads, fruit salads and macaroni salads, mashed potatoes, scalloped potatoes, macaroni and cheese, and oyster stuffing. There was asparagus and green-bean casserole and sweet potatoes and candied yams. There was hollandaise for the ham, and gravies for the turkeys, the mashed potatoes and the pork roasts. There were pies and cakes and cheesecakes and Christmas cookies and fudge for every sweet tooth. And there were drinks galore, too—soda and punch and wine and beer and eggnog—spiked and unspiked.

Regardless of what troubles might have been hanging on for anyone, they seemed to be suspended for the time being in smiles and laughter as folks mingled and talked and ate of the plentiful food. Dallas's three sons and a number of other children dressed in party clothes ran around and played and let out some of their pent-up excitement over the holiday.

One by one, each of the Traubs made their way to Nina and Dallas, and there was no rancor to be found in any of the encounters. Instead, Nina was welcomed warmly by Ellie and Bob, and found herself chatting amiably enough with each of Dallas's five brothers at one point or another.

His brother Forrest and Forrest's fiancée, Angie, were in from Thunder Canyon, and so was Clay, along with his wife, Antonia, and their two children, her baby daughter, Lucy, and his slightly older son, Bennett.

Of course Collin Traub and his wife, Willa, were there. Collin, the new mayor, was polite, but it was Willa who actually did the talking while they shared an eggnog with Dallas and Nina.

The still-single Braden even came up to say hello and tell Nina he was glad she could make it. And Sutter and his fiancée, Paige, stayed to talk quite a while, with Paige seeming overly interested in Nina's pregnancy.

The entire evening was so amiable that, as it wore on,

Nina began to wonder if anyone there even remembered that she was a Crawford. And she certainly had yet another occasion to forget that the Traubs were supposed to be her sworn enemies.

It was nearly ten o'clock before the crowd thinned. While the rest of the family helped Ellie and Bob clean up, Dallas enlisted Nina to join him in getting his boys upstairs to bed.

"Not *home* to bed?" she asked quietly.

"Everybody's spending the night here so we can have one big Christmas morning. We thought maybe if we did it that way it might keep the boys from thinking too much about being without their mother this year."

"Ah…" Nina said in understanding, happy for Ryder, Jake and Robbie that their family all cared so much for them that they were willing to do that.

"Besides," Dallas added with a mischievous smile. "I still have some things to get ready at my house—a bike to finish assembling and some packages that need to be wrapped. Since you're so good at that—" his smile turned into an incorrigible grin "—I thought maybe I could talk you into lending me a hand before I take you back to your place."

"You're going to make me work for my supper?"

"Just a little. If you wouldn't mind…"

As pleasant as the evening had been—and even though Dallas had been true to his word and stayed by her side throughout —it didn't seem as if they'd had much alone time. And while Nina knew—especially after the way the previous evening had ended—that she shouldn't have any alone time with Dallas, when it was suddenly right there for the taking, she couldn't make herself not take it.

So she said, "I don't mind." Which was, in fact, an enormous understatement.

Because the prospect of that alone time had just made her whole night.

"That quiet sounds pretty good, doesn't it?" Dallas commented as he let himself and Nina into his house after they'd gotten Ryder, Jake and Robbie to bed at their grandparents' place and said good-night to the rest of the Traubs.

"Oh, yeah," Nina agreed, not having realized until now the level of noise they'd been in through the party, especially with so many family members remaining to stay overnight. But they were alone at Dallas's place.

Alone with a half-assembled bicycle and several toys waiting to be wrapped.

It was already late, so they wasted no time getting to work—Dallas in the middle of the family room floor and Nina at the kitchen table—after kicking off the shoes that she'd been standing in too long tonight.

"Visions of Christmas future," Dallas said as they went about their separate tasks.

Nina's first thought was that he meant that tonight was her glimpse of future Christmases—with him. And her glance shot to Dallas.

Then she realized he was referring to the many Christmas Eves to come when she'd be assembling toys and wrapping packages for her own child, and she deflated. And relaxed, too, because while there had been the oddest sense of hope in what he'd said, there had also been alarm that he might be suggesting something… Some kind of proposal she didn't want to have to reject…

"I can't wait to tuck in my own little boy or girl and then do this for them," she said to narrow her focus.

"Next Christmas…" Dallas said unnecessarily.

Next Christmas she would have her own child. An almost one-year-old.

It seemed so strange….

And wonderful, too….

It was just difficult to imagine that by this time next year so much would be different. She would have delivered the baby and would know that baby well. Son or daughter. *Her* son or daughter. And so many stages of babydom and parenting would already be past.

"Will I be sorry that the year has gone by, or glad?" she wondered out loud.

"A little of both," he answered, as the voice of experience. "You won't be sorry for getting full nights of sleep again. And you'll be an old hand at diapering and feeding and baths and washing hair—that's an improvement over the first few times when you'll be all thumbs. You'll know hungry cries from fussy cries, tired cries from cries that are just temper and cries that mean you better come quick—that helps. But you'll also look back and feel sad that some things are over and done with."

"It's so weird to think that in just a year's time anything will be over and done with."

"Some things go fast, though. The newborn stage—sure, you're exhausted, but at the same time you get to have this soft little ball of baby in your arms, snuggled there like an angel. You'll have seen a lot of firsts come and go—the first time they hold your finger, the first smile that says they really recognize you, the first time they roll over or sit up or crawl—"

"I guess that's part of why people have more than one—so they can do it all again," Nina mused.

"Part of it, yeah," he agreed. "Do you have plans for that? More artificial insemination for more babies...?"

Why did it sound as if he might care what the answer to that was?

Nina wasn't quite sure, so she merely answered honestly. "No, no plans. What about you? Do you want more kids?"

And why did *she* care what *his* answer might be?

She didn't know. She just knew that if he said he didn't want any more it was going to bother her....

"Three kids doesn't seem like so many when you come from a family with six. And this is a big house—it could handle a couple more. So I guess I wouldn't rule anything out."

Nina smiled without meaning to.

"How about Rust Creek?" he asked then. "Could you see yourself leaving here?"

"No," Nina responded without having to think about it. "I love it here. I love small-town living. The store. Knowing almost everyone—"

"Yeah, but you're only twenty-five. A lot can change between your twenties and your thirties..." he mused, sounding slightly melancholy, so Nina knew he was thinking of his ex-wife's change of heart.

It also served as a reminder to her, though. The more she learned about Dallas the more she found that they had in common and the less aware she was of their age difference. But that gap never narrowed, and she knew she needed not to forget about it.

"What about you?" she asked. "Could you see yourself leaving here?"

"Not me. Never. My roots here are deep," he said, also without pause.

"And you're set in your ways…" she teased, only to reinforce the reminder that he was so much older than she was. Like Leo, who had used the set-in-his-ways excuse for so much….

But Dallas heard her and laughed. "Go ahead and have that baby—see how set in your ways you get to be once it's here," he challenged. "You'll be in a state of change to meet every change that kid makes from now until… well, I was going to say from now until it goes to college, but come to think of it, not even my folks have the luxury of being set in their ways. Not with the six of us getting engaged and married and bringing kids of our own around. And then if divorce rears its ugly head? That shook things up for them, too, believe me. I don't think they know what's coming at them from one day to the next. I know I don't."

And he adapted to everything he needed to adapt to… *unlike* Leo.

But she was trying hard to remind herself why she needed to resist her attraction to him—why she needed to resist him—and finding him *unlike* Leo didn't help matters.

And she *was* trying to resist what she was feeling for Dallas.

Because, despite so many people being around them tonight at his parents' party, despite the half-a-room distance that separated them now, there still hadn't been a single moment tonight when she hadn't been ultra-aware of him. When she hadn't glanced at him and been struck by how handsome he was. When she hadn't wanted to have her hands on him. Or his hands on her…

Actually there hadn't been a moment since she'd stopped things between them last night that her body had seemed to calm down, to stop craving going right back to what had happened between them and letting it find a conclusion.

A conclusion that was beginning to seem like the only way to get what he'd stirred up in her to die down again....

"In case no one has told you yet," Dallas said then, grinning as if he knew something she didn't. "Once that baby gets here, your life as you've known it will be *forever* changed and changing. Kiss what you've known goodbye, darlin'," he joked. "And embrace whatever comes your way because you'll never know what's next, and there's no use fighting it."

Kissing and embracing...

She heard what he'd said and knew what he was talking about, but those two words really rang in her ears. Because they were what she really wanted to be doing at that moment.

She'd finished the last of the wrapping, so she didn't even have that to do to keep her hands busy.

Or to keep her distance from Dallas.

She went around the island and crossed to him, standing slightly behind him to survey his work.

"Done?" he asked.

"I am."

"Me, too. Just about..."

He gave a few more turns of a screwdriver and sat back on his haunches. "There! I'm getting to be a bike-assembling master!"

"You've done this before," Nina said even though she wasn't looking at the bicycle anymore but at his hair. Not too long. Not too short. Carelessly combed. Clean and shiny and sexy...

She wanted to bury her face in it.

That wasn't something she'd ever considered doing before.

Oh, she just had it so bad for this man!

And it was getting worse by the minute.

All on its own her hand went to his head, smoothing his hair.

But at least not burying her face in it...

Dallas froze.

Then he flipped down the bicycle's kickstand and set the bike upright before he took her hand from his head, stood and turned to face her, releasing her hand the moment he was.

He inhaled noticeably and sighed, looking raptly at her. And, with only two fingers that never actually touched her skin, he raised her sweater's neckline from where it had fallen off her left shoulder and gave it a more demure positioning.

"What're you doing, lady?" he asked, his voice raspy.

Nina shrugged. She couldn't give him any other answer because she wasn't completely sure *what* she was doing. Being carried away, she guessed.

All she knew with any certainty was that her body was screaming for him. It had been for the past twenty-four hours. And while this was certainly not an ideal time for her to enter into anything with Dallas or anyone else, she'd never been in the throes of a desire so persistent, so undeniable, so intense.

A desire he'd said last night that he didn't think he would regret satisfying.

Sounding accepting—reluctantly—he said, "I get that

you might not be so interested in…" He obviously wasn't sure how to say *having sex,* but the involuntary glance down at breasts that were contained by a strapless bra tonight made it clear what was on his mind.

And she could only smile at how wrong he was.

"But, Nina," he went on in a tone that rang with frustration. "I want you in the worst way, and if you come any closer or so much as lay another hand on me…I'm gonna bust wide-open."

"That sounds painful," she said in a voice that was pure seductress. She raised a hand to mold to the side of that sculpted face and looked into his blue eyes. "What if I want you in the worst way, too?" she whispered, then glanced at her protruding belly and back at him. "This wouldn't bother you?"

"No," he said with a wry laugh that left no doubt it wasn't an issue for him at all. "But you…last night…"

"Yeah… It made me feel a little…shy…" she confessed. "But that hasn't seemed to…quench anything."

He laughed, then reiterated what he'd said the night before. "You are amazingly beautiful. That baby bump is nothing but—" he took a turn at shrugging "—nature at work. It doesn't make me want you any less."

He leaned forward and kissed her, as if to prove that. A hopeful kiss that was tentative, too, as if he was afraid of getting where they'd been the night before and then having her pull the plug again.

But there was some kind of something—something indescribable, something almost magical—in whatever it was that was between them. Because all it took was him moving only those inches nearer. All it took was getting one whiff of his cologne. All it took was that simple press of his lips to hers, and to Nina nothing mattered

as much as he did. As wanting him did. As getting to
have him did…

Just this once, a little voice in the back of her mind
rationalized.

Just this once because there were too many reasons
why it couldn't be anything *but* this once.

But just this once, as her Christmas gift to herself.

Because she couldn't resist anymore…

She placed a hand on the side of his neck and let her
lips part to invite more of that kiss, and Dallas followed
suit.

A sound rumbled in his throat, and even without words
Nina knew what it meant. He did want her, and his re-
sistance was down, too, so he had to trust that she really
would go through with it tonight.

But Nina had every intention of it. There was no way
the needs coursing through her would allow anything
less.

All tentativeness evaporated from that kiss then, as it
grew more fervent, and hunger was unleashed.

Dallas's arms circled her, pulling her to him as his
mouth opened wide over hers and his tongue really came
to play.

At least for a little while, until it ended and he took
her hand. "You're sure?" he asked, giving her one last
chance to opt out.

"I'm sure if you are," she told him. "And if you know
how it's done at this stage…" she added, a bit insecure
about the fact that she didn't have a clue.

He grinned. "I do," he said confidently before he took
her upstairs to his room.

It was a big master bedroom and so clean that Nina

had the fleeting thought that he must have expected this tonight—or at least held out hope.

He didn't turn on any lights. Instead, he left the room in only the white glow of a full moon reflected off the snow outside and coming in through large windows exposed by open curtains.

Then he spun her around to face him again at the foot of his king-size bed and recaptured her mouth with his in a kiss that held nothing back now. Instead it started very much where they'd left off the previous night, as if his own needs and desires had been simmering barely beneath the surface since then, too, waiting to be unleashed.

Feverish—that was what that kiss was. Hot and intense and burning bright. And it was everything Nina had been dying for since she'd stopped him from kissing her like that in the store.

He cradled her head in his left hand and braced her back with his right as mouths reclaimed each other and Nina realized she now had free rein...

She slipped her hands under his sweater to his bare back, drinking in the feel of sleek skin over massive muscles. She was up to his shoulders when the thought struck that she didn't have to leave him dressed, and so she tore away from the kiss long enough to pull his sweater off over his head.

He smiled and went right back to kissing her, letting her have her way, exploring him.

And now that she had the chance, Nina didn't leave anything unexplored. She sent her palms on a quest that went from his narrow waist, expanding from there to broad, broad shoulders that she dug her fingers into just a little. She went to biceps that were cut and carved, squeezing those, too, reveling in the feel of power and strength there. And then there were his pectorals and the tiny male nibs that were almost as hard as she could feel her own nipples growing even as she discovered his.

Apparently Dallas decided to continue what she'd begun because he reached down to the very bottom of her sweater and went under, too. But rather than what she'd expected—and hoped for—rather than returning to breasts that were yearning for his attention, he found the waistband of her leather pants and slid them down.

Ah, the advantage of an easy-off waistband…because down they went without incident. Nina kicked them aside and was left in the lacy string bikini panties she'd chosen tonight just because they were comfortable and not because she'd had this in mind as an endgame.

Or so she told herself.

Her sweater had fallen so far down her right arm that the part of her breast that swelled above the strapless bra was exposed. It made her feel sexy and bold. So she let her hands glide from Dallas's chest to his washboard abs. All the way down to the waistband of his slacks.

He really did want her, and that made her smile beneath the onslaught of the kissing that was still going on, and growing hotter and hotter with every passing moment.

And she wanted him to be free to want her….

So she unfastened the hook that held his waistband closed and then unzipped his pants with the help of his own burgeoning needs.

It was such a turn-on to have the evidence of how much he really did yearn for her that Nina felt her own desire take a leap to another level even as she closed her hand around the steely length of him.

He groaned from deep in his throat, and that was when one of his hands slid under her sweater again. Up the back, he went straight for the hook of her bra, undoing it and then pulling it out to drop on the floor.

Then he did two things at once. He abandoned her mouth and nuzzled the top of her sweater to dip low enough to expose one breast to his seeking mouth as his hand found the other breast from inside the sweater.

And suddenly there was so much that was so deliciously sweet all at once…

He kneaded and massaged and toyed with her nipple while sucking the other breast deeply into the warm, wet velvet of his mouth, flicking the crest with the tip of his tongue, nipping with tender teeth and giving Nina her reason for moaning.

It all felt so divine that her spine arched and let him know she just wanted more. More and more and more, and maybe nothing would be enough when she wanted him as much as she did.

His other hand located the string of her panties and he disposed of those, too, bringing his hand back to the side of what used to be her waist. And just like that, mounting desire mingled just a bit with self-consciousness.

But his hand was big and warm, and so, so adept, too, and the way he slid it to the underside of her belly— gently, lovingly, adoringly—dissolved some of the awkwardness.

Just before he slipped lower still and his hand ended up between her legs…

The gasp at that first touch took her by surprise, and when his fingers slipped into her she very nearly turned to mush. Her knees actually did weaken enough for her to rely more on leaning into Dallas's big body, and her grip around him tightened, too, apparently giving him the signal that it was time to get her off her feet.

But not without getting rid of her sweater first.

He returned to kissing her after he did that, giving her a deep, poignant kiss laced with so much passion that it was the sexiest kiss she'd ever had, and it washed away every last reservation about being naked with him.

Then he scooped her up into his arms much the way he had that day in the blizzard—only so much better this time—and he laid her on his bed, joining her there.

That was when the urgency that had been growing in Nina since the night before burst to the surface. And apparently the same thing happened for Dallas because a new concentration, a new intensity, came to everything then. To his mouth at her breasts, to his hands all over her body, to her hands all over him…

Until she knew she couldn't last much longer, not without the full feel of him inside her. Not without the release that her body was beyond needing…

Then he wasn't lying facing her anymore, he was behind her, spooning her, kissing her shoulder, flicking his tongue there. One hand still worked its magic at her breasts and the other shifted her legs just so, freeing a way for him to find his home right where she craved him to be.

Part surprise, part sigh, part moan was what sounded from her then as he taught her the delights of a position she'd never known before. He moved carefully into her and retreated, carefully in even more, all the while continuing to arouse with the wonders of his hands on her, giving her nipples his palms to kernel ever more tightly into, kneading and taking her on a ride that was so incredibly not set in its way that she didn't know what to do but let him take her on it.

And take her on it he did. Coming deeply and more deeply into her. Delving gently, carefully, but still faster and faster into the core of her, building white-hot flames to burn and fuel her. To drive her higher and higher, striving for that peak that he seemed to know exactly when to bring.

Because just when she was desperate for it, one hand deserted her breasts and reached down below instead…

He definitely knew what he was doing because he sent her right over the top into a climax so incredible she lost herself in it. In it, and in that man and what he was doing to her, even as she felt him plunge into her and shudder with a culmination of his own that made him catch his breath, too, and kept them both suspended in pure, exquisite ecstasy…

Then Dallas melded his body around hers so seamlessly it was as if they were two pieces of clay formed to fit together.

He kissed her shoulder once more. "You okay?" he asked in a gravelly voice.

"Wow…" was all she could whisper in response as she slowly came back to her senses.

"But are you okay…?" he asked again.

"Oh, yeah. Better than that…"

He laughed a relieved, replete laugh and placed a trail of kisses along the length of her shoulder and up the side of her neck before he laid his head on the mattress above hers, making a nest for her head under his chin.

They stayed that way for a while before Nina recalled that it was Christmas Eve. That even though she'd accepted his mother's invitation to Christmas dinner the next day because her own family continued to be quarantined, Dallas still needed to have Christmas morning with his boys, with his family.

"You have to get me home," she reminded him softly.

"I don't want you to *go* home," he said.

"I don't want to go home," she commiserated with a laugh. "But I have to. I don't think me and my being here in the same clothes I wore tonight is quite what anyone is expecting Santa to bring."

He laughed. "It's what *I* want Santa to bring," he insisted.

But then he sighed in resignation, kissed the top of her head and said, "I know, I know..." And he did the last thing Nina wanted him to do—he took his arms from where they were wrapped so warmly around her, he took the long, heavy leg he had locked over her hips away, and he got up to retrieve their clothes.

He brought her hers first, unashamedly giving her a pretty terrific Christmas gift in the view of his magnificent body naked in the moonlight. Then he sat on the end of the bed and put his own clothes on with his back to her.

Nina appreciated that and wasted no time dressing herself, not really eager to give him the same unfettered view of her.

And once they were both decent again, Dallas came to her to kiss her once more—a long, leisurely, sexy kiss that only made it more difficult to go out into the cold night for the drive back to her apartment.

A long, leisurely, sexy kiss that was probably the reason that, once they got there and he gave her another one, he didn't end up leaving her at her door.

Instead Nina did what she'd been sorry she hadn't done the previous night.

She took him to her bed.

For just one more time…

Chapter Ten

After his night with Nina, and slipping into his parents' house at three in the morning, and very few hours of rest after that, Dallas was still the first one up on Christmas morning. Mainly because he was just too elated to sleep much.

He lit the Christmas tree lights and a fire in the fireplace. He sorted all the gifts into piles specific to each person. And he was humming Christmas carols as he made coffee in the kitchen, feeling better than he had in longer than he could remember. Maybe since soon after Robbie was born, when he'd given up thinking that anything was going to please Laurel.

And it was all because of Nina.

"Merry Christmas," a sleepy-sounding Ryder said from behind him.

Dallas glanced over his shoulder to see his oldest son

standing in the doorway in his flannel pajamas, surprised that it was Ryder who was first to rise and not Robbie.

"Merry Christmas!" Dallas answered. "Anybody else up?"

"Just me," Ryder informed him.

"Did you check out the presents?"

"Mmm, a little," Ryder said, as if he wasn't sure it was all right if he had. "I saw a baseball mitt…"

One of the things he'd asked for.

"…and that swamp creature Jake wanted and Robbie's bike."

Those were the gifts left unwrapped, as if Santa had set them out.

"I hope Robbie got the deluxe neon alien invasion spaceship, too," Ryder added with a hint of warning, as if Dallas might have overlooked the toy the youngest of the Traub sons had asked for repeatedly—and without omitting a single word of the lengthy description.

"I don't think he'll be disappointed," Dallas said, silently thanking Paige for that contribution early on, when he'd still been too muddled in his own misery to be paying as much attention as he should have been to what his kids were saying.

Sutter had spent a lot of time in Rust Creek Falls in November and had done some babysitting for him. The boys had gone along several times to do things with Paige, such as make cookies and help sort food for the food drives.

Paige had also helped Robbie write a letter to Santa asking for his mom to come back. Or, if he couldn't have that, then a new mom. Or, if he couldn't have that, then a deluxe neon alien invasion spaceship.

Dallas had been more stuck on the mom issue, but

Paige had kept the spaceship in mind and picked one of the season's hot items up when she'd had the opportunity. By the time Dallas had even begun to think about gifts, it likely would have been too late to get one at all, which would have disappointed his youngest.

The alien spaceship was in one of the wrapped packages from Santa—Paige hadn't even wanted the credit—and Dallas made a mental note to thank her again for that kindness and consideration.

He just had to hope that the spaceship was enough to compensate for Robbie's other requests not being met because there was no mom—new or old—under that tree.

Ryder came to stand beside him. "I like the way coffee smells, but it tastes like licking a dirty ashtray."

"When have you ever licked a dirty ashtray?" Dallas asked with a smile.

"You know, I just think it's what it would taste like. Yuck."

"Well you're a little young for coffee yet, so it's probably better that you don't like the taste of it. How about some juice while we wait for everyone else to get up?"

Ryder shrugged his concession to that.

"Your grandmother has a big breakfast planned for after we open gifts but I don't think anybody would notice if we hit that cookie tray," Dallas suggested.

Ryder reached far back on the counter for the tray of Christmas goodies and slid it forward while Dallas poured his juice.

As they ate iced cut-out cookies, Ryder said, "This has been a pretty good Christmas."

He sounded surprised by that, which confirmed what had seemed to be the case—that the ten-year-old hadn't been looking forward to this holiday. Understandable, under the circumstances.

"It was tomorrow when Mom left last year," Ryder said then, as if Dallas might not realize that.

"I know," Dallas said.

"And her not bein' here this year made it kind of… not much fun…"

"I know," Dallas repeated sympathetically. "It's hard. I know you guys miss her."

"Do you?"

"I did," Dallas confided. "Then I just got pretty sad. And mad. And in kind of a bad mood I couldn't get out of."

Ryder nodded his head knowingly. "But Nina made some of the things better. It was fun when she brought the Christmas tree and helped decorate it. And the rest of the stuff we did with her. She's, like…you know, kind of happier than mom was."

Dallas wasn't sure what to say to that. Should he talk about Laurel's unhappiness and discontent with her life? Should he explain that Ryder and Jake and Robbie weren't to blame? Should he get into all of that now, on Christmas morning?

It just didn't seem as though he should. It was a subject he obviously needed to address, but not right there and then. And likely not with Ryder alone.

So he said, "Yeah, I think Nina is a happier person than your mom. Some people are, you know? We're all just different—look at you and Jake and Robbie. There are things about you that are the same but there's a lot about you that's different from your brothers."

"I don't play jokes like Jake, and Robbie's a baby," Ryder summed up the only differences he seemed to see.

"Well, that's one way to look at it. But maybe because you're closer to being a man you take things more seriously, too. That could make you seem a little less happy than Jake or a little more mature than Robbie," Dallas offered, hoping to put some sort of positive spin on Ryder's introversion and his more obvious sorrow at the loss of his mother.

Ryder shrugged. "We all like Nina, though," he said. "When she's around…I don't know, I guess maybe because she's happier than mom was, we're happier then, too."

"I know she makes me feel better," Dallas admitted, realizing just how true that was. How true it had been since that day in the blizzard. "But I'm glad to hear that she makes you guys feel better, too."

"I think Robbie wants her to be our new mom," Ryder said as if he wasn't sure he should say that, the same way he hadn't been sure he should say he'd looked at the presents around the tree.

"I don't think moms are like shoes—you don't just get new ones."

"Yeah. But you can get second ones. Lots of kids have stepmoms or stepdads—that's what those are. Like Uncle Clay and Aunt Antonia—Uncle Clay is Lucy's stepfather and Aunt Antonia is Bennett's stepmom," he explained, as if Dallas had somehow missed that fact. "But they're a real family."

"True," Dallas said.

"Maybe Nina might not be so bad for that."

High praise coming from Ryder.

And for some reason, Dallas appreciated that stamp of approval.

But all he did was ruffle his son's hair and say, "Well, today is Christmas and let's just enjoy that for now, huh?"

"Yeah," Ryder agreed, showing some restrained enthusiasm."

Robbie charged into the kitchen just then. "There you guys are! Santa came! When can we open presents?"

"We have to wait—"

"No more waiting," Ellie Traub said wearily, coming up behind Robbie. "He has us all up. Just pour out cups of that coffee I smell, and we can get this show on the road."

Christmas morning was the best kind of chaos. It was a houseful of family injected with the delight of children—Dallas's three boys, and his brother Clay's small son, Bennett, and Clay's stepdaughter, baby Lucy.

After the melee of gift opening Dallas's mother headed up breakfast preparations, putting everyone to work.

Dallas sneaked away then to call Nina, to wish her a Merry Christmas and make sure she was doing all right, that there hadn't been any ill-effects from their night together.

Just as she was assuring him she was fine, Jake found him and Dallas was forced to cut the call short.

"It's okay. *I'm* okay," Nina said. "Go and have Christmas morning with your boys!"

"I'll see you soon," he said, thinking that it couldn't be soon enough.

"See you soon," Nina echoed, and he thought she just might sound as if she felt the same way.

When it was ready, breakfast was shared with everyone sitting around the expanded dining room table.

Disagreements that had arisen between the brothers recently and in times gone by were put aside for the holiday, and breakfast was accompanied by laughing and joking and teasing, and reminiscing about Christmases past in the Traub family.

Even though they'd all been together at Thanksgiving, Dallas knew that a part of why they'd all made sure to come together again for Christmas was for him and the boys, to help distract them from thoughts of Laurel and the anniversary of her leaving. And he appreciated that.

But he also knew that another part of communing over both holidays was that the damage, destruction and disruption caused by Rust Creek's flood had shaken everyone up in one way or another. It had left them all with a need to come together, to regroup and touch home base, to be reassured that there was still that place and those people to go home to.

When breakfast was over and the mess cleaned, everyone went their separate ways to visit other friends and family.

Dallas took the boys and all their gifts home for a few hours of playing with their new things before he oversaw three baths, washed three heads of hair and dispatched his sons to dress for Christmas dinner back at their grandparents' house.

The Christmas dinner that they would go and pick Nina up for...

"Get a move on—no messing around," he commanded his sons, because he felt as though he'd been without her for far, far too long already today, and he couldn't wait to get to her, to see her again, to have her by his side.

He showered, shampooed and shaved to get ready, too, then dressed in a pair of tan corduroy pants and an espresso-colored polo sweater, wishing that there had been a way of including Nina all day long. Because, as good as the day had been, he'd still missed her more than he thought it was possible to miss anyone.

"Come on, boys—I need to see how you look before we go and we *need* to go," he called as he left his own room and headed downstairs.

The sound of his three sons tussling to get out of their shared room and down the steps was familiar. And then there they were in the entryway, dressed in the slacks he'd set out for them.

But none of them had on the sweaters he'd also decided they should wear.

Instead, each of them wore the shirt he'd bought and pretended had come from their mother.

"Oh…" Dallas said when he first saw them.

"We wanted to wear Mom's shirts," Robbie announced proudly.

So they really had needed to believe that she'd thought of them.

It stabbed Dallas through the heart and at the same time made him grateful to Nina for having come up with the idea.

"Is that okay?" Ryder asked, sounding tentative but hopeful.

"Sure it is," Dallas answered without hesitation.

"Ryder says just 'cuz she sent 'em doesn't mean she's comin' back—like it said on the tags," Robbie informed him.

"No, it doesn't," Dallas confirmed.

"But she didn't forget us like we're nothin', either," Jake said.

"You guys are not nothing. You're not nothing at all. You're great kids," Dallas assured them, hating that that's what their mother had caused them to feel and needing to bear hug them all together right then, for his own sake if not for theirs.

They barely suffered his hug before wiggling free.

"And we wanted to look nice for Nina," Robbie added then.

"Yeah, me, too," Dallas said.

"'Cuz she helped us have this Christmas," his youngest pointed out matter-of-factly.

"Yes, she did." And they'd never know to what extent she'd helped them have this Christmas. But something swelled in his heart for her, just the same.

"So let's go get 'er," Jake said, as if he didn't know why they were wasting time.

"Yeah, let's," Dallas said, thinking that, once they did, he wasn't sure how he was going to let go of her again.

Ever.

Nina spoke to her mother on the phone to wish everyone a Merry Christmas. Laura Crawford was still feeling just fine, convinced that she'd had what the rest of the family had the month before, so was at no risk of getting it. But she again told Nina to stay away, assuring her they would have Christmas when the bug was gone.

So Nina spent the day putting the final touches on the nursery. And thinking about Dallas more than about her coming baby because she was still in the rosy glow of the night they'd spent together.

Once the nursery was in order, she showered and got ready for Christmas dinner with the Traubs.

She wore a black velvet jumper, cut just A-line enough to camouflage what Dallas liked to call her baby bump, over a high-necked white blouse. Black tights and a simple pair of black patent-leather Mary Janes finished the

Christmassy and very prim look that belied the not-at-all-prim memories she kept having about the night before. Memories that inspired desire to spring to life again as if it hadn't been quenched, twice.

"Last night was supposed to take care of that," she lectured herself as she brushed out her hair and left it loose, then applied blush, mascara, just a hint of eye shadow and a little lip gloss.

But rather than squelching those cravings for Dallas, being with him had only added fuel to the fire.

And when she heard a knock on the door to her apartment that told her he was there, squelching anything went by the wayside as she rushed just to get to see him again.

"Merry Christmas!" he greeted her for the second time that day when she opened the door.

"Merry Christmas," Nina answered, just as jovially.

Then he produced a sprig of mistletoe from behind his back, held it over her head and grinned.

"We have to behave," she warned, speaking as much to herself as to him.

"I know," he agreed, ignoring it all anyway as he stepped over her threshold, wrapped his nonmistletoe-bearing arm around her to pull her to him and kissed her soundly.

"Now *that's* what I needed," he breathed when the kiss ended. "Well, the beginning of it, anyway. Too bad the boys are down in the truck…"

Or, Nina knew, she and Dallas would have ended up in bed again despite her resolve that last night be their only night together.

And while she told herself this was the perfect opportunity to let him know her intentions, her mind was already wandering to that night.

After dinner.

To the possibility that the boys wouldn't tag along when he brought her home…

Then it wouldn't only be a one-night stand, she reasoned, knowing she was just looking for an excuse.

But they had a dinner to get to and his sons were waiting, and after he kissed her again he let go of her and held her coat for her to slip into.

The ride to the Triple T ranch was filled with all three boys talking about what they'd received for Christmas.

"And these shirts," Robbie pointed out, holding open his coat to display what he was wearing. "Our mom sent 'em to us."

Nina glanced at Dallas, who smiled gratefully at her. Then she said, "Let me see yours, Ryder and Jake."

They showed them off, just as pleased as the youngest Traub had, breaking Nina's heart yet again to see how thrilled they were to have what they believed were gifts from their mother.

"Oh, yeah, those are really nice shirts," she decreed, glad that Robbie moved on right away to telling her about the deluxe neon alien invasion spaceship he'd also received.

"We took all our new stuff to our house, but I brought that back with us so I could show you."

"Oh, good, I've been wanting to see one of those," Nina told him just as they arrived at the elder Traubs' home.

Except for Nina, Christmas dinner was only family, and Dallas's parents and siblings welcomed her once again with open arms.

The meal began with squash soup with a dollop of crème fraiche and a sprinkling of crispy fried pancetta on top. That was followed by a giant prime rib roast, cooked to perfection, garlic mashed potatoes, a mélange of vegetables in butter sauce, a green salad, a fruit ambrosia and homemade rolls.

Dessert was to be a seven-layer chocolate cake, but just as they were getting to that Nina felt a little odd and excused herself to go to the bathroom.

Luckily she made it just in time, so that when her water broke it wasn't on one of the Traub's dining room chairs.

With her pulse racing, she cleaned herself up, then slipped out of the bathroom. Robbie was nearby, and that seemed like a godsend when a surprisingly strong pain began to build.

"Would you go get your dad for me, please?" she managed to ask the little boy before the pain doubled her over.

Dallas was there just as it did. "Oh-oh," he breathed when he saw her leaning against the bathroom door frame.

Nina nodded through the pain, and when it was over she said, "My water broke and I think...I think I'm going to have this baby now."

"No thinking about it, sweetheart. You are."

Nina hadn't thought that she would ever be as grateful to Dallas as she had been through the blizzard. But from the moment of that first contraction, she was.

He took over again the way he had that day and before she knew it, he'd called to tell her family what was happening, and that he would take care of everything, and she was in his truck being raced to the hospital in Kalispell.

Along the way he kept things light, he talked her

through pains that were intense, regular and started at ten minutes apart. He joked with her; he reassured her that everything was going to be all right.

And he swore that nothing was going to pry him away from her side until that baby was born.

The tales Nina had heard about many first babies requiring long hours of labor were the complete opposite of her experience. As soon as they reached the hospital in Kalispell the doctor in the emergency room examined her and she was rushed to a delivery room while the nursing staff hurried Dallas into a surgical gown and booties.

Then he was ushered in to sit at her head, where he kept her hair out of her eyes and helped her raise up when she needed to push, all the while being referred to as "Dad" since there was no chance to explain that he wasn't the father of her baby.

And after hors d'oeuvres at six o'clock, dinner at seven and missing dessert at eight, at 10:10 on Christmas night—gripping Dallas's hand in a bone-crushing grip—Nina delivered a five-pound, nine-ounce healthy baby girl, who brought tears to her mother's eyes the moment her new daughter was placed in her arms.

And, Nina thought, she brought a suspicious glimmer of moisture to Dallas's eyes, too…

Chapter Eleven

"Good morning, little Noelle," Dallas whispered to the tiny bundle he was holding.

The sun was just coming up on the day after Christmas and he could hear the sounds of the hospital beginning its morning routine.

But inside that room all was quiet.

Nina was sleeping exhaustedly, the way she had been since she'd been taken from delivery to the maternity ward and finally finished what it involved to be admitted and settled into her room.

But when her daughter—whom Nina had spontaneously named Noelle in honor of the Christmas birth—had stirred in her own hospital bassinet beside her mother's bed, Dallas had picked her up, hoping to buy Nina a little more sleep.

Noelle was small, but pink and perfect, with just a

smattering of hair the color of Nina's. And gazing down at her made him smile.

"You're a beauty, like your mama," he told her in that same, almost inaudible whisper. "But you must be tired, too, so why don't you go back to sleep for a little while?"

As if obeying, the newborn balled up her fists under her chin, closed her eyes and did just that, making Dallas smile all over again.

But he didn't put her back in her bassinet. He continued to hold her, to look down at her. To marvel at the wonders of new life.

And to feel things for her that he had no right to feel.

Weary and sleep-deprived himself, he glanced at Nina.

Still sleeping. And she *was* a beauty—it struck him all over again.

Actually, it struck him almost every time he looked at her. And what he felt for her washed through him with the force of the flood that had nearly leveled Rust Creek Falls.

He'd told her he would stay by her side through the delivery, but he hadn't left her side yet, despite her telling him he could. And not because he thought it was the right thing to do, like when he'd brought her here after their near-collision in the blizzard.

No, he'd stayed by her side because that was where he wanted to be. So much that nothing could have torn him away from it while Noelle was being born. So much that he couldn't even tear himself away the rest of the night, either. Away from Nina or away from Noelle.

You're not mine....

You're neither one mine, he reminded himself.

But somehow it felt as if they were. Or, at least, as if they should be. And the thought of walking away from either of them was something he just couldn't find it in himself to do.

He let his head rest against the back of the lounger he'd been sitting in for the past few hours. He thought that this might have been the room that Laurel was in when Ryder was born, but unlike being here with Nina after their near collision, that thought didn't disturb him now. Now it was Nina's room, and being there with her seemed so natural that nothing that had come before it could have an impact.

After marveling—and reveling—in that fact for a moment, he closed his eyes the way he had for brief catnaps while watching over these two.

But this time he had no intention of sleeping. This time he tried to mentally remove himself from this picture the way he knew he should.

You already have three kids waiting for you at the ranch. Three kids you need to go home to. Three kids to think of...

And after spending the past year being the voice of reason every time anyone he knew had fallen in love—the voice of doom, some would say—he tried to be the voice of reason again now. With himself.

There was no doubt that Laurel had left him gun-shy when it came to romance, to relationships, to marriage. For himself or for anyone else. It could all just so easily go sour, and no matter how hard a person tried, they couldn't sweeten it up again—it was a harsh lesson he'd learned.

He and Laurel had gotten together so young—that was what he'd decided was the main cause of things not working out between them. That, while he might have known exactly what he wanted, Laurel had been more the child doing what she was told, what was expected of her, what had been fairly easy to persuade her to do. Had she been less the child and more the adult, she might not have made the choices she had. The choices she'd regretted and amended when it had hurt so many.

So he'd decided that if he ever got involved with anyone again—and he hadn't been sure he ever would—the woman would have to be mature and stable. Someone whose feet were firmly planted on the ground.

But Nina was only twenty-five. A single year older than Laurel had been when he'd finally talked her into actually marrying him.

What if, a few years from now when Nina was older, she felt stifled the way Laurel had? What if she woke up one day and decided she wasn't happy living in Rock Creek Falls anymore? What if being a parent turned out to be a trial for her the way it had been for Laurel, and she wanted to push the reset button, too? She could even bail and leave him with *her* daughter....

Trust. That was part of this, Dallas realized.

He knew that while Laurel might not have taken the kids away from him, she had taken away some of his ability to trust. To trust another woman. To trust his own judgment when it came to women.

But then he opened his eyes and looked at Nina again, thinking: *This is Nina. Not Laurel...*

And as he started to actually see Nina, he silently, wryly, chuckled at his own thoughts. At how he'd just portrayed her in his mind. The second Laurel...

It was all a damn scary scene he'd painted.

But it wasn't the real Nina, and he knew it.

No, she didn't have the years on her—there was no denying that. And, yes, her venturing into single parenthood might have seemed a little rash to him at the beginning. But now it served as a sign to him that Nina really did know her own mind. That she really did know what she wanted. And that she was strong enough to make the decision to have this baby on her own, to raise this baby on her own, and to take the steps to accomplish it.

And if anyone could handle single parenthood, it was Nina.

If anyone *would* deal with whatever unforeseen difficulties might come of it, it was Nina.

If anyone would dig in her heels and make it work, it was Nina.

Because young or not, she was still a woman of substance, of grit, of everything good and kind and sweet and generous and giving. And she was about as grounded a person as he'd ever met.

He'd seen her in action, he'd seen with his own two eyes how much she loved Rust Creek Falls and what she was willing to do to help it come back from the flood—even being eight months pregnant. And not only was it impressive, not only were her pure will and determination and energy level impressive, but no one did all she'd done for a place they would leave behind, either.

And he'd also seen what she'd done for him and his boys—she was a problem solver, she was someone who hunkered down and did what needed to be done. Someone who thought enough of family, of kids, to want to help them see light again at the end of the divorce tunnel.

Even when it wasn't her own family.

Even when it was a family her own was feuding with.

None of that—not a single thing—would have been Laurel. Not at any age. Laurel was as Laurel had begun—all about herself.

Laurel, who hadn't sent a thing to the boys to remember them at Christmas.

Instead, it was Nina who had saved Christmas—for him and the boys. Both with what she'd done openly and with what she'd done behind the scenes with those shirts his sons were all so delighted to believe were from their mother.

Nina, who showed no jealousy over Laurel. Who hadn't cared about making the other woman look good or bad. Who had only thought about his boys and that it might make them feel better to allow them to think their mother hadn't completely forgotten them. Hadn't thought they were nothing...

Also unlike Laurel.

No, Nina was nothing like his ex-wife and she wouldn't just turn her back on a husband, a marriage, kids, to run off for her own sake, any more than he would.

But what was he thinking? he asked himself. What was he *really* thinking?

About marriage and Nina?

Well, here you are, a small clear voice in the back of his mind said, *fresh out of her delivery room, holding her daughter, not knowing how you're going to be able to leave either of them behind....*

Marriage and Nina.

Where was that gun-shyness he'd hit everyone else with this past year?

Nowhere to be found.

Because, even though he didn't know how it had happened, he'd somehow fallen in love with Nina.

He hadn't let himself categorize the way he was feeling about her before. But there and then, tired and emotionally raw, his guard was down. And it all worked together to leave bare what those feelings genuinely were.

He loved her. In a way he might not have ever loved Laurel.

What he'd felt for Laurel had begun when they were kids. It had begun as what was probably puppy love. And maybe the fact that they'd gone from there had left a certain amount of *im*maturity to it.

He hadn't realized that before, but now, comparing what he'd felt for Laurel with what he felt for Nina, he could tell the difference.

This was something deeper, more intense, stronger and more resilient. It was the adult version. It was *him,* mature and stable, feet firmly planted on the ground, in love with her.

But what about her?

Yes, she was far beyond Laurel when it came to maturity and stability, and the kind of person she was. But did she feel for him what he felt for her? And even if she did, was she willing to take on someone older than she was again? Was she willing to take on someone who already had three kids of his own?

And what about that damn feud?

He wasn't worried so much about his family—he didn't believe that Christmas had been merely a show. He honestly thought that they were willing to accept Nina—even though she was a Crawford—if she made him happy. And she did.

But what about her family?

There wasn't anything warm and fuzzy on that front. Even the night before, when he'd called to say Nina had gone into labor and that he was taking her to the hospital, her mother had been outraged to learn that Nina was with him.

So, no, that would not be an easy road to travel.

And trying to end the generations-old battle between the Crawfords and the Traubs might be an undertaking bigger than Nina would want to deal with.

But what was it she'd told him at the very start of this whole thing, when she'd talked about using artificial insemination to have this baby?

That sometimes a person had to go after what they wanted.

No matter what, and even if not everything is just right, Dallas added himself.

At least he had to try to go after what he wanted.

Which was Nina.

And Noelle.

And a life with them in Rust Creek Falls…

Nothing had ever looked as good to Nina as the sight of Dallas sitting beside her hospital bed holding her tiny new daughter in his big, muscular arms, against his broad chest.

He was gazing down at Noelle, letting her grasp his index finger in one of her tiny fists, beaming at her with a look of such warmth and delight and adoration in his blue eyes.

For a moment, Nina stayed perfectly still, perfectly quiet, just looking at the two of them, trying to burn the image into her brain to keep forever, and marveling at the pure potency of what she felt at that moment.

Then, as if to check on her, Dallas looked up from the baby and when he saw that Nina was awake, he grinned that one-sided grin of his and said a simple "Hey."

"You didn't go home," Nina responded, marveling at that fact, too. And how glad she was that he hadn't. And how safe and secure it made her feel to have him there.

"Nah, couldn't do it," he said, taking a deep breath that expanded his chest.

He stood and came to sit on the side of her bed with Noelle, facing Nina.

Nina couldn't resist reaching out to touch the baby's hand wrapped so tightly around his finger. And his finger, too...

"How come? Wouldn't your truck start or did we have another blizzard or—"

He shook his head. "I couldn't do it because I couldn't *make* myself do it."

Nina smiled, but only tentatively. He seemed to be getting at something and she was a little afraid of what it might be.

Or maybe afraid to hope what it might be...

Then he started to talk about sitting there with Noelle, about the fact that he hadn't been able to make himself leave either one of them, about that getting him to thinking....

And the sweet, sweet things he said about what he felt for her, what he felt for Noelle, what he wanted, brought tears to Nina's eyes.

"I know we're not the same age and never will be," he said, extracting his finger from the newborn so he could stroke Nina's cheek. "And I know I have three kids I'd be asking you to take on, and that's a lot. And even though my family has let you slip through a crack in their side of the feud, that doesn't necessarily mean they're ready to lay down the hatchet completely—although I have some hopes. And your family still hates the idea of anything Traub, but—"

He paused, shook his head and shrugged as if none of that really mattered. "I love you, Nina. I love you so much I'm bowled over by it. I want to move you and this baby into my house before you ever get out of this bed so you both can come home with me when you leave here. I want a whole lifetime with you, with Noelle, that starts right now. I want you to go on looking out for my boys and making their lives better. I even want a couple more of these—" he jiggled Noelle ever so slightly "—that we make ourselves. And I can't leave until I know there's any chance that I might be able to have—"

"Nina!"

"You. To have it all with you," Dallas finished despite the hushed but harsh voice of Laura Crawford coming from behind him, from where Nina's mother stood in the doorway.

"Mom," Nina greeted quietly. "I didn't think you would be able to come…"

Nina had been completely tuned in to Dallas and what he was saying. And his broad shoulders effectively blocked the view of the doorway, so there had been no indication that her mother was standing there or for how long or how much she might have overheard. But apparently it was enough.

"I called the hospital before dawn and talked to them about whether or not I could come over here from a sick house. They said as long as I wasn't sick and I wore this getup and this mask and didn't touch the baby, they'd let me in. I thought you'd be alone…"

Even standing there looking like a green marshmallow, a surgical mask covering her nose and mouth, her mother still managed to convey righteous indignation. Quiet righteous indignation, but still righteous indignation.

"No, Dallas has been with me the whole time," Nina said, infusing her words with a plea to be reasonable.

"And now he wants to move you into his house? He wants to take over my grandbaby?"

So she'd heard plenty. Nina wasn't ready to get into any of that with her yet so she merely said, "Did you come to see your granddaughter or to fight?"

"I didn't come to see her in the hands of a Traub," Laura Crawford muttered under her breath, just loudly enough to be heard.

Nina shook her head disgustedly but said to Dallas, "Maybe you could give us a minute. And take the baby to the nursery, where she doesn't have to be in the middle of this."

"I'll do whatever you want," Dallas assured her.

He took Noelle to the doorway Laura Crawford continued to block, and stood tall and strong and unyielding in front of her when he said, "Mrs. Crawford, this is your granddaughter. I know you have to want a look no matter who's holding her...."

Laura cast him another scathing glare from over the surgical mask and gazed down at Noelle, her eyes filling with tears at that first glimpse of the newborn, despite whatever anger she felt at Dallas.

"Beautiful, isn't she?" Dallas asked calmly, understandingly.

Then he said, "I love your daughter, Mrs. Crawford. I already love this little girl here in my arms. I just want the chance to make Nina as happy as she makes me. I want to look out for her daughter the way she's looked out for my boys, and I want to make a life for us all. Can't we put the rest behind us?"

Nina watched her mother blink back her tears over seeing Noelle for the first time but stubbornly say nothing in response to Dallas. Instead, she stepped aside so he could take the baby out.

Over his shoulder, Dallas cast Nina a glance that asked if she was sure she wanted him to go. And only when Nina nodded in response did he finally disappear down the corridor with Noelle.

Nina raised the head of her bed so she could sit more upright to face what she knew was coming as her mother crossed the room.

"I can't believe this," her mother said despondently, going on to voice her disapproval in no uncertain terms.

But Nina couldn't concentrate on her mother's hushed-for-the-hospital tirade. She was still thinking too much about what Dallas had just said.

He loved her.

He loved her.

He *loved* her...

And still awash in all that had filled her own heart when she'd opened her eyes to see him holding Noelle, it struck her like a bolt of lightning that she loved him, too.

But clearly it wasn't that simple.

Not when she was under the attack of her mother's dislike of the Traubs.

Not when she was envisioning being uprooted from her apartment, taking Noelle home to Dallas's house rather than to the nursery Nina had made for her, *moving* out to Dallas's ranch and stepping into his already established life and family. Not when she was envisioning all the adapting and accommodating that that meant for her.

All the adapting and accommodating that was so much like what she'd had to do for Leo and had sworn to herself that she wouldn't do again for another man. That she would only do for Noelle.

Noelle, who was her first priority, the one she had to think about now.

Wouldn't saying yes to Dallas cause her hours-old daughter to take a backseat? Rather than being the coveted first and only child, the way she'd come into this world, she would instantly be just one of *four* kids. Was that fair to her?

Nina's mind was spinning faster than her mother was talking.

She'd planned to devote herself to this baby she'd wanted so much. She fully intended to dote on Noelle, and she already loved her like she'd never loved anything or anyone. And no, the idea of Noelle taking a backseat to anything or anybody did not appeal to Nina.

But when she thought about the expression on Dallas's handsome face when she'd first opened her eyes to that sight of him holding Noelle such a short while ago, she realized that she'd seen the doting and all she felt for Noelle coming from him, too. Which meant that Noelle could have *two* loving, adoring, doting parents instead of just one.

And when she thought of it that way, it felt a little like she would be denying her daughter something if Nina said no.

But Noelle would still be one of *four* kids.

And Nina couldn't bear to think of her daughter lost in the shuffle.

On the other hand, Nina herself had been the youngest of six and she'd never felt lost in any shuffle.

Instead she'd always had someone to play with, to follow around and torment to amuse herself. She'd always had someone whose bed she could crawl into if she had a nightmare. She'd never been alone in facing bullies or the trials and tribulations of growing up. She'd had brothers and a sister to turn to for comfort after the breakup with Leo. She wasn't alone in dealing with her parents aging, and when she lost her parents, she wouldn't be left alone in the world then, either.

Because she had family.

Yes, there had been some adapting to be done in that family. But they'd adapted to her as much as she'd had to adapt to anyone else. It had only been with Leo that she had found herself needing to be the only one in the relationship to accommodate.

And now that she thought about it, it occurred to her that Leo had been an only child. Maybe that was why he hadn't learned to do anything other than expect someone else to meet his needs while putting their own on the back burner. Maybe that had contributed to his expectations that she be flexible while he insisted on remaining a creature of habit. Maybe it hadn't been just the age difference that had put her at a disadvantage.

But Dallas came from the same kind of upbringing she did. From a big family. And, yes, he was older than she was—almost as much older as Leo had been. But he was a kind, caring, generous, compassionate man who had sacrificed himself more than once to step in and take care of her.

Dallas was faultlessly thoughtful and considerate of her—something that could never have been said of Leo. And Dallas hadn't given the impression that he expected her, or anyone else, to put anything on hold or on the back burner for him. He'd even embraced her having this baby despite the fact that, early on, he'd clearly been confused by why she was doing it this way.

Never once had she felt taken advantage of, the way she had with Leo, and not until Dallas's request that she and Noelle move into his house had she felt as if she had to do more compromising than Dallas had done or was willing to do.

Yes, to be with him would mean uprooting herself. It would mean taking Noelle home to his house rather than to her apartment. But that wasn't because he was set in his ways or because he used that as an excuse to control what went on. It was just the best, most logical way for things to work out.

And other than that, she thought that Dallas was right that having kids made being set in his ways impossible. And he was okay with that. He was even okay with adding her baby to his family. And having more...

More that could come out of nights like the one they'd spent together. The night that had left her wanting nothing so much as to be back in his arms.

"Are you even listening to me?" her mother asked.

She wasn't.

But now that her mother had forced her to, Nina knew that even if she was willing to move into Dallas's house and life, even if she was willing to be a replacement mother to his boys and give her new daughter three big brothers, there was still the issue of the animosity between his family and hers.

Especially the obviously flaming animosity her family held on to, even if his had backed away from the feud enough to allow her in....

"Please don't, Mom," Nina said in a quiet voice when

her mother had gone on to disparage Dallas and the rest of the Traubs. "I love that man. Please don't make me choose—"

"Choose!" her mother repeated as if the possibility of that hadn't occurred to her. "Are you telling me that you would pick *him* over us? *Them* over us?"

"I don't want to pick anyone over anyone. And I don't think I should have to. Especially when you can't tell me—right here and now, without any question—why you hate the Traubs. And don't bring up the election because Nate's gone on just fine not being mayor and can run again if he wants to. Even against a Traub if it was done less mean-spiritedly, which it could be."

"I can't believe what I'm hearing."

"The Traubs are just like us, Mom," Nina went on. "They're a family who care about each other. And about Rust Creek Falls. Just like us. They're making their way through life the same way we are. There's no reason, no sense in hating them because somebody got mad at somebody a gazillion years ago."

"You wouldn't really turn your back on us? Take that baby away from us…?" Laura Crawford asked in a whisper full of disbelief, obviously not in agreement with anything Nina had said but beginning to fear she might actually lose her daughter or her new—and first—grandchild.

"No, I wouldn't turn my back on you or take Noelle away from you. But I want to be with Dallas." And as Nina said that, she knew just how true it was. True enough to weather whatever conflicts arose from joining the two families because she suddenly couldn't see her life without him. She couldn't see herself raising Noelle without him. She couldn't see anything without him.

"And if I'm with Dallas, then it's up to you," she continued, thinking to illustrate what that would mean for her mother, should her family opt to go on the way they had been. "Will you not come to Noelle's christening or her birthday parties because the Traubs do? Will you only see Noelle when I can bring her to you because you won't visit her and see Dallas or his boys? Will you keep us at arm's length just for some fight that took place generations before any of us were even born?"

"So what is it you see, Nina?" her mother demanded angrily. "The Traubs and the Crawfords just getting together and hugging and kissing and pretending we haven't hated each other for decades? Becoming bosom buddies?"

Sadly, no, she didn't see that.

But Nina refused to just bow to the status quo.

"At first they were only civil to me," Nina informed her mother, outlining the course of her own path to the Traubs. "Then things became a little more friendly because they were glad that Dallas was happier when he was with me—the way I feel when I'm with him," she said pointedly. "And when they found out I was going to be alone on Christmas they invited me to join them. The same way you've invited more people than I can count to join us whenever you've heard of anyone we know spending a holiday alone. No, there hasn't been any hugging and kissing—" *well, with Traubs other than Dallas, anyway* "—but they opened their door to me, they were nice and hospitable, and it's gotten easier as it's gone along."

"So put a good face on it, is that what you're saying? And pretend we haven't been at each other's throats forever?"

"Yes," Nina said. "Start that way. For my sake. For *Noelle's* sake. Do what Dallas asked—just put the stupid rift behind us and try something else."

Laura Crawford was still frowning over that surgical mask but her tone was more resigned when she said, "You're serious about this? About this man? Isn't he as old as Leo?"

Ah, an attempt to throw a wrench into the works, because her mother knew Nina's thinking about that…

"Yes, he's almost as old as Leo, but he's a completely different person," Nina said, knowing that as a fact, pure and simple, and not daunted at all anymore by their age difference.

"And three kids, Nina," her mother said, trying again. "He already has *three* kids."

"Three kids who need a mom. Three kids who I already love and want to be a mom to."

"And you'd leave your little apartment and let yourself be swallowed up in his life. Isn't that what you did with Leo? What you weren't going to do again?"

"I'd leave my apartment to live in a nice house, but it isn't the same as what I had to do with Leo because nothing is the same with Dallas. He left his kids, his family on *Christmas* to do what needed to be done for me because he takes care of what needs to be taken care of. Like I do. He goes with the flow—that makes him the exact opposite of Leo."

"But they're Traubs…" her mother said, sounding defeated.

"They're just people. A family. The same as we are."

"I don't know how this will work," her mother lamented.

"I think that if you try, and they try, eventually it can."

Her mother rolled her eyes, shook her head, frowned

mightily. And yet there was still some semblance of acceptance. Unwilling and resentful, but acceptance on some level. "And I thought artificial insemination and having a baby without a husband was over-the-top enough. Leave it to you to add Traubs to the mix," she grumbled.

But, for now, that was concession enough for Nina, and she realized that she just had to have faith that something better would come later, that even if both families began by just going through the motions of peace, eventually maybe peace would become a reality and grow into something better. Something that could genuinely put behind them whatever it was that had kept them at odds.

Her mother had just taken her hand to squeeze and leaned over to place a kiss to her forehead through the surgical mask when Dallas knocked on the door, tentatively poking just his head into the room.

"I thought you might want to know, Mrs. Crawford— they're about to change Noelle's diaper. If you want, they'll do it at the nursery window so you can see all ten fingers and all ten toes, and that she really is just perfect."

And maybe what the two families could be brought together for.

"I need to go see that," Laura Crawford said, tearing up again at the mere thought of the baby.

"Go," Nina encouraged her.

She watched as her mother returned to the door and stopped in front of Dallas, where he'd remained just to the outside of it.

For a moment Laura Crawford didn't speak, she merely stood there, proudly, stubbornly. But then she straightened her shoulders and raised her chin to the big man and said, "Thank you for taking care of my daughter and my granddaughter."

It was slightly begrudging, only coolly courteous, but an improvement nonetheless.

"You're welcome. It was my pleasure," Dallas answered with more warmth.

Then Nina's mother went past him and down the corridor, and Dallas came back to sit on the side of Nina's bed.

He took her hand in both of his, raised it to kiss and when he'd tucked it against his thigh, he said, "Poor Noelle has to have a diaper change whether she needs it or not because there's one more thing I have to say, and I had to get back here to say it."

Nina smiled at him. "You said quite a bit before."

"But there's one more thing—if it isn't too late…" He glanced over his shoulder at the door to see if the coast was still clear. Then, looking at her again, his blue eyes delving into hers, he said, "I love you, Nina, and I'd really, really—*really*—like it if you'd say yes, you'll marry me…"

Nina teared up herself for the umpteenth time, smiled and didn't even need another moment to think about it before she said, "Yes, I will marry you."

A shocked sort of happiness infused Dallas's expression. "You will?"

Nina laughed. "My mother had a lot to say and it gave me a while to think when I was supposed to be listening," she confided, going on to tell him how she'd resolved her own issues and the realizations she'd come to about him, about everything.

"I love you, too," she told him. "I don't know how it happened when I was trying to make sure it didn't, but it did…"

"I know, I was fighting it, too. It was just bigger and stronger than I am."

And that was saying something.

"But what about your mom and the rest of your family?" Dallas asked, nodding in the direction of the hospital room door.

"I told her how I feel about you. That I want to be with you. So seeing her granddaughter might be more limited if she and everyone else keeps up the way they have been. And she doesn't want that. So I'm hoping that she and everyone else will come around."

"That's why she was nicer a minute ago?"

Nina laughed. "Well, yes, that's why she's trying. If everybody just tries—"

"We'll make it work out," Dallas assured her, reaching a hand to the back of her neck as he leaned forward to kiss her. Deeply, profoundly, oh-so-sweetly and yet with passion right there, too…

And that was what Nina really needed. The touch of Dallas's hands. The heat and strength of his body. The feel of his mouth pressed to hers. And that connection that had formed between them despite every obstacle and issue that should have prevented it.

She truly loved this man and wanted to spend the rest of her life with him.

When the kiss ended and she looked more closely at him, she saw the fatigue lurking behind his eyes and knew he needed some rest.

"Go home and sleep," she urged in a quiet voice filled with her own reluctance to lose his company.

"I'd rather round up some of my brothers and start to move you and Noelle to my place," he said, more question than statement. "Are you gonna let me do that?"

Nina smiled. "I don't think you and three boys will fit into my apartment, so yes, you can do that." Because even though she'd been looking forward to bringing her new baby home to the bright yellow nursery she'd decorated, the thought of going anywhere Dallas wasn't didn't appeal to her. "But you must know better than anyone that that means you're signing on for sleepless nights."

He smiled back at her. "Consider me signed on."

"But get some rest before you start moving day," she decreed.

"A couple of hours," he agreed. "A couple more to move things. Then I'll be back."

She already couldn't wait.

But he still didn't seem eager to leave because he stayed there, studying her awhile longer, kissing her again, telling her how much he loved her.

And only when Nina reminded him that her mother would be back any minute, and told him it was probably better if she was alone with her to tell her they were engaged, did he give Nina one last, lingering kiss, and actually go.

But not without leaning in first and whispering, "We're going to have a great life together…"

And leaving Nina certain that they would.

Epilogue

"Welcome, everyone, to the grand reopening of our elementary school, and thank you for coming out before you get your New Year's Eve parties started!" Mayor Collin Traub said over the microphone.

He was standing at a podium set up in the school cafeteria in front of a hundred occupied folding chairs while the rest of the audience filled the perimeters of the room because there weren't enough seats.

Nina was sitting in the center of the third row. It was Noelle's first outing and the newborn was sleeping peacefully beside her in Dallas's arms—which had become Noelle's favorite place to snooze.

To Nina's left were her parents and those of her siblings who could make the event, and to Dallas's right was his family, with Ryder, Jake and Robbie interspersed between uncles.

During the week since Nina and Noelle had left the hospital and moved in with Dallas and the boys, the Crawfords and the Traubs had crossed paths and reached an unspoken truce of sorts. At first, barely civil hellos had been the only exchanges. As the week progressed, "How are you?" had been added on both sides. And with most of their focus on Noelle, Ryder, Jake and Robbie, so far the two families seemed to be tolerating each other.

It wasn't great, but it was something.

And having them all in that room at that moment, sitting in the same row of chairs, was enough to have caused a buzz throughout the cafeteria when townsfolk began to notice that a détente between the families had been reached.

"The flood cost us dearly." Rust Creek's new mayor began what sounded like a prepared speech. "Including the life of our former mayor, Hunter McGee, and I'd like us to spend a moment in silent remembrance."

That request was honored by everyone except a few fussy babies and very small children.

When the moment had been observed, Collin picked up where he'd left off.

"As you can see, thanks to the involvement of the New York organization Bootstraps, and the volunteers who came to Rust Creek Falls, the mission to bring our school back from the flood damage and make it better than ever has been accomplished. We want to thank everyone for their efforts and generosity of time and energy."

Applause and cheers went up.

When it died down, Collin said, "We want to particularly thank Lissa Roarke, who brought our situation to the attention of the whole country and whose television appearance and writings on our behalf have generated donations and help and—" the mayor smiled "—the interest—I hear—of any number of single women who just might like to find a Rust Creek cowboy of their own. Like my brother Braden, for instance, who is now the only one of us left single."

The crowd laughed at the brotherly goad.

"Sorry, Braden," Collin apologized remorselessly. "But I wanted a lead into making some announcements and congratulations, and your status as an available bachelor got to be it."

More chuckles from the audience.

"While we aren't all out from under the destruction the flood left," Collin said, "I think we should note that from the bad came some good. And as this New Year is upon us, I want to take the time to recognize and celebrate that good the same way we're here celebrating our resurrected and improved school."

There were mutterings of agreement to that.

"I know you're all looking at that third row, there," Collin went on, "where the Crawfords and the Traubs are actually sitting together. If you'll notice, my brother Dallas and Nina Crawford—and Nina's not-quite-a-week-old daughter, Noelle—are right there in the middle, and that says it all because they're the connecting link. Seems like Christmas brought them together and—in keeping with the holiday theme—Dallas and Nina are engaged and have set a Valentine's Day wedding date."

More clapping and cheers of congratulations rang through the room. Nina wasn't sure how much of it might be for the ending of the feud between the two families, but she knew that some of it was for her and Dallas. So she smiled and glanced at Dallas, who smiled back, leaned over and kissed her.

"But they're not the only two pairing up," Mayor Traub went on. "As you all know, your kindergarten teacher, Willa Christensen, and I came together over the flood and ended up tying the knot, and so did Dean Pritchett and Shelby Jenkins, and our newest addition to veterinary medicine—Brooks Smith and Jazzy Cates.

"And not only did we come out with three weddings, but Gage Christensen has the flood to thank for bringing him Lissa," the young mayor continued. "And my brother Sutter and our fifth-grade teacher, Paige Dalton, have reunited after five years, and just announced to us that they'll be having a January wedding—so that makes three engagements, too."

Collin winked at Sutter and Paige, who had also told the family that Paige was pregnant—although they didn't think it was good for her image as a schoolteacher to let that news get around until after the wedding.

"The efforts to help Rust Creek Falls survive and come back better than ever have brought out the best in us all, I think," Collin said. "It's even offered an opportunity for redemption for some—particularly for Arthur Swinton."

Nina saw the reservations that name raised in the crowd that was clearly unsure what was to come, since the Thunder Canyon former city councilman and mayor had taken such a big fall from grace in the past few years.

"Due to the persistence of Arthur's newfound son, Shane Roarke, and Shane's adopted family, Arthur's sentence has been commuted and he's been released from jail."

There were mutterings about that that weren't all favorable.

But before they got out of hand, Collin said, "I know some of you won't agree with that, but Arthur has vowed to devote the rest of his life to positive change and I, for one, wish him the best in that pursuit. Arthur has set about proving his intentions by raising—legally—a large sum of money that he's donating to our town renovation project to ensure that Rust Creek Falls continues to rebuild and grow!"

Collin's victorious tone was answered with more applause, though even that held some reserve.

When it died down once more, Collin concluded his speech, reminding them all of a few humorous moments during the past year, sending out some tongue-in-cheek congratulations and lightening the tone from there.

Then he said, "That's about it for me tonight. But DJ's Rib Shack, owned by my cousin DJ Traub in Thunder Canyon, has provided us with a full meal to mark this occasion. We'll be setting up for that while you all tour the school, and when you get back here dinner'll be served."

Enthusiasm for that was unmistakable.

"And just let me be the first to wish us all a Happy New Year!" Collin concluded.

"Happy New Year!" the crowd echoed as everyone stood to take the school tour.

A beautiful job had been done restoring, rejuvenating and restocking the building, and that was all pointed out by the principal, who gave the tour.

Along the way, Robbie took the hand of Laura Crawford—whom he'd developed a fondness for—on one side, and his own grandmother on the other. Nina saw it and couldn't help smiling at how both women put aside their differences to indulge the little boy—a sign of the future, she hoped.

By the time everyone returned to the school cafeteria it had been transformed back into just that, with bench-lined tables all set out and the kitchen open and ready to serve the delicious meal that was one of several gifts the Thunder Canyon branch of the Traub family had sent to help its neighbors during these long months of struggle.

And as Nina sat with Dallas by her side, who was still cradling Noelle in one arm while keeping his other arm around her, she felt such a sense of happiness and contentment come over her that it made her well up.

Rust Creek Falls would survive and go on providing the home she'd always known, the home she never wanted to leave. And now, not only did she have the child she'd wanted and been denied for too long, but she had Dallas and Ryder and Jake and Robbie—an entire family—to share it with.

"What are you thinking about, Miss-Nina-with-the-tears-in-her-eyes?" Dallas asked, leaning close to her ear so that she alone could hear him, he alone noticing that she was in the throes of emotions.

"I was just thinking how much I love you," she said. "And Noelle and the boys, and this whole town. And how glad I am to spend the rest of my life here with you."

Dallas pressed a warm kiss to her cheek and stayed there a long moment before he nuzzled her ear with his nose and whispered, "If anyone had told me a year ago that I'd be where I am now, I'd have called them a liar. But the truth is, you've made me the luckiest man on earth."

Nina could only smile at that and turn to kiss him, knowing that luck had shone down on them both through the blinding blizzard and opened their eyes to what was right there waiting for them in each other.

* * * * *

Merry Christmas

& A Happy New Year!

Thank you for a wonderful
2013…

A sneaky peek at next month...

Cherish™

ROMANCE TO MELT THE HEART EVERY TIME

My wish list for next month's titles...

In stores from 20th December 2013:

❏ The Final Falcon Says I Do – Lucy Gordon

& The Greek's Tiny Miracle – Rebecca Winters

❏ Happy New Year, Baby Fortune! – Leanne Banks

& Bound by a Baby – Kate Hardy

In stores from 3rd January 2014:

❏ The Man Behind the Mask – Barbara Wallace

& The Sheriff's Second Chance – Michelle Celmer

❏ English Girl in New York – Scarlet Wilson

& That Summer at the Shore – Callie Endicott

Available at WHSmith, Tesco, Asda, Eason, Amazon and Apple

Just can't wait?

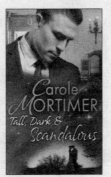

Come in from the cold this Christmas with two of our favourite authors. Whether you're jetting off to Vermont with Sarah Morgan or settling down for Christmas dinner with Fiona Harper, the smiles won't stop this festive season.

Visit:
www.millsandboon.co.uk

MILLS & BOON®
Book Club

Join the Mills & Boon Book Club

Want to read more **Cherish**™ books?
We're offering you **2 more** absolutely **FREE!**

We'll also treat you to these fabulous extras:

- ❧ **Exclusive offers and much more!**

- ❧ **FREE home delivery**

- ❧ **FREE books and gifts with our special rewards scheme**

Get your free books now!

**visit www.millsandboon.co.uk/bookclub
or call Customer Relations on 020 8288 2888**